Joanne Harris is the author of the Whitbread-shortlisted *Chocolat* (made into a major film starring Juliette Binoche), *Blackberry Wine*, *Five Quarters of the Orange*, *Coastliners*, *Holy Fools*, *Jigs & Reels*, *Sleep, Pale Sister* and, with Fran Warde, two cookbooks, *The French Kitchen* and *The French Market*. She lives in Huddersfield, Yorkshire, with her husband and daughter.

GENTLEMEN & PLAYERS

Joanne Harris

Doubleday

LONDON · TORONTO · SYDNEY · AUCKLAND · JOHANNESBURG

TRANSWORLD PUBLISHERS
61–63 Uxbridge Road, London W5 5SA
a division of The Random House Group Ltd

RANDOM HOUSE AUSTRALIA (PTY) LTD
20 Alfred Street, Milsons Point, Sydney,
New South Wales 2061, Australia

RANDOM HOUSE NEW ZEALAND LTD
18 Poland Road, Glenfield, Auckland 10, New Zealand

RANDOM HOUSE SOUTH AFRICA (PTY) LTD
Isle of Houghton, Corner Boundary Road and Carse O'Gowrie,
Houghton 2198, South Africa

Published 2005 by Doubleday
a division of Transworld Publishers

A catalogue record for this book is available from the British Library.
ISBNs 0385 603665 (cased)
0385 609523 (tpb)

Typeset in Goudy by
Kestrel Data, Exeter, Devon.

Printed in Australia by
Griffin Press.

1 3 5 7 9 10 8 6 4 2

Papers used by Transworld Publishers are natural, recyclable products made
from wood grown in sustainable forests. The manufacturing processes conform
to the environmental regulations of the country of origin.

To Derek Fry
One of the old school

When an old cricketer leaves the crease you never know
   whether he's gone
If sometimes you're catching a fleeting glimpse of a twelfth
   man at silly mid-on
And it could be Geoff, and it could be John, with a new-ball
   sting in his tail
And it could be me and it could be thee—
       Roy Harper, *When an Old Cricketer Leaves the Crease*

Any skool is a bit of a shambles.
       Geoffrey Willans, *Down with Skool!*

PAWN

1

IF THERE'S ONE THING I'VE LEARNED IN THE PAST FIFTEEN years, it's this; that murder is really no big deal. It's just a boundary, meaningless and arbitrary as all others – a line drawn in the dirt. Like the giant NO TRESPASSERS sign on the drive to St Oswald's, straddling the air like a sentinel. I was nine years old at the time of our first encounter, and it loomed over me then with the growling menace of a school bully.

NO TRESPASSERS
NO UNAUTHORIZED ENTRY BEYOND THIS POINT
BY ORDER.

Another child might have been daunted by the command. But in my case curiosity overrode the instinct. By *whose* order? Why *this* point and not another? And most importantly, what would happen if I crossed that line?

Of course I already knew the school was out of bounds. By then I'd been living in its shadow for six months, and already that tenet stood tall among the commandments of my young life, as laid down by John Snyde. *Don't be a sissy. Look after your own. Work hard, play hard. A little drink never did anyone any harm.* And, most importantly: *Stay clear of St Oswald's*, occasionally punctuated by a *Stay bloody clear if you know what's good for you,* or a warning punch to the upper arm. The punches were supposed to be friendly, I knew. All the same, they hurt. Parenting was not one of John Snyde's special skills.

Nevertheless, for the first few months I obeyed without question. Dad was so proud of his new job as Porter; such a fine old school, such a great reputation, and we were going to live in the Old Gatehouse, where generations of Porters before us had lived. There would be tea on the lawn on summer evenings, and it would be the beginning of something wonderful. Perhaps, when she saw how well we were doing now, Mum might even come home.

But weeks passed and none of that happened. The Gatehouse was a Grade 2 listed building, with tiny, latticed windows that let in hardly any light. There was a perpetual smell of damp, and we weren't allowed a satellite dish because it would have lowered the tone. Most of the furniture belonged to St Oswald's – heavy oak chairs and dusty dressers – and next to them our own things – salvaged from the old council flat on Abbey Road – looked cheap and out of place. My dad's time was entirely taken up with his new job and I quickly learned to be self-reliant – to make any demand, such as regular meals or clean sheets, qualified as *being a sissy* – not to trouble my father at weekends, and always to lock my bedroom door on Saturday nights.

Mum never wrote; any mention of her also counted as *being a sissy*, and after a while I started to forget what she had looked like. My dad had a bottle of her perfume hidden under his mattress, though, and when he was out on his rounds, or down the Engineers' with his mates, I would sometimes sneak into his bedroom and spray a little of that perfume – it was called Cinnabar – on to my pillow and maybe pretend that Mum was watching TV in the next room, or that she'd just popped into the kitchen to get me a cup of milk and that she'd be back to read me a story. A bit stupid, really: she'd never done those things when she was home. Anyway, after a bit, Dad must have thrown the bottle away, because one day it was gone, and I couldn't even remember how she'd smelled any more.

Christmas approached, bringing bad weather and even more work for the Porter to deal with, so we never did get to have tea on the lawn. On the other hand, I was happy enough. A solitary child even then; awkward in company; invisible at school. During the first term I kept to myself; stayed out of the house; played in the snowy woods behind St Oswald's and explored every inch of the school's perimeter – making sure never to cross the forbidden line.

I discovered that most of St Oswald's was screened from public view; the main building by a long avenue of linden trees – now bare – which bordered the drive, and the land surrounded on all sides by walls and hedges. But through the gates I could see those lawns – mowed to banded perfection by my father – the cricket grounds with their neat hedges; the chapel with its weathervane and its inscriptions in Latin. Beyond that lay a world as strange and remote in my eyes as Narnia or Oz; a world to which I could never belong.

My own school was called Abbey Road Juniors; a squat little building on the council estate, with a bumpy playground built on a slant and two entrance gates with BOYS and GIRLS written above them in sooty stone. I'd never liked it; but even so I dreaded my arrival at Sunnybank Park, the sprawling comprehensive which I was destined by postcode to attend.

Since my first day at Abbey Road I'd watched the Sunnybankers – cheap green sweatshirts with the school logo on the breast, nylon rucksacks, fag-ends, hairspray – with growing dismay. They would hate me, I knew it. They would take one look at me and they would hate me. I sensed it immediately. I was skinny; undersized; a natural hander-in of homework. Sunnybank Park would swallow me whole.

I pestered my father. 'Why? Why the Park? Why there?'

'Don't be a sissy. There's nothing wrong with the Park, kid. It's just a school. They're all the bloody same.'

Well, *that* was a lie. Even I knew that. It made me curious; it made me resentful. And now, as spring began to quicken over the bare land and white buds burst from the blackthorn hedges, I looked once more at that NO TRESPASSERS sign, painstakingly lettered in my father's hand, and asked myself: Whose ORDER? Why *this* point and not another? And, with an increasing sense of urgency and impatience: What would happen if I crossed that line?

There was no wall here, no visible boundary of any kind. None was needed. There was simply the road, the blackthorn hedge running alongside it and, a few yards to the left, the sign. It stood there arrogantly, unchallenged, certain of its authority. Beyond it on the other side I imagined perilous, uncharted territory. Anything could be waiting there – land-mines, mantraps, security guards, hidden cameras.

Oh, it *looked* safe enough: no different, in fact, from the near side. But that sign told me otherwise. Beyond it, there was Order. There was authority. Any infringement of that order would result in retribution as mysterious as it was terrible. I did not doubt it for a moment; the fact that no details were given merely strengthened the air of menace.

So I sat at a respectful distance and observed the re-stricted area. It was strangely comforting to know that here, at least, Order was being enforced. I'd seen the police cars outside Sunnybank Park. I'd seen the graffiti on the sides of the buildings and the boys throwing stones at cars in the lane. I'd heard them yelling at the teachers as they came out of school, and I'd seen the generous sheaves of razor-wire above the staff car-park.

Once I had watched as a group of four or five cornered a boy on his own. He was a few years older than I was, and dressed with greater care than the majority of Sunny-bankers. I knew he was in for a beating as soon as I saw the library books under his arm. Readers are always fair game at a place like Sunnybank.

St Oswald's was another world. Here I knew there would be no graffiti, no litter, no vandalism – not so much as a broken window. The sign said so; and I felt a sudden inarticulate conviction that *this* was where I truly belonged; this place where young trees could be planted without somebody snapping their heads off in the night, where no one was left bleeding in the road; where there were no surprise visits from the community police officer, or posters warning pupils to leave their knives at home. Here would be stern masters in old-fashioned black gowns; surly Porters like my father; tall prefects. Here to do one's homework was not to be *a poof*, or *a swot*, or *a queer*. Here was safety. Here was home.

I was alone; no one else had ventured this far. Birds came and went on the forbidden ground. Nothing happened to them. Some time later a cat swaggered out from under the hedge and sat facing me, licking its paw. Still nothing.

I came closer then, daring first to breach the shadow, then to crouch between the sign's great feet. My own shadow crept stealthily forward. My shadow trespassed.

For a time that was thrilling enough. But not for long: there was already too much of the rebel in me to be content with a technical misdemeanour. With my foot I jabbed lightly at the grass on the other side, then pulled away with a delicious shiver, like a child taking its first step into the ocean. Of course I had never seen the ocean, but the instinct was there, and the sensation of having moved into an alien element where anything might happen.

Nothing did.

I took another step and this time, did not pull away. Still nothing. The sign towered over me like a monster from a late-night movie, but it was strangely frozen, as if outraged at my impudence. Seeing my chance, I made a break for it and ran across the windy field towards the hedge, running low, tensed for an attack. Reaching the hedge, I flung myself into its shadow, breathless with fear. Now I had done it. Now they would come.

There was a gap in the hedge only a few feet away from me. It looked to be my best chance. I inched towards it, keeping to the shadow, and crammed myself into the tiny space. They might come at me from either side, I thought; if they came from both, then I would have to run for it. I had observed that given time, adults had a tendency to forget things, and I felt reasonably confident that if I could get away quickly enough, then I might possibly escape retribution.

Expectantly, I waited. The tightness in my throat gradually subsided. My heart slowed to a near-normal pace. I became aware of my surroundings, first with curiosity, then with increasing discomfort. There were thorns sticking through my T-shirt into my back. I could smell sweat, and soil, and the sour smell of the hedge. From somewhere close by came birdsong, a distant mower, a drowsy burr like insects in the grass. Nothing more. At first I grinned with pleasure – I had trespassed, and escaped capture – then I became aware of a feeling of dissatisfaction, a flutter of resentment beneath my ribs.

Where were the cameras? The land-mines? The guards? Where was the ORDER, so sure of itself that it had to be written in capital letters? Most importantly, *where was my father?*

I stood up, still wary, and left the shadow of the hedge. The sun hit me in the face and I threw up a hand to shield my eyes. I took a step away into the open, then another.

Surely *now* they would come, these enforcers: these shadowy figures of order and authority. But seconds passed, and then minutes, and nothing happened. No one came, not a prefect, a teacher – not even a Porter.

A kind of panic clutched at me then, and I ran into the middle of the field and waved my arms, like someone on a desert island trying to flag down a rescue plane. Didn't they care? I was a trespasser. Didn't they *see* me?

'Here!' I was delirious with indignation. 'Here I am! Here! *Here!*'

Nothing. Not a sound. Not even the barking of a dog in the distance or the faintest whoop of a warning siren. It was then that I realized, with anger and a clammy kind of excitement, that it had all been a big lie. There was nothing in the field but grass and trees. Just a line in the dirt, daring me to cross it. And I had dared. I had defied the ORDER.

All the same I felt somehow cheated, as I often did when faced with the threats and assurances of the adult world, which promises so much and delivers so little.

They lie, kid. It was my father's voice – only slightly slurred – in my head. *They promise you the world, kid, but they're all the same. They lie.*

'They do not! Not always—'

Then try it. Go on. I dare you. See how far you get.

And so I went further, following the hedge up a small hill towards a stand of trees. There was another sign there: TRESPASSERS WILL BE PROSECUTED. Of course by then the first step had been taken, and the implicit threat barely slowed me down.

But beyond the trees was a surprise. I'd expected to see a road, a railway line perhaps, a river – something to show that there was a world outside of St Oswald's. But from where I was standing, and as far as I could see, *everything* was St Oswald's: the hill, the little wood, the tennis courts, the cricket green, the sweet-smelling lawns and the long, long stretches of meadow beyond.

And here behind the trees I could see people; I could see boys. Boys of all ages; some barely older than myself, others dangerously, swaggeringly adult. Some were dressed in cricket whites, some wore running shorts and coloured singlets with numbers written on them. In a square of sand some distance away, some were practising jumps. And beyond them I could see a big building of soot-mellowed stone; rows of arched windows reflecting the sun; a long slate roof punctuated by skylights; a tower; a weathervane; a sprawl of outbuildings; a chapel; a graceful stairway leading down towards a lawn, trees, flowerbeds, asphalt courtyards separated from each other by railings and archways.

Here too were boys. Some sat on the steps. Some stood talking under the trees. Some were in navy-blue blazers and grey trousers, others in sports kit. The sound they made – a sound I had not even registered until now – reached me like a flock of exotic birds.

I understood at once that they were a different race to myself; gilded not only by the sunlight and their proximity to that lovely building but by something less tangible; a slick air of assurance; a mysterious shine.

Later, of course, I saw it as it really was. The genteel decay behind the graceful lines. The rot. But that first forbidden glimpse of St Oswald's seemed like unattainable glory to me then; it was Xanadu, it was Asgard and Babylon all in one. Within its grounds young gods lounged and cavorted.

I understood then that this was far more than a line in the dirt, after all. It was a barrier no amount of bravado or desire would permit me to cross. I was an intruder; suddenly I felt very conscious of my dirty jeans, my scuffed sneakers, my pinched face and lank hair. I no longer felt like a daring explorer. I had no right to be there. I had become something *low*; common; a spy, a prowler, a dirty little sneak with hungry eyes and light fingers. Invisible or not, that was how they would always see me. That was what I was. A Sunnybanker.

You see, it had already begun. *That* was St Oswald's; that's what it does to people. Rage flared in me like an ulcer. Rage, and the beginnings of revolt.

So I was an outsider. So what? Any rule can be broken.

Trespass, like any crime, goes unpunished when there's no one to see it. Words – however talismanic – are only ever words.

I didn't know it then, but that was the moment I declared war against St Oswald's. It wouldn't have me? Then I would have *it*. I would take it, and no one, nothing – not even my father – would stop me. The line had been drawn. Another boundary to be crossed, a more sophisticated bluff this time, secure in its ancient arrogance, unaware that therein lay the germ of its destruction. Another line, daring me to cross it.

Like murder.

KING

1

St Oswald's Grammar School for Boys
Monday, 6th September, Michaelmas Term

THAT'S NINETY-NINE BY MY RECKONING, SMELLING OF WOOD
and old chalk dust and disinfectant and the incompre-
hensibly biscuity, hamsterish smell of boys. Ninety-nine
terms strung across the years like dusty paper-lanterns.
Thirty-three years. It's like a prison sentence. Reminds me
of the old joke about the pensioner convicted of murder.

'Thirty years, Your Honour,' he protests, 'It's too much!
I'll never manage it!' And the judge says: 'Well, just do as
many as you can . . .'

Come to think of it, that's not funny. I'll be sixty-five in
November.

Not that it matters. There's no compulsory retirement at
St Oswald's. We follow our own rules. We always have. One
more term, and I'll have scored my Century. One for the

Honours Board at last. I can see it now; in Gothic script: Roy Hubert Straitley (BA), Old Centurion of the School.

I have to laugh. I never imagined I'd end up here. I finished a ten-year stretch at St Oswald's in 1954, and the last thing I expected then was to find myself there again – a master, of all things – keeping order, doling out lines and detentions. But to my surprise I found that those years had given me a sort of natural insight into the teaching business. By now there isn't a trick I don't know. After all, I've played most of them myself; man, boy and somewhere in between. And here I am again, back at St Oswald's for another term. You'd think I couldn't keep away.

I light a Gauloise; my one concession to the influence of the Modern Languages. Technically, of course, it's not allowed; but today, in the privacy of my own form-room, no one's likely to pay very much attention. Today is traditionally free of boys and reserved for administrative matters; the counting of textbooks; allocation of stationery; last-minute revisions to the timetable; collection of form- and set-lists; induction of new staff; departmental meetings.

I am, of course, a department in myself. Once Head of Classics, in charge of a thriving section of respectful menials, now relegated to a dusty corner of the new Languages section, like a rather dull first edition no one quite dares to throw away.

All my rats have abandoned ship – apart from the boys, that is. I still teach a full timetable, to the bafflement of Mr Strange – the Third Master, who considers Latin irrelevant – and to the covert embarrassment of the New Head. Still, the boys continue to opt for my irrelevant subject, and their results remain on the whole rather good. I like to think it's my personal charisma that does it.

Not that I'm not very fond of my colleagues in Modern Languages, though I do have more in common with the subversive Gauls than with the humourless Teutons. There's Pearman, the Head of French – round, cheery, occasionally brilliant, but hopelessly disorganized – and Kitty Teague, who sometimes shares her lunch-time biscuits with me over a cup of tea, and Eric Scoones, a sprightly half-Centurion (also an Old Boy) of sixty-two who, when the mood takes him, has an uncanny recollection for some of the more extreme exploits of my distant youth.

Then there's Isabelle Tapi, decorative but rather useless in a leggy, Gallic sort of way, the subject of a good deal of admiring graffiti from the locker-room fantasy set. All in all a rather jolly department, whose members tolerate my eccentricities with commendable patience and good humour, and who seldom interfere with my unconventional methods.

The Germans are less congenial on the whole; Geoff and Penny ('League of') Nations, a mixed double-act with designs on my form-room; Gerry Grachvogel, a well-meaning ass with a predilection for flashcards, and finally, Dr 'Sourgrape' Devine, Head of Department and a staunch believer in the further expansion of the Great Empire, who sees me as a subversive and a pupil-poacher, has no interest in Classics and who doubtless thinks *carpe diem* means 'fish of the day'.

He has a habit of passing my room with feigned briskness whilst peering suspiciously through the glass, as if to check for signs of immoral conduct, and I know that today of all days it will only be a matter of time before I behold his joyless countenance looking in on me.

Ah. What did I tell you?

Right on cue.

'Morning, Devine!'

I suppressed the urge to salute, whilst concealing my half-smoked Gauloise under the desk, and gave him my broadest smile through the glass door. I noticed he was carrying a large cardboard box piled high with books and papers. He looked at me with what I later knew to be ill-concealed smugness, then moved on with the air of one who has important matters to attend to.

Curiously, I got up and looked down the corridor after him, just in time to see Gerry Grachvogel *and* the League of Nations disappearing furtively in his wake, all carrying similar cartons.

Puzzled, I sat down at my old desk and surveyed my modest empire.

Room 59, my territory for the last thirty years. Oft-disputed but never surrendered. Now only the Germans continue to try. It's a large room, nice in its way, I suppose, though its elevated position in the Bell Tower gives me more stairs to climb than I would have chosen, and it lies about half a mile as the crow flies from my small office on the Upper Corridor.

You'll have noticed that as over time dogs and their owners come to resemble each other, so it is with teachers and classrooms. Mine fits me like my old tweed jacket, and smells almost the same – a comforting compound of books, chalk and illicit cigarettes. A large and venerable blackboard dominates the room – Dr Devine's endeavours to introduce the term 'chalkboard' having, I'm happy to report, met with no success whatever. The desks are ancient and battle-scarred, and I have resisted all attempts to have them replaced by the ubiquitous plastic tables.

If I get bored, I can always read the graffiti. A flattering amount of it concerns me. My current favourite is *Hic magister podex est*, written – by some boy or other – oh, more years ago than I like to remember. When *I* was a boy no one would have dared to refer to a master as a *podex*. Disgraceful. And yet for some reason it never fails to make me smile.

My own desk is no less disgraceful; a huge time-blackened affair with fathomless drawers and multiple inscriptions. It sits on an elevated podium – originally built to allow a shorter Classics master access to the blackboard – and from this quarterdeck I can look down benevolently upon my minions and work on the *Times* crossword without being noticed.

There are mice living behind the lockers. I know this because on Friday afternoons they troop out and sniff around under the radiator pipes while the boys do their weekly vocabulary test. I don't complain; I rather like the mice. The Old Head once tried poison, but only once;

the stench of dead mouse is far more noxious than anything living could ever hope to generate, and it endured for weeks until finally, John Snyde, who was Head Porter at the time, had to be called in to tear out the skirting-boards and remove the pungent dead.

Since then the mice and I have enjoyed a comfortable live-and-let-live approach. If only the Germans could do the same.

I looked up from my reverie to see Dr Devine passing the room again, with his entourage. He tapped his wrist insistently, as if to indicate the time. Ten thirty. Ah. Of course. Staff Meeting. Reluctantly I conceded the point, flicked my cigarette-stub into the waste-paper basket, and ambled off to the Common Room, pausing only to collect the battered gown hanging on a hook by the stock-cupboard door.

The Old Head always insisted on gowns for formal occasions. Nowadays I'm virtually the only one who still wears one to meetings, though most of us do on Speech Day. The parents like it. Gives them a sense of tradition. I like it because it provides good camouflage and saves on suits.

Gerry Grachvogel was locking his door as I came out. 'Oh. Hello, Roy.' He gave me a more than usually nervous smile. He is a lanky young man, with good intentions and poor classroom control. As the door closed I saw a pile of flat-packed cardboard boxes propped up against the wall.

'Busy day today?' I asked him, indicating the boxes. 'What is it? Invading Poland?'

Gerry twitched. 'No, ah – just moving a few things around. Ah – to the new departmental office.'

I regarded him closely. There was an ominous ring to that phrase. '*What* new departmental office?'

'Ah – sorry. Must get along. Headmaster's Briefing. Can't be late.'

That's a joke. Gerry's late to everything. '*What* new office? Has someone died?'

'Ah – sorry, Roy. Catch you later.' And he was off like a homing pigeon for the Common Room. I pulled on my gown and followed him at a more dignified pace, perplexed and heavy with foreboding.

I reached the Common Room just in time. The New Head was arriving, with Pat Bishop, the Second Master, and his secretary, Marlene, an ex-parent who joined us when her son died. The New Head is brittle, elegant and slightly sinister, like Christopher Lee in *Dracula*. The Old Head was foul-tempered, overbearing, rude and opinionated; exactly what I enjoy most in a Headmaster. Fifteen years after his departure, I still miss him.

On my way to my seat I stopped to pour myself a mug of tea from the urn. I noticed with approval that although the Common Room was crowded and that some of the younger members of staff were standing, my own seat had not been taken. Third from the window, just under the clock. I balanced the mug on my knees as I sank into the cushions, noticing as I did that my chair seemed rather a tight fit.

I think I may have put on a few pounds during the holidays.

'Hem-hem.' A dry little cough from the New Head, which most of us ignored. Marlene – fifty-ish, divorced, ice-blond hair and Wagnerian presence – caught my eye and frowned. Sensing her disapproval, the Common Room settled down. It's no secret, of course, that Marlene runs the place. The New Head is the only one who hasn't noticed.

'Welcome back, all of you.' That was Pat Bishop, generally acknowledged to be the human face of the School. Big, cheery, still absurdly youthful at fifty-five, he retains the broken-nosed and ruddy charm of an oversized schoolboy. He's a good man, though. Kind, hardworking, fiercely loyal to the School, where he too was once a pupil – but not overly bright, in spite of his Oxford education. A man of action, our Pat, of compassion, not of intellect; better suited to classroom and rugby pitch than to management committee and Governors' Meeting. We don't hold that against him, however. There is more than enough intelligence in St Oswald's; what we really need is more of Bishop's type of humanity.

'Hem-hem.' The Head again. It comes as no surprise that there is tension between them. Bishop, being Bishop, tries hard to ensure that this does not show. However, his popularity with both boys and staff has always been irksome to the New Head, whose social graces are less than obvious. 'Hem-*hem*!'

Bishop's colour, always high, deepened a little. Marlene, who has been devoted to Pat (secretly, she thinks) for the past fifteen years, looked annoyed.

Oblivious, the Head stepped forward. 'Item one: fund-raising for the new Games Pavilion. It has been decided to create a second administrative post to deal with the issue of fund-raising. The successful candidate will be chosen from a shortlist of six applicants and will be awarded the title of Executive Public Relations Officer in Charge of—'

I managed to tune out most of what followed, leaving the comforting drone of the New Head's voice sermonizing in the background. The usual litany, I expect; lack of funds, the ritual post-mortem of last summer's results, the inevitable New Scheme for pupil recruitment, another attempt to impose Computer Literacy on all teaching staff, an optimistic-sounding proposal from the girls' school for a joint venture, a proposed (and much-dreaded) School Inspection in December, a brief indictment of government policy, a little moan about Classroom Discipline and Personal Appearance (at this point Sourgrape Devine gave me a sharp look), and the ongoing litigations (three to date, not bad for September).

I passed the time looking around for new faces. I was expecting to see some this term; a few old lags finally threw in the towel last summer and I suppose they'll have to be replaced. Kitty Teague gave me a wink as I caught her eye.

'Item eleven. Reallocation of form-rooms and offices. Due to the renumbering of rooms following the completion of the new Computer Science Suite . . .'

Ah-ha. A fresher. You can usually spot them, you know, by the way they stand. Rigidly to attention, like army cadets. And the suits of course, always newly pressed and virgin of chalk dust. Not that *that* lasts long; chalk dust is a perfidious substance, which persists even in those politically correct areas of the school where the blackboard – and his smug cousin, the chalkboard – have both been abolished.

The fresher was standing by the computer scientists. A bad sign. At St Oswald's all computer scientists are bearded; it's the rule. Except for the Head of Section, Mr Beard, who, in half-hearted defiance of convention, has only a small moustache.

'. . . As a result, rooms 24 to 36 will be renumbered as rooms 114 to 126 inclusive, room 59 will be known as room 75, and room 75, the defunct Classics office, will be reallocated as the German Departmental Workroom.'

'*What?*' Another advantage of wearing gowns to staff meetings; the contents of a mug of tea, intemperately jerked across the lap, barely leave a mark. 'Headmaster, I believe you may have misread that last item. The Classics office is still in use. It is most certainly not *defunct*. And neither am I,' I added *sotto voce*, with a glare at the Germans.

The New Head gave me his chilly glance. 'Mr Straitley,' he said. 'All these administrative matters have already been discussed at last term's Staff Meeting, and any points you wanted to make should have been raised then.'

I could see the Germans watching me. Gerry – a poor liar – had the grace to look sheepish.

I addressed Dr Devine. 'You know perfectly well I wasn't at that meeting. I was supervising exams.'

Sourgrape smirked. 'I e-mailed the minutes to you myself.'

'You know damn well I don't *do* e-mail!'

The Head looked chillier than ever. He himself likes technology (or so he purports); prides himself on being up to date. I blame Bob Strange, the Third Master, who has made it clear that there is no room in today's educational system for the computer illiterate, and Mr Beard, who has helped him to create a system of internal communication of such intricacy and elegance that it has completely over-ridden the spoken word. Thus, anyone in any office may contact anyone else in any other office without all that unfortunate business of standing up, opening the door, walking down the corridor and actually *talking* to somebody (such a perverse notion, with all the nasty human contact that implies).

Computer refuseniks like myself are a dying breed, and as far as the administration is concerned, deaf, dumb and blind.

'Gentlemen!' snapped the Head. 'This is not the appropriate moment to debate this. Mr Straitley, I suggest you put any objections you may have in writing and e-mail them to Mr Bishop. Now shall we continue?'

I sat down. '*Ave, Caesar, morituri te salutant.*'

'What was that, Mr Straitley?'

'I don't know. Maybe it was the gentle crumbling of civilization's last outpost that you heard, Headmaster.'

Not an auspicious start to the term. A reprimand from the New Head I could bear, but the thought that Sourgrape Devine had managed to steal my office right from under my nose was intolerable. In any case, I told myself, I would not go gently. I intended to make Occupation very, very difficult for the Germans.

'And now to welcome our new colleagues.' The Head allowed a fractional warmth to colour his voice. 'I hope that you will make them at home, and that they will prove to be as committed to St Oswald's as the rest of you.'

Committed? They should be locked up.

'Did you say something, Mr Straitley?'

'An inarticulate sound of approval, Headmaster.'

'Hm.'

'Precisely.'

There were five freshers in all: one a computer scientist, as I had feared. I didn't catch his name, but Beards are interchangeable, like Suits. Anyway, it's a department into which, for obvious reasons, I seldom venture. A young woman to Modern Languages (dark hair, good teeth, quite promising so far); a Suit to Geography, who seem to have started a collection; a Games teacher in a pair of loud and disquieting Lycra running-shorts; plus a neat-looking young man for English who, for the moment, I have yet to categorize.

When you've seen as many Common Rooms as I have you begin to recognize the fauna that collect in such places. Each school has its own ecosystem and social mix, but the same species tend to predominate everywhere. Suits, of course (more and more of these since the arrival of the New

Head – they hunt in packs), and their natural enemy, the Tweed Jacket. A solitary and territorial animal, the Tweed Jacket, though enjoying the occasional bout of revelry, tends not to pair up very often, which accounts for our dwindling numbers. Then there's the Eager Beaver, of which my German colleagues Geoff and Penny Nation are typical specimens, the Jobsworth, who reads the *Mirror* during Staff Meetings, is rarely seen without a cup of coffee and is always late to lessons, the Low-Fat Yoghurt (invariably female, this beast, and much preoccupied with gossip and dieting), the Jackrabbit of either gender (who bolts down a hole at the first sign of trouble), plus any number of Dragons, Sweeties, Strange Birds, Old Boys, Young Guns and eccentrics of all kinds.

I can usually fit any fresher into the appropriate category within a few minutes' acquaintance. The geographer, Mr Easy, is a typical Suit: smart, clean-cut and built for paperwork. The Games man, gods help us, is a classic Jobsworth. Mr Meek, the computer man, is rabbity beneath his fluffy beard. The linguist, Miss Dare, might be a trainee Dragon if not for the humorous twist to her mouth; I must remember to try her out, see what she's made of. The new English teacher – Mr Keane – might not be as straightforward – not actually a Suit, not quite a Beaver, but far too young for the tweedy set.

The New Head makes much of this pursuit of Young Blood; the future of the profession, he says, lies with the influx of new ideas. Old lags like myself, of course, are not fooled. Young blood is cheaper.

I said as much to Pat Bishop later, after the meeting.

'Give them a chance,' he said. 'At least let them settle in before you have a go.'

Pat likes young folk, of course; it's part of his charm. The boys can sense it; it makes him accessible. It also makes him immensely gullible, however; and his inability to see the bad side of anyone has often caused annoyance in the past. 'Jeff Light's a good, straight sportsman,' he said. I thought of the Lycra-shorted Games teacher. 'Chris Keane comes highly recommended.' That, I could more readily believe. 'And the French teacher seems to have a lot of sense.'

Of course, I thought, Bishop would have interviewed everyone. 'Well, let's hope so,' I said, heading for the Bell Tower. Following that full-frontal attack by Dr Devine, I didn't want any more trouble than I had already.

2

YOU SEE; IT WAS ALMOST TOO SIMPLE. AS SOON AS THEY SAW
my credentials they were hooked. It's funny, how much
trust some people lay in pieces of paper: certificates,
diplomas, degrees, references. And at St Oswald's it's worse
than anywhere. After all, the whole machine runs on paperwork. Runs rather badly too, from what I gather, now that
the essential lubricant is in such short supply. It's money
that greases the wheels, my father used to say; and he was
right.

It hasn't altered much since that first day. The playing-
fields are less open now that the new housing developments
have begun to spread; and there's a high fence – wire on
concrete posts – to reinforce the NO TRESPASSERS signs.
But the essential St Oswald's is quite unchanged.

The right way to approach is from the front, of course.
The façade, with its imposing driveway and wrought-iron
gates, is built to impress. And it does – to the tune of six

thousand per pupil per year – that blend of old-style arrogance and conspicuous consumption never fails to bring in the punters.

St Oswald's continues to specialize in sententious titles. Here the Deputy Head is the Second Master; the Staff Room is the Masters' Common Room; even the cleaners are traditionally called Bedders, although St Oswald's has had no boarding pupils – and therefore no beds – since 1918. But the parents love this kind of thing; in Old Oswaldian (or 'Ozzie', as tradition has it), homework becomes Prep; the ancient dining-hall is still referred to as the New Refectory, and the buildings themselves – dilapidated as they remain – are subdivided into a multitude of whimsically named nooks and crannies: the Rotunda, the Buttery, the Master's Lodge, the Portcullis, the Observatory, the Porte-Cochère. Nowadays, of course, hardly anyone uses the official names – but they do look very nice in the brochures.

My father, to give him credit, was extraordinarily proud of his title of Head Porter. It was a caretaker's job, pure and simple; but that title – with its implied authority – blinded him to most of the snubs and petty insults he was to receive during his first years at the School. He'd left school at sixteen, with no academic qualifications, and to him St Oswald's represented a pinnacle to which he dared not even aspire.

As a result, he regarded the gilded boys of St Oswald's with both admiration and contempt. Admiration for their physical excellence; their sporting prowess; their superior bone structure; their display of money. Contempt for their softness; their complacency; their sheltered existence. I knew he was comparing us, and as I grew older I became more and more conscious of my inadequacy in his eyes, and of his silent – but increasingly bitter – disappointment.

My father, you see, would have liked a son in his own image; a lad who shared his passion for football and scratch-cards and fish and chips, his mistrust of women, his love of the outdoors. Failing that, a St Oswald's boy; a gentleman player, a cricket captain, a boy with the guts to transcend his class and make something of himself, even if it meant leaving his father behind.

Instead, he had me. Neither fish nor fowl; a useless daydreamer, a reader of books and watcher of B-movies, a secretive, skinny, pallid, insipid child with no interest in sports and whose personality was as solitary as his own was gregarious.

He did his best, though. He tried, even when I did not. He took me to football matches, during which I was heartily bored. He bought me a bicycle, which I rode with dutiful regularity around the outer walls of the School. More significantly, for the first year of our life there he kept reasonably and dutifully sober. I should have been grateful, I suppose. But I was not. Just as he would have liked a son in his image, I longed desperately for a father in mine. I already had the template in my mind, culled from a hundred books and comics. Foremost he would be a man of authority, firm but fair. A man of physical courage and fierce intelligence. A reader, a scholar, an intellectual. A man who understood.

Oh, I looked for him in John Snyde. Once or twice I even thought I'd found him. The road to adulthood is filled with contradictions, and I was still young enough to half-believe the lies with which that road is paved. *Dad knows best. Leave it to me. Elders and betters. Do as you're told.* But in my heart I could already see the widening gulf between us. For all my youth I had ambitions, while John Snyde, for all his experience, would never be anything but a Porter.

And yet I could see he was a good Porter. He performed his duties faithfully. He locked the gates at night, walked the grounds in the evening, watered plants, seeded cricket lawns, mowed grass, welcomed visitors, greeted staff, organized repairs, cleaned drains, reported damage, removed graffiti, shifted furniture, gave out locker keys, sorted post and delivered messages. In exchange some of the staff called him John, and my father glowed with pride and gratitude.

There's a new Porter now – a man called Fallow. He is heavy, discontented, lax. He listens to the radio in the Lodge instead of watching the entrance. John Snyde would never have stood for that.

My own appointment was made St Oswald-style, in isolation. I never met the other candidates. I was interviewed by the Head of Section, the Head and both the Second and Third Masters.

I recognized them at once, of course. In fifteen years Pat Bishop has grown fatter and redder and cheerier, like a cartoon version of his earlier self, but Bob Strange looks just the same despite his thinning hair; a lean, sharp-featured man with dark eyes and a poor complexion. Of course back then he'd only been an ambitious young English master with a flair for administration. Now he is the School's *éminence grise*; a master of the timetable; a practised manipulator; a veteran of countless INSET days and training courses.

Needless to say, I recognized the Head. The New Head, he'd been in those days; late thirties, though prematurely greying even then, tall and stiff and dignified. He didn't recognize me – after all, why should he? – but shook my hand in cool, limp fingers.

'I hope you have had time to look around the School to your satisfaction.' The capital letter was implicit in his voice.

I smiled. 'Oh yes. It's very impressive. The new IT department especially. Dynamic new tools in a traditional academic setting.'

The Head nodded. I saw him mentally filing away the phrase, maybe for next year's prospectus. Behind him Pat Bishop made a sound that might have been derision or approval. Bob Strange just watched me.

'What struck me particularly—' I stopped. The door had opened and the secretary had walked in with a tea-tray. It stalled me mid-phrase – the surprise of seeing her more than anything else, I suppose; I had no real fear *she* would recognize *me* – then I carried on: 'What struck me particularly was the seamless way the modern has been grafted on to the old to create the best of both worlds. A school that isn't afraid to give out the message that although it *can* afford the latest innovations, it hasn't merely succumbed to popular fads, but has used them to strengthen its tradition of academic excellence.'

The Head nodded again. The secretary – long legs, emerald ring, whiff of Number Five – poured tea. I thanked her in a voice that managed to be both distant and appreciative. My heart was beating faster; but in a way I was enjoying myself.

It was the first test, and I knew I had passed.

I sipped my tea, watching Bishop as the secretary removed the tray. 'Thank you, Marlene.' He drinks his tea as my father did – three sugars, maybe four – and the silver tongs looked like tweezers in his big fingers. Strange said nothing. The Head waited, his eyes like pebbles.

'All right,' said Bishop, looking at me. 'Let's get down to the nitty-gritty, shall we? We've heard you talk. We all know you can spout jargon at interview. My question is, what are you like in the classroom?'

Good old Bishop. My father liked him, you know; saw him as one of the lads, completely failing to see the man's real cunning. *Nitty-gritty.* A typical Bishop expression. You can almost forget that there's an Oxford degree (if only an upper Second) behind the Yorkshire accent and the rugby-player's face. No. It doesn't do to underestimate Bishop.

I smiled at him and put down my cup. 'I have my own methods in the classroom, sir, as I'm sure you do. Outside it,

I make it my business to know every bit of jargon that comes my way. It's my belief that if you can do the talk, and you get the results, then whether or not you've been following the latest government guidelines becomes irrelevant. Most of the parents don't know anything about teaching. All they want is to be sure they're getting their money's worth. Don't you agree?'

Bishop grunted. Frankness – real or faked – is a currency he understands. I sensed a grudging admiration in his expression. Test two – I'd passed again.

'And where do you see yourself in five years' time?' That was Strange, who had remained silent for most of the interview. An ambitious man, I knew, clever beneath his prissy exterior, eager to safeguard his little empire.

'In the classroom, sir,' I replied at once. 'That's where I belong. That's what I enjoy.'

Strange's expression did not alter, but he nodded, once, reassured that I was no usurper. Test three. Another pass.

There was no doubt in my mind that I was the best candidate. My qualifications were excellent; my references first-rate. They ought to be: I spent long enough forging them. The nicest touch was the name, carefully selected from one of the smaller Honours Boards on the Middle Corridor. I think it suits me, plus I'm sure my father would have been pleased that I'd re-created him as an Ozzie – an Old Boy of St Oswald's.

The John Snyde business was a long time ago; not even

the oldsters like Roy Straitley or Hillary Monument are likely to remember much about it now. But for my father to have been an Old Boy accounts for my familiarity with the School: my affection for the place: my desire to teach there. Even more than the Cambridge First, the reassuring accent and the discreetly expensive clothes, it makes me suitable.

I invented a few convincing details to carry the story – a Swiss mother, a childhood overseas. After such long practice I can visualize my father quite easily: a neat, precise man with musician's hands and a love of travel. A brilliant scholar at Trinity – that's where he met my mother, in fact – later to become one of the leading men in his profession. Both killed, tragically, in a cable-car accident near Interlaken, last Christmas. I added a couple of siblings for good measure: a sister in St Moritz, a brother at university in Tokyo. I did my probationary year at Harwood's Grammar School in Oxfordshire, before opting to move north into a more permanent post.

As I said, it was almost too easy. A few letters on impressive-looking headed paper, a colourful CV, an easy-to-fake reference or two. They didn't even check the details – disappointing, as I had gone to such lengths to get them right. Even the name tallies with an equivalent degree given out the same year. Not to myself, of course. But these people are so easily blinded. Even greater than their stupidity, there's the arrogance, the certainty that no one would cross the line.

Besides, it's a game of bluff, isn't it? It's all to do

with appearances. If I'd been a Northern graduate with a common accent and a cheap suit, I could have had the best references in the world and never have stood a chance.

They phoned me the same evening.

I was in.

3

St Oswald's Grammar School for Boys
Monday, 6th September

THE NEXT THING I DID AFTER THE MEETING WAS TO GO looking for Pearman. I found him in his office, with the new linguist, Dianne Dare.

'Don't mind Straitley,' Pearman told her cheerily as he introduced us. 'He's got a thing about names. He'll have a field day with yours, I know he will.'

I ignored the unworthy comment. 'You're letting your department be overrun by women, Pearman,' I said severely. 'Next you'll be picking out chintz.'

Miss Dare gave me a satirical look. 'I've heard all about you,' she said.

'All of it bad, I expect?'

'It wouldn't be professional for me to comment.'

'Hm.' She is a slender girl, with intelligent brown

eyes. 'Well, it's too late to back out now,' I said. 'Once St Oswald's gets you, you're here for life. It saps the spirit, you know. Look at Pearman, a shadow of his former self; he's actually surrendered my office to the Boche.'

Pearman sighed. 'I thought you wouldn't like that.'

'Oh, you did?'

'It was either that, Roy, or lose room 59. And since you never use your office—'

He was right, in a way, but I wasn't going to say so. 'What do you mean, lose room 59? That's been my form-room for thirty years. I'm virtually a part of it. You know what the boys call me? Quasimodo. Because I look like a gargoyle and I live in the Bell Tower.'

Miss Dare kept a straight face, but only just.

Pearman shook his head. 'Look, take it up with Bob Strange if you like. But this was the best I could do. You get to keep room 59 for most of the time, and there's still the Quiet Room if someone else is teaching there and you want to do some marking.'

That sounded ominous. I always mark in my own room when I'm free. 'Do you mean to say I'm going to be *sharing* room 59?'

Pearman looked apologetic. 'Well, most people share,' he said. 'We don't have the space otherwise. Haven't you seen your timetable?'

Well, of course I hadn't. Everyone knows I never even look at it until I need to. Fuming, I rummaged through my pigeon-hole and came up with a crumpled piece of computer paper and a memo from Danielle, Strange's secretary. I braced myself for bad news.

'Four people? I'm sharing my room with four upstarts and a House Meeting?'

'It gets worse, I'm afraid,' said Miss Dare meekly. 'One of the upstarts is me.'

It says a lot for Dianne Dare that she forgave me what I said then. Of course it was all in the heat of the moment: words spoken in haste, and all that. But anyone else – Isabelle Tapi, for instance – might have taken umbrage. I know; it's happened before. Isabelle suffers from delicate nerves, and any claim – for emotional trauma, for instance – is taken very seriously by the Bursar's office.

But Miss Dare held her ground. And to do her justice, she never left my room in disorder when she'd been teaching there, or rearranged my papers, or screamed at the mice, or commented on the bottle of medicinal sherry at the back of my cupboard, so I felt I hadn't done too badly with her.

All the same, I did feel resentful of this attack on my small empire; and I had no doubt who had been behind it. Dr Devine, Head of German and, perhaps more relevantly, Head of Amadeus House: which House was now scheduled, coincidentally, to meet in my form-room every Thursday morning.

Let me explain. There are five Houses at Saint Oswald's. Amadeus, Parkinson, Birkby, Christchurch and Stubbs. They deal principally with sporting fixtures, clubs and Chapel, so of course I don't have much to do with them. A

House system that runs principally on Chapel and cold showers doesn't have a lot going for it in my book. Still, on Thursday mornings these Houses meet in the largest rooms available to discuss the week's events, and I was most annoyed at this choice of my room as their meeting-place. Firstly, it meant that Sourgrape Devine would have the chance to poke around in all my desk drawers, and secondly it meant hideous confusion as a hundred boys struggled to cram into a room designed for thirty.

I told myself mournfully that it was only once a week. Still, I felt uneasy. I didn't like the speedy way Sourgrape had managed to get a foot in the door.

The other intruders, I have to say, concerned me less. Miss Dare I already knew. The other three were all freshers: Meek, Keane and Easy. It isn't unusual for a new staff member to teach in a dozen or more different rooms; there's always been a shortage of space at St Oswald's, and this year the conversion of the new Computer Science Suite had brought things to a crisis. Reluctantly I prepared to open my fortress to the public. I anticipated little difficulty from the new staff. Devine was the man to watch.

I spent the rest of the day in my sanctum, brooding over the paperwork. My timetable was a surprise – only twenty-eight teaching periods a week compared to thirty-four last year. My classes, too, seemed to have decreased in size. Less work for me, of course; but I didn't doubt that I'd be on cover every day.

Several people called: Gerry Grachvogel put his head

round the door and nearly lost it (he asked when I was planning to clear out my office); Fallow, the Porter, came to change the number on the door to 75; Hillary Monument, the Head of Maths, came to smoke a quiet cigarette out of the way of his disapproving deputies; Pearman to drop off some textbooks and to read me an obscene poem by Rimbaud; Marlene to bring my register; and Kitty Teague to ask how I was.

'All right, I suppose,' I said glumly. 'It isn't even the Ides of March yet. God knows what'll happen then.' I lit a Gauloise. I might as well do it while I still could, I told myself. There'd be precious little chance of a quiet smoke when Devine got in.

Kitty looked sympathetic. 'Come down to Hall with me,' she suggested. 'You'll feel better when you've had a bite to eat.'

'What, and have Sourgrape leering at me over his lunch?' In fact I had been planning to pop over to the Thirsty Scholar for a pint, but I didn't have the heart for it now.

'Do it,' urged Kitty, when I told her so. 'You'll feel better out of this place.'

The Scholar is, in theory at least, out of bounds to students. But it's only half a mile up the road from St Oswald's, and you'd have to be a complete innocent to believe that half the Sixth Form doesn't go there at lunch-times. In spite of grim lectures from the Head, Pat Bishop, who enforces discipline, tends to ignore the infringement. So do I, as long as they take their ties and blazers off; that way both they and I can pretend I don't recognize them.

It was quiet this lunch-time. There were only a few people in the bar. I caught sight of Fallow, the Porter, with Mr Roach – a historian who grows his hair long and likes the boys to call him Robbie – and Jimmy Watt, the School's man-of-all-work, skilful with his hands, but not much of an intellect.

He beamed on seeing me. 'Mr Straitley! Good holiday?'

'Yes, thank you, Jimmy.' I have learned not to tax him with long words. Some people are not so kind; seeing his moon face and gaping mouth, it's easy to forget his good nature. 'What are you drinking?'

Jimmy beamed again. 'Half a shandy, thanks, boss. Gotta get some wiring done this after.'

I carried his drink and my own to a free table. I noticed Easy, Meek and Keane sitting together in the corner with Light, the new Games man, Isabelle Tapi, who always enjoys socializing with new staff, and Miss Dare, slightly aloof, a couple of tables away. I wasn't surprised to see them together. There's safety in numbers, and St Oswald's can be intimidating to the newcomer.

Putting Jimmy's drink down, I ambled over to their table and introduced myself. 'It looks as though some of you are going to be sharing my room,' I said. 'Though I don't see how you're going to teach Computer Studies in it' – this was to the bearded Meek – 'or is it just another stage in your plan to inherit the earth?'

Keane grinned. Light and Easy just looked puzzled.

'I – I'm a part-timer,' said Meek nervously. 'I – t–teach M–maths on F–Fridays.'

Oh dear. If *I* frightened him, 5F on a Friday afternoon would eat him alive. I hated to think of the mess they would make in my room. I made a mental note to be on call if there were any signs of a riot.

'Bloody good place to have a pub, though,' said Light, gulping his pint. 'I could get used to this at lunch-time.'

Easy raised an eyebrow. 'Won't you be training, or supervising extracurricular, or rugby, or something?'

'We're all entitled to a lunch-break, aren't we?'

Not just a Jobsworth, but a Union man. Dear gods. That's all we need.

'Oh. But the Headmaster was – I mean, I said I'd take charge of the Geography Society. I thought everyone was supposed to do extracurricular.'

Light shrugged. 'Well, he would say that, wouldn't he? I'm telling you, there's no way I'm going to do after-school sports and weekend matches *and* give up my lunch-time pint as well. What is this, bloody Colditz?'

'Well, you don't have lessons to prepare, or marking—' began Easy.

'Oh, that's typical,' said Light, his face reddening. 'Typical bloody academic. Unless you've got it on paper it doesn't count, is that it? I'll tell you this for free, those lads'll get more from my lessons than they would learning the bloody capital of Khazistan, or whatever it is—'

Easy looked taken aback. Meek put his face into his lemonade and refused to come out. Miss Dare stared out of the window. Isabelle shot Light an admiring glance from beneath her smoky eyelashes.

Keane grinned. He seemed to be enjoying the fracas.

'What about you, then?' I said. 'What do you think of St Oswald's?'

He looked at me. Mid to late twenties; slim; dark-haired, with a fringe; black T-shirt under a dark suit. He seems very assured for such a young man, and his voice, though pleasant, has an edge of authority. 'When I was a boy I lived near here for a while. Spent a year at the local comp. Sunnybank Park. Compared to that, St Oswald's is another world.'

Well, *that* didn't surprise me much. Sunnybank Park eats kids alive, especially the bright ones. 'Good thing you escaped,' I said.

'Yeah.' He grinned. 'We moved down south, and I changed schools. I was lucky. Another year and that place would have finished me off. Still, move over Barry Hines; it's all good material if I ever write a book.'

Oh dear, I thought. Not a Budding Author. You get them from time to time, especially among the English staff, and though not as awkward as Union men or Jobsworths, they rarely bring anything but trouble. Robbie Roach was a poet in the days of his youth. Even Eric Scoones once wrote a play. Neither has ever quite recovered.

'You're a writer?' I said.

'Strictly a hobby,' said Keane.

'Yes, well – I understand the horror genre isn't as lucra-tive as it used to be,' I said, with a glance at Light, who was demonstrating a biceps curl to Easy with the aid of his pint of beer.

I looked back at Keane, who had followed my gaze. At first sight, he showed potential. I hoped he wouldn't turn out to be another Roach. English teachers so often have the fatal tendency; that thwarted ambition to be something more, something other than a simple schoolmaster. It usually ends in tears, of course; escape from Alcatraz looks positively childish in comparison with escape from teaching. I looked at Keane for signs of rot; I have to say that at first sight I didn't notice any.

'I wrote a b–book once,' said Meek. 'It was called *Java-script and other*—'

'I *read* a book once,' said Light, smirking. 'Didn't think much of it, though.'

Easy laughed. He seemed to have got over his initial faux pas with Light. At the next table, Jimmy grinned and moved a little closer to the group, but Easy, face half-averted, managed to avoid eye contact.

'Now if you'd said the *internet*—' Light moved his chair a few inches, blocking Jimmy, and reached for his half-finished beer. 'Plenty to read *there* – if you're not afraid of going *blind*, know what I mean—'

Jimmy slurped his shandy, looking slightly crestfallen. He isn't as slow as some people take him for, and besides, the snub was plain enough for anyone to see. I was suddenly reminded of Anderton-Pullitt, the loner of my form, eating his sandwiches alone in the classroom while the other boys played football in the Quad.

I shot a sideways glance at Keane, who was watching, neither approving nor disapproving, but with a gleam of appreciation in his grey eyes. He winked at me, and I smiled back, amused that the most promising of our freshers so far had turned out to be a Sunnybanker.

4

THE FIRST STEP IS ALWAYS THE HARDEST. I MADE MANY MORE illicit forays into St Oswald's, gaining confidence, moving closer into the grounds, the courtyards, then at last the buildings themselves. Months passed; terms; and little by little my father's vigilance diminished.

Things had not turned out quite how he'd hoped. The teachers who called him John remained no less contemptuous than the boys who called him Snyde; the Old Gatehouse was damp in winter, and between the beer and the football and his passion for scratchcards, there was never quite enough money. In spite of his great ideas, St Oswald's had turned out to be just another caretaker's job, filled with daily humiliations. It took up all his life. There never was time for tea on the lawn, and Mum never did come home.

Instead, my father took up with a brassy nineteen-year-old called Pepsi, who ran a beauty parlour in town, wore too much lip gloss and liked to party. She had her own place, but she often stayed at ours, and in the mornings my father was heavy-eyed and short-tempered, and the house smelt of cold pizza and beer. On those days – and others – I knew to keep out of his way.

Saturday nights were the worst. My father's temper was exacerbated by beer and, pockets empty after a night on the tiles, he most often chose me as the butt of his resentment. 'Yer little bastard,' he would slur at me through the bedroom door. 'How do I know you're mine, eh? How do I know you're even mine?' And if I was foolish enough to open the door, then it would start: the pushing, the shouting, the swearing, and finally the big slow roundhouse punch that, nine times out of ten, would strike the wall and send the drunkard sprawling.

I wasn't afraid of him. I had been once; but you can get used to anything in time, you know, and nowadays I paid as little attention to his rages as the inhabitants of Pompeii to the volcano that was one day to extinguish them. Most things, repeated often enough, can become routine; and mine was simply to lock the bedroom door, whatever came, and to keep well out of his way the morning after.

At first Pepsi tried to get me on her side. Sometimes she would bring me little presents, or try to make dinner, though she wasn't a great cook. But I remained stubbornly aloof. It wasn't that I disliked her – with her false nails and overplucked eyebrows, I considered her too stupid to dislike – or even that I resented her. No, it was her dreadful *palliness* which offended me; the implication that she and I could have something in common, that one day perhaps, we could be friends.

It was at this point that St Oswald's became my playground. It was still officially out of bounds, but by then my father had begun to lose his initial evangelism for the place, and he was happy to turn a blind eye to my occasional infringement of the rules, so long as I was discreet and drew no attention to myself.

Even so, as far as John Snyde was concerned, I only ever played in the grounds. But the Porter's keys were carefully labelled, each in its place in the glass box behind the Gatehouse door, and as my curiosity and my obsession grew I found it harder and harder to resist the challenge.

One small theft, and the School was mine. Now no door was closed to me; passkey in hand, at weekends I roamed the deserted buildings while my father watched TV, or went down the local with his mates. As a result, by my tenth birthday I knew the School better than any pupil, and I was able to pass – invisible and unheard – without so much as raising dust.

I knew the cupboards where the cleaning equipment was kept; the medical room; the electrical points; the archives. I knew all the classrooms; the south-facing Geography rooms, unbearably hot in summer; the cool, panelled Science rooms; the creaking stairs; the odd-shaped rooms in the Bell Tower. I knew the pigeon-loft, the Chapel, the Observatory with its round glass ceiling, the tiny studies with their rows of metal cabinets. I read ghost phrases from half-cleaned blackboards. I knew the staff – at least by reputation. I opened lockers with the master key. I smelt chalk and leather and cooking and wood polish. I tried on discarded Games kit. I read forbidden books.

Better still, and more dangerous, I explored the roof. The roof of St Oswald's was a huge, sprawling thing, ridged like a brontosaurus in stony overlapping plates. It was a small city in itself, with towers and quads of its own that mirrored the towers and quads of the School below. Great chimneys, imperially crowned, soared above the crooked ridges; birds nested; rogue elders sank their roots into damp crevices and flourished improbably, dripping blossom into the cracks between the slates. There were channels and gullies and monkey-puzzle ledges leading over the rooftops; there were skylights and balconies, perilously accessible from high parapets.

At first I was cautious, remembering my clumsiness in school gymnastics. But left to my own devices I gained in confidence; learned balance; taught myself to scramble silently over smooth slates and exposed girders; learned how to use a metal rail to vault from a high ledge on to a small balcony, and there down a thick, hairy elbow of creeper into a sallow-throated chimney of ivy and moss.

I loved the roof. I loved its peppery smell; its dankness in wet weather; the rosettes of yellow lichen that bloomed and spread across the stones. Here, at last, I was free to be myself. There were maintenance ladders leading out from various openings, but these were mostly in poor condition, some of them reduced to a lethal filigree of rust and metal, and I'd always scorned them, finding my own entrances to the rooftop kingdom, unblocking windows that had been painted shut decades before, looping pieces of rope around chimney stacks to aid ascent, exploring the wells and crawl-spaces and the great leaded stone gutters. I had no fear of heights or falling. I found to my surprise that I was naturally agile; on the roof my light build was a real advantage, and up here there were no bullies to mock my skinny legs.

Of course I had long known that maintaining the roof was a job my father detested. He could just about cope with a broken slate (as long as it was accessible from a window), but the leadwork that sealed the gutters was quite another matter. To reach that, one had to crawl down a slated incline towards the far edge of the roof, where there was a stone parapet that circled the gutter, and from there, to kneel, with three hundred feet of bluegreen St Oswald's air between himself and the ground, to check the seal. He never did this necessary duty; gave a multitude of reasons for failing to do so, but after the excuses had run dry I finally, gleefully guessed the truth. John Snyde was afraid of heights.

Already, you see, secrets fascinated me. A bottle of sherry at the back of a stock-cupboard, a packet of letters in a tin box behind a panel, some magazines in a locked filing-cabinet, a list of names in an old accounts book. For me, no secret was mundane; no titbit too small to escape my interest. I knew who was cheating on his wife; who suffered from nerves; who was ambitious; who read romantic novels; who used the photocopier illicitly. If knowledge is power, I owned the place.

By then I was in my last term at Abbey Road Juniors. It had not been a success. I had worked hard, kept out of trouble, but had consistently failed to make any friends. In an effort to combat my father's Northern vowels I had tried – disastrously – to imitate the voices and mannerisms of the St Oswald's boys, thereby earning myself the nickname 'Snobby Snyde'. Even some of the teachers used it; I'd heard them in their staff room, the heavy door swinging open into a fug of smoke and laughter. *Snobby Snyde*, pealed a woman's voice. *Oh, that's priceless. Snobby Snyde.*

I had no illusions that Sunnybank Park would be any better. Most of its intake was from the Abbey Road estate, a depressing block of pebble-dashed council houses and cardboard flatblocks with washing at the balconies and dark stairwells that smelt of piss. I'd lived there myself. I knew what to expect. There was a sandpit filled with nuggets of dogshit; a playground with swings and a lethal scattering of broken glass; walls of graffiti; gangs of boys and girls with foul mouths and grubby, inbred faces.

Their fathers drank with my father down at the Engineers'; their mothers had gone with Sharon Snyde to Cinderella's Dance-a-rama on Saturday nights. 'You want to make an effort, kid,' my father told me. 'Give 'em a chance, and you'll soon fit in.'

But I didn't want to make the effort. I didn't want to fit in at Sunnybank Park.

'Then what *do* you want?'

Ah. *That* was the question.

Alone in the echoing corridors of the School, I dreamed

of having my name on the Honours Boards, of sharing jokes with the St Oswald's boys, of learning Latin and Greek instead of woodwork and technical drawing, of doing prep instead of homework at the big wooden desks. In eighteen months, my invisibility had changed from a talent to a curse; I longed to be *seen*; I strove to belong; I went out of my way to take ever greater risks in the hope that one day, perhaps, St Oswald's would recognize me and take me home.

So I carved my initials alongside those of generations of Old Oswaldians on the oak panels in the Refectory. I watched weekend sports fixtures from a hiding-place at the back of the Games Pavilion. I struggled to the top of the sycamore tree in the centre of the Old Quad and made faces at the gargoyles at the edge of the roof. After school I ran back as fast as I could to St Oswald's and watched the boys as they left; heard their laughter and their complaints, spied on their fights, breathed the exhaust fumes of their parents' expensive cars as if it were incense. Our own school book-room was poorly stocked, mostly with paperbacks and comics, but in St Oswald's huge cloistered library I read avidly – *Ivanhoe* and *Great Expectations* and *Tom Brown's Schooldays* and *Gormenghast* and *The Arabian Nights* and *King Solomon's Mines*. Often I smuggled books home – some of them hadn't been taken out of the library since the forties. My favourite was *The Invisible Man*. Walking along the corridors of St Oswald's at night, smelling the day's chalk and the bland lingerings of the kitchen, hearing the dead echoes of happy voices and watching the shadows of the trees fall on to the newly polished floors, I knew exactly, and with a deep ache of longing, how he had felt.

All I wanted, you see, was to *belong*. Abbey Road Juniors had been shabby and rundown, a failing tribute to sixties liberalism. But Sunnybank Park was infinitely worse. I took regular beatings for my leather briefcase (everyone that year was carrying Adidas bags); for my contempt of sports; for my smart mouth; for my love of books; for my clothes; and for the fact that my father worked at *that posh school* (it didn't seem to matter that he was only the caretaker). I learned to run fast and to keep my head down. I imagined myself an exile, set apart from the others, who would one day be called back to where I belonged. Deep down I thought that if I *proved* myself, somehow, if I could withstand the bullying and the petty humiliations, then St Oswald's would one day welcome me.

When I was eleven and the doctor decided I needed glasses, my father blamed my reading. But secretly I knew that I had reached another milestone on the way to St Oswald's, and although 'Snobby Snyde' quickly became 'Speccy Snyde', still I was obscurely pleased. I scrutinized myself in the bathroom mirror and decided that I almost looked the part.

I still do; though the glasses have been replaced by contact lenses (just in case). My hair is a little darker than it was then, and better cut. My clothes too, are well cut, but not too formal – I don't want to look as if I'm trying too hard. I'm especially pleased with the voice; no trace of my father's accent remains, but the fake refinement which made Snobby Snyde such a dreadful little upstart has vanished. My new persona is likeable without being intrusive; a good listener; precisely the qualities needed in a murderer and a spy.

All in all, I was pleased with my performance today. Perhaps some part of me still expects to be recognized, for the thrill of danger was vivid in me all day as I tried not to seem too familiar with the buildings, the rules, the people.

The teaching part, surprisingly, is the easiest. I have my subject's lower sets throughout, thanks to Strange's unique timetabling methods (senior staff invariably get the better classes, leaving the new appointees with the rabble), and this means that, although my timetable is full, it is not intellectually taxing. I know enough about my subject to fool the boys, at least; when in doubt I use the teacher's books to help me.

It is enough for my purpose. No one suspects. I have no top sets or sixth-formers to challenge me. Nor do I anticipate any discipline problems. These boys are very different to the pupils of Sunnybank Park, and I have the whole disciplinary infrastructure of St Oswald's to reinforce my position, should I need it.

I sense that I will not, however. These boys are paying customers. They are used to obeying their teachers; their misbehaviour is limited to the occasional missed prep, or whispering in the classroom. The cane is no longer used – it is no longer necessary in the face of the greater, unspecified threat. It's rather comic, really. Comic and ridiculously simple. It's a game, of course; a battle of wills between myself and the rabble. We all know that there is nothing I could do if they all decided to leave the room at once. We all know, but no one dares to call my bluff.

All the same, I must not be complacent. My cover is good, but even a small misstep at this stage might prove disastrous. That secretary, for instance. Not that her presence changes anything, but it just goes to show that you can't anticipate every move.

I am wary, too, of Roy Straitley. Neither the Head, nor Bishop, nor Strange have spared me a second glance. But Straitley is different. His eyes are still as keen as they were fifteen years ago – and his brain, too. The boys always respected him, even if his colleagues didn't. Much of the gossip I overheard during those years at St Oswald's was in some way to do with him, and though his role in what happened was small, it was nevertheless significant.

He has aged, of course. He must be close to retirement now. But he hasn't changed; still the same affectations, the gown, the tweed jacket, the Latin phrases. I felt almost fond of him today, as if he were an old uncle I hadn't seen for years. But I can see him behind his disguise, even if he does not see me. I know my enemy.

I'd almost expected to hear of his retirement. In a way it would have made things easier. But after today, I'm glad he's still here. It adds excitement to the situation. Besides, the day I bring St Oswald's down, I want Roy Straitley to be there.

5

St Oswald's Grammar School for Boys
Tuesday, 7th September

THERE'S ALWAYS A SPECIAL KIND OF CHAOS ON THE FIRST day. Boys late, boys lost, books to be collected, stationery to be distributed. The classroom changes didn't help; the new timetable had failed to take into account the renumbering of the rooms, and had to be followed by a memo that no one read. Several times I intercepted columns of boys marching towards the new German departmental office instead of towards the Bell Tower, and had to redirect them.

Dr Devine was looking stressed. I had still not cleared out my old office, of course; all the filing cabinets were locked, and only I had the key. Then there were registers, pieces of holiday work to collect, fee cheques to be sent to the Bursar's office, locker keys to distribute, seating arrangements to be made, law to be enforced.

Luckily, I don't have a new form this year. My boys –
thirty-one of them in all – are old lags, and they know what
to expect. They have got used to me, and I to them. There's
Pink, a quiet, quirky lad with a strangely adult sense of
humour, and his friend Tayler; then there are my Brodie
Boys, Allen-Jones and McNair, two extravagant jokers who
earn themselves fewer detentions than they deserve because
they make me laugh; then red-headed Sutcliff; then Niu, a
Japanese boy, very active in the school orchestra; then
Knight, whom I do not trust; little Jackson, who has
to prove himself on a daily basis by picking fights; large
Brasenose, who is easily bullied; and Anderton-Pullitt,
a clever, solitary, ponderous boy who has many allergies
including, if we are to believe him, a very special form of
asthma which means that he should be excused from all
kinds of sports, as well as Maths, French, RE, homework on
Mondays, House Meetings, Assemblies and Chapel. He also
has a habit of following me around – which has caused Kitty
Teague to make jokes at the expense of my *Special Little
Friend* – and bending my ear about his various enthusiasms
(First World War aircraft, computer games, the music of
Gilbert and Sullivan). As a rule I don't mind too much –
he's an odd boy, excluded by his peers, and I think he may
be lonely – but on the other hand, I have work to do, and
no desire to spend what free time I have in socializing with
Anderton-Pullitt.

Of course, schoolboy crushes are a fact of teaching, with
which we learn to deal as best we can. We've all been on
the receiving end at some time or another – even people

like Hillary Monument and myself, who, let's face it, are about as unsightly a pair as you're likely to find out of captivity. We all have our ways of dealing with it, though I believe Isabelle Tapi actually encourages the boys – certainly, she has any number of *Special Little Friends*, as do Robbie Roach and Penny Nation. As for myself, I find that a brisk manner and a policy of benevolent neglect usually discourage overfamiliarity in the Anderton-Pullitts of this world.

Still, all in all, not a bad lot, 3S. They have grown over the holidays; some look almost adult. That ought to make me feel old, but it does not; instead I feel a kind of reluctant pride. I like to think that I treat all the boys equally, but I have developed an especial fondness for this form, which has been with me for the past two years. I like to think we understand each other.

'Oh, *sii–iiiiir!*' There were moans as I handed out Latin tests to everyone.

'It's the first day, sir!'

'Can't we have a quiz, sir?'

'Can we do hangman in Latin?'

'When I have taught you everything I know, Mr Allen-Jones, then perhaps we may find time to indulge in trivial pursuits.'

Allen-Jones grinned, and I saw that in the space marked 'Form-Room' on the cover of his Latin book, he had written 'Room formerly known as 59'.

There was a knock, and Dr Devine put his head around the door.

'Mr Straitley?'

'*Quid agis, Medice?*'

The class sniggered. Sourgrape, who never did Classics, looked annoyed. 'I'm sorry to trouble you, Mr Straitley. Could I have a quick word, please?'

We went out into the corridor, while I kept watch on the boys through the panel in the door. McNair was already beginning to write something on his desk, and I gave the glass a warning tap.

Sourgrape eyed me disapprovingly. 'I was really hoping to reorganize the departmental workroom this morning,' he said. 'Your filing cabinets—'

'Oh, I'll deal with those,' I replied. 'Just leave it all to me.'

'Then there's the desk – and the books – not to mention all those enormous *plants*—'

'Just make yourself at home,' I said in an airy tone. 'Don't mind my stuff at all.' There was thirty years of assorted paperwork in that desk. 'Perhaps you'd like to transfer some of the files to the archive, if you're free,' I suggested helpfully.

'I would not,' snapped Sourgrape. 'And while we're at it, perhaps you can tell me who has removed the new number 59 from the door of the departmental workroom and replaced it by this?' He handed me a piece of card, upon which someone had written: 'Room formerly known as 75' in an exuberant (and rather familiar) young scrawl.

'I'm sorry, Dr Devine. I don't have the slightest idea.'

'Well, it's nothing more than theft. Those door plaques

cost £4 each. That comes to £113 in all for twenty-eight rooms, and six of them are gone already. I don't know what you're grinning at, Straitley, but—'

'Grinning, did you say? Not at all. Tampering with room numbers? Deplorable.' This time I managed to keep a straight face, though Sourgrape seemed unconvinced.

'Well, I shall be making enquiries, and I'd be grateful if you could keep an eye out for the culprit. We can't have this kind of thing happening. It's disgraceful. This school's security has been a shambles for years.'

Dr Devine wants surveillance cameras on the Middle Corridor – ostensibly for security, but actually because he wants to be able to watch what everyone gets up to: who lets the boys watch Test Cricket instead of doing exam revision; who does the crossword during reading comprehensions; who is always twenty minutes late; who nips out for a cup of coffee; who allows indiscipline; who prepares his work materials in advance, who makes it up as he goes along.

Oh, he'd *love* to have all those things on camera; to possess hard evidence of our little failures, our little incompetencies. To be able to demonstrate (during a School Inspection, for instance) that Isabelle is often late to lessons; that Pearman sometimes forgets to arrive at all. That Eric Scoones loses his temper and occasionally cuffs a boy across the head, that I rarely use visual aids, and that Grachvogel, in spite of his modern methods, has difficulty controlling his class. I know all those things, of course. Devine merely suspects.

I also know that Eric's mother has Alzheimer's disease, and that he is fighting to keep her at home; that Pearman's wife has cancer; and that Grachvogel is homosexual, and afraid. Sourgrape has no idea of these things, closeted as he is in his ivory tower in the old Classics office. Furthermore, he does not care. Information, not understanding, is the name of his game.

After the lesson I discreetly used the master key to get into Allen-Jones' locker. Sure enough, the six door plaques were there, along with a set of small screwdrivers and the discarded screws, all of which I removed. I would ask Jimmy to replace the plaques at lunch-time. Fallow would have asked questions, and might even have reported back to Dr Devine.

There seemed no point in taking further action. If Allen-Jones had any sense, he wouldn't mention the matter either. As I closed the locker I caught sight of a packet of cigarettes and a lighter concealed behind a copy of *Julius Caesar*, but decided not to notice them.

I was free for most of the afternoon. I would have liked to stay in my room, but Meek was in there with a third-year Maths class, so I retreated to the Quiet Room (sadly a no-smoking area) for a comfortable chat with any colleagues who happened to be available.

The Quiet Room is, of course, a misnomer. A kind of communal office with desks in the middle and lockers around the edges, it is here that the staff grapevine has its roots. Here, under the pretext of marking, news is disseminated, rumours spread. It has the added advantage of being precisely *underneath* my room, and this lucky coincidence means that if required, I can leave a class to work in silence while I have a cup of tea or read *The Times* in congenial surroundings. Any sound from above is distinctly audible, including individual voices, and it is the work of an instant for me to rise, apprehend and swiftly punish any boy who creates a disturbance. In this way I have acquired a reputation for omniscience, which serves me well.

In the Quiet Room I found Chris Keane, Kitty Teague, Robbie Roach, Eric Scoones and Paddy McDonaugh, the RE master. Keane was reading, occasionally making notes in a red-bound notebook. Kitty and Scoones were going through departmental report cards. McDonaugh was drinking tea whilst flicking through the pages of *The Encyclopaedia of Demons and Demonology*. Sometimes I think that man takes his job a little too seriously.

Roach was engrossed in the *Mirror*. 'Thirty-seven to go,' he said.

There was a silence. When no one questioned his statement he elaborated. 'Thirty-seven working days,' he said. 'Till half-term.'

McDonaugh snorted. 'Since when did *you* ever do any work?' he said.

'I've already done my share,' said Roach, turning a page. 'Don't forget I've been at camp since August.' Summer camp is Robbie's contribution to the school's extracurricular programme: for three weeks a year he goes to Wales with a minibus of boys to lead walking expeditions, canoeing, paintballing and go-karting. It's what he enjoys; he gets to wear jeans every day and have the boys call him by his first name, but still he maintains that it is a great sacrifice, and claims his right to take it easy for the rest of the year.

'Camp,' scoffed McDonaugh.

Scoones eyed them with disapproval. 'I thought this was supposed to be the *Quiet* Room,' he pointed out in chilling tones, before returning to his report cards.

There was silence for a moment. Eric's a good chap, but moody; on another day he might be full of gossip himself; today he looked glum. It was probably the new addition to the French department, I thought to myself. Miss Dare is young, ambitious and bright – one more person to beware of. Plus, she's a woman, and an old-timer like Scoones doesn't like working alongside a woman thirty years younger than he is. He has been expecting promotion at any time these past fifteen years, but he won't get it now. He's too old – and not half amenable enough. Everybody knows it but Scoones himself, and any change to the departmental line-up only serves to remind him that he isn't getting any younger.

Kitty gave me a humorous look, which confirmed my suspicions. 'Lots of admin to catch up on,' she whispered. 'There was a bit of a mix-up last term and for some reason, these records got overlooked.'

What she means is that *Pearman* overlooked them. I've seen his office – overflowing with neglected paperwork, important files drowning in a sea of unread memos, lost coursework, exercise books, old coffee cups, exam papers, photocopied notes and the intricate little doodles he makes when he's on the phone. My own office may *look* the same, but at least I know where everything is. Pearman would be completely at sea if Kitty wasn't there to cover up for him.

'How's the new girl?' I asked provocatively.

Scoones huffed. 'Too smart for her own bloody good.'

Kitty gave an apologetic smile. 'New ideas,' she explained. 'I'm sure she'll settle down.'

'Pearman thinks the world of her,' said Scoones with a sneer.

'He would.'

Pearman has a lively appreciation of feminine beauty. Rumour has it that Isabelle Tapi would never have been employed at St Oswald's but for the minidress she wore at interview.

Kitty shook her head. 'I'm sure she'll be fine. She's full of ideas.'

'I could tell you what she's full of,' muttered Scoones. 'But she's *cheap*, isn't she? Before we know it, they'll be replacing all of us with spotty-faced upstarts with ten-a-penny degrees. Save a bloody fortune.'

I could see that Keane was listening to this; he was grinning as he made his notes. More material for the Great British Novel, I supposed. McDonaugh studied his demons. Robbie Roach nodded with sour approval.

Kitty was conciliatory, as ever. 'Well, we're all having to cut back,' she said. 'Even the textbook budget—'

'Tell me about it!' interrupted Roach. 'History's lost forty per cent, my form-room's a disgrace, there's water coming in through the ceiling, I'm working all hours and what do they do? Blow thirty grand on computers no one wants. What about fixing the roof? What about a paint job on the Middle Corridor? What about that DVD player I've been asking for since God knows when?'

McDonaugh grunted. 'Chapel needs work too,' he reminded us. 'Have to put school fees up again, that's all. No getting round it this time.'

'The fees won't go up,' said Scoones, forgetting his need for peace and quiet. 'We'd lose half the pupils if we did that. There's other grammar schools, you know. Better than this one, if truth be told.'

'*There is a world elsewhere*,' I quoted softly.

'I heard there's been some pressure to sell off some of the School's land,' said Roach, draining his coffee cup.

'What, the playing-fields?' Scoones, a staunch rugby man, was shocked.

'Not the rugby pitch,' explained Roach soothingly. 'Just the fields behind the tennis courts. No one uses them any more, except when boys want to sneak off for a fag. They're useless for sports anyway – always waterlogged. We'd be just as well selling them off for development, or something.'

Development. That sounded ominous. A Tesco's, perhaps, or a Superbowl where the Sunnybankers could go after school for their daily dose of beer and skittles.

'HM won't like that idea,' said McDonaugh drily. 'He doesn't want to go down in history as the man who sold St Oswald's.'

'Perhaps we'll go co-ed,' suggested Roach wistfully. 'Think of it . . . all those girls in uniform.'

Scoones shuddered. 'Ugh! I'd rather not.'

In the lull that followed, I suddenly became aware of a noise above my head; a stamping of feet, scraping of chairs and raised voices. I looked up.

'That your form?'

I shook my head. 'That's the new Beard from Computer Studies. Meek, his name is.'

'Sounds like it,' said Scoones.

The banging and stamping continued, rising to a sudden crescendo, within which I thought I could just make out the dim bleating of Their Master's Voice.

'Perhaps I'd better have a look.'

It's always a bit embarrassing to have to discipline another master's class. I wouldn't do it normally – we tend to mind our own business at St Oswald's – but it was my room, and I felt obscurely responsible. I charged up the stairs to the Bell Tower – not, I suspected, for the last time.

Halfway up, I met Dr Devine. 'Is that your class in there, making that frightful racket?'

I was offended. 'Of course not,' I huffed. 'That's the rabbit Meek. This is what happens when you try to bring Computer Studies to the masses. Anorak frenzy.'

'Well, I hope you're going to deal with it,' said Sourgrape. 'I could hear the noise all the way from the Middle Corridor.'

The nerve of the man. 'Just getting my breath back,' I said with dignity. Those stairs get steeper every year.

Devine sneered. 'If you didn't smoke as much, you'd be able to handle a few stairs.' Then he was off, brisk as ever.

My encounter with Sourgrape didn't do anything to improve my temper. I started on the class at once, ignoring the poor rabbit at the master's desk, and was enraged to find some of my own pupils among their number. The floor was littered with paper aeroplanes. A desk had been toppled. Knight was standing by the window, apparently enacting some farce, because the rest of the class was in paroxysms of laughter.

As I entered silence fell almost instantly – I caught a hiss – *Quaz!* – and Knight attempted – too late – to pull off the gown he had been wearing.

Knight faced me and straightened up at once, looking frightened. As well he might. Caught wearing *my* gown, in *my* room, impersonating *me* – for there was no doubt as to whom that simian expression and hobbling walk was supposed to represent – he must have been praying for the Underworld to swallow him up.

I have to say I was surprised at Knight – a sly, underconfident boy, he was usually happy to let others take the lead while he enjoyed the show. The fact that even *he* had dared to misbehave said little for Meek's discipline.

'You. Out.' A percussive whisper in these cases is far more effective than a raised voice.

Knight hesitated briefly. 'Sir, it wasn't—'

'*Out!*'

Knight fled. I turned on the rest of the group. For a moment I let the silence reverberate between us. No one caught my eye. 'As for the rest of you, if I ever have to come in like this again, if I hear as much as a raised voice coming from this room, I will put you all in after-school detention, culprits, associates and tacit supporters alike. Is that clear?'

Heads nodded. Among the faces I saw Allen-Jones and McNair, Sutcliff, Jackson and Anderton-Pullitt. Half my form. I shook my head in disgust. 'I had thought better of you, 3S. I thought you were gentlemen.'

'Sorry, sir,' muttered Allen-Jones, looking fixedly at his desk lid.

'I think it is Mr Meek who should be receiving the apology,' I said.

'Sorry, sir.'

'Sir.'

'Sir.'

Meek was standing very straight on the podium. My over-large desk made him seem even smaller and less significant. His doleful face looked to be all eyes and beard, not so much rabbit as capuchin monkey.

'I – hm – thank you, Mr Straitley. I – think I c–can – hm – m–manage from here now. Boys – ah, hm—'

As I left the room I turned to close the glass-panelled door behind me. For a second I caught Meek watching me from his perch. He turned away almost instantly, but not soon enough for me to have missed the look on his face.

No doubt about it – I made an enemy today. A quiet one, but an enemy nevertheless. Later he will come up to me in the Common Room and thank me for my intervention, but no amount of pretence from either of us can hide the fact that he has been humiliated in front of a class, and that I was the one to see it happen.

Still, that look startled me. It was as if a secret face had opened up behind the comic little beard and bushbaby eyes; a face of weak but implacable hatred.

6

I FEEL LIKE A CHILD IN A SWEETSHOP ON POCKET-MONEY DAY.
Where shall I start? Will it be Pearman, or Bishop, or
Straitley, or Strange? Or should I begin lower down, with
fat Fallow, who took my father's place with such boneless
arrogance? That stupid half-wit Jimmy? One of the newbies?
The Head himself?

I have to admit that I like the idea. But that would be too
easy; besides, I want to strike at the heart of St Oswald's,
not the Head. I want to bring it *all* down; simply knocking
off a few gargoyles won't do. Places like St Oswald's have a
habit of coming back to life; wars pass; scandals fade; even
murders are eventually forgotten.

Awaiting inspiration, I think I'll bide my time. I find that
I feel the same pleasure in being here that I experienced as
a child: that feeling of delicious trespass. Very little has
changed; the new computers sit uneasily on the new plastic
desks whilst the names of Old Oswaldians glare down from

the Honours Boards. The smell of the place is slightly different – less cabbage and more plastic, less dust and more deodorant – although the Bell Tower (thanks to Straitley) has retained the original formula of mice, chalk and sun-warmed trainers.

But the rooms themselves remain the same; and the platforms on which the masters strode like buccaneers on their quarterdecks; and the wooden floors, inked purple with time and polished to a lethal gloss every Friday night. The Common Room is the same with its dilapidated chairs; and the Hall; and the Bell Tower. It is a genteel decrepitude which St Oswald's seems to relish – and, more importantly, whispers *tradition* to the fee-paying parents.

As a child I felt the weight of that tradition like a physical ache. St Oswald's was so different from Sunnybank Park with its bland classrooms and abrasive smell. I felt uneasy at Sunnybank; shunned by the other pupils; contemptuous of the teachers, who dressed in jeans and called us by our first names.

I wanted them to call me Snyde as they would have done at St Oswald's; I wanted to wear a uniform and call them 'Sir'. St Oswald's masters still used the cane; by comparison my own school seemed soft and lax. My form-teacher was a woman, Jenny McCauleigh. She was young, easy-going and quite attractive (many of the boys had crushes on her), but all I felt was a deep resentment. There were no women teachers at St Oswald's. Yet again I had been given a second-rate substitute.

Over months I was bullied; mocked; scorned by staff as

well as pupils. My lunch money stolen; my clothes torn; my books thrown on to the floor. Very soon Sunnybank Park became unbearable. I had no need to feign illness; I had flu more often during my first year than I'd ever had in my life before; I suffered from headaches; nightmares; every Monday morning brought an attack of sickness so violent that even my father began to notice.

Once, I remember, I tried to talk to him. It was a Friday night, and he'd decided to stay at home for a change. These evenings in were rare for him, but Pepsi had got a part-time job in a pub in town, I'd been ill with flu again for a while and he'd stayed in and made dinner – nothing special, just boil-in-the-bag and chips, but to me it showed he was making an effort. For once, too, he was mellow; the six-pack of lager half-finished at his side seemed to have taken some of the edge off his perpetual rage. The TV was on – an episode of *The Professionals* – and we were watching it in a silence that was for a change companionable rather than sullen. The weekend lay ahead – two whole days away from Sunnybank Park – and I too felt mellow, almost content. There were days like that as well, you know; days when I could have almost believed that to be a Snyde was not the end of the world, and when I thought I could see some kind of a light at the end of Sunnybank Park, a time when none of it would really matter. I looked across at my dad and saw him watching me with a curious expression, a bottle held between his thick fingers.

'Can I have some?' I said, emboldened.

He considered the bottle. 'All right,' he said, handing

it over. 'No more, mind. I don't want you getting pissed.'

I drank, relishing the bitter taste. I'd had lager before, of course; but never with my father's approval. I grinned at him, and to my surprise he grinned back, looking quite young for a change, I thought, almost like the boy he must have been once, when he and Mum first met. For the first time really, it crossed my mind that if I'd met him then, I might even have liked that boy as much as she had – that big, soft, skylarking boy – that he and I could perhaps have been friends.

'We do all right without her, kid, don't we?' said my father, and I felt a jolt of astonishment in the pit of my stomach. He'd read my mind.

'I know it's been tough,' he said. 'Your mum and all that – and now that new school. Bet it's taken some getting used to, eh, kid?'

I nodded, hardly daring to hope.

'Them headaches, and all that. Them sick notes. You been having trouble at school? Is that it? Other kids been messing you about?'

Once more I nodded. Now, I knew, he would turn away. My father despised cowards. *Hit first and hit fast* was his personal mantra, along with *The bigger they are, the harder they fall*, and *Sticks and stones may break my bones*. But this time he didn't turn away. Instead he looked straight at me and said, 'Don't worry, kid. I'll sort it. I promise.'

Now it bloomed, appalling, in my heart. The relief; the hope; the beginnings of joy. My father had guessed. My father had understood. He had promised to sort it. I had a sudden, astonishing vision of him striding up to the gates of Sunnybank Park, my father, eighteen feet tall and splendid in his rage and purpose. I saw him walking up to my principal tormentors and bashing their heads together; running up to Mr Bray, the Games teacher, and knocking him down; best and most delightful of all, facing up to Miss McCauleigh, my form-teacher, and saying, 'You can stuff yer bloody school, dearie – we've found somewhere else.'

Dad was still watching me with that happy smile on his face. 'You might not think it, kid, but I've been through it, just like you. Bullies, bigger lads, they're always out there, always ready to give it a try. I wasn't that big when I was a kid, either; I didn't have many friends at first. Believe it or not, I know how you feel. And I know what to do about it, an'all.'

I can still remember that moment now. That blissful feeling of confidence, of order re-established. In that instant I was six years old again, a trusting child, secure in the knowledge that Dad Knows Best. 'What?' I said, almost inaudibly.

My father winked. 'Karate lessons.'

'Karate lessons?'

'Right. Kung Fu, Bruce Lee, all that? I know a bloke, see him down the pub from time to time. Runs a class on Saturday mornings. Ah, come on kid,' he said, seeing my expression. 'Couple of weeks of karate lessons and you'll be right as rain. Hit first and hit fast. Don't take any shit from anyone.'

I stared at him, unable to speak. I remember the bottle of beer in my hand, its cold sweat; on screen, Bodie and Doyle were taking shit from no one. Opposite me on the sofa, John Snyde was still watching with gleeful anticipation, as if awaiting my inevitable reaction of pleasure and gratitude.

So *this* was his wonderful solution, was it? Karate lessons. From a man down the pub. If my heart had not been breaking, I might have laughed aloud. I could see it now, that Saturday class; two dozen toughs from the council estate, weaned on *Street Fighter* and *Kick Boxer II* – with luck I might even run across a few of my principal tormentors from Sunnybank Park, give them the chance to beat me up in an entirely different environment.

'Well?' said my father. He was still grinning, and without much effort I could still see the boy he'd been; the slow learner; the bully-in-waiting. He was so absurdly pleased with himself, and so very far from the truth, that I felt, not contempt or anger as I'd expected, but a deep, unchildish sorrow.

'Yeah, OK,' I said at last.

'Told you I'd figure something out, didn't I, eh?'

I nodded, tasting bitterness.

'C'm'ere, kid, give yer old dad a hug.'

And I did, still with that taste at the back of my throat, smelling his cigarettes and his sweat and his beery breath and the mothball smell of his woolly jumper; and as I closed my eyes I thought to myself – *I am alone.*

Surprisingly enough, it didn't hurt as much as I'd

expected. We went back to *The Professionals* after that, and for a while I pretended to go to the karate lessons, at least until my father's attention turned elsewhere.

Months passed, and my life at Sunnybank Park settled into a dismal routine. I coped with it as best I could – mostly, increasingly, with avoidance. At lunch-times I would play truant and lurk in the grounds of St Oswald's. In the evenings I would run back to watch after-school games fixtures or to spy through the windows. Sometimes I even entered the buildings during school hours. I knew every hiding-place there was; I could always go unseen or, wearing a uniform pieced together from lost or pilfered items, in a corridor I could even pass for a pupil.

Over months I grew bolder. I joined the crowd at a school Sports Day, wearing an overlarge House singlet stolen from a locker on the Upper Corridor. I lost myself in the general mill and, emboldened by my success, even crashed a Lower School 800-metre race, presenting myself as a first-year from Amadeus House. I'll never forget how the boys cheered when I crossed the finishing-line, or the way the Duty Master – it was Pat Bishop, younger then; athletic in his running shorts and school sweatshirt – scruffed my cropped hair and said: *Well done, lad, two House points and report for the Team on Monday!*

Of course, I knew that there could be no question of my joining a team. I was tempted, but even I didn't dare go as far as that. My visits to St Oswald's were already as frequent as I could make them, and although my face was nondescript to the point of invisibility, I knew that if I wasn't careful I would one day be recognized.

But it was an addiction; as time passed I ran greater risks. I went into School at Break and bought sweets from the tuck-shop. I watched football matches, waving my St Oswald's scarf against supporters of the rival school. I sat in the shadow of the cricket pavilion, a perpetual Twelfth Man. I even joined the yearly full-School photograph, tucking myself into a corner among the new first-years.

In my second year I found a way to visit the School during lesson-time, missing my own Games period to do so. It was easy; on Monday afternoons we always had a five-mile cross-country run, which took us right around St Oswald's playing-fields and back in a wide loop to our own school. The other pupils hated it. It was as if the grounds themselves were an insult to them, provoking jeers and catcalls. Sometimes graffiti appeared on the brick walls of the perimeter after their passage, and I felt a fierce and penetrating shame that anyone watching us might imagine that I had been among those responsible. Then I discovered that if I hid behind a bush until the others had passed I could quite easily double back across the fields, thereby giving myself an entire free afternoon at St Oswald's.

At first I was careful; I hid in the grounds and timed the arrival of the Games class. I planned things meticulously. I had a good two hours before most of the runners arrived back at the school gates. It would be easy enough to change back into my kit and rejoin the tail of the group unnoticed.

Two teachers accompanied us – one in front, one at the

back. Mr Bray was a failed sportsman of colossal vanity and bludgeoning wit, who favoured athletic boys and pretty girls and held everyone else in utter contempt. Miss Potts was a student teacher, usually to be found at the tail of the group, holding court – she called it 'counselling' – to a little clique of admiring girls. Neither paid much attention to me; neither would notice my absence.

I hid my stolen St Oswald's uniform – grey jumper, grey trousers, school tie, navy blazer (with the School crest and the motto – *Audere, agere, auferre* – stitched across the pocket in gold) – under the steps of the Games Pavilion and changed there. No one saw me – St Oswald's Games afternoons were on Wednesdays and Thursdays, so I would not be disturbed. And as long as I was back for the end of my own school day, my absence would remain unnoticed.

At first the novelty of being in the School during lesson-time was enough. Unquestioned, I walked down the corridors. Some classes were uproarious. Others were eerily silent. I peered through glass panels at heads bent over their desks; at paper darts thrown surreptitiously behind a master's back; at notes passed in secret. I put my ear to closed doors and locked studies.

But my favourite haunt was the Bell Tower. A warren of little rooms, most rarely used – boxrooms, pigeon lofts, storage cupboards – with two teaching rooms, one large, one small, both belonging to the Classics department, and a rickety stone balcony from which I could gain access to the roof and lie there unseen on the warm slates, listening to the drone of voices from the open windows along the

Middle Corridor and making notes in my stolen exercise books. In that way I furtively followed a number of Mr Straitley's first-year Latin lessons; Mr Bishop's second-form Physics; Mr Langdon's History of Art. I read *Lord of the Flies* with Bob Strange's third form and even handed in a couple of essays to his Middle Corridor pigeon-hole (I collected them in secret the next day from Strange's locker, marked, graded, and with the word NAME?? scrawled across the top in red pen). At last, I thought, I'd found my place. It was a lonely place, but that didn't matter. St Oswald's – and all its treasures – were at my disposal. What else could I want?

Then I met Leon. And everything changed.

It was a dreamy, sunny late spring day – one of those days when I loved St Oswald's with a violent passion no mere pupil could have hoped to duplicate – and I was feeling unusually bold. Since our first encounter, my one-sided war against the School had gone through many stages. Hatred; admiration; anger; pursuit. That spring, though, we had reached a kind of truce. As I rejected Sunnybank Park I had begun to feel that St Oswald's was coming to accept me, slowly; my movement through its veins no longer that of an invader, but almost a friend – like an inoculation of some apparently toxic material that later turns out to be of use.

Of course I was still angry at the unfairness of it; at the fees that my father could never have afforded; at the fact that, fees or not, I could never hope to be accepted. But in spite of that, we had a relationship. A benign symbiosis, perhaps, like the shark and the lamprey. I began to understand that I need not be a parasite; I could let St Oswald's use me as I used it. Lately I had begun to keep records of things to be done around the School; cracked panes, loose tiles, damaged desks. I copied the details into the Repairs Book in the Porter's Lodge, signing them with the initials of various teachers to avoid suspicion. Dutifully, my father dealt with them; and I felt proud that in a small way I too had made a difference; St Oswald's thanked me; I was approved.

It was a Monday. I had been wandering along the Middle Corridor, listening at doors. My afternoon Latin class was over and I was considering going to the library, or the art block, and mingling with the study-period boys there. Or perhaps I could go to the Refectory – the kitchen staff would have gone by then – and sneak some of the biscuits left out for the teachers' after-school meeting.

I was so absorbed by my thoughts that as I rounded the bend into the Upper Corridor I almost bumped into a boy who was standing, hands in pockets, face to the wall, beneath an Honours Board. He was a couple of years older than I was – I guessed fourteen – with a sharp, clever face and bright grey eyes. His brown hair, I noticed, was rather long for St Oswald's, and the end of his tie, which was hanging disreputably out of his jumper, had been scissored off. I gathered – with some admiration – that I was looking at a rebel.

'Watch where you're going,' said the boy.

It was the first time any St Oswald's boy had bothered to speak to me directly. I stared at him, fascinated.

'What are you here for?' I knew that the room at the end of the Upper Corridor was a master's study. I'd even been in once or twice; a small airless place, knee-deep in papers, with several huge and indestructible plants sprawling ominously from a high and narrow window.

The boy grinned. 'Quaz sent me. I'll get off with a caution, or DT. Quaz never canes anyone.'

'Quaz?' I was familiar with the name; overheard in after-school conversations between boys. I knew it was a nickname, and could not put a face to it.

'Lives in the Bell Tower? Looks like a gargoyle?' The boy grinned again. 'Bit of a *podex*, but he's all right really. I'll talk him round.'

I stared at the boy with growing awe. His confidence fascinated me. The way he spoke of a master – not as a creature of terrifying authority, but as a figure of fun – made me inarticulate with admiration. Better still, this boy – this rebel who dared to flout St Oswald's – was talking to me as an equal, and *he didn't have the slightest idea who I was!*

I had never until then imagined that I might find an ally there. My visits to St Oswald's were painfully private. I had no schoolfriends to tell; confiding in my father or Pepsi would have been unthinkable. But this boy—

At last I found my voice. 'What's a *podex*?'

The boy's name was Leon Mitchell. I gave my own as Julian Pinchbeck, and told him I was a first-year. I was rather small for my age, and I thought it would be easier for me to pass as a member of another year group. That way Leon would not question my absence from Year Assemblies or Games.

I felt almost faint at the enormity of my bluff, but I was elated too. It was really so easy. If one boy could be convinced, then why not others – maybe even masters?

I suddenly imagined myself joining clubs, teams, openly attending lessons. Why not? I knew the School better than any of the pupils. I wore the uniform. Why should anyone question me? There must have been a thousand boys at the School. No one – not even the Head – could be expected to know them all. Better still, I had all the precious tradition of St Oswald's on my side; no one had ever heard of such a deception as mine. No one would ever suspect such an outrageous thing.

'Don't you have a lesson to go to?' There was a malicious gleam in the boy's grey eyes. 'You'll get bollocked if you're late.'

I sensed this was a challenge. 'I don't care,' I said. 'Mr Bishop sent me with a message for the office. I can say the secretary was on the phone, and I had to wait.'

'Not bad. I'll have to remember that one.'

Leon's approval made me reckless. 'I bunk off all the time,' I told him. 'No one's ever caught me.'

He nodded, grinning. 'So what is it today?'

I almost said Games, but stopped myself just in time. 'RE.'

Leon pulled a face. '*Vae!* Don't blame you. Give me the pagans any day. At least they were allowed to have sex.'

I sniggered. 'Who's your form-teacher?' I asked. If I knew that, I could find out for sure what year he was in.

'Slimy Strange. English. A real *cimex*. What about yours?'

I hesitated. I didn't want to tell Leon anything that could too easily be disproved. But before I could answer there was a sudden shuffle of footsteps in the corridor behind us. Someone was approaching.

Leon straightened up immediately. 'It's Quaz,' he advised in a quick undertone. 'Better scat.'

I turned towards the approaching footsteps, torn between relief at not having to answer the form-master question and disappointment that our conversation had been so short. I tried to imprint Leon's face into my memory; the lock of hair falling casually across his forehead; the light eyes; the ironic mouth. Ridiculous to imagine that I would ever see him again. Dangerous even to try.

I kept my expression neutral as the master entered the Upper Corridor.

I knew Roy Straitley by his voice alone. I'd followed his classes, laughed at his jokes, but only at a distance had I ever glimpsed his face. Now I saw him; a hunched silhouette in a battered gown and slip-on leather shoes. I ducked my head as he approached, but I must have looked guilty, because he stopped and looked at me sharply. 'You, boy. What are you doing here out of lessons?'

I mumbled something about Mr Bishop, and a message.

Mr Straitley didn't seem convinced. 'The office is on the Lower Corridor. You're miles away!'

'Yes, sir. Had to go to my locker, sir.'

'What, during lessons?'

'Sir.'

I could tell he didn't believe me. My heart raced. I dared a glance, and saw Straitley's face, his ugly, clever, good-natured face frowning down at me. I was afraid, but behind my apprehension lay something else; an irrational, breath-taking sense of hope. Had he seen me? Had someone finally seen me?

'What's your name, son?'

'Pinchbeck, sir.'

'Pinchbeck, eh?'

I could tell he was thinking what to do. Whether to question me further, as instinct dictated, or simply to let it go and deal with his own pupil. He studied me for a few seconds more – his eyes were the faded yellow-blue of dirty denim – and then I felt the weight of his scrutiny drop. I was not important enough, he'd decided. A Lower School boy, out of lessons without permission; no threat; somebody else's problem. For a second my anger eclipsed my natural caution. No threat, was I? Not worth the effort? Or had I, in all these years of hiding and skulking, at last become completely and irrevocably invisible?

'All right, son. Don't let me see you here again. Now scat.'

And I did, shaking now with relief. As I ran I distinctly heard Leon's voice behind me, whispering: 'Hey, Pinchbeck! After school. OK?'

I turned, and saw him wink at me.

7

St Oswald's Grammar School for Boys
Wednesday, 8th September

DRAMA BELOW DECKS; THE GREAT BLUNDERING FRIGATE
which is St Oswald's has hit the reef early this year. Firstly,
the date of the imminent School Inspection has been
announced for 6 December. This always causes disruption
on a massive scale, especially among the higher echelons of
the administrative staff. Secondly – and from my point
of view, much more disruptive – next term's unusual fee
increases were announced this morning by second-class
post, causing consternation at breakfast tables throughout
the county.

Our Captain continues to maintain that this is perfectly
normal and all in keeping with the rate of inflation, though
he remains at present unavailable for comment. Some
reprobates have been heard to mumble that if we, the staff,

had been informed of the prospective increase, then perhaps we would not have been taken so much by surprise by this morning's influx of angry phone calls.

Bishop, when questioned, supports the Head. He is a poor liar, however. Rather than face the Common Room this morning, he ran laps around the athletics track until Assembly, claiming that he felt unfit and needed the exercise. No one believed this, but as I walked up the steps to room 59 I saw him through the Bell Tower window, still running and dwarfed to forlorn proportions by the elevated perspective.

My form received the news of the fee increase with the usual healthy cynicism. 'Sir, does this mean we get a proper teacher this year?' Allen-Jones appeared unmoved by either the room-numbering incident or my own dire threats of the previous day.

'No, it just means a better stocked drinks cabinet in the Head's secret study.'

Sniggers from the form. Only Knight looked sullen. Following yesterday's unpleasantness, this would be his second day of punishment duty, and he had already been the object of ridicule as he paced the grounds in a bright orange jumpsuit, picking up discarded papers and stuffing them into an enormous plastic sack. Twenty years ago it would have been the cane and the respect of his peers; it goes to show that not all innovations are bad.

'My mum says it's a disgrace,' said Sutcliff. 'There're other schools out there, you know.'

'Yes, but any zoo would be happy to take you,' I said

vaguely, searching in my desk for the register. 'Dammit, where's the register? I know it was here.'

I always keep the register in my top drawer. I may *look* disorganized, but I usually know where everything is.

'When will *your* salary go up, sir?' That was Jackson.

Sutcliff: 'He's a millionaire already!'

Allen-Jones: 'That's because he never wastes money on clothes.'

Knight, in a low voice: 'Or soap.'

I straightened up and looked at Knight. Somehow his expression managed to be insolent and cringing at the same time. 'How did you enjoy your litter round yesterday?' I said. 'Would you like to volunteer for another week?'

'You didn't say that to the others,' muttered Knight.

'That's because the others know the line between humour and rudeness.'

'You pick on me.' Knight's voice was lower than ever. His eyes did not meet mine.

'*What?*' I was genuinely amazed.

'You pick on me, sir. You pick on me because—'

'Because what?' I snapped.

'Because I'm Jewish, sir.'

'What?' I was annoyed with myself. I'd been so pre-occupied with the missing register that I'd fallen for the oldest trick in the book, and allowed a pupil to draw me into a public confrontation.

The rest of the class was silent, watching us both expectantly.

I regained my composure. 'Rubbish. I don't pick on you

because you're *Jewish*. I pick on you because you can never keep your trap shut and you've got *stercus* for brains.'

McNair, Sutcliff or Allen-Jones would have laughed at that, and things would have been all right. Even Tayler would have laughed, and he wears a *yarmulke* in class.

But Knight's expression did not change. Instead I saw something there that I had never noticed before; a new kind of stubbornness. For the first time, Knight held my gaze. For a second I thought he was going to say something more, then he dropped his eyes in the old familiar way and muttered something inaudible under his breath.

'What was that?'

'Nothing, sir.'

'Are you sure?'

'Quite sure, sir.'

'Good.'

I turned back to my desk. The register might have gone astray, but I know all my boys; I would have known the moment I entered the room if one of them were missing. I intoned the list anyway – the schoolmaster's mantra – it never fails to calm them down.

Afterwards I glanced at Knight, but his face was lowered, and there was nothing about his sullen expression that suggested revolt. Normality had been resumed, I decided. The small crisis was over.

8

I DEBATED FOR A LONG TIME BEFORE KEEPING LEON'S appointment. I *wanted* to meet him – more than anything, I wanted to be his friend – though this was a line I had never crossed before, and on this occasion, there was more at stake than ever. But I liked Leon – had liked him from the first – and that made me reckless. At my own school, anyone who spoke to me risked persecution from my schoolyard tormentors. Leon was from another world. Despite his long hair and mutilated tie, he was an insider.

I did not rejoin the cross-country group. The next day, I would forge a letter from my father, saying that I'd had an asthma attack during the run, and forbidding me to take part again.

I had no regrets. I hated Games. I especially hated Mr Bray, my teacher, with his fake tan and his gold neck-chain, flaunting his Neanderthal humour to that little circle of sycophants at the expense of the weak; the clumsy; the inarticulate: the losers like me. And so I hid behind the pavilion, still dressed in my St Oswald's clothes, and waited, with some apprehension, for the end-of-school bell.

No one spared me a look; no one questioned my right to be there. All around me, boys – some in blazers or shirtsleeves, some still in their sports kit – jumped into cars; tripped over cricket bats; exchanged jokes, books, prep notes. A bulky, boisterous-looking man took charge of the bus queue – it was Mr Bishop, the Physics master – while an older man in a black and red gown stood at the Chapel gates.

This, I knew, was Dr Shakeshafte, the Head. My father spoke of him with respect and some awe – after all, he had given him his job. *One of the old school*, my father would say with approval: *Tough but fair. Let's hope the new man's half as good.*

Officially, of course, I knew nothing of the events that had led to the New Head's appointment. My father could be oddly puritanical about some things, and I suppose he felt it was disloyal to St Oswald's to discuss the matter with me. Already, however, some of the local papers had caught the scent, and I had learned the rest from overheard remarks between my father and Pepsi: to avoid adverse publicity, the Old Head was to remain until the end of term – ostensibly to induct the new man and to help him settle in – after which he would leave on a comfortable pension provided by the Trust. St Oswald's looks after its own: and there would be a generous out-of-court settlement for the injured parties – on the understanding, of course, that no mention was made of the circumstances.

As a result, I observed Dr Shakeshafte with some curiosity from my position at the School gates. A craggy-faced man of about sixty, not as bulky as Bishop, but with the same ex-rugbyman's build, he loomed over the boys like a gargoyle. A cane evangelist, I gathered from my father – *Good thing, too, teach these boys some discipline.* At my own school, the cane had already been outlawed for years. Instead, such people as Miss Potts and Miss McCauleigh favoured the empathic approach, whereby bullies and thugs were invited to discuss their feelings before being let off with a caution.

Mr Bray, himself a veteran bully, preferred the direct approach, so like my father's, in which the complainant was advised to *Stop whingeing to me and fight your own battles, for Christ's sake.* I pondered the exact nature of the battle that had resulted in the Head's involuntary retirement, and wondered how it had been fought. I was still wondering when, ten minutes later, Leon arrived.

'Hey, Pinchbeck.' He was carrying his blazer over one shoulder, and his shirt was hanging out. The scissored tie poked impudently from his collar like a tongue. 'What're you doing?'

I swallowed, trying to look casual. 'Nothing much. How did it go with Quaz?'

'*Pactum factum,*' said Leon, grinning. 'DT on Friday, as predicted.'

'Bad luck,' I shook my head. 'So what did you do?'

He made a dismissive gesture. 'Ah, nothing,' he said. 'Bit of basic self-expression on my desk lid. Want to go into town?'

I made a quick mental calculation. I could afford to be an hour late; my father had his rounds to do – doors to lock, keys to collect – and would not be home before five. Pepsi, if she was there at all, would be watching TV, or maybe cooking dinner. She had long since stopped trying to befriend me; I was free.

Try to imagine that hour, if you can. Leon had some money, and we had coffee and doughnuts in the little tea-shop by the railway station, then we went around the record shops, where Leon dismissed my musical tastes as 'banal', and expressed a preference for such bands as the Stranglers and Squeeze. I had a bad moment when we passed a group of girls from my own school, and a worse one when Mr Bray's white Capri stopped at some lights as we were crossing the road, but I soon realized that in my St Oswald's uniform, I might as well really have been invisible.

For a few seconds Mr Bray and I were close enough to touch. I wondered what would happen if I tapped at the window and said, 'You are a complete and utter *podex*, sir.'

The thought made me laugh so much and so suddenly that I could hardly breathe.

'Who's that?' said Leon, noticing me noticing.

'No one,' I said hastily. 'Some bloke.'

'The *girl*, you prat.'

'Oh.' She was sitting in the passenger seat, turned slightly towards him. I recognized her: Tracey Delacey, a couple of years older than I was, the current fourth-form pin-up. She was wearing a tennis skirt, and sat with her legs crossed very high.

'Banal,' I said, using Leon's word.

'*I'd* give her one,' said Leon.

'You would?'

'Wouldn't you?'

I thought of Tracey, with her teased hair and lingering smell of Juicy Fruit gum. 'Uh. Maybe,' I said, without enthusiasm.

Leon grinned as the little car pulled away.

My new friend was in Amadeus House. His parents – a university PA and a civil servant – were divorced ('but that's OK, I get double the pocket money'). He had a younger sister, Charlotte; a dog called Captain Sensible; a personal therapist; an electric guitar; and, it seemed to me, limitless freedom.

'Mum says I need to experience learning beyond the confines of the patriarchal Judaeo-Christian system. She doesn't really approve of St Oz – but Dad's the one who foots the bill. He was at Eton. Thinks day-schoolers are proles.'

'Right.' I tried to think of something honest to say about my own parents, but could not; in less than an hour's acquaintance I already sensed that this boy held more of a place in my heart than John or Sharon Snyde ever had.

Ruthlessly, then, I reinvented them. My mother was dead; my father was a police inspector (the most important-sounding job I could think of at the time). I lived with my father for part of the year, and for the rest of the time with my uncle in town. 'I had to come to St Oswald's mid-term,' I explained. 'I've not been here long.'

Leon nodded. 'That right? I thought you might be a newbie. What happened with the other place? D'you get expelled?'

The suggestion rather pleased me. 'It was a dump. My dad pulled me out.'

'I got thrown out of my last school,' said Leon. 'Dad was livid. Three grand a year, they were getting, and they chucked me out on a first offence. Talk about banal. You'd think they'd make more of an effort, wouldn't you? Anyway, we could do worse than St Oz. Specially now Shakeshafte's leaving, the old bugger—'

I saw my chance. 'Why's he going, anyhow?'

Leon's eyes widened humorously. 'You really are a newbie, aren't you?' He lowered his voice. 'Let me put it this way; I heard he was doing a bit more than just *shaking* his shaft . . .'

Things have changed since then, even at St Oswald's. In those days you could throw money at a scandal and it would go away. All that's changed now. We are no longer over-awed by the burnished spires: we can see the corruption beneath the shine. And it is fragile; a well-placed stone might bring it down. A stone, or something else.

I can identify with a boy like Knight. Small, lank, in-articulate, an obvious outsider. Shunned by his classmates, not for any question of religion, but for a more basic reason. It isn't anything he can alter; it's in the contours of his face, the no-colour of his limp hair, the length of his bones. His family may have money now, but generations of poverty lie bone-deep in him. I know. St Oswald's accepts his kind with reluctance in a time of financial crisis, but a boy like Knight will never fit in. His name will never appear on the Honours Boards. Masters will persistently forget his name. He will never be chosen for teams. His attempts to gain acceptance will always end in disaster. There is a look in his eyes that I recognize too well; the wary, resentful look of a boy who has long since stopped trying for acceptance. All he can do is hate.

Of course I heard about the scene with Straitley almost at once. The St Oswald's grapevine runs fast; any incident is reported within the day. Today had been a particularly bad one for Colin Knight. At registration, the spat with Straitley; at break, an incident with Robbie Roach over missing homework; at lunch-time, a flare-up with Jackson – also of 3S – which resulted in Jackson being sent home with a broken nose and Knight suspended for the week.

I was on duty in the grounds when it happened. I could see Knight in his protective overalls, gloomily picking up litter from the rosebeds. A clever, cruel punishment; far more humiliating than lines or detention. As far as I know, only Roy Straitley uses it. It's the same kind of overall my father used to wear and which the half-wit Jimmy wears now: large, bright orange and visible from right across the playing-fields. Anyone who wears it is fair game.

Knight had tried unsuccessfully to hide behind an angle of the building. A knot of smaller boys had gathered there and they were making fun of him, pointing out scraps of litter he had missed. Jackson, a small, aggressive boy who knows that only the presence of a loser like Knight prevents him from being bullied, was hanging around close by with a couple of other third-years. Pat Bishop was on duty, but out of earshot, surrounded by boys, on the other side of the cricket pitch. Roach, the history master, was on duty too, but seemed more interested in talking to a group of fifth-formers than sorting out discipline.

I went up to Knight. 'That can't be much fun.'

Knight shook his head sullenly. His face was pale and sallow, except for a red spot on each cheekbone. Jackson, who had been observing me, broke away from the little group and edged warily closer. I could see him measuring me with his eyes, as if to determine the threat I represented. Jackals do much the same thing when circling a dying animal.

'Want to join him?' I said sharply, and Jackson scuttled back to his group.

Knight gave me a look of furtive gratitude. 'It's not fair,' he said in a low voice. 'They're always picking on me.'

I nodded sympathetically. 'I know.'

'You know?'

'Oh yes,' I said quietly. 'I've been watching.'

Knight looked at me. His eyes were hot and dark and absurdly hopeful.

'Listen to me, Colin. Isn't that your name?'

He nodded.

'You have to learn to fight back, Colin,' I said. 'Don't be a victim. Make them pay.'

'Pay?' Knight looked startled.

'Why not?'

'I'd get into trouble.'

'Aren't you already?'

He looked at me.

'Then what's to lose?'

The end-of-break bell went then, and I had no time to say anything else, but in any case I didn't have to; the seeds were sown. Knight's hopeful gaze followed me across the schoolyard, and by lunch-time, the deed was done; Jackson was on the ground with Knight on top of him and Roach running towards them with his whistle bouncing against his chest and the others standing by in slack-jawed amazement at the victim who finally decided to fight back.

I need allies, you see. Not among my colleagues, but further down in the substrata of St Oswald's. Strike at the base, and the head will finally topple. I felt a fleeting stab of pity for the unsuspecting Knight, who will be my sacrifice, but I have to remind myself that in any war there must be casualties, and that if things go according to plan there will have to be many more before St Oswald's founders in a crash of broken idols and shattered dreams.

KNIGHT

1

St Oswald's Grammar School for Boys
Thursday, 9th September

THE CLASS WAS UNUSUALLY SUBDUED THIS MORNING AS I took the register (still missing) on a piece of paper: Jackson absent, Knight suspended and three others implicated in what was rapidly growing into a very messy incident.

Jackson's father had complained, of course. So had Knight's: according to their son, all he had done was to respond to intolerable provocation from the others, abetted – so claimed the boy – by their form-tutor.

The Head – still rattled by the numerous complaints about fees – had responded weakly, promising to investigate the incident, with the result that Sutcliff, McNair and Allen-Jones spent most of my Latin lesson standing outside Pat Bishop's office, having been named amongst Knight's chief tormentors, and I had received a summons via Dr

Devine, inviting me to explain the situation to the Head at my earliest convenience.

Of course, I ignored it. Some of us have lessons to teach; duties to perform; papers to read – not to mention clearing the filing cabinets from the new German office, as I pointed out to Dr Devine when he delivered the message.

Still, I was annoyed at the Head's unwarranted interference. This was a domestic matter – something which could and should be resolved by a form-tutor. Gods preserve us from an administrator with too much time on his hands; when a Head starts getting involved in matters of discipline, the results can be catastrophic.

Allen-Jones said as much to me at lunch-time. 'We were only winding him up,' he told me, looking awkward. 'We just went a bit far. You know what it's like.'

I did. Bishop did. I also knew that the Head did not. Ten to one he suspects some kind of conspiracy. I can see weeks of phone calls, letters home, multiple detentions, suspensions and other administrative nuisances before the matter can be laid to rest. It annoys me. Sutcliff is on a scholarship, which can be withdrawn in a case of serious misbehaviour; McNair's father is quarrelsome and will not submit meekly to a suspension; and Allen-Jones senior is an Army man whose exasperation with his bright, rebellious son too often tends to violence.

Left to my own devices, I would have dealt with the culprits rapidly and efficiently, without the need for parental intrusion – for although listening to boys is bad enough, to listen to their parents is fatal – but it's too late for that now. I was in a dark mood as I descended the stairs towards the Common Room, and when the idiot Meek bumped into me on the way in, almost knocking me over, I sent him on his way with a choice epithet.

'Bloody hell, who rattled your cage?' said Jeff Light, the Games teacher, sprawling from beneath his copy of the *Mirror*.

I looked at where he was sitting. Third from the window, under the clock. It's stupid, I know, but the Tweed Jacket is a territorial creature, and I had been goaded almost beyond endurance already. Of course I didn't expect the freshers to know, but Pearman and Roach were there, drinking coffee, Kitty Teague was marking books nearby, and McDonaugh was in his usual place, reading. All four of them glanced at Light as if he were a spillage someone had forgotten to clean up.

Roach coughed helpfully. 'I think you're in Roy's chair,' he said.

Light shrugged, but did not move. Next to him, Easy, the sandy-faced geographer, was eating cold rice pudding out of a Tupperware box. Keane, the would-be novelist, was looking out of the window, from which I could just see the lonesome figure of Pat Bishop, running laps.

'No, really, mate,' said Roach. 'He always sits there. He's practically a fixture.'

Light stretched his interminable legs, earning himself a smouldering glance from Isabelle Tapi in the yoghurt corner. 'Latin, isn't it?' he said. 'Queers in togas. Give me a good cross-country any day.'

'*Ecce, stercus pro cerebro habes*,' I told him, causing

McDonaugh to frown and Pearman to nod in a remote fashion, as if it were a quotation he vaguely recognized. Penny Nation gave me one of her pitying smiles and patted the seat next to her.

'It's all right,' I said. 'I'm not staying.' Gods help me, I wasn't that desperate. Instead, I put the kettle on and opened the sink cupboard to find my mug.

You can tell a lot about a teacher's personality from his coffee mug. Geoff and Penny Nation have twin mugs with CAPITAINE and SOUS-FIFRE written across them. Roach has Homer Simpson; Grachvogel has the *X-Files*. Hillary Monument's gruff image is belied daily by a pint mug with WORLD'S BEST GRANDPA in shaky young letters. Pearman's was bought on a school French trip to Paris and bears a photograph of the poet Jacques Prévert smoking a cigarette. Dr Devine disdains the humble mug altogether and uses the Headmaster's china – a privilege reserved for visitors, senior Suits and the Head himself – Bishop, always popular with the boys, has a different cartoon character every term (this term, Yogi Bear); gifts from his form.

My own is a St Oswald's Jubilee mug, limited edition 1990. Eric Scoones has one, as do several of the Old Guard, but mine has a chipped handle which enables me to distinguish it from the rest. We built the new Games Pavilion with the proceeds of that mug, and I carry mine with pride. Or would, if I could find it.

'Damn it. First the damn register and now the damn mug.'

'Borrow mine,' said McDonaugh (Charles and Diana, slightly chipped).

'That isn't the point.'

And it wasn't; to remove a master's coffee mug from its rightful place is almost as bad as taking his chair. The chair, the office, the classroom and now the mug. I was beginning to feel distinctly under siege.

Keane gave me a satirical look as I poured tea into the wrong mug. 'It's good to know that I'm not the only one having a bad day,' he said.

'Oh?'

'Lost both my free periods today. 5G. Bob Strange's English lit. class.'

Ouch. Of course everyone knows that Mr Strange has much to do; being Third Master and in charge of the timetable, he has over the years managed to construct for himself a system of courses, duties, meetings, admin periods and other necessaries, which leave him scarcely any time for actual pupil contact. But Keane seemed capable enough – after all, he'd survived Sunnybank Park – and I'd seen strong men reduced to jelly by those fifth-formers.

'I'll be all right,' said Keane, when I expressed due sympathy. 'Besides, it's all good material for my book.'

Ah, yes, the book. 'Whatever gets you through the day,' I said, wondering whether or not he was serious. There's a kind of quiet facetiousness about Keane – a whiff of the upstart – that makes me want to question everything he says. Even so I prefer him infinitely to the muscular Light, or the sycophantic Easy, or the timorous Meek.

'By the way, Dr Devine was asking for you,' Keane went on. 'Something about old filing cabinets?'

'Good.' It was the best news I'd had all day. Though after the fracas with 3S, even German-baiting had lost some of its flavour.

'He asked Jimmy to put them in the yard,' said Keane. 'Said to get them moved as soon as possible.'

'*What?*'

'Obstructing a thoroughfare, I think he said. Something to do with Health and Safety.'

I cursed. Sourgrape must *really* have wanted that office. The Health and Safety Manoeuvre is one to which only a few dare to sink. I finished my tea and strode purposefully towards the ex-Classics office, only to find Jimmy, screwdriver in hand, fixing some kind of an electronic attachment to the door.

'It's a buzzer, boss,' explained Jimmy, seeing my surprise. 'So Dr Devine knows if there's someone at the door.'

'I see.' In my day, we just knocked.

Jimmy, however, was delighted. 'When you see the red light, he's with someone,' he said. 'If it's green, he buzzes you in.'

'And the yellow light?'

Jimmy frowned. 'If it's yellow,' he said at last, 'then Dr Devine buzzes through to see who it is – ' he paused, wrinkling his brow – 'and if it's someone important, then he lets them in!'

'Very Teutonic.' I stepped past him into my office.

Inside, a conspicuous and displeasing order reigned. New

cabinets – colour-coded; a handsome water-cooler; a large mahogany desk with computer, pristine blotter and a framed photograph of Mrs Sourgrape. The carpet had been cleaned; my spider-plants – those scarred and dusty veterans of drought and neglect – tidily disposed of; a smug NO SMOKING sign and a laminated timetable showing departmental meetings, duties, clubs and workgroups, hung on the wall.

For a time, there was nothing to say.

'I've got your stuff, boss,' said Jimmy. 'Shall I bring it up for you?'

Why bother? I knew when I was beaten. I slouched off back to the Common Room to drown my sorrows in tea.

2

OVER THE NEXT FEW WEEKS, LEON AND I BECAME FRIENDS. IT was not as risky as it sounds, partly because we were in different Houses – he in Amadeus, whilst I claimed to be in Birkby – and in different years. I met him in the mornings – wearing my own clothes under my St Oswald's uniform – and arrived to my own classes late, with a series of ingenious excuses.

I missed Games – the asthma ploy had worked very well – and spent my breaks and lunches in St Oswald's grounds. I began to think of myself almost as a genuine Ozzie; through Leon I knew the masters on duty, the gossip, the slang. With him I went to the library, played chess, lounged on the benches in the Quad like any of the others. With him, I belonged.

It would not have worked if Leon had been a more outgoing, more popular pupil; but I had soon learned that he too was a misfit – though unlike me, he remained aloof by choice rather than necessity. Sunnybank Park would have killed him in a week; but St Oswald's values intelligence above everything else, and he was clever enough to use his to good advantage. To masters he was polite and respectful – at least, in their presence – and I found that this gave him an immense advantage in times of trouble – of which there were many. For Leon seemed actively to *court* trouble wherever he went: he specialized in practical jokes, small neat revenges, covert acts of defiance. He was rarely caught. If I was Knight, then he was Allen-Jones: the charmer, the trickster, the elusive rebel. And yet he liked me. And yet we were friends.

I invented tales of my previous school for his amusement, giving myself the role I sensed he expected of me. From time to time I introduced characters from my other life: Miss Potts, Miss McCauleigh, Mr Bray. I spoke of Bray with real hatred, remembering his taunts and his posturing, and Leon listened with an attentive look that was not quite sympathy.

'Pity you couldn't get your own back on this guy,' he commented on one occasion. 'Pay him back in kind.'

'What do you suggest?' I said. 'Voodoo?'

'No,' said Leon thoughtfully. 'Not quite.'

By then I had known Leon for over a month. We could smell the end of the summer term, its scent of cut grass and freedom; in another month all schools would break up (eight and a half weeks; limitless, unimaginable time) and there would be no need for changes of uniform or perilous truancies, forged notes or excuses.

We had already made plans, Leon and I; for trips to the cinema; walks in the woods; excursions into town. At Sunnybank Park exams – such as they were – were already over. Lessons were ramshackle, discipline, lax. Some teachers dispensed with their subjects altogether and showed Wimbledon on television, while others devoted their time to games and private study. Escape to Oz had never been easier. It was the happiest time of my life.

Then, disaster struck. It should never have happened; a stupid coincidence, that was all. But it brought my world crashing down, threatened everything I had ever hoped for – and its cause was the Games teacher, Mr Bray.

In the excitement of everything else, I had almost forgotten Mr Bray. I no longer went to Games – had never shown aptitude in any case – and I had assumed that I was not missed. Even without him, Games had been a weekly torment: my clothes tossed into the shower, my sports kit hidden or stolen; my glasses broken; my lukewarm efforts to participate greeted with laughter and contempt.

Bray himself had been the principal instigator of these jeering sessions, repeatedly singling me out for 'demonstrations' in which my every physical shortcoming was pointed out with relentless precision.

My legs were skinny, with prominent knees; and when I had to borrow games kit from school (mine had 'disappeared' once too often and my father refused to buy a new set), Bray provided me with a giant pair of flannel shorts, which flapped ludicrously as I ran, earning me the nickname 'Thunderpants'.

His admirers found this exquisitely amusing, and Thunderpants I remained. This had led to a general understanding among the other pupils that I had a flatulence problem; Speccy Snyde became Smelly Snyde; I was bombarded on a daily basis with jokes about baked beans, and in form matches (during which I was always last to be picked) Bray would cry to the other players, *Watch out, team! Snyde's been on the beans again!*

As I said, I was no loss to the subject, or, I thought, to the teacher. But I had failed to take into account the man's essential malice. It was not enough for him to hold court to his little clique of admirers and sycophants. It was not even enough to ogle the girls (and, on occasion, to dare a quick fumble under cover of a 'demonstration'), or to humiliate the boys with his trollish humour. Every performer needs an audience; but Bray needed more. Bray needed a victim.

I had already missed four Games lessons. I imagined the comments:

Where's Thunderpants, then, kids?

Dunno, sir. In the library, sir. Down the toilet, sir. Excused Games, sir. Asthma, sir.

Asshole, more like.

It would have been forgotten eventually. Bray would have found himself another target – there were plenty of them around. Fat Peggy Johnsen, or spotty Harold Mann, or muffin-faced Lucy Robbins, or Jeffrey Stuarts, who ran like a girl. In the end he would have turned his gaze on one of *them* – and they knew it, watching me with increasing hostility in class and Assembly, hating me for having escaped.

It was they, the losers, who would not let it go; who perpetuated the Thunderpants jokes; who harped incessantly on beans and asthma until every lesson without me seemed like a freakshow without the freak, and at last Mr Bray began to feel suspicious.

I'm not sure where he spotted me. Maybe he had me watched as I slipped away from the library. I had grown reckless; already Leon filled my life and Bray and his ilk were nothing but shadows in comparison. In any case he was waiting for me the next morning; I found out later that he had swapped supervision duties with another teacher to make sure he caught me.

'Well, well, you're looking very full of beans for someone with such terrible asthma,' he said as I ran in through the late entrance.

I stared at him, half-paralysed with fear. He was smiling viciously, like the bronzed totem of a sacrificial cult.

'Well? Cat got your tongue?'

'I'm late, sir,' I stammered, playing for time. 'My dad was—'

I could feel his contempt as he towered over me. 'Perhaps your dad could tell me more about this asthma of yours,' he said. 'Caretaker, isn't he, at the grammar school? Comes into our local from time to time.'

I could hardly breathe. For a second I almost believed that I *did* have asthma; that my lungs would burst with the terror of it. I hoped it would happen – at that time death seemed infinitely preferable to the possible alternatives.

Bray saw it, and his grin hardened. 'See me outside the changing-rooms after school tonight,' he said. 'And don't be late.'

I went through the day in a haze of dread. My bowels loosened; I couldn't concentrate; I went to the wrong classrooms; I couldn't eat my lunch. At afternoon break I was in such a state of panic that Miss Potts, the teacher trainee, noticed and asked me about it.

'Nothing, miss,' I said, desperate to avoid further attention. 'Just a bit of a headache.'

'More than a headache,' she said, coming closer. 'You're very pale—'

'It's nothing, miss. Really.'

'I think maybe you should go home. You might be coming down with something.'

'No!' I could not prevent my voice from rising. That would make things infinitely worse; if I didn't turn up, Bray would talk to my father; any chance I had of evading discovery would be lost.

Miss Potts frowned. 'Look at me. Is anything wrong?'

Silently, I shook my head. Miss Potts was just a student teacher, not much older than my father's girlfriend. She liked to be popular – to be important; a girl in my class, Wendy Lovell, had been making herself sick at lunch-times and when Miss Potts had found out about it, she had phoned the Eating Disorders Helpline.

She often talked about Gender Awareness; was an expert

on Racial Discrimination; had attended courses on Self-assertion and Bullying and Drugs. I sensed that Miss Potts was looking for a Cause, but knew that she would only be at school until the end of term, and that in a few weeks' time, she would be gone.

'Please, miss,' I whispered.

'Come on, sweetheart,' said Miss Potts, wheedling. 'Surely you can tell *me*.'

The secret was simple, like all secrets. Places like St Oswald's – and even to some extent, Sunnybank Park – have their own security systems, built, not on smoke detectors or hidden cameras, but on a thick stratum of bluff.

No one brings down a teacher – no one *thinks* to bring down a school. And why? The instinctive cringing in the face of authority – that fear that by far outstrips the fear of discovery. A master is always 'sir' to his pupils, however many years have passed; even in adulthood we find the old reflexes have not been lost, but have only been subdued for a time, emerging unchanged at the right command. Who would dare call that giant bluff? Who would dare? It was inconceivable.

But I was desperate. On one side there was St Oswald's; Leon; everything I had longed for; everything I had built. On the other, Mr Bray, poised over me like the word of God. *Did* I dare? Could I possibly carry it off?

'Come on, dear,' said Miss Potts gently, seeing her chance. 'You can tell me – I won't tell a soul.'

I pretended to hesitate. Then, in a low voice, I spoke. 'It's Mr Bray,' I said, meeting her eyes. 'Mr Bray and Tracey Delacey.'

3

St Oswald's Grammar School for Boys
Friday, 10th September

IT HAS BEEN A LONG FIRST WEEK. IT ALWAYS IS; BUT THIS year especially the silly season seems to have started early. Anderton-Pullitt is away today (one of his allergic reactions, says his mother), but Knight and Jackson are back in lessons, Jackson sporting an impressive black eye to go with his broken nose; McNair, Sutcliff and Allen-Jones are on behaviour report (Allen-Jones with a bruise to the side of his face which distinctly shows the marks of four fingers, and which he claims he got from playing football).

Meek has taken over the Geography Society, which, thanks to Bob Strange, now meets weekly in my room; Bishop has damaged an Achilles' tendon in the course of an overenthusiastic running session; Isabelle Tapi has taken to hanging around the Games department in a series of increasingly daring skirts; Dr Devine's invasion of the Classics office has suffered a temporary setback following the discovery of a mouse's nest behind the wainscoting; my coffee mug and register are still missing, which has earned me Marlene's disapproval, and when I returned to my room after lunch on Thursday I discovered that my favourite pen – green casing, Parker, with a gold nib – had disappeared from my desk drawer.

It was the loss of this last item that really annoyed me; partly because I only stepped out of my room for a half-hour or so, and more importantly, because it happened at lunch-time, which suggested to me that the thief was a member of the form. My very own 3S – good lads, or so I thought, and loyal to me. Jeff Light was on corridor duty at the time, and so, by chance, was Isabelle Tapi, but (unsurprisingly) neither of them noticed any unusual visitors to room 59 during that lunch-hour.

I mentioned the loss to 3S in the afternoon, hoping that someone might have borrowed the pen and forgotten to return it; only to be met with blank stares from the boys.

'What, no one saw anything? Tayler? Jackson?'

'Nothing, sir. No, sir.'

'Pryce? Pink? Sutcliff?'

'No, sir.'

'Knight?'

Knight looked away, smirking.

—*Knight?*

I took the register on a piece of paper and sent the boys away, now feeling distinctly uneasy. It hurt me to have to do it, but there was only one way to discover the culprit, and that was to search the boys' lockers. As it happened I was free that afternoon, and so I took my passkey and list of locker numbers, left Meek in charge of room 59 and a small group of lower-sixths unlikely to cause any disruption, and made my way to the Middle Corridor and the third-form locker room.

I searched in alphabetical order, taking my time and with especial attention to the contents of pencil-cases, finding nothing but half a carton of cigarettes in Allen-Jones' locker and a girlie magazine in Jackson's.

Then came Knight's; almost overflowing with papers, books and assorted junk. A silver pencil-box shaped like a calculator slid out from between two files; I opened it, but there was no pen. The next was Lemon's; then Niu's; Pink's; Anderton-Pullitt's – piled high with books on his all-consuming passion, First World War aircraft. I searched through all the lockers; found a stash of forbidden playing-cards and a pin-up or two, but no Parker pen.

I spent over an hour in the locker rooms, long enough for the class-change bell to go and the corridor to fill up though, fortunately, no pupil decided to visit his locker between lessons.

Left feeling more annoyed than before; not so much for the loss of the pen – which could, after all, be replaced – but for the fact that some of my pleasure in the boys had been spoilt by the incident, and the fact that until the thief was identified, I would not be able to trust any of them again.

*　　*　　*

Now I was on after-school duty, watching the bus queue; Meek was in the main Quad, barely visible in the mass of departing boys, and Monument was at the Chapel steps, supervising the proceedings from on high.

'Bye, sir! Have a good weekend!' That was McNair, racing by with his tie at half-mast and his shirt hanging out of his trousers. Allen-Jones was with him, running, as always, as if his life were in peril. 'Slow down,' I called. 'You'll break your necks.'

'Sorry, sir,' yelled Allen-Jones, without checking his pace.

I had to smile. I remember running like that – surely not so long ago, when weekends seemed as long as playing-fields. Nowadays they're gone in a blink: weeks, months, years – all gone into the same conjuror's hat. All the same, it makes me wonder. Why do boys always run? And when did I stop running?

'Mr Straitley.'

There was so much noise that I had not heard the New Head walk up behind me. Even on a Friday afternoon he was immaculate; white shirt, grey suit; tie knotted and positioned at precisely the correct angle.

'Headmaster.'

It annoys him to be called Headmaster. It reminds him that in the history of St Oswald's he is neither unique nor irreplaceable. 'Was that a member of your form,' he said, 'dashing past us with his shirt untucked?'

'I'm sure it wasn't,' I lied. The New Head has an adminis-trator's fixation on shirts, socks and other uniform trivia. He looked sceptical at my reply. 'I have noticed a certain disregard for the uniform regulations this week. I hope you'll be able to impress upon the boys the importance of making a good impression outside the School gates.'

'Of course, Headmaster.'

In view of the impending School Inspection, Making a Good Impression has become one of the New Head's main priorities. King Henry's Grammar School boasts a stringent dress code – including straw boaters in summer and top hats for members of the Chapel choir – which he feels contributes to their superior position in the league tables. My own ink-stained reprobates have a less flattering view of their rivals – or *Henriettas*, as St Oswald's tradition names them – with which I must admit to having some sympathy. Sartorial rebellion is a rite of passage, and members of the School – and of 3S in particular – express their revolt by means of untucked shirts, scissored ties and subversive socks.

I tried to say as much to the New Head, but was met with a look of such abhorrence that I wished I hadn't. '*Socks*, Mr Straitley?' he said, as if I had introduced him to some new and hitherto undreamed-of perversion.

'Well, yes,' I said. 'You know, Homer Simpson, *South Park*, Scooby-Doo.'

'But we have *regulation* socks,' said the Head. 'Grey wool, calf-length, yellow-and-black stripe. Eight ninety-nine a pair from the school outfitters.'

I shrugged helplessly. Fifteen years as Head of St Oswald's, and he still hasn't realized that no one – *no one!* – ever wears the uniform socks.

'Well, I expect you to put a stop to it,' said the Head, still looking rattled. 'Every boy should be in uniform, *full* uniform, at all times. I shall have to send a memo.'

I wondered if the Head, as a boy, had been in uniform, full uniform, at all times. I tried to imagine it, and found that I could. I gave a sigh. '*Fac ut vivas*, Headmaster.'

'What?'

'Absolutely, sir.'

'And speaking of memos . . . My secretary e-mailed you three times today asking you to see me in my office.'

'Really, Headmaster?'

'Yes, Mr Straitley.' His tone was glacial. 'We've had a complaint.'

It was Knight, of course. Or rather, Knight's mother, a bottle-blonde of indeterminate age and volatile temperament, blessed with a large alimony settlement and subsequent leisure time to lodge complaints on a termly basis. This time it was my victimization of her son on the grounds of his Jewishness.

'Anti-Semitism is a very serious complaint,' announced the Head. 'Twenty-five per cent of our customers – *parents*, that is – belong to the Jewish community, and I don't have to remind you—'

'No, you *don't*, Headmaster.' That was going too far. To take a boy's side against a master – and in a public place, where anyone might be listening – was beyond disloyal. I could feel my temper rising. 'This is a matter of personalities, that's all, and I expect you to back me fully in the face of this completely unfounded accusation. And while we're at it, may I remind *you* that there is a pyramid structure of discipline, beginning with the form-tutor, and that I don't relish having my duties taken over by someone else without being consulted.'

'Mr Straitley!' The Head was looking rather shaken.

'Yes, Headmaster.'

'There's more.' I waited for it, still seething. 'Mrs Knight says that a valuable pen, a bar mitzvah present to her son, vanished from his locker some time yesterday afternoon. And you, Mr Straitley, were seen opening third-form lockers at just about exactly the same time.'

Vae! I cursed myself mentally. I should have been more careful; should – according to the regulations – have searched the lockers in the presence of the boys themselves. But 3S are my own form – in many ways, my favourite form. Easier to do as I always did: to visit the culprit in secret – to remove the evidence – to leave it at that. It had worked with Allen-Jones and his door plaques; it would have worked with Knight. Except that I had found nothing in Knight's locker – though my gut still told me he was guilty – and had certainly not removed anything.

The Head had hit his stride. 'Mrs Knight not only accuses you of repeatedly victimizing and humiliating the boy,' he said, 'but of more or less accusing him of theft, then, when he denied it, of removing an item of value from his locker in secret – perhaps in the hope of making him confess.'

'I see. Well, this is what *I* think of Mrs Knight—'

'The School's insurance will cover the loss, of course. But it raises the question—'

'*What?*' I was almost at a loss for words. Boys lose things every day. To provide compensation in this case was tantamount to accepting that I was guilty. 'I won't have it. Ten to one the damn thing will turn up under his bed or something.'

'I'd rather deal with it at this level than have the complaint go to the Governors,' said the Head, with unusual frankness.

'I bet you would,' I said. 'But if you do, you'll have my resignation on your desk by Monday morning.'

HM blanched. 'Now take it easy, Roy—'

'I'm not taking it at all. A Headmaster's duty is to stand by his staff. Not to go running scared at the first piece of malicious tittle-tattle.'

There was a rather cold silence. I realized that my voice – long trained in the acoustics of the Bell Tower – had become rather loud. Several boys and their parents were loitering within earshot, and little Meek, who was still on duty, was watching me open-mouthed.

'Very good, Mr Straitley,' said the New Head in a stiff voice.

And at that he went on his way, leaving me with the sense that I had scored at best, a pyrrhic victory, and at worst, the most devastating kind of own goal.

4

POOR OLD STRAITLEY. HE WAS LOOKING SO DEPRESSED WHEN
he left today that I almost felt sorry I'd sneaked his pen. He
looked old, I thought – no longer fearsome but simply *old*, a
sad, baggy-faced comedian past his prime. Quite wrong, of
course. There's real grit in Roy Straitley; a real – and
dangerous – intelligence. Still – call it nostalgia if you
like, or perversity – today I liked him better than ever
before. Should I do him a favour, I wonder? For old times'
sake?

Yes, perhaps. Perhaps I will.

I celebrated my first week with a bottle of champagne.
It's still very early in the game, of course, but I have already
sown a good number of my poison seeds, and this is just the
beginning. Knight is proving to be a valuable tool – almost
a *Special Little Friend*, as Straitley calls them – talking to me
now almost every break, drinking in my every word. Oh,
nothing that might be directly incriminating – I of all

people, should know better than that – but with the help of hints and anecdotes I think I can guide him in the right direction.

His mother didn't complain to the Governors, of course. I didn't really expect her to, in spite of her histrionics. Not this time, anyway. Nevertheless, all these things are being filed away. Deep down, where it matters.

Scandal, the rot that makes foundations crumble. St Oswald's has had its share – neatly excised for the most part by the Governors and Trustees. The Shakeshafte affair, for instance – or that nasty business with the caretaker, fifteen years ago. What was his name? Snyde? Can't remember the details, old chap, but it just goes to show, you can't trust anyone.

In the case of Mr Bray and my own school, there were no Trustees to take matters in hand. Miss Potts listened with widening eyes and a mouth that went from pouty-persuasive to crabapple-sour in less than a minute. 'But Tracey's fifteen,' said Miss Potts (who had always made an effort to look nice in Mr Bray's lessons, and whose face was now rigid with disapproval). '*Fifteen*!'

I nodded. 'Don't tell anyone,' I said. 'He'll kill me if he finds out I've told you.'

That was the bait, and she took it, as I had known she would. 'Nothing's going to happen to you,' said Miss Potts firmly. 'All you have to do is tell me everything.'

I did not keep my after-school appointment with Bray. Instead, I sat outside the Headmaster's office, shaking with fear and excitement, and listening to the drama unfolding within. Bray denied it all, of course; but the besotted Tracey wept violently at his public betrayal; compared herself to Juliet; threatened to kill herself and finally declared that she was pregnant – at which announcement the meeting dissolved into panic and recrimination, Bray scuttled off to call his Union rep and Miss Potts threatened to inform the local newspapers if something was not done *at once* to protect more innocent girls from being led astray by this pervert – whom, she said, she had always suspected, and who should be locked up.

The next day, Mr Bray was suspended from school pending an inquiry, and in the light of its findings never came back. The next term, Tracey revealed that she wasn't pregnant after all (to the open relief of more than one of the fifth-formers), there was a new and very young PE teacher called Miss Applewhite who accepted my asthma excuse without question or curiosity, and even without the benefit of karate lessons, I found I had gained a dubious kind of respect among some of my peers as the pupil who had dared stand up to that bastard Bray.

As I said, a well-placed stone can bring down a giant. Bray was the first. The test case, if you like. Perhaps my classmates sensed it, sensed that I had somehow acquired a taste for fighting back, because after that, much of the bullying which had made my life at school unbearable came to a quiet end. I was no more popular than before, of course; but whereas people had hitherto gone out of their way to torment me, they now left me to my own devices, staff and pupils alike.

Too little, too late. By then I was going to St Oswald's almost every day. I lurked in corridors; I talked to Leon during breaks and lunch-times; I was recklessly happy. Exam week came, and Leon was allowed to revise in the library when he had no exam to sit, so together we escaped into town, looked at records – and sometimes stole them, although Leon had no need to do so, having more than enough pocket money of his own.

I, however, did not. Virtually all my own money – and this included my small weekly allowance as well as the lunch money I no longer spent at school – went on perpetuating my deception at St Oswald's.

The incidental expenses were astonishing. Books; stationery; drinks and snacks from the tuck-shop; bus fare to away matches, and, of course, uniform. I had soon discovered that although all boys wore the same uniform, there was still a certain standard to be maintained. I had presented myself to Leon as a new pupil; the son of a police inspector; unthinkable, then, that I should continue to wear the second-hand clothes I had pilfered from Lost Property, or the scuffed and muddy trainers I wore at home. I needed *new* uniform; shiny shoes; a leather satchel.

Some of these items I stole from lockers outside school hours, removing the nametags and replacing them with my own. Some I bought with my savings. On a couple of occasions I raided my father's beer money when he was out, knowing that he would come home drunk and hoping that he would forget exactly how much he had spent. It worked, but my father was more careful of these things than I had expected, and on the second try I was almost caught out. Fortunately, there was another suspect more likely than I was; a terrific row ensued; Pepsi wore sunglasses for the next two weeks; and I never risked stealing from my father again.

Instead I stole from shops. To Leon I pretended that I did it for fun; we had record-stealing competitions and divided the loot between us in our 'clubhouse' in the woods behind the school. I proved unexpectedly good at the game, but Leon was a natural; totally unafraid, he adapted a long coat especially for the purpose, slipping records and CDs into large pockets in the lining until he could hardly walk with their combined weight. Once, we were very nearly caught; just as we came to the doorway the lining of Leon's coat split, spilling records and their sleeves everywhere. The girl at the checkout gaped at us; customers stared open-mouthed; even the store detective seemed paralysed with astonishment. I was ready to run; but Leon just smiled apologetically, picked up his records with care and only then bolted for it, the wings of his coat flapping out behind him as he ran. It was a long time before I dared visit the shop again – though we did eventually, at Leon's insistence – but, as he said, we'd brought most of it with us anyway.

It's a question of attitude. Leon taught me that, though if he'd known of my imposture I suspect even he would have conceded my superiority at the game. That was im-possible, however. To Leon, most people counted as 'banal'. Sunnybankers were 'rabble'; and the people who lived on the council estates (including the flats on Abbey Road, where my parents and I had once lived) were 'pram-faces', 'slappers', 'toerags' and 'proles'.

Of course, I shared his contempt; but if anything my hatred ran deeper. I knew things that Leon, with his nice house and his Latin and his electric guitar, could not possibly know. Our friendship was not a friendship of equals. The world we had made between us would not support any child of John and Sharon Snyde.

It was my only regret that the game could not last for ever. But at twelve one does not think often of the future, and if there were dark clouds on my horizon, I was still too dazzled by my new friendship to notice them.

5

St Oswald's Grammar School for Boys
Wednesday, 15th September

THERE WAS A DRAWING TACKED TO MY FORM NOTICEBOARD when I came in after yesterday's lunch; a crude caricature of myself sporting a Hitler moustache and a speech bubble saying *'Juden 'raus!'*

Anyone could have placed it there – some member of Devine's set, who were in after Break, or one of Meek's geographers, even a duty prefect with a warped sense of humour – but I knew it was Knight. I could tell from the smug, bland look on his face, from the way he never met my eye, from the small delay between his 'Yes' and his 'Sir' – an impertinence only I observed.

I removed the picture, of course, and crumpled it into the waste-basket without even seeming to look at it, but I could smell the insurrection. Otherwise, all is calm, but I have been here too many years to be fooled; this is only the specious calm of the epicentre; the crisis is yet to come.

I never did find out who saw me in the locker room. It might have been anyone with an axe to grind; Geoff and Penny Nation are both the type, always reporting 'procedural anomalies' in that pious way which hides their real malice. I'm teaching their son this year, as it happens – a clever, colourless first-year boy – and ever since the set lists were printed they have paid an unhealthy amount of attention to my methods in class. Or it might have been Isabelle Tapi, who has never liked me, or Meek, who has his reasons – or even one of the boys.

Not that it matters, of course. But since the first day back I've had the feeling that someone was watching me, closely and without kindness. I imagine Caesar must have felt the same when the Ides of March came around.

In the classroom, business as usual. A first-year Latin group, still fatally under the impression that a verb is a 'doing word'; a sixth-form group of no-more-than-average students, ploughing their well-meaning way through *Aeneid* IX; my own 3S, struggling with the gerund (for the third time) between smart comments from Sutcliff and Allen-Jones (irrepressible, as ever) and more ponderous observations from Anderton-Pullitt, who considers Latin a waste of time better spent on the study of First World War aircraft.

No one looked at Knight, who got on with his work without a word, and the little test I gave them at the end of the lesson satisfied me that most of them were now as comfortable with the gerund as any third-year can reasonably expect to be. As a bonus to his main test, Sutcliff had added a number of impertinent little drawings, showing 'species of gerund in their natural habitat', and 'what happens when a gerund meets a gerundive'. I must remember to talk to Sutcliff some day. Meanwhile the drawings are Sellotaped on to the lid of my desk, a small, cheery antidote to this morning's mystery caricaturist.

In the department, there is good and bad. Dianne Dare seems to be shaping up nicely, which is just as well, as Pearman is at his least efficient. It isn't altogether his fault – I have a soft spot for Pearman, in spite of his lack of organization; the man has a brain, after all – but in the wake of the new appointment, Scoones is becoming a thorough nuisance, baiting and backbiting to such an extent that the quiet Pearman is perpetually on the verge of losing his temper, and even Kitty has lost some of her sparkle. Only Tapi seems unaffected; perhaps as a result of her burgeoning intimacy with the obnoxious Light, with whom she has been seen on numerous occasions in the Thirsty Scholar, as well as sharing a tell-tale sandwich in the Refectory.

The Germans, on the other hand, are enjoying their spell of supremacy. Much good may it do them. The mice may have gone – victims of Dr Devine's Health and Safety regulations – but Straitley's ghost endures, rattling his chains at the inmates and causing occasional mayhem.

For the price of a drink in the Scholar I have acquired a key to the new German office, into which I now retire every time Devine has a House Meeting. It's only ten minutes, I know, but in that time I usually find that I can cause enough inadvertent disorder – coffee cups on the desk, phone out of alignment, crosswords completed in Sourgrape's personal copy of *The Times* – to remind them of my continued presence.

My filing cabinets have been annexed to the nearby Book Room – this also troubles Dr Devine, who was until recently unaware of the existence of the door which divides the two rooms, and which I have now reinstated. He can smell my cigarette smoke from his desk, he says, and invokes Health and Safety with an expression of pious self-satisfaction; so many books must surely present a fire hazard, he protests, and speaks of installing a smoke detector.

Fortunately, Bob Strange – who in his capacity as Third Master, oversees all departmental spending – has made it clear that until the Inspection is over there must be no more unnecessary expenditure, and Sourgrape is forced to endure my presence for the moment, whilst no doubt planning his next move.

Meanwhile, the Head continues his offensive on socks. Monday's Assembly was entirely constructed around the subject, with the result that since then, virtually all the boys in my form have taken to wearing their most controversial socks to school – with, in some cases, the additional extravagance of a pair of brightly coloured sock suspenders.

So far I have counted: one Bugs Bunny, three Bart Simpsons, a *South Park*, four Beavis and Buttheads and, from Allen-Jones, a shocking-pink pair with the Powerpuff Girls embroidered on them in sequins. It's fortunate, then, that my eyes aren't as good as they once were, and that I never notice that kind of thing.

Of course, no one is fooled by the New Head's sudden interest in anklewear. The date of the School Inspection is approaching steadily, and after the disappointing exam results of last summer (thanks to an overburdening of coursework and the latest governmental scheme), he knows that he cannot afford a lacklustre report.

As a result, socks, shirts, ties and such will be prime targets this term, as will graffiti, Health and Safety, mice, computer literacy and walking on the left-hand side of the corridor at all times. There will be in-school assessment for all staff in preparation; a new brochure is already being printed; a subcommittee has been formed to discuss possibilities for improving the image of the school; and an additional row of disabled parking-spaces has been introduced in the visitors' car-park.

In the wake of this unusual activity, the Porter, Fallow, is at his most officious. Blessed with the ability to seem very busy whilst actually avoiding work of any kind, he has taken to lurking in corners and outside form-rooms, clipboard in hand, overseeing Jimmy's repairs and renovations. In this way he gets to overhear a great deal of staff conversation, most of which, I suspect, he passes on to Dr Devine. Certainly, Sourgrape, though he outwardly scorns the gossip of the Common Room, seems remarkably well informed.

Miss Dare was in my form-room this afternoon, covering for Meek, who is ill. Stomach flu, or so Bob Strange tells me, though I have my suspicions. Some people were born to teach, others not, and though Meek won't beat the all-time record – that belongs to a Maths teacher called Jerome Fentimann, who vanished at Break on his first day, never to be seen again – I wouldn't be surprised if he left us mid-term, as a result of some nebulous affliction.

Fortunately, Miss Dare is made of stronger stuff. I can hear her from the Quiet Room, talking to Meek's computer scientists. That calm manner of hers is deceptive; underneath it, she is intelligent and capable. Her aloofness has nothing to do with being shy, I realize. She simply enjoys her own company, and has little to do with the other newcomers. I see her quite often – after all, we share a room – and I have been struck by the speed with which she has adapted to the messy topography of St Oswald's; to the multitude of rooms; to the traditions and taboos; to the infrastructure. She is friendly with the boys without falling into the trap of intimacy; knows how to punish without provoking resentment; knows her subject.

Today before school I found her marking books in my form-room, and was able to observe her for a few seconds before she became conscious of my presence. Slim; business-like in a crisp white blouse and neat grey trousers; dark hair short and discreetly well cut. I took a step forwards; she saw me and stood up at once, vacating my chair.

'Good morning, sir. I wasn't expecting you so early.'

It was seven forty-five. Light, true to type, arrives at five to nine every morning; Bishop gets in early, but only to run his interminable laps, and even Gerry Grachvogel is never in his room before eight. And that *sir* – I hoped the woman wasn't going to be a crawler. On the other hand, I don't like freshers to make free of my first name, as if I were the plumber, or someone they'd met down the pub. 'What's wrong with the Quiet Room?' I said.

'Mr Pearman and Mr Scoones were discussing recent appointments. I thought it might be more tactful to retire.'

'I see.' I sat down and lit an early Gauloise.

'I'm sorry, sir. I should have asked your permission.' Her tone was polite, but her eyes gleamed. I decided that she was an upstart, and liked her the better for it.

'Cigarette?'

'No, thanks, I don't smoke.'

'No vices, eh?' Please gods, not another Sourgrape.

'Believe me, I have plenty.'

'Hm.'

'One of your boys was telling me you'd been in this room for over twenty years.'

'Longer, if you count the years as an inmate.' In those days there had been a whole Classics empire; French was a single Tweed Jacket weaned on the *méthode Assimil*; German was unpatriotic.

O tempora! O mores! I gave a deep sigh. Horatius at the bridge, single-handedly holding back the barbarian hordes.

Miss Dare was grinning. 'Well, it makes a change from plastic desks and whiteboards. I think you're right to hold out. Besides, I like your Latinists. I don't have to teach them grammar. *And* they can spell.'

Clearly, I thought, an intelligent girl. I wondered what

she wanted with me. There are far quicker ways up the greasy pole than via the Bell Tower, and if that was her ambition, then her flattery would have worked better on Bob Strange, or Pearman, or Devine. 'You want to be careful, hanging around this place,' I told her. 'Before you know it, you're sixty-five, overweight and covered with chalk.'

Miss Dare smiled and picked up her marking. 'I'm sure you have work to do,' she said, making for the door. Then she stopped. 'Excuse me for asking, sir,' she said. 'But you're not planning retirement this year, are you?'

'Retirement? You must be joking. I'm holding out for a Century.' I looked at her closely. 'Why? Has someone said anything?'

Miss Dare looked awkward. 'It's just that—' She hesitated. 'As a junior member of the School, Mr Strange has asked me to edit the school magazine. And as I was going over the staff and departmental lists I happened to notice—'

'Notice what?' Now her politeness was beginning to get on my nerves. 'Out with it, for gods' sakes!'

'It's just that – you don't seem to have an entry this year,' said Miss Dare. 'It makes it look as if the Classics department has been—' She paused again, searching for the word, and I found myself reaching the limits of my patience.

'What? What? Marginalized? Amalgamated? Damn the terminology and tell me what you think! What's happened to the bloody Classics department?'

'Good question, sir,' said Miss Dare, unruffled. 'As far as the School's literature is concerned – publicity brochures, department listings, school magazine – it just isn't there.' She paused again. 'And, sir . . . According to the staff listings, neither are you.'

6

Monday, 20th September

IT WAS ALL OVER THE SCHOOL BY THE END OF THE WEEK. Given the circumstances, you might have expected old Straitley to keep quiet for a while, to review his options and maintain a low profile, but it isn't in his nature to do that, even when it's the only wise thing to do. But being Straitley, he marched straight down to Strange's office as soon as he had confirmed the facts, and forced a confrontation.

Strange, of course, denied having done anything under-hand. The new department, he said, would simply be known as Foreign Languages, which included Classical *and* Modern Languages, as well as two new subjects, Language Awareness and Language Design, which were to take place in the computer labs once a week as soon as the relevant software arrived (it would, he was assured, be in place for the School Inspection on 6 December).

Classics had neither been demoted nor marginalized, said Strange; instead the entire profile of Foreign Languages had been upgraded to meet curriculum guidelines. St Henry's, he understood, had already done so four years before, and in a competitive market—

What Roy Straitley thought of that is not on record. Thankfully, from what I heard, most of the abuse was in Latin, but even so, there remains a polite and meticulous coldness between them.

'Bob' has become 'Mr Strange'. For the first time in his career, Straitley has adopted a work-to-rule attitude to his duties; insists on being informed no later than eight-thirty the same morning if he is to lose a free period, which, though correct according to regulations, forces Strange to arrive at work more than twenty minutes earlier than he would in normal circumstances. As a result, Straitley gets more than his fair share of rainy-day Break duties and Friday-afternoon cover sessions, which does nothing to ease the tension between them.

Still, amusing though it may be, this remains a small diversion. St Oswald's has withstood a thousand petty dramas of the same ilk. My second week has passed; I am more than comfortable in my role; and although I am tempted to enjoy my new-found situation for a little longer, I know that there will be no better time to strike. But where?

Not Bishop; not the Head. Straitley? It's tempting, and he'll have to go sooner or later; but I'm enjoying the game too much to lose him so soon. No. There's really only one place to start. The Porter.

*   *   *

That had been a bad summer for John Snyde. He had been drinking more than ever before, and at last it was beginning to show. Always a big man, he had thickened gradually and almost imperceptibly over the years, and now, quite suddenly, it seemed, he was fat.

For the first time I was conscious of it; conscious of the St Oswald's boys passing the gates; conscious of my father's slowness, of his bloodshot eyes, of his bearish, sullen temper. Though it rarely came out in work hours, I knew it was there, like an underground wasps' nest waiting for something to disturb it.

Dr Tidy, the Bursar, had commented on it, although so far my father had avoided an official reprimand. The boys knew it too, especially the little ones; over that summer they baited him mercilessly, shouting; *John! Hey, John!* in their girlish voices, following him in groups as he attended to his duties, running after the ride-on lawn-mower as he drove it methodically around the cricket fields and football pitches, his big bear's rump hanging off either side of the narrow seat.

He had a multitude of nicknames: Johnny Fatso; Baldy John (he had become sensitive about the thinning patch on top of his head, which he tried to camouflage by greasing a long strip of hair to his crown); Doughball Joe; Big John the Chip-Fat Don. The ride-on lawn-mower was a perpetual source of merriment; the boys called it the Mean Machine or John's Jalopy; it was continually breaking down; rumour had it that it ran off the chip-fat which John used to grease his hair; that he drove it because it was faster than his own car. A few times, boys had noticed a beery, stale smell on my father's breath in the mornings, and since then there had been numerous halitosis jokes; boys pretending to become inebriated on the fumes from the caretaker's breath; boys asking how far over the limit he was, and whether he was legal to drive the Mean Machine.

Needless to say I usually kept my distance from these boys during my forays into School; for although I was certain my father never even saw beyond the St Oswald's uniform to the individuals beneath, his proximity made me uneasy and ashamed. It seemed at these times that I had never really *seen* my father before; and when, goaded finally into undignified response, he lashed out – first with his voice, and then with his fists – I writhed with embarrassment, shame and self-loathing.

Much of this was the direct result of my friendship with Leon. A rebel he might have been, with his long hair and his shoplifting forays, but in spite of all that, Leon remained very much a product of his background, speaking with contempt of what he called 'the proles' and 'the mundanes', mocking my Sunnybank Park contemporaries with vicious and relentless accuracy.

For my own part, I joined in the mockery without reserve. I had always loathed Sunnybank Park; I felt no loyalty to the pupils there, and embraced the cause of St Oswald's without hesitation. *That* was where I belonged, and I made certain that everything about me – hair, voice, manners – reflected that allegiance. At that time I wished more than ever for my fiction to be true, longed for the police-inspector father of my imagination and hated more than words could say the fat caretaker with his foul mouth and thick, beery gut. With me he had grown increasingly irritable; the failure of the karate lessons had compounded his disappointment, and on several occasions I found him watching me with frank and open dislike.

Still, once or twice, he made a feeble, half-hearted effort. Asked me to a football match; gave me money for the pictures. Most of the time, however, he did not. I watched him sink deeper every day into his routine of television, beer, takeaways, and fumbling, noisy (and increasingly unsuccessful) sex. After a while even that stopped, and Pepsi's visits grew less and less frequent. I saw her in town a couple of times, and once in the park with a young man. He was wearing a leather jacket and had one of his hands up Pepsi's pink angora sweater. After that she hardly came to see us at all.

It was ironic that the one thing that saved my father during those weeks was the thing he was growing to hate. St Oswald's had been his life, his hope, his pride; now it seemed to taunt him with his own inadequacy. Even so, he endured it; performed his duties faithfully, if without love; squared his stubborn back to the boys who taunted him and sang rude little chants about him in the playground. For me, he endured it; for me, he held out almost to the last. I know that, now that it's too late; but at twelve so many things are hidden; so many things still to be discovered.

'Hey, Pinchbeck!' We were sitting in the Quad under the beech trees. The sun was hot, and John Snyde was mowing the lawn. I remember that smell, the smell of schooldays; of mown grass, dust and of things growing too fast and out of control. 'Looks like Big John's having a spot of bother.'

I looked. So he was; at the limit of the cricket lawn the Mean Machine had broken down again, and my father was trying to restart it, swearing and sweating, as he pulled at the sagging waistband of his jeans. The little boys had already begun to close in; a cordon of them, like pigmies around a wounded rhino.

John! Hey, John! I could hear them across the cricket lawn, budgie voices in the hazy heat. Darting in, darting out, daring each other to get a little closer every time.

'*Geddout of it!*' He waved his arms at them like a man scaring crows. His beery shout reached us a second later; high-pitched laughter followed. Squealing, they scattered; seconds later they were already creeping back, giggling like girls.

Leon grinned. 'Come on,' he said. 'We'll have a laugh.'

I followed him reluctantly, keeping back, removing the glasses that might have marked me. I needn't have bothered; my father was drunk. Drunk and furious, goaded by the heat and the juniors who wouldn't leave him alone.

'Excuse me, Mr Snyde, sir,' said Leon, behind him.

He turned, gaping – taken by surprise by that 'sir'.

Leon faced him, polite and smiling. 'Dr Tidy would like to see you in the Bursar's office,' he said. 'He says it's important.'

My father hated the Bursar – a clever man with a satiric tongue, who ran the School's finances from a spotless little office near the Porter's Lodge. It would have been hard to miss the hostility between them. Tidy was neat, obsessive, meticulous. He attended Chapel every morning; drank camomile tea to soothe his nerves; bred prize-winning orchids in the School conservatory. Everything about John Snyde seemed calculated to upset him; his slouch; his boorishness; the way his trousers came down well over the waistband of his yellowing underpants.

'Dr Tidy?' said my father, eyes narrowed.

'Yes, sir,' said Leon.

'Shit.' He slouched off, towards the office.

Leon grinned at me. 'I wonder what Tidy'll say when he smells that breath?' he said, running his fingers over the Mean Machine's battered flank. Then he turned, his eyes bright with malice. 'Hey, Pinchbeck. Want a ride?'

I shook my head, appalled – but excited, too.

'Come on, Pinchbeck. It's too good an opportunity to miss.' And with one light step he was on the machine, pressing the starter button, revving her up—

'Last chance, Pinchbeck.'

I could not refuse the challenge. I jumped up on to the wheel rim, balancing as the Mean Machine lurched into motion. The juniors scattered, squealing. Leon was laughing wildly; grass sprayed out from behind the wheels in a triumphant green spume and across the lawn John Snyde came running, too slow for it to matter but furious, feather-spitting crazy with rage: 'You boys, there! You fucking *boys*!'

Leon looked at me. We were nearing the far end of the lawn now; the Mean Machine was making the most terrible noise; behind us we could see John Snyde, helplessly out-distanced, and behind him, Dr Tidy, his face a blur of outrage.

For a second joy transfixed me. We were magical; we were Butch and Sundance, leaping from the cliff's edge, leaping from the mower in a haze of grass and glory and running for it, running like hell as the Mean Machine kept going in majestic, unstoppable slo-mo towards the trees.

We were never caught. The juniors never identified us, and the Bursar was so irate at my father's behaviour – at his foul language on School premises, even more than at his drunkenness or his dereliction of duty – that he omitted to follow up whatever leads he might have had. Mr Roach, who had been on duty, was given a ticking-off by the Head, and my father received an official warning and a bill for repairs.

None of this had any effect on me, however. Another line had been crossed, and I was elated. Even sticking it to that bastard Bray had never felt as good as this, and for days I walked on a rosy cloud, through which nothing but Leon could be seen, felt or heard.

I was in love.

At the time I dared not think so in as many words. Leon was my friend. That was all he ever *could* be. And yet that's what it was: blazing, purblind, triple-infatuated, sleepless, self-sacrificing love. Everything in my life was filtered through its hopeful lens; he was my first thought in the morning; my last at night. I was not quite besotted enough to believe that my feelings were in any way reciprocated; to him, I was just a first-year; amusing enough, but by far his inferior. Some days he would spend his lunch-break with me; at other times he might keep me waiting for the entire hour, completely unaware of the risks I ran daily for the chance of being with him.

Nevertheless, I was happy. I did not need Leon's constant presence for my happiness to flourish; for the time it was enough simply to know he was close by. I had to be clever, I told myself; I had to be patient. Above all I sensed that I must not become tiresome, and hid my feelings behind a barrier of facetiousness whilst evolving ever more ingenious ways to worship him in secret.

I exchanged school sweaters with him and for a week I wore his around my neck. In the evenings I opened his locker with my father's master key and went through Leon's things, reading his class notes, his books, looking at the cartoon doodles he drew when he was bored, practising his signature. Outside of my role as a St Oswald's pupil I watched him from afar, sometimes passing by his house in the hope of catching a glimpse of him – or even his sister, whom I worshipped by association. I memorized the number plate on his mother's car. I fed his dog in secret. I combed my lank brown hair so that I fancied it looked like his, cultivated his expressions and his tastes. I had known him for just over six weeks.

I anticipated the approaching summer holidays at the same time as a relief and a further source of anxiety. Relief, because the effort of attending two schools – albeit erratically – was beginning to take its toll. Miss McCauleigh had complained about missing homework and frequent absences, and although I had become skilled at forging my father's signature, there was always the danger that someone might meet him by chance and blow my cover. Anxiety, because although I would soon be free to meet Leon as often as I wished, it meant running even more risks, as I continued my imposture as a civilian.

Fortunately, I had already completed the spadework within the School itself. The rest was a question of timing, location and a few well-chosen props, mainly costumes, which would establish me as the well-off, middle-class individual I pretended to be.

I stole a pair of expensive trainers from a sports shop in town, and a new racing bike (my own would have been quite impossible) from outside a nice house a comfortable distance away. I repainted it, just to be sure, and sold my own on the Saturday market. If my father had noticed, I would have told him I had traded in my old bike for a second-hand model because it was getting too small for me. It was a good story, and would probably have worked, but by then, with the end of term, my father was at last beginning to unravel, and he never noticed anything any more.

Fallow has his place now. Fat Fallow, with his loose lips and ancient donkey-jacket. He has my father's slouch, too, from years of driving the ride-on mower, and, like my father's, his gut spills out obscenely from over his narrow, shiny belt. There is a tradition that all School Porters are called John, and this is true of Fallow, too, though the boys do not call after him and bait him as they did my father. I'm glad; I might have to intervene if they did, and I do not want to make myself conspicuous at this stage.

But Fallow offends me. He has hairy ears and reads the *News of the World* in his little Lodge, wearing ancient slippers on his bare feet, drinking milky tea and ignoring what happens around him. Halfwit Jimmy does the real work; the building, the woodwork, the wiring, the drains. Fallow takes the phone calls. He enjoys making the callers wait – anxious mothers asking after their sick sons, rich fathers detained at a last-minute meeting with the directors – sometimes for minutes on end, as he finishes his tea and scrawls the message on a piece of yellow paper. He likes to travel, and sometimes goes on day-trips to France, organized by his local working men's club, during which he goes to the supermarket, eats chips by the side of the tour bus and complains about the locals.

At work he is by turns rude and deferential, depending on the status of his visitor; he charges boys a pound for opening their locker with the master key; he gloats at the legs of female teachers as they walk up the stairs. With lesser staff he is pompous and opinionated; says *Know what I mean?* and *I'll tell you this for nothing, mate.*

With the higher echelons he is obsequious; with veterans, nauseatingly pally; with juniors like myself, brusque and busy, with no time to waste on chat. He goes up to the Computer Science Suite on Fridays after school, ostensibly to turn off the machines, but actually to surf internet porn sites after hours, while outside in the corridor,

Jimmy uses the floor polisher, passing it slowly across the boards, bringing the old wood to a mellow shine.

It takes less than a minute to obliterate an hour's work. By eight thirty on Monday morning the floors will be as dusty and scuffed as if Jimmy had never been there at all. Fallow knows this; and though he does not perform these cleaning duties himself, he nevertheless feels an obscure resentment, as if staff and boys were an impediment to the smooth running of things.

As a result, his life consists of small and spiteful revenges. No one really observes him – a Porter lives below the salt, and so may take such liberties with the system that remain unnoticed. Members of staff are mostly unaware of this, but I have been watching. From my position in the Bell Tower I can see his little Lodge; I can observe the comings and goings without being seen.

There is an ice-cream van parked outside the School gates. My father would never have allowed that, but Fallow tolerates it, and there is often a queue of boys there after school or at lunch-time. Some buy ice-cream there; others return with bulging pockets and the furtive grin of one who has balked the system. Officially, junior boys are not supposed to leave the School grounds, but the van is only a few yards away, and Pat Bishop accepts it as long as no one crosses the busy road. Besides, he likes ice-cream, and I've seen him several times, munching on a cone as he supervises the boys in the yard.

Fallow, too, visits the ice-cream van. He does it in the morning, when lessons have already begun, making sure to circle the buildings clockwise and thereby avoid passing under the Common Room window. Sometimes he has a plastic bag with him – it is not heavy, but quite bulky – which he leaves under the counter. Sometimes he returns with a cone, sometimes not.

In fifteen years, many of the School's passkeys have been changed. It was to be expected – St Oswald's has always been a target, and security must be maintained – but the Porter's Lodge, among others, is one of the exceptions. After all, why would anyone want to break into a Porter's Lodge? There's nothing there except an old armchair, a gas heater, a kettle, a phone and a few girlie magazines hidden under the counter. There's another hiding-place, too, a rather more sophisticated one, behind the hollow panel which masks the ventilation system, though this is a secret passed on jealously from one Porter to another. It is not very large, but will easily take a couple of six-packs, as my father discovered, and as he told me then, the bosses don't always have to know everything.

I was feeling good today as I drove home. Summer is almost at an end, and there is a yellowness and a grainy texture to the light which reminds me of the television shows of my adolescence. The nights are getting cold; in my rented flat, six miles from the city centre, I will soon have to light the gas fire. The flat is not an especially attractive place – one room, a kitchen annexe and a tiny bathroom – but it's the cheapest I could find, and, of course, I do not mean to stay for long.

It is virtually unfurnished. I have a sofa-bed; a desk; a light; a computer and modem. I shall probably leave them all behind when I go. The computer is clean – or will be, when I have wiped the incriminating stuff from its hard drive. The car is rented, and will also have been thoroughly cleaned by the rental firm by the time the police trace it back to me.

My elderly landlady is a gossip. She wonders why a nice, clean, professional person such as myself should choose to stay in a low-rent flatblock filled with druggies and ex-convicts and people on the dole. I've told her that I am a sales coordinator for a large international software company; that my firm has agreed to provide me with a house, but that the contractors have let them down. She shakes her head at this, bemoaning the ineptitude of builders everywhere, and hopes I'll be in my new home by Christmas.

'Because it must be miserable, mustn't it, love, not having your own place? And especially at Christmas—' Her weak eyes mist over sentimentally. I consider telling her that most deaths among old people occur during the winter months; that three-quarters of would-be suicides will take the plunge during the festive season. But I must maintain the pretence for the moment; so I answer her questions as best I can; I listen to her reminiscences; I am beyond reproach. In gratitude, my landlady has decorated my little room with chintz curtains and a vase of dusty paper flowers. 'Think of it as your little home away from home,' she tells me. 'And if you need anything, I'm always here.'

7

St Oswald's Grammar School for Boys
Thursday, 23rd September

THE TROUBLE BEGAN ON MONDAY, AND I KNEW SOMETHING had happened when I saw the cars. Pat Bishop's Volvo was there, as usual – always first in, he even spends the night in his office at busy times – but it was almost unheard of to see Bob Strange's car there before eight o'clock, and there was the Head's Audi, too, and the Chaplain's Jag, and half a dozen others, including a black-and-white police car, all parked in the staff car-park outside the Porter's Lodge.

For myself, I prefer the bus. In heavy traffic it's quicker, and in any case, I never need to go more than a few miles to work or to the shops. Besides, I have my bus pass now, and though I can't help thinking that there must be some mistake (sixty-four – how can I be *sixty-four*, by all the gods?), it does save money.

I walked up the long drive to St Oswald's. The lindens are on the turn, gilded with the approach of autumn, and there were little columns of white vapour rising from the dewy grass. I looked into the Porter's Lodge as I walked by. Fallow wasn't there.

No one in the Common Room seemed to know exactly what was going on. Strange and Bishop were in the Head's office with Dr Tidy and Sergeant Ellis, the liaison officer. Still Fallow was nowhere to be seen.

I wondered if there had been a break-in. It happens occasionally, though for the most part Fallow does a reasonable job of looking after the place. A bit of a crawler with the management, and of course he's been on the take for years. Small things – a bag of coal, a packet of biscuits from the kitchens, plus his pound-a-go racket for opening lockers – but he's loyal enough, and when you consider that he earns about a tenth of even a junior master's salary, you learn to turn a blind eye. I hoped there was nothing the matter with Fallow.

As always, the boys knew it first. Rumours had been flying wildly throughout the morning; Fallow had had a heart attack; Fallow had threatened the Head; Fallow had been suspended. But it was Sutcliff, McNair and Allen-Jones who found me at Break and asked me, with that cheery, disingenuous air they adopt when they know someone else is in trouble, whether it was true that Fallow had been arrested.

'Who told you that?' I said with a smile of deliberate ambiguity.

'Oh, I heard someone say something.' Secrets are currency in any school, and I hadn't expected McNair to reveal his informant, but obviously, some sources are more reliable than others. From the boy's expression I gathered that this had come from somewhere near the top.

'They've ripped out some panels in the Porter's Lodge,' said Sutcliff. 'They took out a whole bunch of stuff.'

'Such as?'

Allen-Jones shrugged. 'Who knows?'

'Cigarettes, maybe?'

The boys looked at each other. Sutcliff flushed slightly. Allen-Jones gave a little smile. 'Maybe.'

Later, the story came out; Fallow had been using his cheap day-trips to France to bring back illicit, tax-free cigarettes, which he had been selling – via the ice-cream man, who was a friend of his – to the boys.

The profits were excellent – a single cigarette costing up to a pound, depending on the age of the boy – but St Oswald's boys have plenty of money, and besides, the thrill of breaking the rules right under the nose of the Second Master was almost irresistible. The scheme had been going on for months, possibly years; the police had found about four dozen cartons hidden behind a secret panel in the Lodge, and many hundreds more in Fallow's garage, stacked floor to ceiling behind a set of disused bookcases.

Both Fallow and the ice-cream man confirmed the cigarette story. Of the other items found in the Lodge, Fallow denied all knowledge, although he was at a loss to explain their presence. Knight identified his bar mitzvah pen; later, and with some reluctance, I claimed my old green Parker. I was relieved in one sense that no boy in my form had taken them; on the other hand I knew that this was yet another small nail in the coffin of John Fallow, who had at one blow lost his home, his job, and quite possibly, his freedom.

I never did find out who had tipped off the authorities. An anonymous letter, or so I heard; in any case, no one came forward. It must have been someone on the inside, says Robbie Roach (a smoker, and erstwhile good friend of Fallow); some little snitch keen to make trouble. He's probably right; though I hate the thought of a colleague being responsible.

A boy, then? Somehow that seems even worse; the thought that one of our boys could single-handedly do so much damage.

A boy like Knight, perhaps? It was only a thought; but there is a new smugness in Knight, a look of *awareness*, that I like even less than his natural sullenness. Knight? There was no reason to think so. All the same I *did* think so; deep down, where it matters. Call it prejudice; call it instinct. The boy knew something.

Meanwhile, the little scandal runs its course. There will be an investigation by Customs and Excise; and although it is very unlikely that the School will press charges – any suggestion of bad publicity sends the Head into spasms – Mrs Knight has so far refused to withdraw her own complaint. The Governors will have to be informed; there will be questions asked concerning the role of the Porter, his appointment (Dr Tidy is already on the defensive, and is demanding police reports on all ancillary staff), and his probable replacement. In short, the Fallow incident has created ripples all over the school, from the Bursar's office to the Quiet Room.

The boys feel it and have been unusually disruptive, testing the boundaries of our discipline. A member of the School has been disgraced – albeit only a Porter – and a breath of revolt stirs; on Tuesday Meek emerged from his fifth-form Computer Studies classes looking pale and shaken; McDonaugh gave out a series of vicious detentions; Robbie Roach fell mysteriously ill, incensing the whole department, who had to cover for him. Bob Strange set cover for all his classes on the grounds that he was too busy with Other Things, and today the Head took a disastrous Assembly in which he announced (to general, if unvoiced amusement) that there was no truth whatever in the malicious rumours concerning Mr Fallow, and that any boy perpetrating such rumours would be Dealt With Most Severely.

But it is Pat Bishop, the Second Master, who has been most affected by Fallowgate, as Allen-Jones has named the unfortunate affair. Partly, I think, because such a thing is completely outside his comprehension; Pat's loyalty to St Oswald's reaches back for more than thirty years, and what-ever his other faults, he is scrupulously honest. His whole philosophy (such as it is; for our Pat is no philosopher) is based on the assumption that people are fundamentally good and wish, at heart, to do good, even when they are led astray. This ability to see good in everyone is at the core of his dealings with boys, and it works very well; weaklings and villains are shamed by his kind, stern manner, and even staff are in awe of him.

But Fallow has caused a kind of crisis. First, because Pat was fooled – he blames himself for not noticing what was going on – and second, because of the contempt implicit in the deception. That Fallow – whom Pat had always treated with politeness and respect – should repay him in such spiteful coin dismays and shames him. He remembers the John Snyde business, and wonders whether he is somehow at fault in this case. He does not say these things, but I have noticed that he smiles less than usual, keeps to his office during the day, runs even more laps in the mornings, and often works late.

As for the Languages department, it has suffered less than most. This is partly thanks to Pearman, whose natural cynicism serves as a welcome foil for the aloofness of Strange or the anxious bluster of the Head. Gerry Grachvogel's classes are somewhat noisier than usual, though not enough to require my intervention. Geoff and Penny Nation are saddened, but unsurprised, shaking their heads at the beastliness of human nature. Dr Devine uses the Fallow affair to terrorize poor Jimmy. Eric Scoones is bad-tempered, though not much more than usual. Dianne Dare, like the creative Keane, follows the whole thing with fascination.

'This place runs like a complicated soap opera,' she told me this morning in the Common Room. 'You never know what's going to happen next.'

I admitted that there was occasionally some entertainment value to be had from the dear old place.

'Is that why you stayed on? I mean—' She broke off, aware, perhaps, of the unflattering implication.

'I *stayed on*, as you so kindly put it, because I am old-fashioned enough to believe that our boys may derive some small benefit from my lessons, and most importantly, because it annoys Mr Strange.'

'I'm sorry,' she said.

'Don't be. It doesn't suit you.'

It's hard to explain St Oswald's; harder still from across a gulf of more than forty years. She is young, attractive, bright; one day she will fall in love, maybe have children. She will have a house, which will be a home rather than a secondary annexe of the Book Room; she will take holidays in far-flung locations. At least, I hope so; the alternative is to join the rest of the galley slaves and stay chained to the ship until someone pitches you overboard.

'I didn't mean to offend you, sir,' said Miss Dare.

'You didn't.' Perhaps I'm going soft in my old age, or perhaps the business with Fallow has troubled me more than I knew. 'It's just that I'm feeling rather Kafkaesque this morning. I blame Dr Devine.'

She laughed at that, as I thought she might. And yet there remained something in her expression. She has adapted rather well to life at St Oswald's; I see her going to lessons with her briefcase and an armful of books; I hear her talking to the boys in the crisp, cheerful tones of a staff nurse. Like Keane, she has a self-possession that serves her well in a place like this, where everyone must fight his corner and to ask for help is a sign of weakness. She can feign anger or hide it when she needs to, knowing that a teacher must be above all a performer, always master of his audience and always in command of the stage. It's unusual to see that quality in such a young teacher; I suspect that both Miss Dare and Mr Keane are naturals, just as I know poor Meek is not.

'You've certainly come in interesting times,' I said. 'Inspections, restructurings, treason and plot. The bricks and mortar of St Oswald's. If you can survive this—'

'My parents were teachers. I know what to expect.'

That explained it. You can always tell. I picked up a mug (not mine; still missing) from the rack by the side of the sink. 'Tea?'

She smiled. 'The teacher's cocaine.'

I inspected the contents of the tea urn and poured for both of us. Over the years I have become accustomed to drinking tea in its most elementary form. Even so, the brown sludge which settled in my cup looked distinctly toxic. I shrugged and added milk and sugar. *That which does not kill me makes me stronger.* An appropriate motto, perhaps, for a place like St Oswald's, perpetually on the brink of tragedy or farce.

I looked around at my colleagues, sitting in groups around the old Common Room, and felt a deep and unexpected stab of affection. There was McDonaugh, reading the *Mirror* in his corner; Monument, by his side, reading the *Telegraph*; Pearman, discussing nineteenth-century French pornography with Kitty Teague; Isabelle Tapi checking her lipstick; the League of Nations sharing a chaste banana. Old friends; comfortable collaborators.

As I said, it's hard to explain St Oswald's; the sound of the place in the mornings; the flat echo of boys' feet against the stone steps; the smell of burning toast from the Refectory; the peculiar sliding sound of overfilled sports bags being dragged along the newly polished floor. The Honours Boards, with gold-painted names dating back from before my great-great-grandfather; the war memorial; the team photographs; the brash young faces, tinted sepia with the passing of time. A metaphor for eternity.

Gods, I'm getting sentimental. Age does that; a moment ago I was bemoaning my lot and now here I am getting all misty-eyed. It must be the weather. And yet, Camus says, we must imagine Sisyphus happy. Am I unhappy? All I know is that something has shaken us; shaken us to the foundations. It's in the air, a breath of revolt, and somehow I know that it goes deeper than the Fallow affair. Whatever it may be, it is not over. And it's still only September.

EN PASSANT

1

Monday, 27th September

IN SPITE OF THE HEAD'S BEST EFFORTS, FALLOW MADE THE papers. Not the *News of the World* – that would have been too much to expect – but our own *Examiner*, which is almost as good. The traditional rift between School and Town is such that bad news from St Oswald's travels fast, and is received for the most part with a fierce and unholy glee. The ensuing piece was both triumphant and vitriolic, simultaneously portraying Fallow as a long-term employee of the School, dismissed (summarily and without Union representation) for a crime as yet unproved and, at the same time, as a likeable rogue who for years had been getting his own back on a system comprising Hooray Henrys, faceless bureaucrats and out-of-touch academics.

It has become a David and Goliath situation, with Fallow as a symbol of the working classes, fighting the monstrous machines of wealth and privilege. The writer of the piece, who signs his name simply as 'Mole', also manages to convey the impression that St Oswald's is filled with similar scams and small corruptions, that the teaching is hopelessly out of date, that smoking (and possibly drug abuse) is rife and that the buildings themselves are so badly in need of repair that a serious accident is almost inevitable. An editorial, entitled: 'Private Schools – Should They be Scrapped?' – flanks the piece, and readers are invited to send in their own thoughts and grievances against St Oswald's and the Old Boy network which protects it.

I'm rather pleased with it. They printed it almost un-edited, and I have promised to keep them informed of any further developments. In my e-mail I hinted that I was a source close to the School – an Old Boy, a pupil, a Governor, perhaps even a member of staff – keeping the details fluid (I may have to change them later).

I used one of my secondary e-mail addresses – Mole@hot-mail.com – to foil any attempt to discover my identity. Not that anyone at the *Examiner* is likely to try – they're more accustomed to dog shows and local politics than investigative journalism – but you never know where a story like this is going to end. I don't entirely know myself; which is, I suppose, what makes it fun.

It was raining when I arrived in school this morning. Traffic was slower than usual, and I had to make an effort to control my annoyance as I inched through town. One of the things which makes the locals resent St Oswald's is the traffic it generates at rush hour; the hundreds of clean, shiny Jags and sensible Volvos and four-wheel drives and people-carriers which line the roads every morning with their cargo of clean, shiny boys in blazers and caps.

Some take the car even when their home is less than a mile away. God forbid that the clean, shiny boy should have to jump puddles or breathe pollutants or (worse still) experience contamination by the dull, grubby pupils of the nearby Sunnybank Park; the loud-mouthed, loose-limbed boys with their nylon jackets and scuffed trainers; the yawping girls in their short skirts and dyed hair. When I was their age I walked to school; I wore those cheap shoes and grubby socks; and sometimes as I drive to work in my rented car I can still feel the rage mounting in me, the terrible rage against who I was and who I longed to be.

I remember a time, late that summer. Leon was bored; school was out, and we were hanging around the public playground (I remember the roundabout, its paint worn clean through to the metal by generations of young hands), smoking Camels (Leon smoked, so I did too) and watching the Sunnybankers go by.

'Barbarians. Rabble. Proles.' His fingers were long and slender, deeply stained with ink and nicotine. On the path, a little knot of Sunnybankers approaching, dragging their schoolbags, shouting, dusty-footed in the hot afternoon. No threat to us, though there were times when we'd had to run, pursued by a gang of Sunnybankers.

Once, when I wasn't there, they'd cornered Leon, down

by the bins at the back of the school, and given him a kicking. I hated them all the more for that; even more than Leon did – they were *my* people, after all. But these were just girls – four of them together and a straggler from my own year – raucous, gum-chewing girls, skirts hiked up blotchy legs, giggling and screaming as they ran down the path.

The straggler, I saw, was Peggy Johnsen, the fat girl from Mr Bray's Games class, and I turned away instinctively, but not before Leon had caught my eye, and winked.

'Well?'

I knew that look. I recognized it from our forays into town; our record-shop thefts; our small acts of rebellion. Leon's gaze brimmed with mischief; his bright eyes pinned Peggy as she half-ran to keep up.

'Well, what?'

The other four were far ahead. Peggy, with her sweaty face and anxious look, was suddenly alone. 'Oh no,' I said. The truth was I had nothing against Peggy; a slow, harmless girl only a step removed from mental deficiency. I even pitied her a little.

Leon gave me a scornful look. 'What is she, Pinchbeck, your girlfriend?' he said. 'Come *on*!' And he was off at a run, arcing across the playground with an exuberant whoop. I followed him; I told myself there was nothing else I could have done.

We snatched her bags – Leon took her Games kit in its Woolworth's carrier, I grabbed her canvas satchel with the little hearts drawn on in Tipp-Ex. Then we ran, far too fast for Peggy to follow, leaving her squalling in our dust. I'd simply wanted to get away before she recognized me; but my momentum had sent me crashing against her, knocking her to the ground.

Leon had laughed at that, and I did too, viciously, knowing that in another life it could have been me sitting there on the path, it could have been me yelling, 'Ah, come on, you buggers, you lousy bastards,' through my tears as my gym shoes, tied by the laces, were flung into the highest branches of an old tree and my books fluttered their pages like confetti on the warm summer air.

I'm sorry, Peggy. I nearly meant it, too. She wasn't the worst of them, not by a long way. But she was there, and she was disgusting – with her greasy hair and red angry face, she could almost have been my father's child. And so I stomped her books; emptied her bags; scattered her PE kit (I can still see those navy-blue knickers, baggy as my fabled Thunderpants) into the yellow dust.

'Ozzie bastards!'

Survival of the fittest, I replied silently, feeling angry for her, angry for myself, but fiercely elated, as if I'd passed a test; as if by so doing I had narrowed the gap still more between myself and St Oswald's, between who I was and who I meant to be.

'Bastards.'

The lights were at green, but the queue ahead was too long to allow me to pass. A couple of boys saw the opportunity to cross – I recognized McNair, one of Straitley's favourites, Jackson, the diminutive bully from the same form, and the sidling, crablike gait of Anderton-Pullitt – and just at that moment the traffic ahead of me began to move.

Jackson crossed at a run. So did McNair. There was a space of fifty yards ahead of me, into which, if I was quick, I could pass. Otherwise the lights would change again and I would have to stand at the junction for another five minutes as the interminable traffic crawled by. But Anderton-Pullitt did not run. A heavy boy, already middle-aged at thirteen, he crossed in leisurely fashion, not looking at me even when I honked my horn, as if by ignoring me he might will me out of existence. Briefcase in one hand, lunchbox in the other, walking fastidiously around the puddle in the middle of the road so that by the time he was out of my way, the lights had changed and I was forced to wait.

Trivial, I know. But there's an arrogance to it, a lazy contempt which is pure St Oswald's. I wondered what he would have done if I had simply driven at him – or over him, in fact. Would he have run? Or would he have stayed put, confident, stupid, mouthing to the last; *You wouldn't – you couldn't—!*

Unfortunately, there was no question of my running down Anderton-Pullitt. For a start, I need the car, and the rental company might get suspicious if I brought it back with a ruined front end. Still, there are plenty of other means, I thought, and I owed myself a little celebration. I smiled as I waited at the frozen lights, and turned the radio on.

*   *   *

I sat in room 59 for the first half-hour of lunch-time. Thanks to Bob Strange, Straitley was out, either lurking in that Book Room of his, or patrolling the corridors on duty. The room was filled with boys. Some did their homework; some played chess or talked, occasionally chugging from cans of fizzy drink or eating crisps.

All teachers hate rainy days; there is nowhere for the pupils to go but indoors, and they have to be supervised; it is muddy and accidents happen; it is crowded and noisy; squabbles turn into fights. I intervened in one myself, between Jackson and Brasenose (a soft, fat boy who has not yet learned the trick of making his size work for him), supervised the tidying of the room, pointed out a spelling mistake in Tayler's homework, accepted a Polo mint from Pink and a peanut from Knight, chatted for a few minutes to the boys eating their packed lunches on the back row, then, my task accomplished, I made once again for the Quiet Room, to await developments over a cup of murky tea.

I do not, of course, have a form. None of the new staff has. It gives us free time and a broader perspective; I can watch from behind the lines and I know the moments of weakness; the dangerous times; the unsupervised sections of the School; the vital minutes – the seconds – during which, if disaster were to strike, the giant's underbelly would be at its most exposed.

The after-lunch bell is one of these. Afternoon registration has not yet begun, although at this point, lunch-time is officially over. In theory, it is a five-minute warning, a changeover time during which staff still sitting in the Common Room make a move towards their classrooms, and staff members on lunch-time duties have a few minutes to collect their belongings (and maybe glance at a newspaper) before registration.

In effect, however, it is a five-minute window of vulnerability in an otherwise smooth-running operation. No one is on duty; many staff – and sometimes pupils – are still moving from one place to another. Little surprise, then, that most mishaps occur at such a time; scuffles; thefts; petty vandalism; random pieces of misbehaviour perpetrated in transit and under cover of the surge of activity which precedes the return to afternoon lessons. This is why it was five minutes before anyone really noticed that Anderton-Pullitt had collapsed.

It might have been less if he had been popular. But he was not: sitting slightly away from the others, eating his sandwiches (Marmite and cream cheese on wheat-free bread, always the same) with slow, laborious bites, he looked more like a tortoise than a thirteen-year-old boy. There is one of his kind in every year; precocious, be-spectacled, hypochondriac, shunned even beyond bullying, he seems impervious to insults or rejection; cultivates an old man's pedantic speech, which gives him a reputation for cleverness; is polite to teachers, which makes him a favourite.

Straitley finds him amusing – but then he would; as a boy, he was probably just the same. I find him annoying; in Straitley's absence he follows me around when I'm on duty in the yard and subjects me to ponderous lectures on his various enthusiasms (science fiction, computers, First World War aircraft) and his ailments real and imagined (asthma, food intolerances, agoraphobia, allergies, anxiety, warts).

As I sat now in the Quiet Room, I amused myself in trying to determine from the sounds that came from above my head, whether or not Anderton-Pullitt had a genuine ailment.

No one else noticed; no one else was listening. Robbie Roach, who was free next period and has no form either (too many extra curricular commitments), was rootling through his locker. I noticed a pack of French cigarettes in there (a present from Fallow), which he quickly hid behind a pile of books. Isabelle Tapi, who teaches part-time and therefore has no form either, was drinking from a bottle of Evian water and reading a paperback.

I heard the five-minute bell followed by a hubbub; the unchained melody of unsupervised boys; the sound of something (a chair?) falling over. Then, raised voices – Jackson and Brasenose resuming their fight – another chair falling, then silence. I assumed Straitley had come in. Sure enough, there came the sound of his voice – a subdued murmur from the boys, then the domestic cadences of registration, familiar as those of the football scores on Saturday afternoons.

—*Adamczyk?*

Sir.

—*Almond?*

Sir.

—*Allen-Jones?*
Yes, sir.
—*Anderton-Pullitt?*
Beat.
—*Anderton-Pullitt?*

2

St Oswald's Grammar School for Boys
Wednesday, 29th September

STILL NO NEWS FROM THE ANDERTON-PULLITTS. I TAKE THIS
as a good sign – I'm told that in extreme cases the reaction
can prove fatal within seconds – but even so, the thought
that one of my boys might have died – actually *died* – in my
room, under my supervision – makes my heart stutter and
my palms sweat.

In all my years of teaching, I have known three of
my boys die. Their faces look out at me every day from the
class photographs along the Middle Corridor: Hewitt, who
died of meningitis in the Christmas holidays of 1972; and
Constable, 1986; run over by a car in his own street as he
ran to retrieve a lost football; and of course, Mitchell, 1989
– Mitchell, whose case has never ceased to trouble me. All
outside of School hours; and yet in every instance (but

especially in his) I feel to blame, as if I should have been watching out for them.

Then there are the Old Boys. Jamestone, cancer at thirty-two; Deakin, brain tumour; Stanley, car crash; Poulson, killed himself, no one knows why, two years ago, leaving a wife and an eight-year-old Down's Syndrome daughter. Still my boys, all of them, and still I feel an emptiness and a grief when I think of them, mingled with that strange, aching inexplicable feeling that I should have been there.

I thought at first he was faking. Spirits were high; Jackson was fighting with someone in a corner; I was in a hurry. Perhaps he had been unconscious when I entered; precious seconds passed as I quietened the form; found my pen. Anaphylactic shock, they call it – heaven knows I'd heard enough about it from the boy himself, though I'd always assumed his ailments were more to do with his overprotective mother than his actual physical condition.

It was all in his file, as I discovered too late; along with the many recommendations she had sent us concerning his diet, exercise, uniform requirements (man-made fabrics gave him a rash), phobias, antibiotics, religious instruction and social integration. Under 'Allergies' wheat (mild intolerance); and, in capital letters marked with an asterisk and several exclamation marks, NUTS!!

Of course, Anderton-Pullitt doesn't eat nuts. He consumes only food that has been declared risk-free by his mother and which, furthermore, corresponds to his own rather limited idea of what is acceptable. Every day the contents of his lunchbox consist of exactly the same things;

two cream cheese and Marmite sandwiches on wheat-free bread, cut into four; one tomato; one banana; a packet of Maynard's Wine Gums (of which he discards all but the red and black sweets); and a can of Fanta. As it is, it takes him all lunch-time to consume this meal; he never goes to the tuck-shop; never accepts food from any other boy.

Don't ask me how I managed to carry him downstairs. It was an effort; boys milled uselessly around me in excitement or confusion; I called for help, but no one came except for Gerry Grachvogel next door, who looked close to fainting and gasped, 'Oh dear, oh dear,' wringing his little rabbity hands and glancing nervously from side to side.

'Gerry, get help,' I ordered, balancing Anderton-Pullitt on one shoulder. 'Call an ambulance. *Modo fac.*'

Grachvogel just gaped at me. It was Allen-Jones who responded, running down the stairs two at a time, almost knocking over Isabelle Tapi, who was coming up. McNair raced off in the direction of Pat Bishop's office, and Pink and Tayler helped me support the unconscious boy. By the time we reached the Lower Corridor I felt as if my lungs were filled with hot lead, and it was with real gratitude that I passed on my burden to Bishop, who seemed cheered to have something physical to do, and who picked up Anderton-Pullitt as if he were a baby.

Behind me, I was vaguely aware that Sutcliff had finished taking the register. Allen-Jones was on the phone to the hospital – 'They say it'll be quicker if you drive him to Casualty yourself, sir!' – Grachvogel was trying to retrieve his form, who had followed *en masse* to see what was happening, and now the New Head emerged from his office, looking aghast, with Pat Bishop at his side and Marlene peering anxiously from over his shoulder.

'Mr Straitley!' Even in such an emergency as this, he retains a certain curious stiffness, as if constructed from some other medium – plaster, maybe whalebone – than flesh. 'Could you perhaps please explain to me—' But the world had become full of noises, among which my heart-beat was the most compelling; I was reminded of the old jungle epics of my childhood, in which adventurers scaled volcanoes to the sinister cacophony of native drums.

I leaned against the wall of the Lower Corridor, as my legs suddenly effected a transformation from bone, vein, sinew, to something more akin to jelly. My lungs hurt; there was a spot, somewhere in the region of my top waistcoat button, which felt as if someone very large were poking it repeatedly with an outstretched forefinger, as if to emphasize some kind of point. I looked round for a chair to sit upon, but it was too late; the world tilted and I began to slide down the wall.

'Mr Straitley!' From the upside-down perspective, the Head looked more sinister than ever. A *shrunken Head*, I thought vaguely. *Just the thing to placate the Volcano God* – and in spite of the pain in my chest I could not quite prevent myself from laughing. 'Mr Straitley! Mr Bishop! Can *someone* please tell me what is going on here?'

The invisible finger poked me again, and I sat down on the floor. Marlene, ever-efficient, reacted first; she knelt down beside me without hesitation and pulled open my jacket to feel my heart. The drums pulsed; now I could sense rather than feel the movement around me.

'Mr Straitley, hang on!' She smelt of something flowery and feminine; I felt I should make some witty remark, but couldn't think of anything to say. My chest hurt; my ear-drums roared; I tried to get up but could not. I slumped a little further, glimpsed the Powerpuff Girls on Allen-Jones' socks, and began to laugh.

The last thing I remember was the New Head's face looming into my field of vision and myself saying; '*Bwana, the natives, they will not enter the Forbidden City,*' before I passed out.

I awoke in the hospital. I had been lucky, the doctor told me; there had been what he called *a minor cardiac incident,* brought on by anxiety and over-exertion. I wanted to get up immediately, but he refused to allow it, saying that I was to remain under supervision for at least three or four days.

A middle-aged nurse with pink hair and a kindergarten manner then asked me questions, the answers to which she wrote down with an expression of mild disapproval, as if I were a child who persisted in wetting the bed. 'Now, Mr Straitley, how many cigarettes do we smoke a week?'

'I couldn't say, ma'am. I'm not sufficiently intimate with your smoking habits.' The nurse looked flustered. 'Oh, you were talking to *me,*' I said. 'I'm sorry, I thought perhaps you were a member of the Royal family.'

Her eyes narrowed. 'Mr Straitley, I have a job to do.'

'So do I,' I said. 'Third-form Latin, set 2, period 5.'

'I'm sure they can do without you for a little while,' said the nurse. 'No one's indispensable.'

A melancholy thought. 'I thought you were supposed to make me feel better.'

'And so I shall,' she said, 'as soon as we've finished with this little bit of paperwork.'

Well, within thirty minutes Roy Hubert Straitley (BA) was summarized in what looked very like a School register – cryptic abbreviations and ticks in boxes – and the nurse was looking suitably smug. I have to say it didn't look good: age, sixty-four; sedentary job; moderate smoker; alcohol units per week, fair to sprightly; weight, somewhere between mild *embonpoint* and genuine *avoirdupois*.

The doctor read it all with an expression of grim satisfaction. It was a warning, he concluded: a sign from the gods. 'You're not twenty-one, you know,' he told me. 'There are some things you just can't do any more.'

It's an old drill, and I'd heard it before. 'I know, I know. No smoking, no drinking, no fish and chips, no hundred-yard dash, no fancy women, no—'

He interrupted. 'I've been speaking to your GP. A Dr Bevans?'

'Bevans. I know him well. 1975 to 1979. Bright lad. Got an A in Latin. Read medicine at Durham.'

'Quite.' The syllable spoke volumes in disapproval. 'He tells me he's been concerned about you for some time.'

'Really?'

'Yes.'

Drat it. That's what comes of giving boys a Classical

education. They turn against you, the little swine, they turn against you and before you know what's happening, you're on a fat-free diet, wearing sweatpants and checking out the old people's homes.

'So, tell me the worst. What does the little upstart recommend this time? Hot ale? Magnetism? Leeches? I remember when he was in my form, little round boy, always in trouble. And now he's telling *me* what to do?'

'He's very fond of you, Mr Straitley.'

Here it comes, I thought.

'But you're sixty-five years old—'

'Sixty-four. My birthday's on November the fifth. Bonfire Night.'

He dismissed Bonfire Night with a shake of his head. 'And you seem to think you can go on for ever as you always have—'

'What's the alternative? Exposure on a rocky crag?'

The doctor sighed. 'I'm sure an educated man like yourself could find retirement both rewarding and stimulating. You could take up a hobby—'

A hobby, forsooth! 'I'm not retiring.'

'Be reasonable, Mr Straitley—'

St Oswald's has been my world for over thirty years. What else is there? I sat up on the trolley bed and swung my legs over the side. 'I feel fine.'

3

Thursday, 30th September

POOR OLD STRAITLEY. I WENT TO SEE HIM, YOU KNOW, AS soon as school finished, and found that he'd already checked himself out of the cardiac ward, to the disapproval of the staff. But his address was in the St Oswald's hand-book, so I went there instead, bringing with me a little pot plant I had bought at the hospital shop.

I'd never seen him out of character before. An old man, I realized, with an old man's white stubble under his chin and an old man's bony white feet in battered leather slippers. He seemed almost touchingly pleased to see me. 'But you needn't have worried,' he declared, 'I'll be back in the morning.'

'Really? So soon?' I almost loved him for it; but I was concerned, too. I'm enjoying our game too much to let him slip away on a stupid principle. 'Shouldn't you rest, at least for a few days?'

'Don't you start,' he said. 'I've had enough of that from the hospital. Take up a hobby, he says – something quiet like taxidermy or macramé – Gods, why doesn't he just hand me the hemlock bowl and have done with it?'

I thought he was over-dramatizing, and said so.

'Well,' said Straitley, pulling a face. 'It's what I'm good at.'

His house is a tiny two-up, two-down mid-terrace about ten minutes' walk from St Oswald's. The hallway is stacked high with books – some on shelves, others not – so that the original colour of the wallpaper is almost impossible to detect. The carpets are worn right down to the weft, except in the parlour, where lurks the ghost of a brown Axminster. It smells of dust and polish and the dog that died five years ago; a big school radiator in the hallway throws out an unforgiving blast of heat; there is a kitchen with a floor of mosaic tiles; and, covering every scrap of uncluttered wall, a multitude of class photographs.

He offered me tea in a St Oswald's mug, and some dubious-looking chocolate digestives from a tin on the mantelpiece. I noticed that he looks smaller at home.

'How's Anderton-Pullitt?' Apparently he'd been asking the same question every ten minutes at the hospital, even after the boy was out of danger. 'Did they find out what happened?'

I shook my head. 'I'm sure no one blames you, Mr Straitley.'

'That isn't the point.'

And it wasn't; the pictures on the walls said as much,

with their double rows of young faces; I wondered whether Leon might be among them somewhere. What would I do if I saw his face now, in Straitley's house? And what would I do if I saw myself beside him, cap crammed over my eyes, blazer buttoned tightly over my second-hand shirt?

'Misfortune comes in groups of three,' said Straitley, reaching for a biscuit, then changing his mind. 'First Fallow, now Anderton-Pullitt – I'm waiting to see what the next one will be.'

I smiled. 'I had no idea you were superstitious, sir.'

'Superstitious? It comes with the territory.' He took the biscuit after all, and dipped it in his tea. 'You can't work at St Oswald's for as long as I have without believing in signs and portents and—'

'Ghosts?' I suggested slyly.

He did not return my smile. 'Of course,' he said. 'The bloody place is full of them.' I wondered for a moment if he was thinking of my father. Or Leon. For a moment, I wondered if I was one myself.

4

IT WAS DURING THAT SUMMER THAT JOHN SNYDE BEGAN – slowly and inconspicuously – to unravel. Small things at first, barely noticeable within the greater picture of my life, where Leon loomed large and everything else was reduced to a series of vague constructions on a far and hazy horizon. But as July waxed and the end of term came closer, his temper, always a presence, became a constant.

Most of all, I remember his anger. That summer, it seemed, my father was always in a rage. At me; at the School; at the mysterious graffiti artists who spray-painted the side of the Games Pavilion. At the junior boys who called out at him as he rode the big lawn-mower. At the two older boys who had ridden it that time, and who had caused him to receive an official reprimand. At the neighbours' dogs, who left small unwanted presents on the cricket lawn, which he had to remove using a rolled-up plastic bag and a paper tissue. At the government; at the landlord of the pub; at the people who moved over to the other side of the pavement to avoid him as he came home, mumbling to himself, from the supermarket.

One Monday morning only a few days from the end of term, he caught a first-year boy searching under the counter in the Porter's Lodge. Ostensibly for a lost bag, but John Snyde knew better than to believe that story. The boy's intentions were clear from his face – theft, vandalism or some other means to disgrace John Snyde – already the boy had discovered the small bottle of Irish whiskey hidden underneath a pile of old newspapers, and his small eyes gleamed with malice and satisfaction. So thought my father; and, recognizing one of his young tormentors – a monkey-faced boy with an insolent manner – he set out to teach him a lesson.

Oh, I don't suppose he really hurt him. His loyalty to St Oswald's was bitter, but true; and although by now he loathed many of the individuals – the Bursar, the Head and especially the boys – the institution itself still commanded his respect. But the boy tried to bluster; told my father, *You can't touch me*; demanded to be let out of the Lodge; and finally, in a voice that drilled into my father's head (Sunday night had been a late one, and this time, it showed), squalled, *Let me out, let me out let me out let me out* – until his cries alerted Dr Tidy in the nearby Bursar's office and he came running.

By this time the monkey-faced boy – Matthews, he was called – was crying. John Snyde was a big man, intimidating even when he was not enraged, and that day he had been very, very angry. Tidy saw my father's bloodshot eyes and rumpled clothing; saw the boy's tearful face and the wet patch spreading across his grey uniform trousers, and drew the inevitable conclusion. It was the last straw; John Snyde was summoned to the Headmaster's office that very morning, with Pat Bishop present (to ensure the fairness of the proceedings), and given a second, final warning.

The Old Head would not have done it. My father was convinced of that. Shakeshafte knew the pressures of working within a school; he would have known how to defuse the situation without causing a scene. But the new man was from the state sector; versed in political correctness and toytown activism. Besides, he was a weakling beneath his stern exterior, and this opportunity to establish himself as a strong, decisive leader (and at no professional risk) was too good to miss.

There would be an inquiry, he said. For the moment Snyde was to continue his duties, reporting every day to the Bursar for instructions, but was to have no contact at all with the boys. Any further *incidents* – the word was uttered with the prissy self-satisfaction of the churchgoing teetotaller – would result in immediate dismissal.

My father remained certain that Bishop was on his side. Good old Bishop, he said; wasted in that office job; should have been Head. Of course, my father *would* have liked him; that big, bluff man with the rugby-player's nose and the proletarian tastes. But Bishop's loyalties were to St Oswald's; much as he might sympathize with my father's grievances, I knew that when it came to a choice, the School had all his allegiance.

Still, he said, the holidays would give my father time to sort himself out. He'd been drinking too much, that he knew; he'd let himself go. But he was a good man at heart; he'd given loyal service to the School for nearly five years; he could get through this.

A typical Bishop phrase, that: *You can get through this.* He talks to the boys in the same soldierly way, like a rugby coach rallying the team. His conversation, like my father's, was riddled with clichés: *You can get through this. Take it like a man. The bigger they are, the harder they fall.*

It was a language my father loved and understood, and for a time it rallied him. For Bishop's sake, he cut down on his drinking. He had his hair cut, and dressed with greater care. Conscious of the accusation of having *let himself go*, as Bishop put it, he even began to work out in the evenings, doing press-ups in front of the TV while I read a book and dreamed he was not my father.

Then, the holidays came, and the pressures on him diminished. His duties were equally reduced; there were no boys to make life unbearable for him; he mowed the lawns unhindered and patrolled the grounds alone, keeping a sharp watch out for spray-paint artists or stray dogs.

At these times I could believe my father was almost happy; keys in one hand, a can of ale in the other, he roamed his little empire secure in the knowledge that he had a place there – that of a small but necessary cog in a glorious machine. Bishop had said as much; therefore it must be true.

As for myself, I had other preoccupations. I gave Leon

three clear days after the end of term before phoning him to arrange a meeting; he was friendly but in no hurry, and told me that he and his mother had some people coming to stay, and that he was expected to entertain them. That came as a blow, after everything I had so carefully planned; but I accepted it without complaint, knowing as I did that the best way to deal with Leon's occasional perverseness was to ignore it and to let him have his way.

'Are these people friends of your mother's?' I enquired, more to keep him talking than for information.

'Yeah. The Tynans and their kid. It's a bit of a drag, but Charlie and I have to rally round. You know, pass the cucumber sandwiches, pour the sherry, and all that.' He sounded regretful, but I couldn't shake the idea that he was smiling.

'Kid?' I said, with visions of a clever, cheery schoolboy who would eclipse me completely in Leon's eyes.

'Hm. Francesca. Little fat girl, mad about ponies. Good job Charlie's here; otherwise I'd probably have to look after *her* as well.'

'Oh.' I couldn't help sounding a little mournful.

'Don't worry,' Leon told me. 'It won't be for long. I'll give you a call, OK?'

That rattled me. Of course, I couldn't refuse to give Leon my phone number. But the thought that my father might answer his call filled me with anxiety. 'Hey, I'll probably see you,' I said. 'No big deal.'

*   *   *

And so I waited. I was at the same time anxious and bored beyond belief: torn between the desire to wait by the phone in case Leon called, and the equally strong compulsion to ride my bicycle out by his house in the hope of 'accidentally' meeting him. I had no other friends: reading made me impatient; I couldn't even listen to my records because they made me think of Leon. It was a beautiful summer, the kind of summer that exists only in memory and in certain books, hot and blue-green and filled with bees and murmurings, but for me it might as well have been raining every day. Without Leon there was no pleasure in it; I lurked in corners; I stole from shops out of sheer spite.

After a while, my father noticed. His good intentions had brought about a new, temporary alertness, and he began to make comments on my listlessness and quick temper. *Growing pains*, he called it, and recommended exercise and fresh air.

Certainly, I *was* growing; I would be thirteen in August and I had entered a development spurt. I remained, as always, skinny and bird-boned, but I was aware that even so, my St Oswald's uniform had grown rather tight, especially the blazer (I'd need to get another before long); and that my trousers left fully two inches of ankle showing.

A week passed, then most of another. I could feel the holidays slipping by, and could do nothing about it. Had Leon gone away? Passing his house on my new bike, I'd seen an open screen door leading to the patio; heard laughter and voices on the warm air, though I could not tell how many they were, nor whether my friend's voice was among them.

I wondered what the visitors were like. A banker, he'd said, and some kind of high-powered secretary, like Leon's mother. Professional people, who ate cucumber sandwiches and took drinks on the veranda. The kind of people John and Sharon Snyde would never be, no matter how much money they had. The kind of parents I would have wanted for myself.

The thought obsessed me; I began to visualize the Tynans – he in a light linen jacket, she in a white summer dress – with Mrs Mitchell standing by with a jug of Pimm's and a tray of tall glasses, and Leon and his sister, Charlie, sitting on the grass, all of them gilded with the light and with something more – the something that made them different from myself, the something I had glimpsed for the first time at St Oswald's, the day I crossed the line.

That line. It loomed ahead of me once more, taunting me once more with its proximity. Now I could almost see it, the golden line that set me apart from everything I desired. What more must I do? Hadn't I spent the last three months in the court of my enemies, like a stray wolf that joins the hunting hounds to steal their food in secret? Why then that sense of isolation? *Why* hadn't Leon called?

Could it be that he somehow sensed my otherness, and was ashamed to be seen in my company? Hiding in the Gatehouse, afraid to come out in case I was seen, I was half-convinced of it. There was something cheap about me – a scent, perhaps, a polyester-shine – that had alerted him.

I had not been good enough; he had spotted me. It was driving me mad; I needed to know; and that Sunday I dressed carefully and rode my bike over to Leon's house.

It was a bold move. I had never actually been to Leon's house before – riding past it didn't count – and I found that my hands were shaking a little as I opened the gate and walked down the long drive towards the porch. It was a big, double-fronted Edwardian house with lawns to the front and side and a wooded back garden with a summerhouse and a walled orchard.

Old money, as my father would have said with envy and contempt; but to me it was the world I'd read about in books; it was *Swallows and Amazons* and the Famous Five; it was lemonade on the lawn; it was boarding-school; it was picnics by the seaside and a jolly Cook who made scones, and an elegant mother reclining on a sofa and a pipe-smoking father who was always right, always benevolent, though rarely at home. I was not yet thirteen and already I felt desperately old, as if childhood had some-how been denied me – *that* childhood, at least; the one I deserved.

I knocked; I could hear voices coming from behind the house. Leon's mother, saying something about Mrs Thatcher and the Unions, a man's voice – *The only way to do it is to*— – and the muted chink of someone pouring from a jug filled with ice-cubes. Then, Leon's voice, sounding very close, saying; 'Vae, anything but politics, please. Any-one want a lemon-vodka ice?'

'Yeah!' That was Charlie, Leon's sister.

Then, another voice, a girl's, low and well modulated;
'Sure. OK.'

That must be Francesca. It had sounded rather a silly
name to me when Leon had told me over the phone, but
suddenly I wasn't sure any more. I edged away from the door
towards the side of the house – if anyone saw me I would
tell them I had knocked, but had received no reply – and
peered around the edge of the building.

It was much as I had imagined it. There was a veranda
behind the house, shaded by a large tree that cast a mosaic
of light and shade over the tables and chairs that had been
placed underneath. Mrs Mitchell was there, blonde and
pretty in jeans and a clean white shirt, which made her look
very young; then Mrs Tynan, in sandals and a cool linen
dress; then there was Charlotte sitting on a home-made
swing, and facing me, in his jeans and battered sneakers and
his faded Stranglers T-shirt, was Leon.

He'd grown, I thought. In three weeks his features had
sharpened, his body lengthened and his hair, which had
already been borderline in terms of St Oswald's regulations,
now fell across his eyes. Out of uniform he might have
been anyone; he looked like any other boy from my own
school but for that *shine*; the patina that comes from a
lifetime of living in a house like this, of learning Latin with
Quaz in the Bell Tower, of eating smoked-salmon blinis and
lemon-vodka ice instead of half a lager and fish and chips,
of never having to lock your bedroom door on Saturday
nights.

A wave of love and longing overwhelmed me; not just for

Leon, but for everything he stood for. It was so powerful, so mystically adult in its intensity, that for a moment I barely noticed the girl at his side, Francesca, the fat little pony girl of whom he'd seemed so contemptuous on the phone. Then I saw her, and for a time, stood watching, forgetting even to hide in my amazement and dismay.

Fat little pony girl she might once have been. But now – there were no words to describe her. All comparisons failed. My own experience of what constituted desirability was limited to such examples as Pepsi, the women in my father's magazines and the likes of Tracey Delacey. I couldn't see it myself – but then again I wouldn't, would I?

I thought of Pepsi and her false nails and perpetual smell of hairspray; of gum-chewing Tracey, with her blotchy legs and sullen face; and of the magazine women, coy but somehow carnivorous, opened up like something on a pathologist's slab. I thought of my mother, and Cinnabar.

This girl was a different race entirely. Fourteen, maybe fifteen; slim; tawny. The embodiment of *shine*; hair tied carelessly back in a ponytail; long, sleek legs beneath khaki shorts. A small gold cross nestled in the hollow of her throat. Dancer's feet kicked out at an angle; dappled face in the summer green. *This* was why Leon hadn't called; it was this girl; this beautiful girl.

'Hey! Hey, Pinchbeck!'

My God, he'd seen me. I considered making a run for it; but Leon was already coming towards me, puzzled but not annoyed, with the girl a few steps behind him. My chest felt tight; my heart shrunk to the size of a nut. I tried a smile; it felt like a mask. 'Hello, Leon,' I said. 'Hello, Mrs Mitchell. I was just passing by.'

Imagine, if you can, that terrible afternoon. I wanted to go home, but Leon would not allow it; instead I endured two hours of utter wretchedness on the back lawn, drinking lemonade that soured my stomach, while Leon's mother asked me questions about my family and Mr Tynan slapped me repeatedly on the shoulder and speculated on all the mischief Leon and I got up to at school.

It was torture. My head ached; my stomach churned; and throughout all of it I was obliged to smile and be polite and reply to questions whilst Leon and his girl – there was no doubt now that she was *his* girl – lounged and whispered to each other in the shade, Leon's brown hand laid almost casually over Francesca's tawny one, his grey eyes filled with summer and with her.

I don't know what I said in answer to their questions. I remember Leon's mother being especially, agonizingly kind: she went out of her way to include me; asked me about my hobbies, my holidays, my thoughts. I replied almost at random, with an animal's instinct to stay hidden, and I must have passed scrutiny, although Charlotte watched me in a silence I might have found suspicious if my mind had not been wholly taken up with my own suffering.

Finally, Mrs Mitchell must have noticed something, because she looked at me closely and observed that I was looking rather pale.

'Headache,' I said, trying to smile, while behind her Leon played with a long strand of Francesca's honey-mink hair. 'I get them sometimes,' I improvised desperately. 'Better go home and lie down for a while.'

Leon's mother was reluctant to let me go. She suggested that I lie down in Leon's room; offered to get me an aspirin; overwhelmed me with kindness so that I was almost reduced to tears. She must have seen something in my face then, because she smiled and patted me on the shoulder. 'All right, then, Julian, dear,' she said. 'Go home and lie down. Perhaps that's best, after all.'

'Thank you, Mrs Mitchell.' I nodded gratefully – I really was feeling ill. 'I've had a lovely time. Honest.' Leon waved at me, and Mrs Mitchell insisted on giving me a large and sticky slice of cake to take home, wrapped in a paper napkin. As I was walking back down the drive I heard her voice, low and carrying from behind the house: 'What a funny little chap, Leon. So polite and reserved. Is he a good friend of yours?'

5

St Oswald's Grammar School for Boys
Tuesday, 5th October

THE OFFICIAL REPORT FROM THE HOSPITAL WAS ANA-phylactic shock, caused by ingestion of peanuts or peanut-contaminated foodstuffs, possibly accidental.

Of course, there was a terrible fuss. It was a disgrace, said Mrs Anderton-Pullitt to Pat Bishop, who was there; school was supposed to be a safe environment for her son. Why hadn't there been any supervision at the time of his collapse? How had his schoolmaster failed to notice that poor James was unconscious?

Pat dealt with the distressed mother as best he could. He's in his element in this kind of situation; knows how to defuse antagonism; has a shoulder of comforting proportions; projects a convincing air of authority. He promised that the incident would be thoroughly investigated, but assured Mrs

Anderton-Pullitt that Mr Straitley was a most conscientious master and that every effort had been made to ensure her son's safety.

By then, the individual concerned was sitting up in bed, reading *Practical Aeronautics* and looking rather pleased with himself.

At the same time, Mr Anderton-Pullitt, School Governor and ex-England cricketer, was pulling rank with the hospital administration in his attempt to have the remains of his son's sandwiches analysed for nut residue. If they yielded as much as a trace, he said, a certain health-food manufacturer would be sued for every penny it possessed, not to mention a certain chain of retailers. But as it happened, the tests were never made, because before they could get started, the peanut was found floating and still mostly intact, at the bottom of James's can of Fanta.

At first, the Anderton-Pullitts were bewildered. How could a peanut have found its way into their son's drink? Their initial reaction was to contact (and sue) the manufacturers, but it soon became obvious that any malpractice on their part was, at best, unprovable. The can had already been opened; anything might conceivably have fallen inside.

Fallen, or been put there.

It was inescapable: if James's drink had been tampered with, then the culprit must have been someone in the form. Worse still, the perpetrator must have known that his act might have dangerous, if not fatal, consequences. The Anderton-Pullitts took the matter straight to the Head, bypassing even Bishop in their rage and indignation, and announced their intention, if he did not pursue the matter, of going directly to the police.

I should have been there. Unforgivable, that I was not; and yet when I awoke the morning after my brief stint in the hospital I felt so exhausted – so wretchedly *old* – that I called the School and told Bob Strange that I wasn't coming in.

'Well, I didn't expect you to,' said Strange, sounding surprised. 'I assumed that they'd keep you in hospital over the weekend, at least.' His prissy, official tone failed to hide his real disapproval that they had not. 'I can have you covered for the next six weeks, no problem.'

'That won't be necessary. I'll be back on Monday.'

But by Monday the news had broken: there had been an investigation of my form; witnesses had been called and questioned; lockers searched; telephone calls exchanged. Dr Devine had been consulted, in his capacity as Health and Safety officer, and he, Bishop, Strange, the Head and Dr Pooley, the Chairman of the Governors, had spent a long time in the Head's office with the Anderton-Pullitts.

Result: I returned on Monday morning to find the class in uproar. The incident with Knight had even eclipsed the recent – and most unwelcome – piece in the *Examiner*, with its sinister implication of a secret informant within the School. The findings of the Head's investigation were irrefutable; on the day of the incident, Knight had bought a packet of peanuts from the school tuck-shop, and had brought them into the form-room for lunch. He denied it at first, but several witnesses remembered it, including a member of staff. Finally Knight had confessed; yes, he *had* bought the peanuts, but he denied tampering with anyone's drink. Besides, he said tearfully, he *liked* Anderton-Pullitt; he would never have done anything to hurt him.

A record sheet had been produced from the day of Knight's suspension, listing the witnesses to the fight between himself and Jackson. Sure enough, Anderton-Pullitt was among them. A motive was now clearly established.

Well, it wouldn't have stood up in the Old Bailey. But a school is not a court of law; it has its own rules and its methods of applying them; it has its own system, its safeguards. Like the Church, like the Army, it looks after its own. By the time I returned, Knight had been judged, found guilty and suspended from School until after half-term.

My problem was that I didn't quite believe he'd done it.

'It's not that Knight isn't capable of something like that,' I told Dianne Dare in the Common Room that lunch-time. 'He's a sly little oik, and far more likely to cause mischief by stealth than to play up in public, but—' I gave a sigh. 'I don't like it. I don't like *him* – but I can't believe that even he could have been *that* stupid.'

'Never underestimate stupidity,' remarked Pearman, who was standing nearby.

'No, but this is *malice*,' said Dianne. 'If the boy knew what he was doing—'

'If he knew what he was doing,' interrupted Light from his place under the clock, 'then he should be bloody well locked up. You read about these kids nowadays – rapes, muggings, murders, God knows what – and they can't even put them away for it because the bloody bleeding-heart liberals won't let 'em.'

'In my day,' said McDonaugh darkly, 'we had the cane.'

'Bugger that,' said Light. 'Bring back conscription. Teach 'em some discipline.'

Gods, I thought, what an ass. He held forth in this muscular, brainless style for a few minutes more, attracting a sultry glance from Isabelle Tapi, who was watching from the yoghurt corner.

Young Keane, who had also been listening, did a quick, comic mime just outside of the Games teacher's line of vision, twisting his sharp, clever face into an exact parody of Light's expression. I pretended not to notice, and hid my smile behind my hand.

'It's all very well to go on about discipline,' said Roach from behind the *Mirror*, 'but what sanctions do we have? Do something bad, and you get detention. Do something worse, you get suspended, which is the opposite. Where's the sense in that?'

'No sense at all,' said Light. 'But we've got to be seen to be doing something. Whether or not Knight did it—'

'And if he didn't?' said Roach.

McDonaugh made a dismissive gesture. 'Doesn't matter. What matters is *order*. Whoever the troublemaker is, you can be bloody sure he'll think twice about stepping out of line again if he knows that the minute he does, he'll get the cane.'

Light nodded. Keane pulled another face. Dianne shrugged and Pearman gave a little smile of vague and ironic superiority.

'It was Knight,' said Roach with emphasis. 'Just the kind of stupid thing he would do.'

'I still don't like it. It feels wrong.'

The boys were unusually reticent on the subject. In normal circumstances, an incident of this type should provide a welcome break from the School's routine; petty scandals and minor mishaps; secrets and fights: the furtive stuff of adolescence. But this, it seemed, was different. A line had been crossed, and even those boys who had never had a good word to say about Anderton-Pullitt viewed the incident with unease and disapproval.

'I mean, he's not all there, is he, sir?' said Jackson. 'You know – not a *mong* or anything, but you can't say he's completely normal.'

'Will he be all right, sir?' asked Tayler, who has allergies himself.

'Fortunately, yes.' The boy was being kept at home for the present, but as far as anyone could tell, he had made a complete recovery. 'But it could have been fatal.'

There was an awkward pause as the boys looked at each other. As yet, few of them have encountered death beyond the occasional dog, cat or grandparent; the thought that one of them could actually have died – right in front of them, in their own form-room – was suddenly rather frightening.

'It must have been an accident,' said Tayler at last.

'I think so too.' I hoped that was true.

'Dr Devine says we can have counselling if we need it,' said McNair.

'*Do* you need it?'

'Do we get to miss lessons, sir?'

I looked at him and saw him grinning. 'Over my dead body.'

Throughout the day the feeling of unrest intensified. Allen-Jones was hyperactive; Sutcliff depressed; Jackson argumentative; Pink anxious. It was windy, too; and the wind, as every schoolteacher knows, makes classes unruly and pupils excitable. Doors slammed; windows rattled; October was in with a blast, and suddenly it was autumn.

I like autumn. The drama of it; the golden lion roaring through the back door of the year, shaking its mane of leaves. A dangerous time; of violent rages and deceptive calm; of fireworks in the pockets and conkers in the fist. It is the season in which I feel closest to the boy I was, and at the same time closest to death. It is St Oswald's at its most beautiful; gold among the lindens, its tower howling like a throat.

But this year, there is more. Ninety-nine terms; thirty-three autumns; half of my life. This year those terms weigh unexpectedly heavy, and I wonder whether young Bevans may not after all be right. Retirement need not be a death sentence. One more term and I will have scored my Century; to withdraw on such a note can carry no shame. Besides, things are changing, and so they should. Only I am too old to change.

On my way home on Monday night I looked into the Porter's Lodge. Fallow's replacement has not yet been found, and in the meantime, Jimmy Watt has taken over as many as he can manage of the Porter's duties. One of these is answering the phone in the Lodge, but his telephone manner is not good, and he has a tendency to hang up by mistake when transferring calls. As a result, calls had been missed throughout the day, and frustrations were running high.

It was the Bursar's fault; Jimmy does what he's told, but has no concept of working independently. He can change a fuse or replace a lock; he can sweep up fallen leaves; he can even climb up a telegraph pole to retrieve a pair of shoes, tied together by their laces and flung across the wires by a school bully. Light calls him Jimmy Forty-Watt and jeers at his moon face and his slow way of talking. Of course, Light was a bully himself a few years ago; you can still see it in his red face and aggressive, oddly careful walk – steroids or haemorrhoids, I'm not sure which. In any case, Jimmy should never have been left in charge of the Lodge, and Dr Tidy knew it; it was simply that it was easier (and cheaper, of course) to use him as a stopgap until a new appointment was made. Besides, Fallow had been with the school for over fifteen years, and you can't turn a man out of his home overnight, whatever the reason. I found myself thinking about this as I passed the Lodge; it wasn't that I'd especially *liked* Fallow; but he had been a part of the School – a small but necessary part – and his absence was felt.

There was a woman in the Lodge as I went past. I never questioned her presence, assuming she was a secretary drafted in through the School's agency to take calls and to cover for Jimmy when he was called upon to perform one of his many other duties. A greying woman in a suit, rather older than the standard agency temp, whose face seemed dimly familiar. I should have asked who she was. Dr Devine is always talking about intruders, about shootings in American schools and how easy it would be for some crazed person to enter the buildings and go on the rampage – but that's just Devine. He's the Health and Safety man, after all, and he has to justify his salary.

But I was in a hurry, and I did not speak to the greying woman. It was only when I saw her byline and her photo in the *Examiner* that I recognized her; and by then it was too late. The mystery informant had struck again, and this time, I was the target.

6

Monday, 11th October

WELL, MRS KNIGHT, AS YOU MIGHT EXPECT, DID NOT TAKE kindly to the suspension of her only son. You know the type: expensive, arrogant, slightly neurotic and afflicted with that curious blindness which only the mothers of teenage sons seem to possess. She marched down to St Oswald's the morning after the Head's decision, demanding to see him. He was out, of course; instead, an emergency meeting was convened, including Bishop (nervous and unwell), Dr Devine (Health and Safety) and, in the absence of Roy Straitley, myself.

Mrs Knight looked murderous in Chanel. In Bishop's office, sitting very straight on a hard chair, she glared at the three of us with eyes like zircons.

'Mrs Knight,' said Devine. 'The boy could have died.'

Mrs Knight was not impressed. 'I can understand your

concern,' she said. 'Given that there seems to have been no supervision at all at the time of the incident. However, regarding the matter of my son's involvement—'

Bishop interrupted. 'Well, that isn't entirely true,' he began. 'Several members of staff were present at different times throughout Break, although—'

'And did anyone *see* my son put a peanut in the other boy's drink?'

'Mrs Knight, it isn't—'

'Well? Did they?'

Bishop looked uncomfortable. It had been the Head's decision to suspend Knight, after all; and I had a feeling that he himself might have handled the matter differently. 'The evidence suggests that he did it, Mrs Knight. I'm not saying he did it with malice—'

Flatly: 'My son doesn't tell lies.'

'*All* boys tell lies.' That was Devine – true enough, as it happened, but hardly calculated to appease Mrs Knight. She levelled her gaze upon him.

'Really?' she said. 'In that case, maybe you should re-examine Anderton-Pullitt's account of the supposed fight between Jackson and my son.'

Devine was taken aback. 'Mrs Knight, I really don't see what relevance—'

'Don't you? I do.' She turned to Bishop. 'What I see is a concerted campaign of victimization against my son. It's common knowledge that Mr Straitley has his little favourites – his Brodie Boys, I understand he calls them – but I didn't expect *you* to take his side in this. My son has been bullied, accused, humiliated and now suspended from school – something that will go on his class record, and perhaps even affect his university prospects – without even being given a chance to clear his name. And do you know why, Mr Bishop? Do you have any idea why?'

Bishop was completely lost in the face of this attack. His charm – real as it is – is his only weapon, and Mrs Knight was armoured against it. The smile that had tamed my father failed to melt her ice; in fact, it seemed to infuriate her still more.

'I'll tell you, shall I?' she said. 'My son has been accused of theft, of assault and now – as far as I can understand – of attempted murder' – at this point Bishop tried to interrupt, but she waved his protest aside – 'and do you know *why* he has been singled out like this? Have you asked Mr Straitley? Have you asked the other boys?' She paused for effect, and as she met my eyes I gave her an encouraging nod and she bugled, just as her son had in Straitley's class:

'Because he is *Jewish*! My son is a victim of discrimination! I want a proper investigation of all this' – she glared at Bishop – 'and if I don't get one, then you can expect a letter from my solicitor.'

There was a resounding silence. Then Mrs Knight swept out in a fusillade of heels; Dr Devine looked shaken; Pat Bishop sat down with his hand over his eyes and I allowed myself the tiniest of smiles.

Of course, it was understood that the matter would not be discussed outside the meeting. Devine made that clear from the start, and I agreed, with becoming earnestness and respect. I should not have been there in the first place, said Devine; I had only been asked to attend as a witness, failing the presence of the boy's form-master. Not that anyone regretted Straitley's absence; both Bishop and Devine were adamant that the old man, engaging as he was, would only have made a foul situation even worse.

'Of course there's no truth in it,' said Bishop, recovering over a cup of tea. 'There's never been any question of anti-Semitism at St Oswald's. Never.'

Devine looked less convinced. 'I'm as fond of Roy Straitley as anyone,' he said. 'But there's no denying he can be rather odd. Just because he's been here longer than anyone, he tends to think he runs the place.'

'I'm sure he doesn't mean any harm,' I said. 'It's a stressful job for a man of his age, and everyone can make the occasional error of judgement from time to time.'

Bishop looked at me. 'What do you mean? Have you heard anything?'

'No, sir.'

'Are you sure?' That was Devine, almost falling over in his eagerness.

'Absolutely, sir. I simply meant—' I hesitated.

'What? Out with it!'

'I'm sure it's nothing, sir. For his age, I think he's remarkably alert. It's just that recently I've been noticing—' And with modest reluctance I mentioned the missing register, the missed e-mails, the ridiculous fuss he'd made over the loss of that old green pen, not forgetting those few vital, register-less moments, when he had failed to notice the unconscious boy gasping out his life on the classroom floor.

Emphatic denial is by far the best tactic when seeking to incriminate an enemy. And so I managed to convey my utmost respect and admiration of Roy Straitley whilst innocently implying the rest. Thus I am shown to be a loyal member of the School – if a trifle naïve – and second, I ensure that doubt remains like a splinter in the minds of Bishop and Devine, preparing them for the next headline, which, as it happened, was to feature in the *Examiner* this very week.

NUTS TO YOU, SIR!

Colin Knight is a studious, shy young man who has found the social and academic pressures of St Oswald's increasingly difficult to deal with. 'There's a lot of bullying,' he told the *Examiner*, 'but most of us don't dare report it. Some boys can do anything they like at St Oswald's, because some of the teachers are on their side, and anyone who makes a complaint is bound to get into trouble.'

Certainly, Colin Knight does not look like a trouble-maker. And yet, if we are to believe the complaints levelled against him this term by his form-master (Roy Straitley, 65), he has, in three short weeks, been guilty of numerous instances of theft, lying and bullying, culminating in his suspension from school following a bizarre accusation of assault, when a fellow student (James Anderton-Pullitt, 13) choked on a peanut.

We spoke to John Fallow, dismissed from St Oswald's two weeks ago after fifteen years' loyal service. 'I'm glad to see young Knight standing up for himself,' Fallow told the *Examiner*. 'But the Anderton-Pullitts are School Governors, and the Knights are just an ordinary family.'

Pat Bishop (54), Second Master and spokesman for St Oswald's, told us: 'This is an internal disciplinary matter which will be thoroughly investigated before any further decision is taken.'

In the meantime, Colin Knight will continue his education from his bedroom, forfeiting his right to attend the classes for which his family pays £7,000 a year. And although for the average St Oswald's pupil this may not count for much, for ordinary people like the Knights, it's very far from peanuts.

I'm rather proud of that little piece: a medley of fact, conjecture and low humour that should rankle suitably in the arrogant heart of St Oswald's. My one regret was that I could not sign my name to it – not even my assumed name, although Mole was certainly instrumental in its construction.

Instead I used a female reporter as my cover, and e-mailed my copy to her as before, adding a few details to facilitate her enquiry. The piece ran, flanked by a photograph of young Knight – clean and wholesome in his school uniform – and a grainy class portrait from 1997, showing Straitley looking blotchy and dissipated, surrounded by boys.

Of course, any criticism of St Oswald's is balm to the *Examiner*. By the weekend it had resurfaced twice in the national press: once as a cheery blip on page 10 of the *News of the World*, and once as part of a more contemplative editorial piece in the *Guardian*, entitled 'Rough Justice in Our Independent Schools'.

All in all, a good day's work. I'd made sure that any mention of anti-Semitism was withheld for the present, and instead, worked on my touching depiction of the Knights as honest folk, but poor. That's what the readers really want – a story of people like themselves (they think), scrimping and saving to send their kids to the best possible school – although I'd like to see any of them actually blowing seven grand in beer money on fees, for God's sake, when the Government's giving out education for free.

My father read the *News of the World*, too, and he was filled with the same ponderous clichés about *School's your best investment* and *Learning is for Life*, though as far as I could see, it never went further than that, and if he saw the irony in his words, he never gave any sign of it.

7

St Oswald's Grammar School for Boys
Wednesday, 13th October

KNIGHT WAS BACK ON MONDAY MORNING. WEARING AN expression of martyred bravery, like an assault victim, and the tiniest of smirks. The other boys treated him with caution, but were not unkind; in fact I noticed that Brasenose, who usually avoids him, went out of his way to be friendly, sitting next to him at lunch-time and even offering him half of his chocolate bar. It was as if Brasenose, the perpetual victim, had spotted a potential defender in the newly vindicated Knight, and was making an effort to cultivate his friendship.

Anderton-Pullitt was back, too; looking none the worse for his near-death experience, and with a new book on First World War aircraft with which to plague us. As for myself, I've been worse. I said as much to Dianne Dare when she questioned the wisdom of my swift return to work, and later, to Pat Bishop, who accused me of looking tired.

I have to say he isn't looking too well himself at the moment. First the Fallow case, then the scene with Anderton-Pullitt and finally this business with Knight . . . I'd heard from Marlene that Pat had slept more than one night in his office; and now I saw that his face was redder than usual, and his eyes bloodshot. From the way he approached me I guessed the New Head had sent him to sound me out, and I could tell Bishop wasn't pleased about this, but as Second Master, his duty is to the Head, whatever his own feelings on the matter.

'You look exhausted, Roy. Are you sure you ought to be here?'

'Nothing wrong with me that a good strict nurse can't cure.'

He did not smile. 'After what happened, I thought you might at least take a week or two.'

I could see where this was leading. 'Nothing happened,' I said shortly.

'That's not true. You had an attack—'

'Nerves. Nothing more.'

He sighed. 'Roy, be reasonable—'

'Don't lecture me, Pat. I'm not one of your boys.'

'Don't be like that,' said Pat. 'We just thought—'

'You, the Head and Strange—'

'We just thought you could do with a rest.'

I looked at him, but he would not quite meet my eye. 'A rest?' I said. I was beginning to feel annoyed. 'Yes, I see that it might be very convenient if I did take a few weeks off.

Give things time to settle down? Give you chance to smooth a few ruffled feathers? Maybe pave the way for some of Mr Strange's new developments?'

I was right, which made him angry. He didn't say anything, though I could tell he wanted to, and his face, already flushed, took on a deeper shade. 'You're slowing down, Roy,' he said. 'Face it, you're forgetting things. And you're not as young as you were.'

'Is anyone?'

He frowned. 'There's been talk of having you suspended.'

'Really?' That would be Strange, or maybe Devine, with his eye to room 59 and the last outpost of my little empire. 'I'm sure you told them what would happen if they tried. Suspension, without a formal warning?' I'm not a Union man, but Sourgrape is, and so is the Head. 'He who lives by the book dies by the book. And they know it.'

Once more, Pat did not meet my eye. 'I hoped I wouldn't have to tell you this,' he said. 'But you haven't left me any choice.'

'Tell me what?' I said, knowing the answer.

'A warning's been drafted,' he said.

'Drafted? By whom?' As if I didn't know. Strange, of course; the man who had already devalued my department, downsized my timetable, and who now hoped to put me to rest while the Suits and Beards took over the world.

Bishop sighed. 'Listen, Roy, you're not the only one with problems.'

'I don't doubt it,' I said. 'Some of us, however—'

Some of us, however, are paid more than others to deal

with them. It's true, though, that we rarely think of our colleagues' private lives. Children, lovers, homes. The boys are always astonished to see us in a context outside of St Oswald's – buying groceries in a supermarket; at the barber's; in a pub. Astonished, and mildly delighted, like spotting a famous person in the street. *I saw you in town on Saturday, sir!* As if they imagined us hanging up behind our form-room doors, like discarded gowns, between Friday night and Monday morning.

To tell the truth, I am somewhat guilty of this myself. But seeing Bishop today – I mean, really *seeing* him; his rugby-man's bulk gone half to fat in spite of that daily run, and his face drawn, the face of a man who has never quite under-stood how easily fourteen slipped away and fifty settled in – I felt an unexpected pang of sympathy.

'Listen, Pat. I know you're—'

But Bishop had already turned to go, slouching off down the Upper Corridor, hands in pockets, broad shoulders slightly bowed. It was a pose I'd seen him adopt many times when the School rugby team lost against St Henry's, but I knew Bishop too well to believe that the grief implicit in his posture was anything other than a pose. No, he was angry. At himself, perhaps – he's a good man, even if he is the Head's man – but most of all, at my lack of cooperation, School spirit and understanding for his own difficult position.

Oh, I felt for him – but you don't get to be Second Master in a place like St Oswald's without encountering the occasional problem or two. He knows that the Head would be only too pleased to make a scapegoat of me – I don't have much of a career ahead of me, after all, plus I'm expensive and nearing retirement. My replacement would come as a relief to many – my replacement a young chap, a corporate Suit; trained in IT; veteran of many courses; streamlined for rapid promotion. My little malaise must have given them hope. At last, an excuse to be rid of old Straitley without causing too much fuss. A dignified retirement on grounds of ill health; silver plaque; sealed envelope; flattering address to the Common Room.

As for the business of Knight and the rest – well! What could be easier than to lay the blame – ever so quietly – on a former colleague? Before your time; one of the old school, you know, awfully good chap, but set in his ways; not a team player. Not one of us.

Well, you were wrong, Headmaster. I have no intention of going gently into retirement. And as for your written warning, *pone ubi sol non lucet*. I'll score my Century, or die in the attempt. One for the Honours Board.

I was still in a martial frame of mind when I got home this evening, and the invisible finger was back, poking gently but persistently at my wishbone. I took two of the pills Bevans had prescribed, and washed them down with a small medicinal sherry before settling down to some fifth-form marking. It was dark by the time I had finished. At seven I stood up to draw the curtains, when a movement from the garden caught my eye. I leaned closer to the window.

Mine is a long, narrow garden, a seeming throwback to the days of strip-farming, with a hedge on one side, a wall on the other and a variety of shrubs and vegetables growing more or less at random in between. At the far end there is a big old horse-chestnut tree, overhanging Dog Lane, which is separated from the back garden by a fence. Under the tree is a patch of mossy grass on which I like to sit in summer (or did, before the process of getting up again became so cumbersome) and a small and decrepit shed in which I keep a few things.

I have never actually been burgled. I don't suppose I have anything really worth stealing, unless you count books, which are generally held to be worthless by the criminal fraternity. But Dog Lane has a reputation: there is a pub at the corner, which generates noise; a fish and chip shop at the far end, which generates litter; and of course, Sunnybank Park Comprehensive close by, which generates almost anything you can think of, including noise, litter and a twice-daily stampede past my house that would put even the most unruly Ozzies to shame. I tend to be generally tolerant of this. I even turn a blind eye to the occasional intruder hopping over the fence during the conker season. A horse-chestnut tree in October belongs to everyone, Sunnybankers included.

But this was different. For a start, school was long past. It was dark and rather cold, and there was something unpleasantly furtive about the movement I had glimpsed.

Pressing my face to the window, I saw three or four shapes at the far end of the garden, not large enough to be fully adult. Boys, then; now I could hear their voices, very dimly, through the glass.

That surprised me. Usually conker-hunters are quick and unobtrusive. Most people on the lane know my profession, and respect it; and the Sunnybankers to whom I have spoken about their littering habits have rarely, if ever, reoffended.

I rapped sharply on the glass. Now they would run, I thought; but instead the figures fell still, and a few seconds later I heard – unmistakably – jeering from under the horse-chestnut tree.

'That does it.' In four strides I was at the door. 'Oy!' I yelled in my best magisterial voice. 'What the hell do you boys think you're doing!'

More laughter from the bottom of the garden. Two ran, I think – I saw their brief outline, etched in neon, as they climbed the fence. The other two remained, secure in the darkness and reassured by the length of the narrow path.

'I said "What are you doing?"' It was the first time in years that a boy – even a Sunnybanker – had defied me. I felt a surge of adrenalin and the invisible finger poked at me again. 'Come here at once!'

'Or what?' The voice was brash and youthful. 'Think you can take me, you fat bastard?'

'Like fuck he can, he's too old!'

Rage gave me speed; I set off down the path like a buffalo, but it was dark, the path was greasy, my foot in its leather-soled slipper shot to the side, taking me off balance.

I did not fall, but it was close. I wrenched my knee, and when I looked back the two remaining boys were climbing over the fence, in a clap and flutter of laughter, like ugly birds taking wing.

8

St Oswald's Grammar School for Boys
Thursday, 14th October

IT WAS A SMALL INCIDENT. A MINOR IRRITANT, THAT'S ALL.
No damage was done. And yet— There was a time when
I would have caught those boys, whatever it took, and
dragged them back by the ears. Not now, of course. Sunnybankers know their rights. Even so, it had been a long time
since my authority had been so deliberately challenged.
Boys scent weakness. They all do. And it had been a
mistake to run like that, in the dark, especially after
what Bevans had told me. It looked rushed, undignified. A
student teacher's mistake. I should have crept out into Dog
Lane and caught them as they climbed over the fence. They
were only boys – thirteen or fourteen, judging by their
voices. Since when did Roy Straitley allow a few boys to
defy him?

I brooded on that for longer than it deserved. Perhaps that was why I slept so badly; perhaps the sherry; or perhaps I was still troubled by my conversation with Bishop. In any case I awoke unrefreshed; washed, dressed, made toast and drank a mug of tea as I waited for the postman. Sure enough, at seven thirty, the letter-box clattered, and sure enough, there was the typed sheet of St Oswald's notepaper, signed E. Gray, Headmaster, BA (Hons), and Dr B. D. Pooley, Chairman of Governors, the duplicate of which (it said) would be inserted into my personal record for a period of 12 (twelve) months, after which time it would be removed from file, on condition that no further complaint(s) had been lodged and at the discretion of the Governing Body, blah, blah, blah-dy bloody blah.

On a normal day, it would not have concerned me. Fatigue, however, made me vulnerable, and it was without enthusiasm – and a knee that still ached from the evening's misadventure – that I set off on foot to St Oswald's. Without quite knowing why, I made a short detour into Dog Lane, perhaps to check for signs of last night's intruders.

It was then that I saw it. I could hardly have missed it: a swastika, sketched on to the side of the fence in red marker pen, with the word 'HITLER' below it in exuberant letters. It was recent, then; almost certainly the work of last night's Sunnybankers – if, indeed, they *were* Sunnybankers. But I had not forgotten the caricature tacked up on to the form noticeboard; the cartoon of myself as a fat little mortar-boarded Nazi, and my conviction at the time that Knight was behind it.

Could Knight have found out where I lived? It wouldn't be hard; my address is in the School handbook, and dozens of boys must have seen me walking home. All the same I couldn't believe that Knight – Knight, of all people – would dare to do something like this.

Teaching's a game of bluff, of course; but it would take a better player than Knight to check me. No, it had to be a coincidence, I thought; some marker-happy Sunnybank Parker slouching home to his fish and chips, who saw my nice clean fence and hated its unblemished surface.

At the weekend, I'll sand and repaint it with wipe-clean gloss. It needed doing anyway, and as any teacher knows, one piece of graffiti invites another. But I couldn't help feeling, as I walked to St Oswald's, that all the unpleasantness of the past few weeks – Fallowgate, the *Examiner* campaign, last night's intrusion, Anderton-Pullitt's ridiculous peanut, even the Headmaster's prim little letter of this morning – were somehow – obscurely, irrationally, *deliberately* – related.

Schools, like ships, are riddled with superstitions, and St Oswald's more than most. The ghosts, perhaps; or the rituals and traditions that keep the old wheels creaking away. But this term has given us nothing but bad luck right from the beginning. There's a Jonah on board. If only I knew who it was.

When I entered the Common Room this morning, I found it suspiciously quiet. Word of my warning must have got around, because conversations fell silent throughout the day every time I entered a room, and there was a certain gleam in Sourgrape's eye that boded ill for someone.

The Nations avoided me; Grachvogel looked furtive; Scoones was at his most aloof; and even Pearman seemed most unlike his cheery self. Kitty, too, looked especially preoccupied – she barely acknowledged my greeting as I came in, and it bothered me rather; Kitty and I have always been chums, and I hoped nothing had happened to change that. I didn't think it had – after all, the little upsets of the past week hadn't touched *her* – but there was definitely something in her face as she looked up and saw me. I sat beside her with my tea (the vanished Jubilee mug having been replaced by a plain brown one from home), but she seemed engrossed in her pile of books, and hardly said a word.

Lunch was a mournful affair of vegetables – thanks to the vindictive Bevans – followed by a sugarless cup of tea. I took the cup with me to room 59, though most of the boys were outside, except for Anderton-Pullitt, happily engrossed in his aeronautics book, and Waters, Pink and Lemon, who were quietly playing cards in one corner.

I had been marking for about ten minutes when I looked up and saw the rabbit Meek, standing beside the desk with a pink slip in his hand and a look of mingled hate and deference on his pale, bearded face.

'I got this slip this morning, sir,' he said, holding out the piece of paper. He has never forgiven me for my intervention in his lesson, or for the fact that I witnessed his humiliation in front of the boys. As a result he addresses me as 'sir', like a pupil, and his tone is flat and colourless, like Knight's.

'What is it?'

'Assessment form, sir.'

'Oh, gods. I'd forgotten.' Of course, the staff appraisals are upon us; Heaven forbid that we should fail to complete all the necessary paperwork before December's official inspection. I supposed I had one too; the New Head has always been a great fan of internal appraisal – as introduced by Bob Strange, who also wants more in-service training, yearly management courses and performance-related pay. Can't see it myself – your results are only as good as the boys you teach, after all – but it keeps Bob out of the classroom, which is the essential thing.

The general principle of appraisal is simple: each junior member of staff is individually observed and appraised in the classroom by a senior master; each Head of Section by a Head of Year; each Head of Year by a Deputy, that is, Pat Bishop or Bob Strange. The Second and Third Masters are assessed by the Head himself (though in Strange's case, he spends so little time in the classroom that you wonder why he bothers). The Head, being a geographer, does hardly any teaching at all, but spends much of his time on courses, lecturing teams of PGCE students on Racial Sensitivity or Drug Awareness.

'It says you'll be observing my lesson this afternoon,' said Meek. He didn't look too pleased about it. 'Third-form computer science.'

'Thank you, Mr Meek.' I wondered which joker had decided to put me in charge of computer science. As if I didn't know. And with Meek, of all people. Oh well, I thought. Bang goes my free period.

There are some days in a teaching career where everything goes wrong. I should know; I've seen a few – days when the only sensible thing to do is to go home and back to bed. Today was one of them; an absurd parade of mishaps and annoyances, of litter and lost books and minor scuffles and unwelcome administrative tasks and extra duties and louche comments in the corridors.

A run-in with Eric Scoones over some misbehaviour of Sutcliff's; my register (still missing, and causing trouble with Marlene); wind (never welcome); a leak in the boys' toilets and the subsequent flooding of part of the Middle Corridor; Knight (unaccountably smug); Dr Devine (equally so); a number of annoying room changes due to the leak and e-mailed (ye gods!) to all staff workstations, with the result that I arrived late to my morning cover period – English, for the absent Roach.

There are many advantages to being a senior master. One is that having established a reputation as a disciplinarian, it is rarely necessary to enforce it. Word gets round – *Don't mess with Straitley* – and a quiet life for all ensues. Today was different. Oh, it happens occasionally; and if it had happened on any other day I might not have reacted as I did then. But it was a large group, a lower third – thirty-five boys, and not a single Latinist among them. They knew me only by reputation – and I don't suppose the recent article in our local press had helped much.

I was ten minutes late, and the class was already noisy. No work had been set, and as I walked in, expecting the boys to stand in silence, they simply glanced in my direction and went right on doing precisely what they'd been doing before. Games of cards; conversations; a rowdy discussion at the back with chairs kicked over and a powerful stench of chewing gum in the air.

It shouldn't have angered me. A good teacher knows that there is fake anger and real anger – the fake is fair game, part of the good teacher's armoury of bluff, but the real must be hidden at all costs, lest the boys – those master manipulators – understand that they have scored a point.

But I was tired. The day had started badly, the boys didn't know me and I was still angry over the incident in my back garden the night before. Those high young voices – *Like fuck he can, he's too old!* – had sounded too familiar, too plausible to be easily dismissed. One boy looked up at me and turned to his desk-mate. I thought I heard the phrase – *Nuts to you, sir!* – amidst a clap of ugly laughter.

And so I fell – like a novice, like a student teacher – for the oldest trick in the book. I lost my temper.

'Gentlemen, silence.' It usually works. This time it didn't; I could see a group of boys at the back laughing openly at the battered gown I had omitted to remove following my mid-morning Break duty. *Nuts to you, sir*, I heard (or thought), and it seemed to me that if anything, the volume increased.

'I said, "Silence!"' I roared – an impressive sound in usual circumstances, but I'd forgotten Bevans and his advice to take it easy, and the invisible finger prodded me in the sternum mid-roar. The boys at the back sniggered, and irrationally I wondered if any of them had been there last night – *Think you can take me, you fat bastard?*

Well, in such a situation there are inevitably casualties. In this case, eight in lunch-time detention, which *was* perhaps a trifle excessive, but a teacher's discipline is his own, after all, and there was no reason for Strange to intervene. He did, however; walking past the room at just the wrong time, he happened to hear my voice and looked through the glass at precisely the moment that I turned one of the sniggering boys around by the sleeve of his blazer.

'Mr *Straitley*!' Of course nowadays, no one touches a pupil.

Silence fell; the boy's sleeve was torn at the armpit. 'You saw him, sir. He hit me.'

They knew he hadn't. Even Strange knew, though his face was impassive. The invisible finger gave another push. The boy – Pooley, his name was – held up his torn blazer for inspection. 'That was brand-new!'

It wasn't; anyone could see that. The fabric was shiny with age; the sleeve itself a little short. Last year's blazer, due for replacement. But I'd gone too far; I could see it now. 'Perhaps you can tell Mr Strange all about it,' I suggested, turning back to the now-silent class.

The Third Master gave me a reptilian look.

'Oh, and when you've finished with Mr Pooley, do please send him back,' I said. 'I need to arrange his detention.'

There was nothing for Strange to do then but to leave,

taking Pooley with him. I don't suppose he enjoyed being dismissed by a colleague – but then, he shouldn't have interfered, should he? Still, I had a feeling he would not let the matter go. It was too good an opportunity – and, as I recalled (though a little late), young Pooley was the eldest son of Dr B. D. Pooley, Chairman of Governors, whose name I had most recently encountered on a formal written warning.

Well, after that I was so rattled that I went to the wrong room for Meek's appraisal, and arrived twenty minutes into the lesson. Everyone turned round to look at me, Meek excepted; his pallid face wooden with disapproval.

I sat down at the back; someone had set out a chair for me, with the pink appraisal form on it. I scanned the sheet. It was the usual box-ticking format: planning, delivery, stimulus, enthusiasm, class control. Marks out of five, plus a space for a comment, like a hotel questionnaire.

I wondered what sort of an opinion I was supposed to have; still, the class was quiet, barring a couple of nudgers at the back; Meek's voice was reedy and penetrating; the computer screens behaved themselves, creating the migraine-inducing patterns which apparently constituted the object of the exercise. All in all, satisfactory enough, I supposed; I smiled encouragingly at the hapless Meek; left early in the hope of a quick cup of tea before the start of the next period; and stuck the pink slip into the Third Master's pigeon-hole.

As I did, I noticed something lying on the floor at my

feet. It was a little notebook, pocket-sized, bound in red. Opening it briefly I saw it half-filled with spindly writing; on the flyleaf I read the name C. KEANE.

Ah, Keane. I looked around the Common Room, but the new English teacher was not there. And so I pocketed the notebook, meaning to give it back to Keane later. Rather a mistake, or so it turned out. Still, you know what they say about listening at doors.

Every teacher keeps them. Notes on boys; notes of lists and duties; notes of grudges small and large. You can tell almost as much about a colleague by his notebook as by his mug – Grachvogel's is a neat and colour-coded plea for order; Kitty's a no-nonsense pocket diary; Devine's an impressive black tome with little inside. Scoones uses the same green accounts-books he has been using since 1961; the Nations have charity planners from Christian Aid; Pearman a stack of odd papers, Post-It notes and used envelopes.

Now, having opened the thing, I couldn't resist a glance at young Keane's notebook; and by the time I realized that I shouldn't be reading it, I was hooked, lined and sinkered.

Of course I already knew the man was a writer. And he has that look; the slight complacency of the casual observer, content to enjoy the view because he knows he won't be staying long. What I hadn't guessed was how much he'd already seen; the tiffs, the rivalries, the little secrets of the Common Room dynamic. There were pages of it; closely written in handwriting so small that it was scarcely legible;

character studies, sketches, overheard remarks, gossip, history; news.

I scanned the pages, straining my eyes to decipher the minuscule script. Fallowgate was mentioned; and Peanuts; and Favourites. There was a little of our School history – I saw the names Snyde, Pinchbeck and Mitchell alongside a folded newspaper cutting of that sad old tale. Next to that, a photocopied snippet from a St Oswald's official School photograph, a colour snapshot of another school's Sports Day – boys and girls sitting cross-legged on the grass – and a bad portrait of John Snyde, looking criminal, as most men do when seen on the front page of a newspaper.

Several more pages, I saw, were given over to cartoons, caricatures for the most part. Here was the Head, rigid and glacial, the Don Quixote to Bishop's Sancho. There was Bob Strange, a hybrid half-human wired into his computer terminal. My own Anderton-Pullitt was there in goggles and flying helmet; Knight's schoolboy crush on a new teacher was mercilessly exposed; Miss Dare portrayed as a bespectacled, bestockinged schoolmarm with Scoones as her growling Rottweiler. Even I was included, hunchbacked and black-robed, swinging from the Bell Tower with Kitty, a plumpish Esmerelda, under my arm.

That made me smile; but there was some unease in it, too. I suppose I've always had a bit of a soft spot for Kitty Teague. All above board, of course, you know – I just never realized it was so damned *obvious*. I wondered, too, whether Kitty had seen it.

Damn the man; I thought to myself. Hadn't I known

from the first that he was an upstart? And yet I'd liked him. Like him still, if truth be told.

R. Straitley: Latin. Devoted Old Boy of St Oswald's. Sixties; smoker; overweight; cuts his own hair. Wears the same brown tweed jacket with elbow-patches every day (well, *that's* a lie, smarty-pants; I wear a blue suit to Speech Days and funerals); *hobbies include baiting the management and flirting with the French teacher. Boys hold him in unexpected affection* (you're forgetting Colin Knight); *albatross around B. Strange's neck. Harmless.*

Well, I like that. Harmless, forsooth!

Still, it could be worse; under Penny Nation's entry I read *poisonous do-gooder*, and under Isabelle Tapi, *French tart*. You can't deny the man has a turn of phrase. I would have read on; but at that moment the bell for registration went, and I put the notebook in my desk drawer, with some reluctance, hoping to finish it at leisure.

I never did. Returning to my desk at the end of school I found the drawer empty and the notebook gone; at the time I assumed that Keane, who, like Dianne, occasionally shares my room, had found it and taken it back. I never asked him, for obvious reasons; and it was only later, when the scandals began to erupt one after the other, that I thought to make the connection between that little red notebook and the ubiquitous Mole, who knew the School so well, and who seemed to have so many insights into our harmless little ways.

9

Friday, 15th October

ANOTHER SUCCESSFUL WEEK, I THINK. NOT LEAST WAS MY
discovery of that notebook, with its incriminating contents.
I believe Straitley may have read some of it, though
probably not all. The handwriting is too spindly for his old
eyes, and besides, if he had drawn any suspicious con-
clusions, I would have seen it in his manner before now.
Still, it would have been unwise to keep the book. I see
that; and I burnt the offending item – not without a pang –
before it could fall under hostile scrutiny. I may yet have to
revisit the problem – but not today. Today I have other
concerns to attend to.

The October half-term is upon us already, and I mean to
be very busy (I'm not just talking about marking books).
No, next week I shall be in School almost every day. I have
cleared it with Pat Bishop, who also finds it hard to keep

away, and with Mr Beard, the Head of IT, with whom I have an unofficial arrangement.

All perfectly innocent – after all, my interest in technology is nothing new, and I know from experience that I am best hidden when I am in the open. Bishop approves, of course; he doesn't really know much about computers, but supervises me in his avuncular way, popping out of his office every once in a while to see if I need help.

I am not a brilliant student. A couple of elementary faux pas have established me as willing, if not especially able, which allows Bishop to feel superior whilst giving me extra cover, should I ever need it. I doubt I shall; if my presence is ever questioned at a later date, I know I can rely on Pat to say that I simply didn't have the expertise.

Every member of St Oswald's staff has an e-mail address. This consists of their first two or three initials followed by the address of the School website. In theory, every member of staff should check his e-mail twice a day, in case of an urgent memo from Bob Strange, but in practice, some never do. Roy Straitley and Eric Scoones are among these; many more use the system but have neglected to personalize their mailboxes, and have kept the default password (PASS-WORD) to access their mail. Even the ones, like Bishop, who imagine themselves to be more computer-literate, are predictable enough: Bishop himself uses the name of his favourite sportsman and even Strange, who should know better, has a series of easy-to-guess codes (his wife's maiden name, his date of birth and so on).

Not that I ever had to do much guessing. Fallow, who used

the facilities every night, kept a list of user codes in a notebook in the Porter's Lodge, along with a box of disks (material downloaded from the internet) that no one had bothered to investigate. By retracing his steps (under a different user identity) I managed to lay quite a convincing trail. Better still, by disabling the firewall on the School's computer network for a few minutes, and then sending a carefully prepared file attachment to admin@saintoswalds.com, from one of my hotmail addresses, I was able to introduce a simple virus designed to lie dormant in the system before awakening into dramatic action a couple of weeks later.

Not the most exciting kind of spadework, I know. All the same, I enjoyed it. This evening I thought I might allow myself a little celebration; a night off, a couple of drinks at the Thirsty Scholar. That turned out to be a mistake; I hadn't realized how many colleagues – and pupils – frequented the place. I was only halfway through my first drink when I spotted a little group of them – I recognized Jeff Light, Gerry Grachvogel and Robbie Roach, the long-haired geographer, with a couple of seventeen- or eighteen-year-olds who might have been St Oswald's sixth-formers.

I shouldn't have been surprised – it's no secret that Roach likes to hang out with the boys. Light, too. Grachvogel, on the other hand, looked slightly furtive, but then he always does, and he at least has the sense to know (as Straitley puts it) that no good ever comes of getting over-friendly with the troops.

I was tempted to stay. There was no reason to be shy; but

the thought of socializing with them, of *letting my hair down*, as the ghastly Light would have put it, *and having a couple of bevvies*, was distinctly unpleasant. Thankfully, I was sitting by the door and was able to make my exit, quick and unobserved.

I recognized Light's car, a black Probe, in the alley beside the pub, and toyed with the idea of putting its side window through; but there might be security cameras in the street, I thought, and it would be pointless to risk exposure on a stupid whim. Instead I walked the long way home – the night was mild, and besides, I'd promised myself another look at Roy Straitley's fence.

He had already removed the graffiti. I wasn't surprised; even though he couldn't actually see it from his house, its simple presence must have irked him, just as it irked him that the boys who had invaded his garden might return. Perhaps I'll arrange it – just to see his face – but not tonight. Tonight I deserved better.

And so I went home to my chintz-hung room, opened my second bottle of champagne (I have a case of six, and I mean to see them all empty by Christmas), caught up with a little essential correspondence, then went down to the payphone outside and made a quick call to the local police, reporting a black Probe (registration LIT 3) driving erratically in the vicinity of the Thirsty Scholar.

It's the sort of behaviour my therapist tends to dis- courage nowadays. I'm too impulsive, or so she says; too judgemental. I don't always consider the feelings of others as I should. But there was no risk to me; I did not give my name, and in any case – you know he deserved it. Like Mr Bray, Light is a braggart; a bully; a natural rule-breaker; a man who genuinely believes that a few pints under his belt make him a better driver. Predictable. They're all so predictable.

That's their weakness. The Oswaldians'. Light, of course, is a complacent fool; but even Straitley, who is not, shares the same foolish complacency. *Who would dare to attack me? To attack St Oswald's?*

Well, gentlemen. I would.

CHECK

1

THE SUMMER OF MY FATHER'S BREAKDOWN WAS THE HOTTEST
in remembered history. At first it cheered him, as if this
were a return to the legendary summers of his childhood,
during which, if I was to believe him, he spent the happiest
days of his life. Then, as the sun continued remorseless and
the grass on St Oswald's lawns veered from yellow to brown,
he soured and began to fret.

The lawns were his responsibility, of course; and it was
one of his duties to maintain them. He set up sprinklers to
water the grass, but the area to be covered was too large
to be dealt with in this way, and he was obliged to restrict
his attentions to the cricket pitch only, while the remainder
of the lawns grew bald under the sun's hot and lidless eye.
But that was only one of my father's concerns. The graffiti
artist had struck again, this time in technicolour; a mural,
fully six foot square, on the side of the Games Pavilion.

My father spent two days scrubbing it off, then another

week repainting the Pavilion, and swore that next time, he'd give the little bastard the thrashing of his life. Still the culprit eluded him; twice more, spray-paintings appeared in and around St Oswald's, crudely colourful, artistic in their way, both of them featuring caricatures of masters. My father began to watch the school at night, lying in wait behind the Pavilion with a twelve-pack of beer, but still there was no sign of the guilty party, although how he managed to avoid detection was a mystery to John Snyde.

Then there were the mice. Every large building has vermin – St Oswald's more than most – but since the end of the summer term, mice had infested the corridors in unusually large numbers. Even I saw them occasionally, especially around the Bell Tower, and I knew that their breeding would have to be checked; poison laid down and the dead mice removed before the new term began and the parents had a chance to complain.

It incensed my father. He was convinced that boys had left food in their lockers; blamed the carelessness of the School cleaners; spent days opening and checking every locker in the School with mounting rage – but no success.

Then there were the dogs. The hot weather affected them as it did my father, making them lethargic by day and aggressive in the evenings. By night their owners – who had usually omitted to walk them in the sweltering daytime – now loosed them on the wasteground at the back of St Oswald's, and they ran in packs there, barking and tearing up the grass. They had no respect for boundaries; despite my father's attempts to keep them out, they would squeeze through the fence into St Oswald's playing-fields and shit on the newly sprinkled cricket pitch. They seemed to have an instinct for choosing the spot that would annoy my father most; and in the mornings he would have to drag himself around the fields with his pooper-scooper, arguing furiously with himself and chugging at a can of flat beer.

Infatuated as I was with Leon, it took me some time to understand – and even longer to care – that John Snyde was losing his mind. I had never been very close to my father, nor had I ever found him easy to read. Now his face was a perpetual slab, its most common expression one of bewildered rage. Once, perhaps, I had expected something more. But this was the man who had thought to solve my social problems with karate lessons. Faced with this infinitely more delicate situation, what could I possibly hope from him now?

Dad, I'm in love with a boy called Leon.

I didn't think so.

All the same, I tried. He'd been young once, I told myself. He'd been in love, in lust, whatever. I brought him beer from the fridge; made tea; sat for hours in front of his favourite TV shows (*Knight Rider, Dukes of Hazzard*) in the hope of something other than blankness. But John Snyde was sinking fast. Depression enfolded him like a crazy quilt; his eyes reflected nothing but the colours from the screen. Like the rest of them, he barely saw me; at home, as at St Oswald's, I had become the Invisible Man.

Then, two weeks into that hot summer holiday, a double catastrophe struck. The first was my own fault: opening a window on to the roof of the School I managed to trip the burglar alarm and it sounded. My father reacted with un-expected speed, and I was nearly caught in the act. As it was, I got back to the house and was just about to replace the passkeys, when along came my father, and saw me with the keys in my hand.

I tried to bluff my way out of it. I'd heard the alarm, I said; and noticing that he had forgotten the keys, had been on my way to deliver them. He didn't believe me. He had been jumpy that day, and he'd already suspected the keys were missing. I had no doubt I was in for it now. There was no way out of the house except past my father, and from the expression on his face, I knew I didn't have a chance.

It wasn't the first time he'd hit me, of course. John Snyde was the champion of the roundhouse punch, a blow which connected maybe three times out of ten and which felt like being hit with a petrified log. Usually I dodged, and by the time he saw me again he had sobered up, or forgotten why I had angered him in the first place.

This time was different. First, he was sober. Second, I had committed the unforgivable offence, a trespass against St Oswald's; an open challenge to the Head Porter. For a moment I saw it in his eyes; his trapped rage; his frustration: it was the dogs, the graffiti, the bald patches on the lawn; it was the kids who pointed at him and called him names; it was the monkey-faced boy; it was the unspoken contempt of people like the Bursar and the New Head. I don't know how many times he punched me, but by the end of it my nose was bleeding, my face was bruised, I was crouching in a corner with my arms over my head and he was standing over me with a dazed expression on his big face, his hands outspread like a stage murderer's.

'My God. Oh my God. Oh my God.'

He was talking to himself, and I was too preoccupied with my busted nose to care, but at last I finally dared to lower my arms. My stomach hurt, and I felt as if I was about to be sick, but I managed to keep the feeling at bay.

My father had moved away and was sitting at the table, his head in his hands. 'Oh God. I'm sorry. I'm sorry,' he repeated, though whether this was addressed to me or to the Almighty, I could not tell. He did not look at me as I slowly stood up. Instead he spoke into his hands, and although I kept my distance, knowing how volatile he could be, I sensed that something had broken in him.

'I'm sorry,' he said, now shaken by sobs. 'I can't take it, kid. I just can't – fucking – take it.' And with that he finally brought it out, the last and most terrible blow of that miserable afternoon, and as I listened, first in astonishment, then in growing horror, I realized that I *was* going to be sick after all, and rushed out into the sunlight, where St Oswald's marched interminably across the blue horizon and the sun trepanned my forehead and the scorched grass smelt like Cinnabar and all the time the stupid birds sang and sang and would not stop singing.

2

I SUPPOSE I SHOULD HAVE GUESSED. IT WAS MY MOTHER. Three months ago she had begun to write to him again, in vague terms at first, then in more and more detail. My father had not told me of her letters, but in retrospect, their arrival must have coincided more or less with my first meeting with Leon and the beginning of my father's decline.

'I didn't want to tell you, kid. I didn't want to think about it. I thought that if I just ignored it, it might just go away. Leave us both alone.'

'Tell me what?'

'I'm sorry.'

'Tell me *what?*'

He told me then, still sobbing, as I wiped my mouth and listened to the idiot birds. For three months he had tried to hide it from me; at a single blow I understood his rages, his renewed drinking, his sullenness, his irrational, homicidal changes of mood. Now he told me everything; still holding his head in his hands as if it might break open with the effort, and I listened with increasing horror as he staggered through his tale.

Life, it seemed, had been kinder to Sharon Snyde than it had to the rest of the family. She had married young, giving birth to me only a few weeks before her seventeenth birthday, and she had been just twenty-five when she left us for good. Like my father, Sharon was fond of clichés, and I gathered that there had been a great deal of hand-wringing psychobabble in her letters; apparently she had *needed to find out who she was*, conceded that there were *faults on both sides*, that she had been in *a bad place emotionally* and claimed a number of similar excuses for her desertion.

But she had changed, she said; finally, she had grown up. It made us sound like a toy she had outgrown, a tricycle perhaps, once loved, but now rather ridiculous. I wondered if she still wore Cinnabar, or whether she had grown out of that, too.

In any case she had remarried, a foreign student she had met in a bar in London, and had moved to Paris to be with him. Xavier was a wonderful man and both of us would really like him. In fact she would love us to meet him; he was an English teacher in a *lycée* in Marne-la-Vallée; was keen on sports; adored children.

And that brought her to her next point; although she and Xavier had tried and tried, they had never been able to have a child. And although Sharon had not had the courage to write to me herself, she had never forgotten her

Munchkin, her sweetheart, or let a single day go by without thinking of me.

Finally, Xavier had been convinced. There was plenty of room in their apartment for three; I was a bright kid and would pick up the language with no difficulty; best of all I would have a family again, a family that cared, and money to make up for everything the years had denied me.

I was appalled. Four years had passed; and in that time the desperate longing I had once felt for my mother had moved towards indifference and beyond. The thought of seeing her again – the reconciliation of which she apparently dreamed – now filled me with a dull and cringing embarrassment. I could see her now, with my altered perspective; Sharon Snyde, now with a new, cheap lacquer-coating of sophistication, offering me a new, cheap, ready-made life in exchange for my years of suffering. The only problem was, I no longer wanted it.

'You do, kid,' said my father. His violence had given way to a mawkish self-pity that offended me almost as much. I was not fooled. It was the banal sentimentality of the hooligan with MUM and DAD tattooed across his bleeding knuckles; the thug's indignation over some child molester in the news; the tears of the tyrant at a run-over dog. 'Ah, kid, you do. It's a chance, see, another chance. Me? I'd take her back tomorrow if I could. I'd take her back today.'

'Well, I wouldn't,' I said. 'I'm happy here.'

'Yeah. Happy. When you could have all that—'

'All what?'

'Paris, and that. Money. A life.'

'I've got a life,' I said.

'And money.'

'She can keep her money. We've got enough.'

'Yeah. All right.'

'I mean it, Dad. Don't let her win. I want to stay here. You can't *make* me—'

'I said, "All right."'

'Promise?'

'Yeah.'

'Really?'

'Yeah.'

But I noticed then that he would not meet my eye, and that night when I took out the rubbish I found the kitchen bin filled with scratchcard stubs – twenty of them, maybe more; Lotto and Striker and *Winner Takes All!* – shining like Christmas trimmings among the tea leaves and spent tin cans.

3

THE SHARON SNYDE PROBLEM WAS THE CULMINATION OF ALL the blows that summer had dealt me. From her letters, which my father had kept from me but which I now read with growing horror, her plans were well advanced. In principle Xavier had agreed to an adoption; Sharon had done some research into schools; she had even been in touch with our local social services, who had relayed such information – concerning my school attendance, academic progress and general attitude to life – as would strengthen her case against my father.

Not that she needed it; after years of struggling, John Snyde had finally given in. He rarely washed; rarely went out except to the chip-shop or the Chinese takeaway; spent most of our money on scratchcards and booze; and during the next couple of weeks, became increasingly withdrawn.

At any other time I might have welcomed the freedom his depression gave me. Suddenly I could go out as late as I wanted, and no one questioned where I had been. I could go to the cinema; to the pub. I could take my keys (I'd finally had a set of duplicates made after that last disastrous episode) and roam St Oswald's whenever I wanted. Not that I did much of that, however. Without my friend, most of the usual pastimes had lost their appeal, and I rapidly abandoned them in favour of hanging out (if you could call it that) with Leon and Francesca.

Every pair of lovers needs a stooge. Someone to keep watch; a convenient third party; an occasional chaperone. I was sickened, but I was necessary; and I nursed my breaking heart in the knowledge that for once, for however brief a time, Leon needed me.

We had a shack (a 'clubhouse', Leon called it) in the wood beyond St Oswald's playing-fields. We had built it off the path, on the remains of someone else's long-abandoned den, and it was a neat little place, well camouflaged, with half-log walls and a roof of thick pine branches. It was there that we went, I keeping watch, smoking and trying not to listen to the sounds that came from the little shack behind me.

At home, Leon played it cool. Every morning I would call for them on my bike, Mrs Mitchell would pack us a picnic and we would make for the woods. It looked quite innocent – my presence made it so – and no one guessed at those languid hours under the leaf-canopy, the muted laughter from inside the shack, the glimpses I had of them together, of his naked rye-brown back and sweetly dappled buttocks in the shadows.

Those were the good days; on bad days Leon and Francesca simply slipped away, laughing, into the woods, leaving me feeling stupid and useless as they ran. We were never a threesome. There was Leon-and-Francesca, an exotic hybrid, subject to violent mood swings, to fierce enthusiasms, to astonishing cruelty; and then there was me, the dumb, the adoring, the eternally dependable stooge.

Francesca was never entirely happy at my presence. She was older than I was – maybe fifteen. No virgin, from what I could tell – that's what Catholic school does to you – and already she was besotted with Leon. He played on that; spoke gently; made her laugh. It was all a pose; she knew nothing about him. She had never seen him throw Peggy Johnsen's trainers across the telegraph wire, or steal records from the shop in town, or pitch ink-bombs over the playground wall on to some Sunnybanker's clean shirt. But he told her things he'd never told me; talked about music and Nietzsche and his passion for astronomy, while I walked unseen behind them with the picnic basket, hating them both, but unable to leave.

Well, of course I hated *her*. There was no justification. She was polite enough to me – the real nastiness always came from Leon himself. But I hated their whispers; that shared heads-together laughter that excluded me and ringed them with intimacy.

Then it was the touching. They were always touching. Not just kissing, not making love, but a thousand little touches: a hand on the shoulder; a brush of knee against knee; her hair on his cheek like silk snagging Velcro. And I could *feel* them, every one; like static in the air; stinging me, making me electric, making me combustible.

It was a delight worse than any torture. After a week of playing gooseberry to Leon and Francesca, I was ready to scream with boredom, and yet at the same time my heart pounded with a desperate rhythm. I dreaded our outings, but lay awake every night, going over every small detail with agonizing care. It was like a disease. I smoked more than I wanted to; I bit my nails until they bled. I stopped eating; my face developed an ugly rash; every step I took felt like walking on glass.

The worst was that Leon knew. He couldn't have failed to see it; played me like a tomcat showing off his mouse, with the same carefree cruelty.

Look! Look what I got! Watch me!

'So what d'you think?' A brief moment out of earshot – Francesca behind us, picking flowers or having a pee, I can't remember which.

'What about?'

'*Frankie*, you moron. What do you think?'

Early days; still stunned by developments. I flushed. 'She's nice.'

'Nice.' Leon grinned.

'Yeah.'

'*You*'d have some, wouldn't you? You'd have some, given half a chance?' His eyes were gleaming with malice.

I shook my head. 'Dunno,' I said, not meeting his gaze.

'*Dunno?* What are you, Pinchbeck, a queer or something?'

'Fuck off, Leon.' The flush deepened. I looked away.

Leon watched me, still grinning. 'Come on, I've seen you. I've seen you watching when we were in the clubhouse. You never talk to her. Never say a word. But you do look, don't you? Look and learn, right?'

He thought *I* wanted her, I realized with a jolt; he thought I wanted her for myself. I almost laughed. He was so wrong, so cosmically, hilariously *wrong*. 'Look, she's OK,' I said. 'Just – not my type, that's all.'

'Your *type*?' But the edge had gone from his voice now. His laughter was infectious. He yelled, 'Hey, Frankie! Pinchbeck says you're not his type!' then he turned to me and touched my face, almost intimately, with the tips of his fingers. 'Give it five years, mate,' he said with mocking sincerity. 'If they haven't dropped by then, see me.'

And then he was off, running through the wood with his hair flying out behind him and the grass whipping crazily against his bare ankles. Not to escape me, not this time; but simply running for the sheer exuberance of being alive, and fourteen, and randy as hell. To me he looked almost in-substantial, half-disintegrated in the light-and-shade from the leaf-canopy, a boy of air and sunshine, an immortal, beautiful boy. I could not keep up; I followed at a distance with Francesca protesting behind and Leon running ahead, shouting and running in great impossible bounds across the white hemlock-mist into the darkness.

I remember that moment so very clearly. A fragment of pure joy, like a shard of dream, untouched by logic or events. In that moment I could believe we would live for ever.

Nothing mattered; not my mother; not my father; not even Francesca. I had glimpsed something, there in the woods, and though I could never hope to keep up with it, I knew it would stay with me for the rest of my life.

'I love you, Leon,' I whispered as I struggled through the weeds. And that, for the moment, was more than enough.

4

IT WAS HOPELESS, I KNEW. LEON WOULD NEVER SEE ME AS I saw him, or feel anything for me but kindly contempt. And yet I was happy, in my way, with the crumbs of his affection; a slap on the arm, a grin, a few words – *You're all right, Pinchbeck* – were enough to lift me, sometimes for hours. I was not Francesca; but soon, I knew, Francesca would be back at her convent school, and I – I—

Well, that was the big question, wasn't it? In the fortnight that had followed my father's revelation, Sharon Snyde had phoned every other night. I had refused to talk to her, locking myself in my room. Her letters, too, remained unanswered, her presents unacknowledged.

But the adult world cannot be shut out for ever. However high I turned up my radio, however many hours I spent away from home, I could not escape Sharon's machinations.

My father, who could perhaps have saved me, was a spent force; drinking beers and shovelling pizza in front of the

television while his duties remained undone and my time –
my precious time – ran out.

Dear Munchkin,

   *Did you like the clothes I sent for you? I wasn't sure what
size to buy, but your father says you're small for your age. I
hope I got it right. I do so want things to be perfect when we
meet again. I can't believe you're going to be thirteen. It
won't be long, now, will it, darling? Your plane ticket should
arrive in the next few days. Are you looking forward to your
visit as much as I am? Xavier is very excited to be meeting
you at last, even though he's a bit nervous, too. I expect he's
afraid of being left out, while we catch up on the last five
years!*

   Your loving mother,
   Sharon.

It was impossible. She believed it, you see; really believed
that nothing had changed, that she could pick up our life
where she had left it; that I could be her Munchkin,
her darling, her little dress-up doll. Worse still, my father
believed it. Wanted it, encouraged it in some perverse way,
as if by letting me go he might somehow alter his own
course, like ballast thrown from a sinking ship.

   'Give it a chance.' Conciliatory now, an indulgent parent
with a recalcitrant child. He had not raised his voice since
the day he struck me. 'Give it a chance, kid. You might
even enjoy yourself.'

   'I'm not going. I won't see her.'

'I tell you. You'll like Paris.'

'I won't.'

'You'll get used to it.'

'I fucking won't. Anyway, it's just a visit. I'm not going to *live* there or anything.'

Silence.

'I *said*, "It's just a visit."'

Silence.

'Dad?'

Oh, I tried to encourage him. But something in him was broken. Aggression and violence had given way to indifference. His weight increased still further; he was careless with his keys; the lawns grew ragged with neglect; the cricket pitch, denied its daily dose of the sprinklers, grew brown and bare. His lethargy – his failure – seemed designed to remove any choice I might still have had between remaining in England and embracing the new life Sharon and Xavier had planned so carefully on my behalf.

And so I was torn between my loyalty to Leon and the increasing need to cover for my father. I took to watering the cricket pitch at night; I even tried to mow the lawns. But the Mean Machine had ideas of its own, and I succeeded only in scalping the grass, which made it worse than ever, whilst the cricket pitch, despite my best efforts, refused to flourish.

It was inevitable that sooner or later, someone would notice. One Sunday I came home from the woods to find Pat Bishop in our living room, sitting uncomfortably on one of the good chairs, and my father, on the sofa, facing him. I could almost feel the static in the air. He turned as I came in; I was about to apologize and leave at once, but the look on Bishop's face stopped me dead. I saw guilt there – and pity, and anger – but most of all I saw profound relief. It was the look of a man willing to seize upon any diversion to get away from an unpleasant scene, and though his smile was as broad as ever and his cheeks were just as pink as he greeted me, I was not fooled for a moment.

I wondered who had made the complaint. A neighbour; a passer-by; a member of staff. A parent, perhaps, wanting his money's worth. There were certainly plenty of things to complain about. The School itself has always attracted attention. It must be beyond reproach at all times. Its servants, too, must be beyond reproach; there is enough resentment between St Oswald's and the rest of the town without giving extra grist to the rumour mill. A Porter knows this; that is why St Oswald's has Porters.

I turned to my father. He would not look at me, but kept his eyes on Bishop, who was already halfway to the door. 'It wasn't my fault,' he said. 'I – we've been going through a bit of a rough patch, me and the kid. You tell them, sir. They'll listen to you.'

Bishop's smile – quite humourless now – could have spanned an acre. 'I don't know, John. You're on a final warning. After that other business – hitting a lad, John—'

My father tried to stand. It took an effort; I saw his face, soft with distress, and felt my insides crawl with shame. 'Please, sir—'

Bishop saw it too. His big frame filled the doorway. For a

second his eyes rested on me and I saw pity in them, but not a glimmer of recognition, though he must have seen me at St Oswald's more than a dozen times. Somehow, that – his failure to see – was worse than anything else. I wanted to speak up, to say: *Sir, don't you recognize me? It's me, Pinchbeck. You gave me two House points once, remember, and told me to report for the cross-country team!*

But it was impossible. I had fooled him too well. I had thought them so superior, the St Oswald's masters; but here was Bishop looking flushed and sheepish, just as Mr Bray had looked, the day I brought him down. What help could he give us? We were alone; and only I knew it.

'Sit tight, John. I'll do what I can.'

'Thank you, sir.' He was shaking now. 'You're a friend.'

Bishop put a large hand on my father's shoulder. He was good; his voice was warm and hearty, and he was still smiling. 'Chin up, man. You can do it. With a bit of luck you'll have it all in order by September, and no one need know any better. But no more messing about, eh? And John—' he swatted my father, in friendly fashion, on the arm, as if he were patting an overweight Labrador. 'Stay off the juice, won't you? One more strike, and even I won't be able to help you.'

To some extent, Bishop kept his word. The complaint was dropped – or at least shelved for the present. Bishop dropped by every few days to ask him how he was, and my father seemed to rally a little in response. More importantly, the Bursar had hired a handyman of sorts; a problem case called Jimmy Watt, who was supposed to take over some of the more irksome of the Porter's duties, leaving John Snyde free to cope with the real work.

It was our last hope. Without his Porter's job, I knew he had no chance against Sharon and Xavier. But he had to *want* to keep me, I thought; and for that, I had to be what he wanted me to be. And so, in my turn, I worked on my father. I watched football on television; ate fish and chips from newspaper; jettisoned my books; volunteered for every household chore. At first he watched me with suspicion, then bemusement, and finally, a sullen kind of approval. The fatalism which had first afflicted him when he learned of my mother's situation seemed to erode a little; he spoke with bitter sarcasm of her Paris lifestyle, her fancy college-boy husband, her assumption that she could re-enter our life on whatever terms she damn well pleased.

Emboldened, I fed him the notion of thwarting her plans; of showing her who was boss, of playing along with her pathetic ambitions only to frustrate her with his final, decisive master-stroke. It appealed to his nature; it gave him direction; he had always been a man's man, with a sour distrust of the machinations of women.

'They're all at it,' he told me one time, forgetting who I was as he launched into one of his frequent rants. 'The bitches. All smiles one minute, and the next they're reaching for the kitchen knife to stab you in the back. Get away with it, too – it's in the papers every day. I mean, what can you do? Big strong man – poor little girlie – I mean it stands to reason he must've *done* something to her, right? Spousal abuse or whatever the fuck – and the next thing you know there she is, in Court, fluttering her eyelashes, getting custody of kids and cash and God knows what else—'

'Not this kid,' I said.

'Ah, come on,' said John Snyde. 'You can't mean it. Paris, a good school, a new life—'

'I told you,' I said. 'I want to stay here.'

'But *why?*' He stared at me befuddled, like a dog denied a walk. 'You could have anything you wanted. Clothes, records—'

I shook my head. 'I don't want them,' I said. 'She can't just come back here after five bloody years and try to buy me with that French bloke's money.' He was watching me now, a crease between his blue eyes. 'I mean, you've been there all the time,' I said. 'Looking out for me. Doing your best.' He nodded then, a tiny movement, and I could tell he was paying attention. 'We've been all right, haven't we, Dad? What do we need them for anyway?'

There was a silence. I could tell that my words had struck a chord. 'You've been all right,' he said. I wasn't sure whether or not he meant it as a question.

'We'll manage,' I said. 'We always have. Hit first and hit fast. Never give up, eh, Dad? Never let the bastards grind you down?'

Another pause, long enough to drown in. Then he laughed, a startling, sunny, young laugh that took me by surprise. 'All right, kid,' he said. 'We'll give it a try.'

* * *

And so, in hope, we entered August. My birthday was in three weeks' time; term started in four. Ample time for my father to restore the grounds to their original perfection, to complete the maintenance work, to set traps for the mice and to repaint the Games Pavilion in time for September. My optimism returned. There was some justification; my father had not forgotten our conversation in the lounge, and this time he really seemed to be making an effort.

It made me hopeful, even a little ashamed at how I'd treated him in the past. I'd had my problems with John Snyde, I thought; but at least he was honest. He'd done his best. He hadn't abandoned me, then tried to bribe me back to his side. In the light of my mother's actions, even the football matches and the karate lessons seemed less ridiculous to me now, and more like clumsy but sincere overtures of friendship.

And so I helped him as best I could: I cleaned the house; I washed his clothes; I even forced him to shave. I was obedient, almost affectionate. I *needed* him to keep this job; it was my only weapon against Sharon; my ticket to St Oswald's, and to Leon.

Leon. Strange, isn't it, how one obsession grows from another? At first it was St Oswald's; the challenge; joy of subterfuge; the need to belong; to be someone more than the child of John and Sharon Snyde. Now it was just Leon; to be with Leon; to know him, possess him in ways I could not yet understand. There was no single reason for my choice. Yes, he was attractive. He had been kind, too, in his careless way; he had included me; he had given me the means of revenge against Bray, my tormentor. And I had been lonely; vulnerable; desperate; weak.

But I knew it was none of that. From the moment I first saw him, standing in the Middle Corridor with his hair in his eyes and the end of his scissored tie poking out like an impudent tongue, I had already known. A filter had lifted from the world. Time had separated into *before-Leon* and *after-Leon*; and now nothing could ever be the same.

Most adults assume that the feelings of adolescence don't count, somehow, and that those searing passions of rage and hate and embarrassment and horror and hopeless, abject love are something you grow out of, something hormonal, a practice run for the Real Thing. This one wasn't. At thirteen, *everything* counts; there are sharp edges on everything, and all of them cut. Some drugs can re-create that intensity of feeling, but adulthood blunts the edges, dims the colours and taints everything with reason, rationalization or fear. At thirteen I had no use for any of those. I knew what I wanted; and I was ready, with the single-mindedness of adolescence, to fight for it to the death. I would not go to Paris. Whatever it took, I would not leave.

5

St Oswald's Grammar School for Boys
Monday, 25th October

ON THE WHOLE, A POOR START TO THE NEW HALF-TERM. October has turned menacing, tearing the leaves from the golden trees and showering the Quad with conkers. Windy weather excites the boys; wind and rain means excited boys in the form-room over Break; and after what happened last time I left them to their own devices, I dare not leave them unsupervised even for a moment. No break for Straitley, then; not even a cup of tea; and my resulting temper was so bad that I snapped at everyone, including my Brodie Boys, who can usually make me laugh even at the worst of times.

As a result the boys kept their heads down, in spite of the windy weather. I put a couple of fourth-formers in detention for failing to hand in work, but apart from that I hardly had to raise my voice. Perhaps they sensed something – some whiff of pre-strike ozone in the air – that warned them that now was not the time for a display of high spirits.

The Common Room, as I understand, has been the scene of a number of small, sour skirmishes. Some unpleasantness about appraisals; a computer breakdown in the office; a quarrel between Pearman and Scoones concerning the new French syllabus. Before half-term Roach lost his credit card, and now blames Jimmy for leaving the Quiet Room door unlocked after school; Dr Tidy has decreed that as of this term, tea and coffee (hitherto provided free of charge) must be paid for to the tune of £3.75 a week; and Dr Devine, in his capacity as Health and Safety representative, has officially called for a smoke detector in the Middle Corridor (in the hope of driving me from my smoker's den in the old Book Room).

On the bright side, there has been no comeback from Strange over Pooley and his torn blazer. I have to say that surprises me a little; I'd have expected that second warning to have arrived in my pigeon-hole by now, and can only suppose that Bob has either forgotten the incident altogether or dismissed it as end-of-term foolishness and decided not to take it further.

Besides, there are other, more important things to deal with than one boy's ripped lining. The offensive Light has lost his driving licence, or so Kitty tells me, following some kind of an incident in town. There's more to it than that, of course, but my enforced restriction to the Bell Tower meant that for most of the day I was out of the mainstream of Common Room gossip, and therefore had to rely on the boys for information.

As usual, however, the rumour mill has been at work. One source declared that Light had been arrested following a police tip-off. Another said that Light had been ten times over the legal limit; yet another, that he had been stopped with St Oswald's boys in the car with him, and that one of them had actually been at the wheel.

I have to say that, at first, none of it troubled me overmuch. Every now and then you come across a teacher like Light; an arrogant buffoon who has managed to fool the system and enters the profession expecting an easy job with long holidays. As a rule they don't last long. If the boys don't finish them off, something else usually does, and life goes on without much of a blip.

As the day wore on, however, I began to realize that there was something more afoot than Light's traffic offences. Gerry Grachvogel's class next to mine was unusually noisy; during my free period I stuck my head around the door and saw most of 3S, including Knight, Jackson, Anderton-Pullitt and the usual suspects, apparently talking amongst themselves whilst Grachvogel sat staring out of the window with an expression of such abstracted misery that I curbed my original impulse – which was to interfere – and simply returned to my own room without a word.

When I got back, Chris Keane was waiting for me. 'I didn't by any chance leave a notebook here before half-term, did I?' he asked as I came in. 'It's a little red one. I keep all my ideas in it.'

For once I thought he was looking less than calm;

recalling some of his more subversive comments, I thought I could understand why.

'I found a notebook in the Common Room before half-term,' I told him. 'I thought you'd reclaimed it.'

Keane shook his head. I wondered whether or not I should tell him I'd glanced inside, then, seeing his furtive expression, decided against.

'Lesson plans?' I suggested innocently.

'Not quite,' said Keane.

'Ask Miss Dare. She shares my room. Maybe she saw it and put it away.'

I thought Keane looked slightly worried at that. As well he might, knowing the contents of that incriminating little book. Still, he seemed cool enough about it and simply said, 'No problem. I'm sure it'll turn up sooner or later.'

Come to think of it, things have had rather a habit of disappearing in the last few weeks. The pens, for instance; Keane's notebook; Roach's credit card. It happens occasionally; a wallet I could understand, but I really couldn't see why anyone would want to steal an old St Oswald's mug, or indeed my form register, which has still not resurfaced – unless it is simply to annoy me, in which case it has more than succeeded. I wondered what other small and insignificant items had disappeared in recent days, and whether the disappearances might be in some way related.

I said as much to Keane.

'Well, it's a school,' he said. 'Things vanish in schools.'

Perhaps, I thought; but not St Oswald's.

I saw Keane's ironic smile as he left the room, almost as if I had spoken aloud.

At the end of school I went back into Grachvogel's room, hoping to find out what was on his mind. Gerry's a good enough chap, in his way, not a natural in the class, but a true academic with a real enthusiasm for his subject, and it bothered me to see him looking so under the weather. However when I stuck my head around his classroom door at four o'clock, he was not there. That too was unusual; Gerry tends to hang around after hours, messing with the computers or preparing his interminable visual aids, and it was certainly the first time I'd ever seen him leave his room unlocked.

A few of my boys remained at their desks, copying up some notes from the board. I was unsurprised to recognize Anderton-Pullitt, always a laborious worker, and Knight, studiously not looking up, but with that smug little half-smirk on his face that told me he had registered my presence.

'Hello, Knight,' I said. 'Did Mr Grachvogel say if he'd be back?'

'No, sir.' His voice was colourless.

'I think he left, sir,' said Anderton-Pullitt.

'I see. Well, pack up your things, boys, quick as you can. Don't want any of you to miss the bus.'

'I don't catch the bus, sir.' It was Knight again. 'My mother picks me up. Too many perverts around nowadays.'

Now I try to be fair. I really do. I pride myself upon it, in fact; my fairness; my sound judgement. I may be rough, but I am always fair; I never make a threat that I would not carry out, or a promise I do not mean to keep. The boys know it, and most of them respect that; you know where you stand with old Quaz, and he doesn't let sentiment interfere with the job. At least I hope so; I'm getting increasingly sentimental with my advancing years, but I don't think that has ever got in the way of my duty.

However, in any teacher's career there are times when objectivity fails. Looking at Knight, his head still lowered but his eyes darting nervously back and forth, I was reminded once more of that failure. I don't trust Knight; the truth is there's something about him that I've always detested. I know I shouldn't, but even teachers are human beings. We have our preferences. Of course we do; it is simply *unfairness* that we must avoid. And I do try; but I am aware that of my little group, Knight is the misfit, the Judas, the Jonah, the one who inevitably takes it too far, mistakes humour for insolence, mischief for spite. A sullen, cosseted, whey-faced little cuss who blames everyone for his inadequacies but himself. All the same, I treat him exactly as I do the rest; I even tend to leniency towards him because I know my weakness.

But today there was something in his manner that made me uneasy. As if he knew something, some unhealthy secret that both delighted him and made him ill. He certainly *looks* ill, in spite of his smugness; there is a new flare of acne across his pallid features, a greasy sheen to his flat brown hair. Testosterone, most likely. All the same I cannot help thinking the boy *knows* something. With Sutcliff or Allen-Jones, the information (whatever it was) would have been mine for the asking. But with Knight . . .

'Did something happen in Mr Grachvogel's class today?'

'Sir?' Knight's face was a cautious blank.

'I heard shouting,' I said.

'Not me, sir,' said Knight.

'No. Of course not.'

It was useless. Knight would never tell. Shrugging, I left the Bell Tower, heading for the Languages office and our first departmental meeting of the new half-term. Grachvogel would be there; maybe I could talk to him before he left. Knight – I told myself – could wait. At least until tomorrow.

There was no sign of Gerry at the meeting. Everyone else was there, which made me more certain than ever that my colleague was ill. Gerry *never* misses a meeting; loves in-service training; sings energetically in Assemblies and always does his prep. Today he wasn't there; and when I mentioned his absence to Dr Devine, the response was so chilly that I wished I hadn't. Still miffy about the old office, I suppose; all the same, there was more in his manner than the usual disapproval; and I was rather subdued during the course of the meeting, going over all the things that I might unwittingly have done to provoke the old idiot. You wouldn't know it, but I'm quite fond of him really, suits and all; he's one of the few constants in a changing world, and there are already too few of those to go round.

And so the meeting wore on, with Pearman and Scoones arguing over the merits of various exam boards; Dr Devine icy and dignified; Kitty unusually lacklustre; Isabelle filing her nails; Geoff and Penny Nation sitting to attention like the Bobbsey Twins; and Dianne Dare watching everything as if departmental meetings were the most fascinating spectacle in the world.

It was dark when the meeting finished, and the School was deserted. Even the cleaners had gone. Only Jimmy remained, walking the polishing-machine slowly and conscientiously over the parquet floor of the Lower Corridor. 'Night, boss,' he told me as I passed. ''Nother one done, eh?'

'You've got your work cut out,' I said. Since Fallow's suspension, Jimmy has carried out all the Porter's duties, and it has been a heavy task. 'When's the new man starting?'

'Fortnight,' said Jimmy, grinning all over his moon face. 'Shuttleworth, he's called. Supports Everton. Reckon we'll get on all right though.'

I smiled. 'You didn't fancy the job yourself, then?'

'Nah, boss.' Jimmy shook his head. 'Too much hassle.'

When I reached the School car-park, it was raining heavily. The Nations' car was already pulling out of their allocated space. Eric doesn't have a car – his eyesight is too bad, and besides, he lives practically next door to the School. Pearman and Kitty were still in the office, going over papers – since his wife's illness, Pearman has been increasingly reliant on Kitty. Isabelle Tapi was redoing her make-up –

Gods knew how long *that* might take – and I knew I could not expect a lift from Dr Devine.

'Miss Dare, I wonder if—'

'Of course. Hop in.'

I thanked her and settled into the passenger seat of the little Corsa. I have noticed that a car, like a desk, frequently reflects the owner's mind. Pearman's is exceptionally messy. The Nations have a bumper sticker that reads: DON'T FOLLOW ME, FOLLOW JESUS. Isabelle's has a Care Bear dashboard toy.

By contrast, Dianne's car is neat, clean, functional. Not a cuddly toy or amusing slogan in sight. I like that; it's the sign of an ordered mind. If I had a car, it would probably be like Room 59; all oak panelling and dusty spider-plants.

I said as much to Miss Dare, and she laughed. 'I hadn't thought of that,' she said, turning on to the main road. 'Like dog owners and their pets.'

'Or teachers and their coffee mugs.'

'Really?' Apparently Miss Dare has never noticed. She herself uses a school mug (plain white, with blue trim) as supplied by the kitchens. She seems remarkably free of whimsy for such a young woman (admittedly, my basis for comparison is not extensive); but this, I think, is a part of her charm. It struck me that she might get on well with young Keane – who is also very cool for a fresher – but when I asked her how she was getting along with the other new staff she simply shrugged.

'Too busy?' I ventured.

'Not my type. Drink-driving with boys in the car. How stupid.'

Well, amen to *that*: the idiot Light had certainly blotted his copybook with his ridiculous antics in town. Easy's just another disposable Suit; Meek a resignation waiting to happen. 'What about Keane?'

'I haven't really spoken to him.'

'You should. Local boy. I've a feeling he might be your type.'

I told you I was getting sentimental. I'm hardly built for it, after all, but there's something about Miss Dare that brings it out, somehow. A trainee Dragon, if ever I saw one (though better-looking than most Dragons I have known), I find that I have no difficulty in imagining her in thirty or forty years' time, looking something like Margaret Rutherford in *The Happiest Days of Your Life*, if rather slimmer, but with the same humorous twist.

It's all too easy to get drawn in, you know; at St Oswald's, different laws apply to those of the world outside. One of these is Time, which passes much faster here than anywhere else. Look at me: approaching my Century, and yet when I look in the mirror I see the same boy I always was – now a grey-haired boy with too much luggage under his eyes and the unmistakable, faintly dissipated air of an old class clown.

I tried – and failed – to communicate some part of this to Dianne Dare. But we were nearing my house; the rain had stopped; I asked her to drop me off at the end of Dog Lane, and explained that I wanted a chance to check the fence; to make sure the graffiti incident had not been repeated.

'I'll come with you,' she said, pulling up to the kerb.

'No need,' I said, but she insisted, and I realized that, ironically, *she* was concerned for *me* – a sobering thought, but a kind one. And perhaps she was right; because as soon as we entered the lane we saw it – certainly it was too big to miss – not just graffiti, but a mural-sized portrait – myself, moustached and swastika'd, larger than life in multicoloured spray-paint.

For half a minute we just stared at it. The paint looked barely dry. And then a rage took hold of me; the sort of transcendent, vocabulary-blocking rage I have felt maybe three or four times in my entire career. I vented it concisely, forgetting the refinements of the *Lingua Latina* for the pure Anglo-Saxon. Because I knew the culprit; knew him this time without a shadow of a doubt.

Quite apart from the small slim object I had spotted lying in the wedge of shadow at the base of the fence, I recognized the style. It was identical to the cartoon that I had removed from the 3S noticeboard; the cartoon that I had long suspected was the work of Colin Knight.

'Knight?' echoed Miss Dare. 'But he's such a little mouse.'

Mouse or not, I knew it. Besides, the boy has a grudge; he hates me, and the support of his mother, the Head, the newspapers and Heaven knows what other malcontents has given him a sly kind of courage. I picked up the slim object at the base of the fence. The invisible finger poked me again; I could feel my blood pounding; and the rage, like some lethal drug, pumped through me, bleaching the world of its colour.

'Mr Straitley?' Now Dianne looked concerned. 'Are you all right?'

'Perfectly so.' I had recovered; I was still trembling, but my mind was sound, and the savage in me checked. 'Look at this.'

'It's a pen, sir,' said Dianne.

'Not *just* a pen.'

I should know; I searched for it long enough, before it was found in the secret cache in the Porter's Lodge. Colin Knight's bar mitzvah pen, as I live and breathe; cost over £500 according to his mother, and conveniently embellished with his initials – CNK – just to be sure.

6

Tuesday, 26th October

NICE TOUCH. THAT PEN. IT'S A MONT BLANC, YOU KNOW; ONE
of the cheaper ones, but even so, quite out of my league.
Not that you'd know it to look at me now; the polyester-
shine is gone, replaced by a slick, impenetrable veneer of
sophistication. One of the many things I picked up from
Leon, along with my Nietzsche and my penchant for lemon-
vodka. As for Leon, he always enjoyed my murals; he
himself was no artist, and it astonished him that I was able
to create such accurate portraits.

Of course I'd had more opportunity to study the masters;
I had notebooks filled with sketches – what was more, I
could forge any signature Leon gave me, which meant
that both of us were able to benefit with impunity from
a number of excuse-notes and out-of-school permission-
slips.

I'm glad to see that the talent has not deserted me. I sneaked out of School during my afternoon free period to finish it off – not as risky as it sounds; hardly anyone ever uses Dog Lane except for the Sunnybankers – and returned in time for Period 8. It worked like a dream; no one saw a thing except the half-wit Jimmy, who was repainting the School gates and who gave me his idiotic grin as I drove through.

I thought at the time I might have to do something about Jimmy. Not that he would ever *recognize* me or anything; but loose ends are loose ends, and this one has remained too long untied. Besides, he offends me. Fallow was fat and lazy, but Jimmy, with his wet mouth and fawning smile, is somehow worse. I wonder that he has survived this long; I wonder that St Oswald's – with its pride in its reputation – tolerates him at all. A care-in-the-community case, as I recall; cheap and disposable as a forty-watt bulb. The word is *disposable*.

That lunch-time I carried out three small and unobtrusive thefts: a tube of valve oil from a pupil's trombone (one of Straitley's pupils, a Japanese boy called Niu); a screwdriver from Jimmy's lock-up; and, of course, Colin Knight's famous pen. No one saw me; and no one saw what I did with those three items when the time came.

Timing – *timing* – is the all-important factor. I knew Straitley and the other linguists would be at the meeting last night (except Grachvogel, who had one of his migraines following that unpleasant little interview with the Head).

By the end of it, everyone else would have gone home, except for Pat Bishop, who can usually be trusted to remain in School until eight or nine. I didn't think he would be a problem, however; his office is on the Lower Corridor, two flights down, too far from the Languages department for him to hear anything.

For a moment I was back in the sweetshop, spoilt for choice. Obviously Jimmy was my primary target, but if this thing worked out I could probably have anyone in the Languages department as a bonus. The question was, who? Not Straitley, of course; not yet. I have my plans for Straitley, and they are maturing very well. Scoones? Devine? Teague?

Geographically, it had to be someone with rooms in the Bell Tower; someone single, who would not be missed; most of all someone *vulnerable*; a lame gazelle that had fallen behind; someone defenceless – a woman, perhaps? – whose misfortune would provoke a real scandal.

There could only be one choice. Isabelle Tapi, with her high heels and tight sweaters; Isabelle who regularly takes time off for PMT and has dated virtually every male member of staff under fifty (except Gerry Grachvogel, who has other preferences).

Her room is in the Bell Tower, just up from Straitley's. It's an odd-shaped, whimsical little space; hot in summer, cold in winter, with windows on four sides and twelve narrow stone steps leading from the door up into the room. Not very practical – it was a store-room in my father's day, and there is barely enough space there to seat an entire class. You can't get a mobile-phone signal there to save your life; Jimmy hates it; the cleaners avoid it – it's almost impossible to get a vacuum up those little steps – and most of the staff – unless they have taught in the Bell Tower themselves – hardly even realize it's there.

For my purpose, then, it was ideal. I waited until after school. I knew Isabelle would not go to the Departmental meeting until she had had a coffee (and a chat with the beastly Light); that gave me five or ten minutes. It was enough.

First, I went into the room, which was empty. Next, I took out my screwdriver and sat down on the steps with my eyes level with the door-handle. It's a simple enough mechanism, based on a single square pin that connects the handle to the latch. Depress the handle, the pin turns, and the latch opens. Nothing could be easier. Remove the pin, however, and however much you pull and push at the handle, the door stays shut.

Quickly, I unscrewed the handle from the door, opened it a crack and removed the pin. Then, keeping my foot wedged in the doorway to stop it closing, I replaced the screws and the handle as before. *There.* From the outside, the door would open perfectly normally. Once inside, however . . .

Of course you can never be *completely* sure. Isabelle might not return to her room. The cleaners might be uncharacteristically thorough; Jimmy might decide to look in. I didn't think so, however. I like to think I know St Oswald's better than most, and I've had plenty of time to get used to its

little routines. Still, not knowing's half the fun, isn't it? –
and if it didn't work, I told myself, I could always start again
in the morning.

7

St Oswald's Grammar School for Boys
Wednesday, 27th October

I SLEPT BADLY LAST NIGHT. PERHAPS THE WIND, OR THE memory of Knight's perfidious behaviour, or the sudden artillery-fire of rain that fell just after midnight, or my dreams, which were more vivid and unsettling than they have been for years.

I'd had a couple of glasses of claret before bed, of course – I don't suppose Bevans would have approved of *that*, or of the tinned steak pie that accompanied them – and I awoke at three thirty with a raging thirst, a sore head and the vague foreknowledge that the worst was yet to come.

I set off early to school, to clear my head and to give myself time to think out a strategy to deal with the boy Knight. It was still pouring, and by the time I reached St Oswald's main gate, my coat and hat were heavy with rain.

It was still only seven forty-five, and there were only a few cars in the staff car-park; the Head's; Pat Bishop's; and Isabelle Tapi's little sky-blue Mazda. I was just considering this (Isabelle rarely gets in before eight thirty; and on most days closer to nine) when I heard the sound of a car pulling in sharply behind me. I turned and saw Pearman's grubby old Volvo swerve across the half-deserted car-park, leaving a quavery stripe of burnt rubber across the wet tarmac in his wake. Kitty Teague was in the passenger seat. Both looked tense – Kitty sheltering under a folded newspaper, Pearman walking very fast – as they approached.

It occurred to me that it might be bad news about Pearman's wife, Sally. I'd only seen her once since her treatment, but she had looked dry and yellow under the big brave smile, and I'd suspected then that her brown hair was a wig.

But when Pearman walked in with Kitty at his heels, I knew that it was worse than that. The man's face was haggard. He did not return my greeting; he barely saw me as he pushed open the door. Behind him, Kitty caught my eye and immediately burst into tears; it took me by surprise, and by the time I had recovered enough to ask what was happening, Pearman had vanished down the Middle Corridor, leaving nothing but a trail of wet footprints across the polished parquet floor.

'For Heaven's sake, what's wrong?' I said.

She covered her face with her hands. 'It's Sally,' she said. 'Someone sent her a letter. It came this morning. She opened it at breakfast.'

'Letter?' Sally and Kitty had always been close, I knew; but even so this distress seemed unwarranted. 'What letter?'

For a moment she seemed incapable of answering. Then she looked at me through the ruins of her make-up and said in a low voice, 'An anonymous letter. About Chris and me.'

'Really?' It took me a while to understand what she was saying. Kitty and *Pearman*? Pearman and Miss Teague?

I really must be getting old, I thought; I had never suspected. I knew they were friends; that Kitty had been supportive – frequently beyond the call of duty. But now it all came out, though I tried hard to stop it; how they had kept it a secret from Sally, who was ill; how they had hoped to marry some day, and now – now—

I took Kitty to the Common Room; made tea; waited with it for ten minutes outside the Ladies'. Finally Kitty came out, looking pink-eyed and rabbity under a fresh coat of beige powder, saw the tea and burst into helpless tears again.

I'd never have thought it of Kitty Teague. She's been at St Oswald's for eight years and I'd never seen her close to this. I offered my handkerchief and held out the tea, feeling awkward and wishing (rather guiltily) for someone more qualified – Miss Dare, perhaps – to take over.

'Are you all right?' (The clumsy gambit of the well-meaning male.)

Kitty shook her head. Of course she wasn't; I knew that much, but the Tweed Jacket is not known for his *savoir faire* with the opposite sex, and I had to say something, after all.

'Do you want me to fetch someone?'

I suppose I was thinking of Pearman; as Head of Department, I thought, the whole thing was really his responsibility. Or Bishop; he's the one who normally deals with emotional crises among the staff. Or Marlene – *yes!* – a sudden wave of relief and affection as I remembered the secretary, so efficient on the day of my own collapse, so approachable with the boys. Capable Marlene, who had endured divorce and bereavement without breaking down. She would know what to do; and even if she didn't, at least she knew the code, without which no male can hope to communicate with a woman in tears.

She was just coming out of Bishop's office as I arrived at her desk. I suppose I take her for granted, as do the rest of the staff. 'Marlene, I wonder if—' I began.

She eyed me with well-feigned severity. 'Mr Straitley.' She always calls me 'Mr Straitley', even though she has been Marlene to all members of the teaching staff for years. 'I don't suppose you've found that register yet.'

'Alas, no.'

'Hmm. I thought not. So what is it now?'

I explained about Kitty, without giving too many details.

Marlene looked concerned. 'It never rains but it pours,' she said wearily. 'Sometimes I wonder why I bother with this place, you know. What with Pat running himself into the ground, everyone on hot bricks over the School Inspection and now this—'

For a moment she looked so harassed that I felt guilty at having asked her.

'No, it's all right,' said Marlene, seeing my expression.

'You leave it to me. I think your department's got enough to be dealing with as it is.'

She was right about that. The department was down to myself, Miss Dare and the League of Nations for most of the day. Dr Devine was off timetable for administrative purposes; Grachvogel was away (again) and during my free periods this morning I took Tapi's first-year French class *and* Pearman's third-year, plus a routine assessment of one of the freshers – this time, the irreproachable Easy.

Knight was absent, and so I was unable to challenge him about the graffiti on my fence, or about the pen I had discovered at the scene. Instead I wrote a complete account of the incident and delivered one copy to Pat Bishop and a second to Mr Beard, who as well as being Head of Computer Science also happens to be Head of the Third Form. I can wait; I have proof of Knight's activities now, and I look forward to dealing with him in my own time. A pleasure deferred, so to speak.

At Break I took Pearman's corridor duty, and after lunch I supervised his group, Tapi's, Grachvogel's and mine in the Assembly Hall, while outside the rain poured down incessantly and, across the corridor, a steady stream of people filed in and out of the Head's office throughout the long afternoon.

Then, five minutes before the end of school, Marlene delivered a summons from Pat. I found him in his office, with Pearman, looking stressed. Miss Dare was sitting by the desk; she gave me a sympathetic look as I came in, and I knew we were in for trouble.

'I take it this is about the Knight boy?' In fact I had been surprised not to see him waiting outside Pat's office; perhaps Pat had already spoken to him, I thought; although by rights no boy should have been questioned before I had had the opportunity to speak to the Second Master.

For a second, Pat's face was blank. Then he shook his head. 'Oh, no. Tony Beard can deal with that. He's the Head of Year, isn't he? No, this is about an incident that happened last night. After the meeting.' Pat looked at his hands, always a sign that he was out of his depth. His nails, I saw, were very bad; bitten down almost to the cuticles.

'What incident?' I said.

For a moment he did not meet my eye. 'The meeting ended just after six,' he said.

'That's right,' I told him. 'Miss Dare gave me a lift home.'

'I know,' said Pat. 'Everyone left at about the same time, except for Miss Teague and Mr Pearman, who stayed for about another twenty minutes.'

I shrugged. I wondered where he was going with this, and why he was being so formal about it. I looked at Pearman, but there was nothing in his expression to enlighten me.

'Miss Dare says you saw Jimmy Watt on the Lower Corridor as you went out,' said Pat. 'He was polishing the floor, waiting to lock up.'

'That's right,' I said. 'Why? What's happened?'

That might explain Pat's manner, I thought. Jimmy, like Fallow, was one of Pat's appointments, and he'd had to put up with a certain amount of criticism about it at the time. Still, Jimmy had always done a reasonable job. No great intellect, to be sure; but he was loyal, and that's what really counts at St Oswald's.

'Jimmy Watt has been dismissed, following the incident last night.'

I didn't believe it. 'What incident?'

Miss Dare looked at me. 'Apparently he didn't check all the classrooms before locking up. Isabelle got shut in somehow, panicked, slipped down the stairs and broke her ankle. She didn't get out till six o'clock this morning.'

'Is she all right?'

'Is she ever?'

I had to laugh. It was typical St Oswald's farce, and the Second Master's mournful expression made it even more ridiculous. 'Oh, you can laugh,' said Pat in a sharp voice, 'but there's been an official complaint. Health and Safety have got involved.' That meant Devine. 'Apparently someone spilt something – oil, she says – on the steps.'

'Oh.' Not so amusing, then. 'Surely you can have a word with her?'

'Believe me, I have.' Pat sighed. 'Miss Tapi seems to think there was more to it than just a mistake on Jimmy's part. She seems to think there was deliberate mischief involved. And believe me, she knows her rights.'

Of course she did. Her type always do. Dr Devine was her Union rep; I guessed that he would already have briefed her on precisely the kind of compensation she could expect. There would be an injury claim; a disability claim (surely no one could expect her to go to work with a broken ankle); plus the negligence claim and the claim for mental distress.

You name it, she'd claim it: trauma, backache, chronic fatigue, whatever. I would be covering for her for the next twelve months.

As for the publicity – the *Examiner* would have a field day with this. Forget Knight. Tapi, with her long legs and expression of martyred bravery, was in another league.

'As if we hadn't enough to deal with, just before an inspection,' said Pat bitterly. 'Tell me, Roy, are there any other little scandals brewing that I should know about?'

8

Friday, 29th October

DEAR OLD BISHOP. FUNNY HE SHOULD ASK. AS A MATTER OF fact I know of at least two; one which has already begun to break with the slow inevitability of a tidal wave, and the second coming along nicely.

Literature, I've noticed, is filled with comforting drivel about the dying. Their patience; their understanding. My experience is that, if anything, the dying can be as vicious and unforgiving as those they leave so reluctantly behind. Sally Pearman is one of these. On the strength of that single letter (one of my best efforts, I have to say) she has set all the usual clichés into motion; locks changed; solicitor called; kids off to Granny; husband's clothes discarded on the lawn. Pearman, of course, cannot lie. It's almost as if he wanted to be found out. That look of misery and relief. Very Catholic. But it comforts him.

Kitty Teague is another matter. There is no one to comfort her now. Pearman, half-crushed beneath his masochistic guilt, barely speaks to her; never catches her eye. Secretly, he holds her responsible – she is a woman, after all – and as Sally recedes, sweetened by remorse, into a mist of nostalgia, Kitty knows she will never be able to compete.

She was away from school today. Stress, apparently. Pearman took his classes, but he looks abstracted, and without Kitty to help him, he is dreadfully disorganized. As a result he makes numerous mistakes; fails to turn up to Easy's appraisal; forgets a lunch-time duty; spends all Break looking for a pile of sixth-form literature papers that he has mislaid (they are actually in Kitty's locker in the Quiet Room; I know because I put them there).

Don't get me wrong. I have nothing in particular against the man. But I do have to keep moving on. And it's more efficient to work in departments – in blocks, if you like – than to diffuse my efforts all over the School.

As for my other projects . . . Tapi's escapade has missed today's papers. A good sign; it means the *Examiner* is saving it for the weekend, but the grapevine tells me that she is very distressed, blames the School in general for her ordeal (and Pat Bishop in particular – seems he wasn't quite sympathetic enough at the crucial time) and expects full Union support and generous settlement, in or out of court.

Grachvogel was away again. I hear the poor chap's prone to migraines, but I believe it may be more to do with the disturbing phone calls he has been receiving. Since his evening out with Light and the boys, he's been looking less than perky. Of course, this is the age of equality – there can be no discrimination on the grounds of race, religion or gender (ha!) – all the same he knows that to be a homo-sexual in a boys' school is to be very vulnerable indeed, and he wonders how he could have given himself away, and to whom.

In normal circumstances he might have approached Pearman for help, but Pearman has troubles of his own, and Dr Devine, technically his boss and Head of Department, would never understand. It's his own fault, really. He should have known better than to hang around with Jeff Light. What *was* he thinking? Light is far less at risk. He oozes testosterone. Tapi sensed it; although I wonder what she will say when the full story eventually breaks. So far, he has been very supportive of Tapi's plight; a keen Union man, he enjoys any situation that involves a challenge to the system. Good. But who knows, maybe that too will backfire. With a little help, of course.

And Jimmy Watt? Jimmy has gone for good, to be replaced by a fresh crew of contract cleaners from town. No one really cares about this except the Bursar (the contract cleaners are more expensive, plus they work to rule and know their rights) and possibly Bishop, who has a soft spot for hopeless cases (my father, for example) and would have liked to have given Jimmy a second chance. Not so the Head, who managed to get the half-wit off the premises with astonishing (and not-quite-legal) speed (that should make an interesting piece for Mole, when Tapi fizzles out), and who has remained shut in his office for most of the past two days, communicating only through his intercom and through Bob Strange, the one member of the upper management who remains completely indifferent to these petty disturbances.

As for Roy Straitley, don't think I have forgotten him. He, most of all, is never far from my thoughts. But his extra duties keep him busy, which is what I need while I enter the next phase of my demolition plan. He is simmering nicely, though; I happened to be in the Computer Science Suite after lunch when I heard his voice in the corridor, and so was able to overhear an interesting conversation between Straitley and Beard regarding (a) Colin Knight and (b) Adrian Meek, the new computer science teacher.

'But I *didn't* write him a rotten report,' Straitley was protesting. 'I sat through his lesson, filled out the form and took a balanced view. That was it.'

'Poor class control,' said Beard, reading from the appraisal form. 'Poor lesson management. Lack of personal appeal? What kind of a balanced view is that?'

There was a pause as Straitley looked at the form. 'I didn't write this,' he said at last.

'Well, it certainly *looks* like your writing.'

There was another, longer pause. I considered coming out of the computer room then, so that I could see the expression on Straitley's face, but decided against it. I didn't want to draw too much attention to myself, especially not at what was soon to be the scene of a crime.

'I didn't write this,' repeated Straitley.

'Well, who did?'

'I don't know. Some practical joker.'

'Roy—' Now Beard was beginning to sound uncomfort-able. I've heard that tone before, the edgy, half-conciliatory tone of one dealing with a possibly dangerous lunatic. 'Look, Roy, fair criticism and all that. I know young Meek isn't the brightest we've ever had—'

'No,' said Straitley. 'He isn't. But I didn't write him a stinker. You can't file that assessment if I didn't write it.'

'Of course not, Roy, but—'

'But what?' There was an edge to Straitley's voice now. He's never liked dealing with Suits, and I could tell the whole thing annoyed him.

'Well, are you sure you didn't just – *forget* what you'd written?'

'What do you mean, *"forget"*?'

He paused. 'Well, I mean, maybe you were in a hurry, or—'

Behind my hand, I laughed silently. Beard is not the first staff member to have suggested that Roy Straitley is *slowing down*, to use a Bishop phrase. I've planted that seed in a couple of minds already, and there have been enough instances of irrational behaviour, chronic forgetfulness and small things going astray to make the idea plausible. Straitley, of course, has never considered this for a moment.

'Mr Beard, I may be nearing my Century, but I am far from senility. Now if we could possibly move on to a matter of some importance' – (I wondered what Meek would say when I told him Straitley considered his assessment to be a matter of no importance) – 'perhaps you have managed to find time in your busy schedule to read my report on Colin Knight.'

At my terminal, I smiled.

'Ah, Knight,' said Beard weakly.

Ah, Knight.

As I said, I can identify with a boy like Knight. In fact I was nothing like him – I was infinitely tougher, more vicious and more streetwise – but with more money and better parents I might have turned out just the same. There's a long streak of resentment in Knight that I can use; and his sullenness means that he is unlikely to confide in anyone else until the point of no return has been passed. If wishes were horses, as we used to say when we were kids, then old Straitley would have been stampeded to death years ago. As it is, I have been tutoring Knight (on quite an extracurricular basis), and in this, if nothing else, he is an apt pupil.

It didn't take much. Nothing at first that could be traced to me; a word here; a push there. 'Imagine *I'm* your form-tutor,' I told him, as he followed me, puppylike, on my duty rounds. 'If you have a problem, and you feel you can't talk to Mr Straitley about it, come to me.'

Knight had. Over three weeks I have been subjected to his pathetic complaints, his petty grievances. No one likes him; teachers pick on him; pupils call him 'creep' and 'loser'. He is miserable all the time, except when rejoicing at some other pupil's misfortune. In fact he has been in-strumental in spreading quite a number of little rumours for me, including a few about poor Mr Grachvogel, whose absences have been noted and eagerly discussed. When he returns – *if* he returns – he is likely to find the details of his private life – with whatever embellishments the boys may have added – emblazoned on desks and toilet walls throughout the School.

Most of the time, though, Knight likes to complain. I provide a sympathetic ear; and although by now I can perfectly understand why Straitley loathes the brat, I have to say I'm delighted with my pupil's progress. In slyness, in sullenness, in sheer unspoken malice, Knight is a natural.

A pity he has to go, really; but as my old dad might have said, you can't make an omelette without killing people.

9

St Oswald's Grammar School for Boys
Friday, 29th October

THAT ASS BEARD. THAT PERENNIAL ASS. WHOEVER THOUGHT *he* could make a decent Head of Year? Began by practically saying I was senile over Meek's idiotic assessment form, then had the temerity to question my judgement on the subject of Colin Knight. Wanted more *evidence*, if you can believe it. Wanted to know whether I had spoken to the boy.

Spoken to him? Of course I'd spoken to him, and if ever a boy was lying . . . It's in the eyes, you know; the way they skitter repeatedly to the left-hand corner of the picture, as if there were something there – toilet paper on my shoe, perhaps, or a big puddle to avoid. It's in the meek look, the exaggerated response, the succession of 'Honestly, sir's and 'I swear, sir's and behind it all, that sneak smug air of knowledge.

Of course I knew all that would end when I produced the pen. I let him talk; swear; swear on his mother's grave; then out it came, Knight's pen with Knight's initials on it, discovered at the scene of the crime.

He gaped. His face fell. We were alone in the Bell Tower. It was lunch-time. It was a crisp, sunny day; the boys were in the yard chasing autumn. I could hear their distant cries, like gulls on the wind. Knight could hear them too, and half-turned longingly towards the window.

'Well?' I tried not to be *too* satisfied. He was only a boy, after all. 'It *is* your pen, isn't it, Knight?'

Silence. Knight stood with his hands in his pockets, shrivelling before my eyes. He knew it was serious, a matter for expulsion. I could see it in his face; the blot on his record; his mother's disappointment; his father's anger; the blow to his prospects. '*Isn't it*, Knight?'

Silently, he nodded.

I sent him to the Head of Year, but he never got there. Brasenose saw him at the bus stop later that afternoon, but thought nothing of it. A dentist's appointment, perhaps, or a quick, unsanctioned jaunt to the record shop or the café. No one else remembers seeing him; a lank-haired boy in St Oswald's uniform, carrying a black nylon rucksack and looking as if the world's troubles had just descended on to his shoulders.

'Oh, I *spoke* to him all right. He didn't say much. Not after I produced the pen.'

Beard looked troubled. 'I see. And what exactly did you say to the boy?'

'I impressed upon him the error of his ways.'

'Was anyone else present?'

I'd had enough of this. Of course there hadn't been; who else would have been present, on a windy lunch-time with a thousand boys playing outside? 'What's going on, Beard?' I demanded. 'Have the parents complained? Is that it? Am I victimizing the boy again? Or is it that they know full well that their son's a liar and that it's only because of St Oswald's that I haven't reported him to the police?'

Beard took a deep breath. 'I think we should discuss this somewhere else,' he said uneasily (it was eight o'clock in the morning, and we were on the Lower Corridor, as yet almost deserted). 'I wanted Pat Bishop to be here, but he isn't in his office and I can't get hold of him on his phone. Oh dear' – at this he tugged at his weak moustache – 'I really think further discussion of this should wait until the proper authorities—'

I was about to make a stinging retort about Heads of Year and proper authorities when Meek came in. He gave me a venomous look, then addressed Beard. 'Problem in the labs,' he said in his colourless voice. 'I think you should have a look.'

Beard looked openly relieved. Computer problems were his field. No unpleasant human contact; no inconsistencies; no lies; nothing but machines to programme and decode. I knew that there had been incessant computer problems this week – a virus, so I'm told – with the result that, to my delight, e-mail had been completely suspended and Computer Science relegated to the library for several days.

'Excuse me, Mr Straitley—' That look again, like a man whose last-minute reprieve has finally come. 'Duty calls.'

I found Bishop's (handwritten) note in my pigeon-hole at the end of the lunch-break. Not before, I'm afraid, though Marlene tells me she delivered it at registration. But the morning had been fraught with problems: Grachvogel absent; Kitty depressed; Pearman pretending nothing was wrong, but looking rumpled and pale, with deep shadows under his eyes. I heard from Marlene (who always knows everything) that he slept in School last night; apparently he hasn't been home since Tuesday, when the anonymous letter had exposed his long-term infidelity. Kitty blames herself, says Marlene; feels she has let Pearman down; wonders if it was her fault that the mystery informant learned the truth.

Pearman says not, but remains aloof. Just like a man, says Marlene; too busy with his own problems to notice that poor Kitty is completely distraught.

I know better than to comment on this. I don't take sides. I just hope that Pearman and Kitty will be able to continue to work together after this. I'd hate to lose either of them, especially this year, when so many other things have already gone bad.

There is one small consolation, however. Eric Scoones is a surprising pillar of strength in a world turned suddenly weak. Difficult at the best of times, he comes into his own at the worst, taking over Pearman's duties without complaint (and with a kind of relish). Of course he would have liked to have been Head of Department. Might even have been good at it – though he lacks Pearman's charm, he is meticulous in all forms of administration. But age has soured him, and it is only in these moments of crisis that I see the real Eric Scoones; the young man I knew thirty years ago; the conscientious, energetic young man; the demon in the classroom; the tireless organizer; the hopeful young Turk.

St Oswald's has a way of eating those things. The energy; the ambition; the dreams. That's what I was thinking as I sat in the Common Room five minutes before the end of lunch-break, with an old brown mug in one hand and a stale digestive in the other (Common Room fund; I feel I should be getting my money's worth, somehow). It's always crowded at that time, like a railway terminal disgorging passengers to a variety of destinations. The usual suspects in their various seats: Roach, Light (unusually subdued) and Easy, all three getting their extra five minutes with the *Daily Mirror* before the beginning of afternoon school. Monument asleep; Penny Nation with Kitty in the girls' corner; Miss Dare, reading a book; young Keane, popping in for a quick breather after his lunch-time duty.

'Oh, sir,' he said, seeing me there. 'Mr Bishop's been looking for you. I think he sent you a message.'

A message? Probably an e-mail. The fellow never learns.

I found Bishop in his office, squinting at the computer screen with his close-work glasses on. He removed them at once (he is self-conscious about the way he looks, and those pebble spectacles seem more suited to an elderly academic than an ex-rugby player).

'Took your bloody time, didn't you?'

'I'm sorry,' I said mildly. 'I must have missed your message.'

'Bollocks,' said Bishop. 'You never remember to check your mail. I'm sick of it, Straitley, I'm sick of having to call you to my office like some member of the Lower Fifth who never hands in his coursework.'

I had to smile. I do like him, you know. He's not a Suit – though he tries, gods help him – and there is a kind of honesty about him when he's angry that you'd never find in someone like the Head. '*Vere dicis?*' I said politely.

'You can cut *that* out for a start,' said Bishop. 'We're in real shit here, and it's your bloody fault.'

I looked at him. He wasn't joking. 'What's the problem? Another complaint?' I suppose I was thinking about Pooley's blazer again – though surely, Bob Strange would have wanted to deal with that himself.

'Worse than that,' said Pat. 'It's Colin Knight. He's done a bunk.'

'What?'

Pat glared at me. 'Yesterday, after his little run-in with you at lunch-time. Took his bag, went off and no one – and I mean *no one*, not his parents, not his friends, not a single bloody soul – seems to have clapped eyes on him since.'

BISHOP

1

Sunday, 31st October

ALL HALLOWS' EVE. I'VE ALWAYS LOVED IT. THAT NIGHT IN particular, rather than Bonfire Night and its gaudy celebrations (and anyway, I've always thought it rather tasteless for children to celebrate the gruesome death of a man guilty of little more than getting ideas above his station).

It's true; I've always had a soft spot for Guy Fawkes. Perhaps because I am in much the same situation: a lone plotter with only my wits to defend me against my monstrous adversary. But Fawkes was betrayed. I have no allies, no one with whom to discuss my own explosive schemes, and if I am betrayed, then it will be by my own carelessness or stupidity rather than by someone else's.

The knowledge cheers me, for my job is a lonely one and I often long for someone with whom to share the triumphs, the anxieties of my day-to-day revolt. But this week marks the end of a new phase in my campaign. The picador's role is ended; time now for the matador to take the stage.

I began with Knight.

A pity, in a way; he has been very helpful to me this term, and of course I have nothing personal against the boy, but he would have had to go some time or other, and he knew too much (whether he was aware of it or not) to be allowed to continue.

I was expecting a crisis, of course. Like all artists, I like to provoke, and Straitley's reaction to my little piece of self-expression on his back fence had certainly exceeded expectations. I knew he'd find the pen, too, and leap to the logical conclusion.

As I said, they're so predictable, these St Oswald masters. Push the buttons, press the switch and watch them go. Knight was ready; Straitley primed. For a few packs of Camels the Sunnybankers had been prepared to feed an old man's paranoia; I had done the same with Colin Knight. Everything was in place; both protagonists poised for battle. All that remained was the final showdown.

Of course I knew he'd come to me. *Imagine I'm your form-tutor,* I'd said, and he had; on Thursday after lunch, he ran straight to me in tears, poor boy, and told me all about it.

'Now calm down, Colin,' I'd said, manoeuvring him into a little-used office off the Middle Corridor. 'What *exactly* has Mr Straitley accused you of?'

He told me, with a great deal of snot and self-pity.

'I see.'

My heart quickened. It had begun. There was no stopping it now. My gambit had paid off; now all I had to do was to watch as St Oswald's began to tear itself apart, limb by limb.

'What do I do?' He was almost hysterical now, his pinched face prunelike with anxiety. 'He'll tell my mum, he'll call the police, I might even be *expelled*—' Ah, expulsion. The ultimate dishonour. In the pecking order of terrible consequences, it even takes precedence over parents and the police.

'You won't be expelled,' I said firmly.

'You don't know that!'

'Colin. Look at me.' A pause, Knight shaking his head hysterically. '*Look* at me.'

He did, still shaking, and slowly the beginnings of hysteria began to subside.

'Listen to me, Colin,' I said. Short sentences, eye contact and an air of conviction. Teachers use this method; so do doctors, priests and other illusionists. 'Listen carefully. You won't be expelled. Do as I say, come with me and you'll be fine.'

He was waiting for me, as instructed, at the bus stop by the staff car-park. It was ten to four, and already it was getting dark. I'd left my class (for once) ten minutes early, and the street was deserted. I stopped the car opposite the bus stop. Knight got in on the passenger side, his face pallid with terror and hope. 'It's all right, Colin,' I told him gently. 'I'm taking you home.'

*   *   *

I didn't plan it quite that way. Really I didn't. Call it foolhardy if you like, but as I pulled out of St Oswald's that afternoon, into a street that was already blurry with thin October rain, I still hadn't *quite* decided what to do with Colin Knight. On a personal level, of course, I'm a perfectionist. I like to have all the bases covered. Sometimes, however, it's best to rely on pure instinct. Leon taught me that, you know, and I have to admit that some of the best moves I have ever made have been the unplanned ones; the impulsive strokes of genius.

So it was with Colin Knight; and it came to me in a sudden inspiration, as I was passing the municipal park.

I told you I've always had a soft spot for Hallowe'en. As a child I much preferred it to the common celebrations of Bonfire Night, which I've always vaguely mistrusted, with its candyfloss commercialism, its trollish good cheer in front of the big barbecue. Most of all I mistrusted the Community Bonfire, an annual event held on Bonfire Night, in the local park, allowing the public to congregate *en masse* before a conflagration of alarming scale and a mediocre firework display. There is often a funfair, staffed by cynical 'travellers' with an eye for the main chance; a hot-dog stand; a Test Your Strength booth (*Every one's a Winner!*); a rifle range, with moth-eaten teddies hanging by their necks like trophies; a toffee-apple salesman (the apples squashy and brown beneath the coating of brittle bright-red candy) and a number of pickpockets pushing their sly way through the holiday crowd.

I've always hated this gratuitous display. The noise; the sweat; the rabble; the heat and the sense of violence about to erupt have always repelled me. Believe it or not, I despise violence. Its inelegance more than anything else, I think. Its crass and bludgeoning stupidity. My father loved the Community Bonfire for the same reasons I detested it; and he was never happier than on such occasions, a bottle of beer in one hand, face purple with the heat from the fire, a pair of alien antennae wagging on his head (or it might have been a pair of devil's horns), neck craned to watch the rockets as they burst *brapp-brapp-brapp* across the smoky sky.

But it was thanks to his memory that I had my idea; an idea so sweetly elegant that it made me smile. Leon would have been proud of me, I knew; my twin problems of dispatch and disposal both sorted at a single blow.

I flicked on the indicator and turned towards the park. The big gates were open – in fact this is the only time of year when access is granted to vehicles – and I drove in slowly on to the main walkway.

'What are we doing here?' asked Knight, his anxiety forgotten. He was eating a chocolate bar from the school tuck-shop and playing a computer game on his state-of-the-art mobile phone. An earpiece dangled languidly from one ear.

'I've got something to drop off here,' I said. 'Something to burn.'

*   *   *

This is, as far as I can see, the only advantage of the Community Bonfire. It gives the opportunity to anyone who so wishes to dispose of any unwanted rubbish. Wood, pallets, magazines and cardboard are always appreciated, but any combustible is more than welcome. Tyres, old sofas, mattresses, stacks of newspapers – all have their place, and the citizens are encouraged to bring whatever they can.

Of course by now the bonfire had already been built: scientifically, and with care. A forty-foot pyramid, marvellous in its construction; layer upon layer of furniture, toys, paper, clothes, refuse sacks, packing crates, and – in deference to centuries of tradition – guys. Dozens of guys; some with placards around their necks; some rudimentary; some eerily human-looking, standing and sitting and reclining in various positions on the unlit pyre. The area had been cordoned off at a distance of fifty yards or so from the structure; when it was lit, the heat would be so intense that to approach any further would be to risk incineration.

'Impressive, isn't it?' I said, parking as close as I could to the cordoned area. A number of skips containing assorted jumble blocked further access; but I reckoned it was near enough.

'It's all right,' said Knight. 'What have you brought?'

'See for yourself,' I said, getting out of the car. 'Anyway, Colin, you might have to help me. It's a bit bulky for me to manage on my own.'

Knight got out, not bothering to remove the phone's earpiece. For a second I thought he was going to complain;

but he followed me, looking incuriously at the unlit pyre as I unlocked the boot.

'Nice phone,' I said.

'Yeah,' said Knight.

'I like a good bonfire, don't you?'

'Yeah.'

'I do hope it doesn't rain. There's nothing worse than a bonfire that won't start. Though they must use something – petrol, I expect – to start it off. It always seems to catch so fast—'

As I spoke I kept my body between Knight and the car. I needn't have bothered, I suspect. He wasn't very bright. Come to think of it, I was probably doing the gene pool a favour.

'Come on, Colin.'

Knight took a step forwards.

'Good lad.' A hand in the small of the back – a gentle push. For a moment I thought of the Test Your Strength (*Every one's a Winner!*) booth of my childhood funfairs; imagined myself lifting the mallet high, smelled popcorn and smoke and the reek of boiled hot-dogs and fried onions; saw my father grinning in his ridiculous alien antennae, saw Leon with a Camel crooked between his ink-stained fingers, smiling encouragement—

And then I brought the boot lid down as hard as I could, and heard that unspeakable – but nonetheless quite reassuringly familiar – *crunch* telling me that once again, I was a winner.

2

THERE WAS RATHER A LOT OF BLOOD.

I'd expected it, and taken precautions, but even so I may have to dry-clean this suit.

Don't imagine I *enjoyed* it; in fact I find any kind of violence repulsive, and would much have preferred to let Knight fall to his death from a high place, or choke on a peanut – anything but this primitive and messy solution. Still, there's no denying that it *was* a solution, and a good one too. Once Knight had declared himself he couldn't be allowed to live; and besides, I need Knight for the next stage.

Bait, if you like.

I borrowed his phone for a moment or two, wiping it clean on the damp grass. After that I switched it off and put it in my pocket. Then I covered Knight's face in a black plastic sack (I always carry a few in the car, just in case), secured in place with an elastic band. I did the same with

Knight's hands. I sat him in a broken armchair near the base of the pile, and anchored him in place with a block of magazines held together with string. By the time I had finished he looked just like the other guys waiting on the unlit bonfire, though perhaps less realistic than some.

An old man walking a dog came along as I was working. He greeted me; the dog barked, and they both passed by. Neither of them noticed the blood on the grass, and as for the body itself – I've discovered that as long as you don't *behave* like a murderer, no one will assume you *are* a murderer, whatever evidence exists to the contrary. If ever I decide to turn to robbery (and one day I might; I'd like to think I have more than one string to my bow), I will wear a mask and a striped jersey, and carry a bag marked SWAG. If anyone sees me, they will simply assume that I am on my way to a fancy-dress party, and think nothing of it. People, I find, are for the most part *very* unobservant, especially of the things that are going on right beneath their noses.

That weekend, I celebrated with fire. It is traditional, after all.

I found the Gatehouse burned rather well, given the old damp problem. My only regret was that the new Porter – Shuttleworth, I think his name is – had not yet moved in. Still, with the house empty and Jimmy suspended, I couldn't have chosen a more convenient time.

There is a certain amount of video security at St Oswald's, though most of it is concentrated on the front gate and its imposing entrance. I was willing to take the risk that the Porter's Lodge would not be under surveillance. All the same, I wore a hooded top, just baggy enough for camouflage. Any camera would simply show a hooded figure, carrying two unlabelled cans and with a school satchel slung over one shoulder, running along the side of the perimeter fence in the direction of the Lodge.

Breaking in was easy. Less easy were the memories that seemed to seep out of the walls: the smell of my father; that sourness; the phantom reek of Cinnabar. Most of the furniture had belonged to St Oswald's. It was still there: the dresser; the clock; the heavy dining table and chairs that we never used. A pale rectangle on the living-room wallpaper where my father had hung a picture (a sentimental print of a little girl with a puppy) unexpectedly tore at my heart.

I was suddenly, absurdly, reminded of Roy Straitley's house, with its rows of school photographs, smiling boys in faded uniforms, the fixed, expectant faces of the brash young dead. It was terrible. Worse, it was *banal*. I had expected to take my time, to splash petrol across the old carpets, the old furniture, with a joyful step. Instead I did what had to be done in furtive haste and ran, feeling like a sneak, like a trespasser, for the first time I could remember since that day at St Oswald's, when I first saw the lovely building, its windows shining in the sun, and wanted it for my own.

That was something Leon never understood. He never really *saw* St Oswald's; its grace, its history, its arrogant *rightness*. To him it was just a school; desks to be carved upon, walls to be graffiti-ed, teachers to be mocked and defied. So wrong, Leon. So childishly, fatally wrong.

And so I burned the Gatehouse; and instead of the elation I had anticipated, I felt nothing but a slinking remorse, that weakest and most useless of emotions, as the gleeful flames pranced and roared.

By the time the police arrived, I had recovered. Having changed my baggy sweatshirt for something more appropriate, I stayed for just long enough to tell them what they wanted to hear (a youth, hooded, fleeing the scene) and to allow them to find the cans and discarded satchel. By which time the fire engines had arrived too, and I stepped aside to let them do their job. Not that there was much for them to do by then.

A student prank, the *Examiner* will say: a Hallowe'en stunt taken criminally far. My champagne tasted a little flat; but I drank it anyway, while making a couple of routine calls with Knight's borrowed phone and listening to the sounds of fireworks and the voices of young revellers – witches, ghouls and vampires – as they ran down the alleys below me.

If I sit in exactly the right position at my window, I can just see Dog Lane. I wonder if Straitley is sitting at *his* window tonight, lights dimmed, curtain drawn. He expects trouble, that's for sure. From Knight, or someone else – Sunnybankers or shadowy spirits. Straitley believes in ghosts – as well he might – and tonight, they are out in force, like memories set loose to prey upon the living.

Let them prey. The dead don't have much to amuse them. I've done my bit; stuck my little spanner in the School's old works. Call it a sacrifice, if you like. A payment in blood. If that doesn't satisfy them, nothing will.

3

St Oswald's Grammar School for Boys
Monday, 1st November

WHAT A SHAMBLES. WHAT AN ALMIGHTY SHAMBLES. I SAW
the fire last night, of course; but thought it was the annual
Guy Fawkes bonfire, a few days early and a few degrees from
its usual spot. Then I heard the fire engines, and all at once
I had to be there. It was so like that other time, you see; I
recalled the sound of sirens in the darkness, Pat Bishop like
a crazed cinema director with his damned megaphone—

It was freezing cold as I stepped outside. I was glad of my
coat, and of the checked scarf – a Christmas present from
some boy, in the days when pupils still did such things –
wound firmly round my neck. The air smelt good, of smoke
and fog and gunpowder, and although it was late, a gang of
trick-or-treaters was pelting down the alley with a carrier
bag of sweets. One of them – a little ghost – dropped a

wrapper as he passed – a mini-Snickers wrapper, I think it was – and I stooped automatically to pick it up.

'Hey, you!' I said in my Bell Tower voice.

The little ghost – a boy of eight or nine – stopped short.

'You dropped something,' I said, handing him the wrapper.

'You *what?*' The ghost looked at me as if I might be mad.

'You dropped something,' I said patiently. 'There's a litter bin over there,' pointing to a dustbin only a dozen yards away. 'Just walk over and put it in.'

'You *what?*' Behind him, there was grinning, nudging. Someone sniggered beneath a cheap plastic mask. Sunny-bankers, I thought with a sigh, or juvenile thugs-in-waiting from the Abbey Road estate. Who else would let their eight- or nine-year-old children roam the streets at half past eleven, without an adult in sight?

'In the bin, please,' I said again. 'I'm sure you were brought up better than to drop litter.' I smiled; for a moment half a dozen little faces looked up wonderingly at mine. There was a wolf; three sheeted ghosts; a grubby vampire with a leaky nose; and an unidentifiable person who might have been a ghoul or a gremlin or some X-rated Hollywood creature without a name.

The little ghost looked at me, then at the wrapper.

'Well done,' I began to say, as he moved towards the bin.

At that he turned and grinned at me, exposing teeth as discoloured as a veteran smoker's. 'Fuck off,' he said, and ran off down the alley, dropping the Snickers wrapper as he went. The others ran the opposite way, scattering papers as they went, and I heard their jeers and insults as they ran off into the freezing mist.

It shouldn't have bothered me. As a teacher, I see all sorts, even at St Oswald's, which is, after all, a somewhat privileged environment. Those Sunnybankers are a different breed; the estates are rife with alcoholism, drug abuse, poverty, violence. Foul language and litter come as easily to them as hello and goodbye. There is no malice in it, not really. Still, it bothered me, perhaps more than it should. I had already given out three bowls of sweets to trick-or-treaters that night; among them, a number of mini-Snickers bars.

I picked up the wrapper and put it in the bin, feeling unexpectedly depressed. I'm getting old, that's all there is to it. My expectations of youth (and of humanity in general, I believe) are quite outdated. Even though I suspected – knew, perhaps, in my heart – that the fire I had seen was something to do with St Oswald's, I did not *expect* it; the absurd optimism that has always been the best and worst part of my nature forbids me to take the gloomy view. That's why a part of me was genuinely surprised when I arrived at the School, saw the fire crew at the blaze and understood that the Gatehouse was on fire.

It could have been worse. It could have been the library. There was a fire there once – before my time, in 1845 – that burned up more than a thousand books, some very rare. A careless candle, perhaps, left unsupervised; there is certainly nothing in the School's records to suggest it was malice.

This was. The Fire Chief's report says petrol was used; a

witness at the scene reports a hooded boy, running away. Most damning of all; Knight's satchel, dropped at the scene, a little charred but still perfectly recognizable, the books within carefully labelled with his name and form.

Bishop was there at once, of course. Pitching in with the firemen so energetically that for a time I thought he was one of them. Then he came looming out at me through the smoke, eyes red, hair in spikes, flushed almost to apoplexy with the heat and the moment.

'No one inside,' he panted, and I saw now that he was carrying a large clock under one arm, running with it like a prop forward about to score a try. 'Thought I'd try to save a few things.' Then he was off again, his bulk somehow pathetic against the flames. I called after him, but my voice was lost; a few moments later I glimpsed him trying to drag an oak chest through the burning front door.

As I said, what a shambles.

This morning the area was cordoned off, the debris still fiercely red and smoking, so that now the whole School smells of Bonfire Night. In the form there is no other topic of conversation; the report of Knight's disappearance, and now this, are enough to fuel rumours of such wild inventiveness that the Head has had no choice but to call an emergency Staff Meeting to discuss our options.

Plausible denial has always been his way. Look at that business with John Snyde. Even Fallowgate was hotly refuted; now HM means to deny Knightsbridge (as Allen-Jones has dubbed it), especially as the *Examiner* has been asking the most impertinent questions in the hope of turning up some new scandal.

Of course it will be all over town by tomorrow. Some pupil will talk, as they always do, and the news will break. A pupil disappears. A revenge attack on the School follows, perhaps provoked – who knows? – by bullying and victimization. No note was left. The boy is at large. Where? Why?

I assumed – we all did – that Knight was the reason the police were there this morning. They arrived at eight thirty; five officers, three in plain clothes; one woman, four men. Our community officer (Sergeant Ellis, a veteran, skilled in public relations and manly tête-à-têtes) was not with them, and I should have suspected something there and then, though in fact I was far too preoccupied with my own affairs to give them much thought.

Everyone was. And with good reason: half the department missing; computers down with a deadly germ; boys infected with revolt and speculation; staff on edge and unable to concentrate. I had not seen Bishop since the previous night; Marlene told me that he'd been treated for smoke inhalation, but had refused to stay in hospital and moreover, had spent the rest of the night in School, going over the damage and reporting to the police.

Of course it is generally, if unofficially, accepted (at least in management circles) that I am to blame. Marlene told me as much, having glanced at a drafted letter dictated by Bob Strange to his secretary, and now awaiting approval from Bishop. I didn't get a chance to read it, but I can guess at the style as well as the content. Bob Strange is a specialist of the bloodless coup-de-grâce, having drafted a dozen or so similar letters in the course of his career. *In the light of recent events . . . regrettable, but unavoidable . . . now cannot be overlooked . . . a sabbatical to be taken on full pay until such time as . . .*

There would be references to my erratic behaviour, my increasing forgetfulness and the curious incident of Anderton-Pullitt, not to mention Meek's bungled assessment, Pooley's blazer and any number of smaller infractions, inevitable in the career of any master, all noted, numbered and set aside by Strange for possible use in instances such as this.

Then would come the open hand, the grudging acknowledgement of *thirty-three years of loyal service* . . . the small, tight-mouthed assurance of personal respect. Beneath it, the subtext is always the same: *You have become an embarrassment.* In short, Strange was preparing the hemlock bowl.

Oh, I can't say I was entirely surprised. But I have given so much to St Oswald's over so many years that I suppose I imagined it made me some kind of an exception. It does not; the machinery that lies at the heart of St Oswald's is as heartless and unforgiving as Strange's computers. There is no malice involved, simply an equation. I am old; expensive; inefficient; a worn cog from an outdated mechanism that in any case serves no useful purpose. And if there is to be a scandal, then who better to carry the blame? Strange knows that I will not make a fuss. It's undignified, for a start; and besides, I would not bring more scandal to St

Oswald's. A generous settlement on top of my pension; a nicely worded speech by Pat Bishop in the Common Room; a reference to my ill health and the new opportunities afforded by my impending retirement; the hemlock bowl cunningly hidden behind the laurels and the paraphernalia.

Damn him to hell. I could almost believe he'd planned this from the start. The invasion of my office; my removal from the prospectus; his interference. He'd held on to the letter until now only because Bishop was unavailable. He needed Bishop on his side. And he'd get him, too, I told myself; I like Pat, but I have no illusions as to his loyalty. St Oswald's comes first. And the Head? I knew he would be more than happy to present the case to the Governors. After that, Dr Pooley could do his worst. And who, I thought, would really care? And what about my Century? From where I was standing, it might have been an age away.

At lunch-time I got a memo from Dr Devine, handwritten for once (I assumed the computers were still down) and delivered by a boy from his fifth form.

R.S. Report to office at once. M.R.D.

I wondered if *he* was in on it, too. I wouldn't have put it past him. So I made him wait; marked a few books, exchanged pleasantries with the boys; drank tea. Ten minutes later Devine came in like a dervish, and on seeing his expression I dismissed the boys with a wave of the hand and gave him my full attention.

Now you may have been under the impression that I've got some kind of a feud going with old Sourgrape. Nothing could be further from the truth; in fact most of the time I quite enjoy our spats, even though we don't always see eye to eye on matters of policy, uniform, Health and Safety, cleanliness or behaviour.

I do know where to draw the line, however, and any thought of baiting the old idiot vanished as soon as I saw his face. Devine looked sick. Not merely pale, which is his natural state, but yellow; haggard; old. His tie was askew; his hair, which is usually immaculate, had been pushed out of place so that now he looked like a man in a high wind. Even his walk, which is usually brisk and automatic, had developed a hitch; he staggered into my room like a clock-work toy and sat down heavily on the nearest desk.

'What's happened?'

There was no trace of banter in my voice now. Someone had died; that was my first thought. His wife; a boy; a close colleague. Only some terrible catastrophe could have affected Dr Devine in this way.

It was a sign of his real distress that he took no opportunity to berate me for my lack of response to his summons. He remained sitting on the desk for a few moments, his thin chest drawn down towards his protuberant knees.

I pulled out a Gauloise, lit it and held it out.

Devine hasn't indulged in years, but he took it without a word.

I waited. I'm not always known for my *savoir faire*, but I know how to deal with troubled boys, and that was exactly what Devine looked like to me then, a grey-haired, very troubled boy, his face raw with anxiety, his knees bunched up against his chest in a desperate protective gesture.

'The police.' It came out as a gasp.

'What about them?'

'They've arrested Pat Bishop.'

It took me some time to get the whole story. For a start, Devine didn't know it. Something to do with computers, he thought, although the details were unclear. Knight was mentioned; boys in Bishop's classes were being questioned, though what the charge against Bishop actually was no one seemed to know.

I could see why Devine was panicked, though. He has always tried very hard to ingratiate himself with the management, and he is naturally terrified of being implicated in this new, unspecified scandal. Apparently the visiting officers questioned Sourgrape at some length; seemed interested to know that on several occasions Pat has played host to Mr and Mrs Sourgrape; and were now about to search the office for any further evidence.

'Evidence!' yawped Devine, stubbing out his Gauloise. 'What are they expecting to find? If only I knew—'

Half an hour later, two of the officers departed, carrying Bishop's computer. When Marlene asked why, no answer was given. The three remaining officers stayed to *carry out further inquiries*, mostly in the Computer Science Suite, which has now been closed to all members of the School. One of the officers (the woman) came into my form-room during Period 8 and asked me when I had last used my workstation there. I informed her curtly that I never used the computers, having no interest at all in electronic games, and she left, looking like a School Inspector about to write an unfriendly report.

The class was completely uncontrollable after that, so we played hangman in Latin for the last ten minutes of the lesson, while my mind raced and the invisible finger (never far away) jabbed at my breastbone with ever-increasing persistence.

At the end of the lesson I went in search of Mr Beard, but I found him evasive, speaking of viruses in the School computer network, of workstations and password pro-tections and internet downloads – all subjects which hold as little fascination for me as do the works of Tacitus for Mr Beard.

As a result, I now know as little about the matter as I did at lunch-time, and was forced to leave School (after waiting over an hour, without success, for Bob Strange to emerge from his office), feeling frustrated and horribly anxious. This isn't over, whatever it is. November it may be, but I have a feeling the Ides of March have just begun.

4

Tuesday, 2nd November

MY PUPIL MADE THE PAPERS AGAIN. THE NATIONALS THIS time, I am proud to say (of course, Mole had a little something to do with that, but he would have found his way in there sooner or later).

The *Daily Mail* blames the parents; the *Guardian* sees a victim; and the *Telegraph* included an editorial on vandalism, and how it should be tackled. All very gratifying: plus Knight's mother has launched a tearful TV appeal to Colin saying that he isn't in any trouble and begging him please to come home.

Bishop has been suspended, pending further inquiry. I'm not surprised; what they found on his computer must certainly have helped. Gerry Grachvogel, too, must have been arrested by now, and very soon, others will follow. The news has hit the School like a bomb – the same time-bomb, as it happens, that I put in place during half-term.

A virus to immobilize the system's defences. A carefully planted set of internet links. A log of e-mails sent to and from Knight's personal station to a hotmail address accessible from the School. A selection of images, mostly stills but with a few interesting webcam clips, sent to a number of staff addresses and downloaded into password-protected files.

Of course, none of this would have come to light if the police had not investigated Colin Knight's e-mail correspondence. But in these days of internet chat-rooms and virtual predators, it pays to cover all the bases.

Knight fitted the victim profile – a solitary youngster, unpopular at school. I knew they would hit upon the idea sooner or later. As it happens, it was sooner. Mr Beard helped it along, going through the systems after the crash, and after that it was just a question of following the thread.

The rest is simple. It's a lesson they still have to learn, the folk of St Oswald's; a lesson I learned over ten years ago. They are so complacent, these people; so arrogant and naïve. They need to understand what I understood in front of the big NO TRESPASSERS sign; that the rules and legislations of the world are all held in place by the same precarious fabric of bluff and complacency; that any rule can be broken; that trespass, like any crime, goes unpunished when there's no one to see it. It's an important lesson in any child's education – and, as my father always said, your education's the most precious thing in the world.

But why? I hear you ask. Sometimes I still ask it myself. Why do I do it? Why so dogged, after all these years?

Simple revenge? I only wish it were that easy. But you and I both know that it goes deeper than that. Revenge, I'll admit, is a part of it. For Julian Pinchbeck, perhaps – for the whingeing, cringing child I was, hiding in the shadows and wishing desperately to be someone else.

But for myself? Nowadays I'm happy with who I am. I'm a solid citizen. I have a job – a job at which I have proved myself unexpectedly talented. I may still be the Invisible Man as far as St Oswald's is concerned, but I have refined my role far beyond that of mere impostor. For the first time I wonder if I could stay here longer.

It's certainly a temptation. I have already made a promising start; and in times of revolution, field officers are quickly promoted. I could be one of those officers. I could have it all – all St Oswald's has to offer: bricks, guns and glory.

Should I take it? I wonder.

Pinchbeck would have jumped at the chance. Of course, Pinchbeck was content, if not happy, to pass unseen. But I am not he.

What do I want, then?

What have I *always* wanted?

If it were simply a matter of revenge, then I could simply have set fire to the main building instead of just the Gatehouse and let the whole wasps' nest go up in flames. I could have put arsenic in the staff tea urn or cocaine in the First Eleven's orange squash. But there wouldn't have been much fun in that, would there? Anyone can do those things. But no one can do what I have done; no one has *ever* done what I am doing. Still, one thing is missing from the victory tableau. My own face. The face of the artist among the crowd of extras. And as time passes, that small absence looms larger and larger.

Regard. In English it implies respect and admiration. In French it simply means 'a look'. That – to be *seen* – is all I ever wanted; to be more than just a fleeting glimpse, a twelfth man in this game of Gentlemen and Players. Even an invisible man may cast a shadow; but my shadow, grown long over years, has been lost among the dark corridors of St Oswald's.

No more. Already it has begun. The name of Snyde has already been mentioned. Pinchbeck, too. And before it ends, as St Oswald's spirals to its inevitable fate, I promise you: *I will be seen.*

Until then, I am content, for a time, to be an educator. But there are no exams to be passed in my subject. The only test is survival. In this I have a certain experience – Sunnybank Park must have taught me *something*, after all – but I like to think that the rest comes from natural talent. As a pupil of St Oswald's, that skill would have been refined out of me, to be replaced by Latin, Shakespeare and all the comfortable assurances of that very privileged world. For most of all, St Oswald's teaches *conformity*; team spirit; playing the game. A game in which Pat Bishop excels; which makes it all the more appropriate that he should be the first real casualty.

As I said before, the way to bring down St Oswald's is a blow to the heart, not the Head. And Bishop is the heart of the School; well-meaning; honest; respected and loved by boys and staff. A friend to those in trouble; a strong arm to the weak; a conscience; a coach; an inspiration. A man's man; a sportsman; a gentleman; a man who never delegates a single task, but works tirelessly and with joy for the good of St Oswald's. He has never married – how could he? Like Straitley, his devotion to the School precludes a normal family life. Base persons might suspect him of having other preferences. Especially in the current climate, where simply the desire to work with children is seen as legitimate cause for suspicion. But Bishop? *Bishop?*

No one believes it; and yet the staff room is already curiously divided. Some speak with bold indignation against the unthinkable charge (Straitley amongst them). Others (Bob Strange, the Nations, Jeff Light, Paddy McDonaugh) converse in lowered voices. Scraps of overheard cliché and conjecture – *There's no smoke without fire; Always thought he was too good to be true; A bit too friendly with the boys, know what I mean* – overhang the Common Room like smoke signals.

It's astonishing, once fear or self-interest has stripped away the veneer of comradeship, how easily one's friends may turn. I should know; and by now it must have begun to dawn on him, too.

There are three stages of reaction to such an accusation. One, denial. Two, anger. Three, capitulation. My father, of course, acted guilty from the start. Inarticulate; angry; confused. Pat Bishop must have given them a better performance. The Second Master of St Oswald's is not a man to be intimidated easily. But the proofs were there, un-deniable. Logs of chat-room conversations conducted after hours from his password-protected station at St Oswald's. A text message sent from Knight's phone to Bishop's own mobile on the evening of the fire. Pictures stored in his computer's memory. Many pictures, all of boys: some showing practices of which Pat, in his innocence, had never even heard.

Of course he denied it. First, with a kind of grim amuse-ment. Then with shock; indignation; rage; and finally a tearful confusion that did more to condemn him than anything else the police had found.

They'd searched his house. A number of photographs had been removed as evidence. School photographs; rugby teams; Bishop's boys throughout the years, smiling from the walls, all unaware that they would one day be used as evidence. Then there were the albums. Dozens of them, filled with boys; school trips, away matches, last-days-of-term, boys paddling in a Welsh stream, boys bare-chested on a day by the sea, lined up, limbs sleek, hair unkempt, young faces grinning at the camera.

So many boys, they'd said. Wasn't that a little – *unusual?*

Of course he'd protested. He was a teacher; all teachers keep such things. Straitley could have told them *that;* how year after year no one is forgotten, how certain faces linger unexpectedly. So many boys, passing like the seasons. It was natural to feel a certain nostalgia; more natural still, in the absence of family, to develop affection for the boys one taught, affection and—

What *kind* of affection? Here was the dirt. They sensed it, despite his protests, closing in like hyenas. He denied it with disgust. But they were gentle; spoke of stress; a breakdown; an offer of help.

His computer had been password-protected. Of course, someone else *might* have learned the password. Someone else might have used his computer. Someone else might even have planted the pictures. But the credit card that had been used to pay for them was his. The bank confirmed it; and Bishop was at a loss to explain how his own card could have been used to download hundreds of pictures on to the hard drive of his office PC.

Let us help you, Mr Bishop.

Ha. I know the type. And now they'd found his Achilles' heel; not lewdness as they'd suspected, but something infinitely more dangerous – his desire for approval. His fatal eagerness to please.

Tell us about the boys, Pat.

Most people don't see this in him at first. They see his size, his strength, his giant devotion. Underneath all that he is a pitiful creature; anxious; insecure; running his endless laps in an eternal effort to get ahead. But St Oswald's is a demanding master, and its memory is long. Nothing is forgotten, nothing put aside. Even in a career such as Bishop's there have been failures; errors of judgement. He knows it, as do I; but the boys are his security. Their

happy faces remind him that he is a success. Their youth
stimulates him—

Dirty laughter from the wings.

No, that wasn't what he'd meant.

Then what exactly *had* he meant? Crowding round now,
like dogs around a bear. Like the little boys around my
father as he cursed and swore, his big bear's rump hanging
off the seat of the Mean Machine as they squealed and
danced.

Tell us about the boys, Pat.

Tell us about Knight.

'Talk about daft,' said Roach today in the Common Room.
'I mean, how stupid can you get, using your own name and
credit card?'

Though he does not know it, Roach himself is in imminent
danger of discovery. Several threads lead to him already,
and his intimacy with Jeff Light and Gerry Grachvogel is
well established. Poor Gerry, so I hear, is already under
investigation, although his excessively nervous state makes
him a less than reliable witness. Internet pornography has also
been found on his workstation, paid for on his credit card.

'I always knew he was a funny bugger,' said Light. 'Bit too
chummy with the lads, know what I mean?'

Roach nodded. 'Just goes to show,' he said. 'You can't be
sure of anyone these days.'

How true that was. I followed the conversation from afar,
with a certain sense of ironic amusement. The gentlemen of
St Oswald's are a trusting lot; keys left in jacket pockets

slung over chairs; wallets in desk drawers; offices left un-locked. The theft of a credit-card number is the work of a moment; no skill is required; and the card can usually be replaced before the owner even suspects it is missing.

Roach's card was the only one I failed to return – he reported it missing before I could act – but Bishop, Light and Grachvogel have no such excuse. My one regret is that I failed to catch Roy Straitley – it would have been elegant to have sent them all to hell in the same handbasket – but the sly old fox doesn't even own a credit card, and besides, I don't think anyone would believe that he is computer-literate enough to turn on a PC.

Still, *that* can change. We've only just begun, he and I, and I've planned this game for so long that I really don't want it all to end too quickly. Already he is poised on the brink of dismissal; he remains only in the absence of the Second Master and because the desperate lack of staff members in his department makes him – but only for the duration of the crisis – indispensable.

It's his birthday on Friday. Bonfire Night: I imagine he's dreading it; old people so often do. I should send him a present; something nice to take his mind off the week's unpleasantness. So far I haven't had any ideas, but then again, I've had a lot on my plate recently.

Give me time.

5

I'VE NEVER LIKED BIRTHDAYS SINCE, YOU KNOW. TOYS, CAKE, paper hats and friends to tea; for years I longed for those things without ever getting them, just as I longed for St Oswald's and its enviable patina of wealth and respectability. For his birthdays, Leon went to restaurants, where he was allowed wine and had to wear a tie. Until I was thirteen I had never even been to a restaurant. *Waste of money*, grumbled John Snyde. Even before my mother left, my birthdays had been hasty occasions; shop-bought cakes and candles that were put away carefully in an old tobacco tin (with last year's icing-sugar crumbs still clinging to the pastel stubs) for next time. My presents came in Woolworth's bags, with the labels still on them; we sometimes sang 'Happy Birthday To You', but with the dogged, undemonstrative embarrassment of the working class.

When she left, of course, even that stopped. If he remembered, my father would give me money for my birthdays, telling me to *get summat you really want* – but I had no friends, no cards, no parties. Once Pepsi made an effort; pizza with birthday candles on it, and a chocolate cake that had sunk along one side. I tried to be grateful, but I knew I'd been cheated; in a way Pepsi's simple-minded endeavour was even worse than nothing at all. When there was nothing, I could at least forget what day it was.

But that year was different. That August – I remember it still with the supernatural clarity of certain dreams – hot and sweet and smelling of pepper and gunsmoke and resin and grass. A rapturous, terrible, illuminated time; I was two weeks shy of my thirteenth birthday, and my father was planning a surprise.

He hadn't said so in as many words; but I could sense it. He was excited; nervous; secretive. He veered from moments of extreme irritation at everything I did to bouts of tearful nostalgia, telling me I was growing up; offering me cans of beer; hoping that when I left home one day I wouldn't forget my poor old dad, who had always done his best for me.

Most surprisingly, he was spending money. John Snyde – who had always been so tight-fisted that he had recycled his used cigarette-butts, twisting the reclaimed tobacco into skinny roll-ups that he called 'Friday freebies' – had finally discovered the joy of retail therapy. A new suit – for interviews, he said. A gold chain with a medallion on it. A whole crate of Stella Artois – this from a man who purported to despise foreign beers – and six bottles of malt whiskey, which he kept in the shed at the back of the

Gatehouse, under an old candlewick bedspread. There were scratchcards – dozens of them; a new sofa; clothes for me (I was growing); underwear; T-shirts; records; shoes.

Then there were the phone calls. Late at night, when he thought I had gone to bed, I could hear him, talking in a low voice for what seemed like hours at a time. For a while I assumed he was calling a sex line – that or he was trying to get back with Pepsi; there was the same air of furtiveness about his whispering. Once, from the landing, I overheard; only a few words, but words that lodged uncomfortably at the back of my mind.

How much, then? Pause. *All right. It's for the best. The kid needs a mother.*

A mother?

Until then my own mother had written daily. Five years without a word, and now there was no stopping her; we were inundated with postcards, letters, parcels. Most of these remained under my bed, unopened. The air ticket to Paris, booked for September, remained sealed in its envelope, and I thought that perhaps my father had finally accepted that I wanted nothing more from Sharon Snyde; nothing that might remind me of my life before St Oswald's.

Then the letters suddenly stopped. In a way that should have troubled me more; it was as if she were planning something, something that she meant to keep from me.

But days passed and nothing happened. The phone calls ceased – or perhaps my father took more care – in any case I heard nothing else, and my thoughts returned, like a compass point, towards my north.

Leon, Leon, Leon; he was never far from my thoughts. Francesca's departure had found him distant and withdrawn. I tried hard to distract him, but nothing seemed to interest him any more; he disdained all our usual games; zigzagged continually from manically happy to sullen and uncooperative; and worse, now seemed to resent my intrusion into his solitary time, asking me with sarcasm whether I had any other friends and constantly making fun of me for being younger and less experienced than he was himself.

If only he had known. As far as that went, I was light-years ahead. I had conquered Mr Bray, after all; soon I was to take my conquests further. But with Leon I had always felt awkward, young, painfully eager to please. He sensed it; and now it made him cruel. He was at that age when everything seems sharp and new and obvious; when adults are immeasurably stupid; when the rule of self overrides all others; and a lethal cocktail of hormones amplifies every emotion to a nightmarish intensity.

Worst of all, he was in love. Nail-bitingly, miserably, cruelly in love with Francesca Tynan, who had gone back to school in Cheshire, and with whom he spoke almost every day in secret on the phone, running up enormous bills that would be discovered – too late – at the end of the quarter.

'Nothing else compares,' he said – not for the first time. He was in his manic phase; soon he would lapse into sarcasm and open contempt. 'You can talk about it, like the rest of them, but you don't know what it's like. Me, I've *done* it. I've actually done it. The closest *you*'ll ever get is a fumble behind the lockers with your friends from Junior Six.'

I made a face, keeping it light, pretending it was a joke. But it was not. There was something vicious, almost feral about Leon on these occasions; his hair hung over his eyes; his face was pale; a sour smell came from his body; and there was a new scattering of pimples around his mouth.

'I bet you'd like that, queerboy, Queenie, bet you'd like that, wouldn't you, eh?' He looked at me, and I saw a lethal kind of understanding in his grey eyes. '*Queenie*,' he repeated, with a nasty snigger, and then the wind changed and the sun came out and he was Leon again, talking about a concert he was planning to see; about Francesca's hair and how it caught the light; a record he had bought; Francesca's legs and how long they were; the new Bond movie. For a time I could almost believe he really had been joking; then I remembered the chilly intelligence in his eyes and wondered uneasily how I had given myself away.

I should have put an end to it right there and then. I knew that it wasn't going to get any better. But I was helpless; irrational; torn. Something in me still believed that I could turn him round; that everything could be as it was before. I *had* to believe it; it was the only speck of hope on my otherwise bleak horizon. Besides, he needed me. He wouldn't see Francesca again until Christmas at least. That gave me almost five months. Five months to cure him of his obsession, to draw the poison that had infected our comfortable fellowship.

Oh, I had to indulge him. More than was good for him, I

suppose. However, there's nothing quite so vicious as a lover, unless you count the terminally ill, with whom they share many unpleasant characteristics. Both are selfish; withdrawn; manipulative; unstable; reserving all their sweetness for the loved one (or themselves) and turning on their friends like rabid dogs. That was Leon; and yet I treasured him more than ever, now that he finally shared my suffering.

There is a perverse satisfaction in picking at a scab. Lovers do it all the time; seeking out the most intense sources of pain and indulging them, sacrificing themselves again and again for the sake of the loved object with a dogged stupidity that poets have often mistaken for selflessness. With Leon, it was talking about Francesca. With me, it was listening to him. After a while it grew unbearable – love, like cancer, tends to dominate the life of the sufferer so fully that they lose the ability to conduct a conversation on any other subject (so numbingly dull for the listener) – and I found myself trying with increasing desperation to find ways of breaking through the tedium of Leon's obsession.

'I dare you.' That was me, standing outside the record shop. 'Go on, I dare you. That is, if you've still got the balls.'

He looked at me, surprised, then looked beyond me into the shop. Something crossed his face – a shadow, perhaps, of pleasures past. Then he grinned, and I now thought I saw a faint reflection of the old, careless, loveless Leon in his grey eyes.

'You talking to *me*?' he said.

*   *   *

And so we played – the one game this new Leon still accepted to play. And with the game, the 'treatment' began; unpleasant, even brutish, perhaps, but necessary, just as aggressive chemotherapy can be used to attack cancers. And there was plenty of aggression in both of us; it was simply a question of turning it outwards rather than in.

We began with theft. Small things first: records; books; clothes that we dumped in our little hideout in the woods behind St Oswald's. The treatment turned to stronger fare. We graffiti-ed walls and smashed bus shelters. We threw stones at passing cars; pushed over gravestones in the old churchyard; shouted obscenities at elderly dog-walkers who entered our domain. During that fortnight I veered between utter wretchedness and overwhelming joy; we were together again, Butch and Sundance – and for minutes at a time Francesca was forgotten; the thrill of her eclipsed by a stronger, more dangerous rush.

But it never lasted. My treatment was good for the symptoms, not the cause, and I discovered to my chagrin that my patient needed increasingly stronger doses of excitement if he was to respond at all. More and more often it fell to me to think of new things to do, and I found myself struggling to imagine more outrageous exploits for the two of us to perform.

'Record shop?'

'Nah.'

'Graveyard?'

'Banal.'

'Bandstand?'

'Done it.' It was true; the night before, we had broken into the municipal park and smashed every seat on the town bandstand as well as the little railings that surrounded it. I'd felt bad doing it; remembered going into the park with my mother when I was very small; the summer smells of cut grass and hot-dogs and candyfloss; the sound of the colliery band. I remembered Sharon Snyde sitting in one of those blue plastic chairs, smoking a cigarette, while I marched up and down going *pom-pom-pom* on an invisible drum, and for a second I felt horribly lost. That was me aged six; that was when I still had a mother who smelt of cigarettes and Cinnabar, and there was nothing braver and more splendid than a town bandstand in summer, and only bad people smashed things up.

'What's up, Pinchbeck?' It was already late; in the moonlight Leon's face was slick and dark and knowing. 'Had enough already?'

I had. More than enough. But I couldn't tell Leon; it was my treatment, after all.

'Come on,' he'd urged. 'Think of it as a lesson in taste.'

I had, and my retaliation had been swift. Leon had ordered me to demolish the bandstand; I reciprocated by daring him to tie tin cans to the exhausts of all the cars parked outside the police station. Our stakes escalated; our outrages grew increasingly complicated, even surreal (a row of dead pigeons tied to the railings of the public park; a series of colourful murals on the side of the Methodist church); we defaced walls, broke windows and frightened small children from one end of town to the other. Only one place remained.

'St Oswald's.'

'No way.' So far we had avoided the School grounds – barring a little artistic self-expression on the walls of the Games Pavilion. My thirteenth birthday was days away, and with it approached my mysterious and long-anticipated surprise. My father played it cool, but I could tell he was making an effort. He was dry; he had started exercising; the house was immaculate; and his face had developed a hard, dry grin that reflected nothing of what was going on inside. He looked like Clint Eastwood in *High Plains Drifter*; a fat Clint, in any case, but with that same slitty-eyed air of concentration on some eventual, apocalyptic showdown. I approved – it showed resolution – and I didn't want to blow it all now over some idiotic stunt.

'Come on, Pinchbeck. *Fac ut vivas*. Live a little.'

'What's the point?' It wouldn't do to seem too reluctant; Leon would think I was afraid to take the dare. 'We've done St Oswald's a million times.'

'Not this.' His eyes were shining. 'I dare you – I dare you to climb to the top of the Chapel roof.' Then he smiled at me, and at that point I saw the man he might have been; his subversive charm; his irrepressible humour. It struck me like a fist, my love for him; the single pure emotion of all my complicated, grubby adolescence. It occurred to me then that if he had asked me to *jump* from the Chapel roof, I would probably have said yes.

'The *roof?*'

He nodded.

I was almost laughing. 'All right, I will,' I said. 'I'll bring you back a souvenir.'

'No need,' he said. 'I'll get it myself. What?' – seeing my surprise – 'You don't think I'd let you go up there on your own, do you?'

6

St Oswald's Grammar School for Boys
Wednesday, 3rd November

FIVE DAYS, AND STILL NO WORD OF KNIGHT. NO WORD OF Bishop either, though I saw him in Tesco's the other day, looking dazed before a trolley piled high with cat food (I don't even think Pat Bishop *has* a cat). I spoke to him, but he didn't answer. He looked like a man under heavy medication, and I have to admit that I didn't have the courage to pursue the conversation.

Still, I know that Marlene calls every day to make sure he is all right – the woman has a heart, which is more than can be said of the Headmaster, who has forbidden any member of the School to communicate with Bishop until matters have been cleared up.

The police were here all day again, three of them, working through the staff, boys, secretaries and such with the machine efficiency of School Inspectors. A helpline has been set up, encouraging boys to confirm anonymously what has already been established. Many boys have called it – most of them to insist that Mr Bishop couldn't possibly have done anything wrong. Others are being interviewed in and out of lesson-time.

It makes the boys unteachable. My form don't want to talk about anything else, but as I have been told quite clearly that to discuss the matter might harm Pat's case, I must insist that they do not. Many of them are deeply upset; I found Brasenose crying in the Middle Corridor toilets during Period 4 Latin, and even Allen-Jones and McNair, who can usually be relied upon to see the ridiculous in most things, were listless and unresponsive. All my form is – even Anderton-Pullitt seems odder than usual, and has developed a new, extravagant limp to go with all his other peculiarities.

The most recent word on the grapevine is that Gerry Grachvogel, too, has been questioned and may be charged. Other, more outrageous rumours are also running, so that according to gossip, all absentee staff members have become suspects.

Devine's name has been mentioned, and he *is* absent today, although that in itself shouldn't mean anything. It's ridiculous; but it was in the *Examiner* yesterday morning, citing 'sources within the School' (boys, most probably) and hinting that a paedophile ring of long duration and un-precedented importance has been uncovered within the 'hallowed portals' [sic] of the Dear Old Place.

As I said, ridiculous. I've been a master at St Oswald's for thirty-three years, and I know what I'm talking about. Such a thing could never have happened here; not because we think we're better than anywhere else (whatever the *Examiner* may think), but simply because in a place like St Oswald's, no secret can be kept for long. From Bob Strange, perhaps; rooted in his office working out timetables; or from the Suits, who never see anything unless it comes to them in an e-mail attachment. But from *me*? From the *boys*? Never.

Oh, I've seen my share of irregular colleagues. There was Dr Jehu (Oxon.), who turned out afterwards to be just plain Mr Jehu, from the University of Durham, and who had a reputation, it seemed. That was years ago, before such things made the news, and he left quietly and without scandal, as most of them do, with no harm done. Or Mr Tythe-Weaver, the art teacher who introduced life modelling *au naturel*. Or Mr Groper, who developed that unfortunate fixation on a young English student forty years his junior. Or even our own Grachvogel, who all the boys know to be homosexual – and harmless – but who fears terribly for his job if the Governors were to find out. A bit late for that, I'm afraid; but he isn't a *pervert*, as the *Examiner* crowingly suggests. Light may well be a boorish ass, but I don't think he is any more of a pervert than Grachvogel. Devine? Don't make me laugh. And as for Bishop – well. I know Bishop. More importantly, the boys know him, love him, and believe me, if there had been any breath of irregularity about him, they would have been the first to scent it out. Boys have an instinct for such things, and in a school like St Oswald's, rumours disseminate at epidemic speed. Understand this: I have been teaching alongside Pat Bishop for thirty-three years, and if there had been any kind of truth in these accusations, I would have known. The boys would have told me.

Within the Common Room, however, the polarization continues. Many colleagues will not speak of the matter at all, for fear of being implicated in the scandal. Some (though not many) are openly contemptuous of the accusations. Others take the opportunity to spread quiet, right-thinking slander.

Penny Nation is one of these. I remember the description of her in Keane's notebook – *poisonous do-gooder* – and I wonder how I could have worked alongside her for so many years without noticing her essential malice.

'A Second Master should be like the Prime Minister,' she was saying in the Common Room this lunch-time. 'Happily married – like Geoff and me' – quick smile at her Capitaine, today attired in navy pin-stripe that perfectly matches Penny's skirt-and-sweater combination. There was a small silver fish in his lapel. 'That way, there's no *possible* cause for suspicion, is there?' Penny went on. 'In any case, if you're going to be working with *children*' – she says the word in a syrupy, Walt Disney voiceover tone, as if the very thought of children makes her want to melt – 'then you really need to have one of your own, don't you?'

That smile again. I wonder if she sees her husband in Pat's job in some not-too-distant future. He's certainly ambitious enough; a devout church-goer; a family man; a gentleman player; a veteran of many courses.

He isn't the only one with ideas. Eric Scoones has been putting the boot in – rather to my surprise, as I'd always thought of Eric as a fair-minded chap in spite of his resentment at being passed over for promotion. It seems I was wrong; listening to the talk in the Common Room this afternoon I was shocked to hear him siding with the Nations against Hillary Monument – who has always been pro-Pat and who, being at the end of his career, has nothing to lose by nailing his colours to the mast.

'Ten to one we'll find it's some ghastly mistake,' Monument was saying. 'These computers – who trusts them? Always breaking down. And that – what d'you call it? Spam. That's it. Ten to one old Pat got some Spam in his computer and didn't know what it was. As for Grachvogel, he hasn't even been *arrested*. Questioning, that's all it is. Helping the police with their inquiries.'

Eric gave a dismissive grunt. 'You'll see,' he said (a man who never uses computers any more than I do myself). 'The trouble with you is that you're too trusting. That's what they all say, isn't it, when some bloke gets up on a motorway bridge and shoots ten people dead. It's always, "And he was such a nice chap", isn't it? Or some scoutmaster who's been fettling little lads for years – "Ooh, and the kids loved him, you know, never thought for a minute." That's the trouble. No one ever thinks. No one thinks it might happen in our own backyard. Besides, what do we really know about Pat Bishop? Oh, he *plays* it straight – well he would, wouldn't he? But what do we really know about him? Or any of our colleagues, for that matter?'

It was a remark that troubled me then, and has continued to do so ever since. Eric's had run-ins with Pat for years, but I'd always thought, like my own little spats with Dr Devine, that it was nothing personal. He's bitter, of course. A good teacher – if a little old-fashioned – and might have made a good Head of Year if he'd made a bit more of an effort with the management. But deep down I'd always thought he was loyal. If ever I'd expected any of my colleagues to stab poor Bishop in the back, it would not have been Eric. Now I'm not so sure; there was a look in his face today in the Common Room that told me more than I'd ever wanted to know about Eric Scoones. He's always been a gossip, of course; but it has taken me all these years to see the gleeful *Schadenfreude* in my old friend's eyes.

I am sorry for it. But he was right. What do we *really* know about our colleagues? Thirty-three years, and what do we know? For me, the unpleasant revelation has not been about Pat at all, but about the rest of them. Scoones. The Nations. Roach, who is terrified that his friendship with Light and Grachvogel might prejudice his case with the police. Beard, who sees the whole business as a personal affront to the Computer Science department. Meek, who merely repeats everything Beard tells him. Easy, who follows the majority. McDonaugh, who announced at Break that only a pervert could have appointed that queer Grachvogel in a teaching post anyway.

The worst of it is that no one speaks against them now;

even Kitty, who has always been friendly with Gerry Grachvogel and who has invited Bishop to dinner several times, said nothing at lunch-time, but simply looked into her coffee mug with faint distaste and would not meet my eye. She has other things on her mind, I know. Still, it was a moment I could have done without. You may have noticed I'm rather fond of Kitty Teague.

Still, I'm relieved to see that in one or two cases at least, sanity still reigns. Chris Keane and Dianne Dare are among the very few not to have been infected. They were standing by the window as I fetched my tea, still raging against the colleagues who had so summarily condemned Bishop without trial.

'I think everyone's entitled to a fair hearing,' said Keane, after I had aired my feelings a little more. 'I don't really know Mr Bishop, of course, but I have to say he doesn't strike me as the type, somehow.'

'I agree,' said Miss Dare. 'Besides, the boys seem genuinely fond of him.'

'They are,' I said loudly, with a defiant glance at the moral majority. 'This is a mistake.'

'Or a set-up,' said Keane thoughtfully.

'A set-up?'

'Why not?' He shrugged. 'Someone with a grudge. A discontented staff member. An ex-pupil. Anyone. All you'd need would be access to the School, plus a certain degree of computer literacy—'

Computers. I knew we were better off without them. But Keane's words had touched a nerve – in fact, I wondered why on earth I hadn't thought of it myself. Nothing damages a school more cruelly than a sex scandal. Hadn't something similar happened once at Sunnybank Park? Hadn't I seen it myself, too, in the days of the Old Head?

Of course, Shakeshafte's tastes ran, not to boys, but to secretaries and young female members of staff. Such affairs seldom go beyond the stage of tittle-tattle; they are resolved between adults; they rarely make it outside the gates.

But this is different. The papers have declared open season on the teaching profession. Paedophile stories dominate the popular press. Not a week passes without some new accusation. Headteacher, scoutmaster, police officer, priest. All fair game.

'It's possible.' That was Meek, who had been following our conversation. I hadn't expected *him* to voice an opinion; so far he'd done little but nod energetically every time Beard spoke. 'I imagine there are plenty of people who might have a grudge against St Oswald's,' went on Meek in his small voice. 'Fallow, for instance. Or Knight.'

'Knight?' There was a silence. In the backwash of the bigger scandal I'd almost forgotten my juvenile runaway. 'Knight couldn't be responsible for any of this.'

'Why not?' said Keane. 'He fits the type.'

Oh yes. He fitted. I saw Eric Scoones' expression darken; he was listening, and I could see from the insouciant looks on my colleagues' faces that they too were following the exchange. 'Staff passwords aren't difficult to get hold of, either,' said Meek. 'I mean, anyone with access to the administration panel—'

'That's ridiculous,' said Mr Beard. 'Those passwords are absolutely secret.'

'Yours is *AMANDA*,' said Keane, smiling. 'Your daughter's name. Mr Bishop's is *GO-JONNY-GO* – not much imagination required there, for such a keen rugby fan. Gerry's is probably something from the *X-Files*. *MULDER*, perhaps, or *SCULLY—*'

Miss Dare laughed. 'Tell me,' she said, 'are you a professional spy or is it just a hobby?'

'I pay attention,' said Keane.

But Scoones was still unconvinced. 'No boy of ours would dare,' he said. 'Especially not that little runt.'

'Why not?' said Keane.

'He just wouldn't,' said Scoones contemptuously. 'You need balls to go up against St Oswald's.'

'Or brains,' said Keane. 'What? You're really telling me it's *never* happened before?'

7

Thursday, 4th November

HOW VERY INCONVENIENT. JUST AS I WAS ABOUT TO DEAL with Bishop, too. To make myself feel better I went to the internet café in town, accessed Knight's hotmail address (the police must surely be monitoring that by now) and sent out a few nicely abusive e-mails to selected members of St Oswald's staff. It gave me an outlet for some of my annoyance; and, I trust, will maintain the hope that Knight is still alive.

I then made my way to my own flat, where I e-mailed a new piece from Mole to the *Examiner*. I sent a text message to Devine's mobile from Knight's, and after that I phoned Bishop, adopting an accent and disguising my voice. I was feeling rather better by then – it's funny how dealing with tedious business can put you in a good mood – and after a bit of initial heavy breathing I delivered my poisonous message.

I thought his voice sounded thicker than usual, as if he were on some kind of medication. Of course it was almost midnight by then, and he might well have been asleep. I myself don't need a great deal of sleep – three or four hours are usually ample – and I rarely dream. I'm always rather surprised at the way other people cave in if they haven't had their eight or ten hours, and most of them seem to spend half the night dreaming; useless, jumbled dreams that they always want to tell other people about afterwards. I guessed Bishop was a heavy sleeper; a colourful dreamer; a Freudian analyser. Not tonight, though. Tonight I thought he might have other things on his mind.

I phoned again an hour later. This time Bishop's voice was as thick as my father's after a night on the town. 'What do you want?' His bull's roar, distorted by the line.

'You know what we want.' That *we*. Always a help when spreading paranoia. 'We want justice. We want you dealt with, you filthy pervert.'

By this time, of course, he should have hung up. But Bishop has never been a quick thinker. Instead he blustered, angry; tried to argue. 'Anonymous calls? That the best you can do? Let me tell you something—'

'No, Bishop. Let me tell *you*.' My telephone voice is thin and spidery, cutting through the static. 'We know what you've been up to. We know where you live. We'll get you. It's just a matter of time.'

Click.

Nothing fancy, as you see. But it has already worked marvellously with Grachvogel – who now keeps the phone permanently off the hook. Tonight, in fact, I made a little trip up to his place, just to make sure. At one point I was almost convinced I saw someone peeping out from between the living-room curtains, but I was gloved and hooded, and I knew he'd never dare to come out of the house.

Afterwards, for the third time, I phoned Bishop.

'We're getting closer,' I announced in my spidery voice.

'Who are you?' He was alert this time, with a new shrillness to his tone. 'What do you want, for God's sake?'

Click.

Then home, and bed, for the next four hours.

This time, I dreamed.

8

'WHAT'S THE MATTER, PINCHBECK?'

August twenty-third; the eve of my thirteenth birthday. We were standing in front of the School portcullis,
a pretentious little add-on from the nineteenth century,
which marks the entrance to the library and the Chapel
gate. It was one of my favourite parts of the School,
straight from the pages of a Walter Scott novel, with
the School crest in red and gilt above the School motto
(quite a recent addition, but a word or two of Latin
speaks volumes to the fee-paying parents). *Audere, agere,
auferre.*

Leon grinned at me, his hair hanging disreputably in his
eyes. 'Admit it, Queenie,' he said in a mocking tone. 'Looks
a lot higher from down here, doesn't it?'

I shrugged. His teasing was harmless enough for the
moment, but I could read the signs. If I weakened, if I
seemed in the least bit annoyed at his use of that silly

nickname, then he would strike with the full force of his sarcasm and contempt.

'It's a long way up,' I said carelessly. 'But I've been there before. It's easy when you know how.'

'Really?' I could see he didn't believe me. 'Show me, then.'

I didn't want to. My father's passkeys were a secret I had never meant to reveal to anyone, not even (and perhaps especially not) Leon. But still I could feel them, deep in my jeans pocket, daring me to say it, to share it, to cross that final, forbidden line.

Leon was watching me like a housecat who isn't sure whether it wants to play with the mouse or unravel its guts. I had a sudden, overpowering memory of him in the garden with Francesca, one hand laid casually over one of hers, his skin tawny-green in the dappled shade. No wonder he loved her. How could I possibly compete? She had shared something with him, a secret, a thing of power that I could never hope to duplicate.

Or maybe now, I could.

'Wow.' Leon's eyes widened as he saw the keys. 'Where did you get *those?*'

'Nicked them,' I said. 'Off Big John's desk, at the end of term.' In spite of myself, I grinned at the look on my friend's face. 'Had them copied at the key place at lunch-time, then put them back right where I found them.' That was mostly true; I'd had it done just after that last disaster, while my father lay despondent and blind drunk in his bedroom. 'Slack bastard never noticed.'

Now Leon was watching me with a new light in his eyes. It was admiring, but it made me a little uneasy, too. 'Well, well,' he said at last. 'And there was I thinking you were just another little Lower School squirt with no ideas and no balls. And you never told anyone?'

I shook my head.

'Well, good for you,' said Leon softly, and slowly his face lit with his tenderest, most captivating smile. 'It's our secret, then.'

There is something ultimately magical in the sharing of secrets. I felt it then, as I showed Leon around my empire, in spite of the accompanying pang of regret. The passage-ways and alcoves, the hidden rooftops and secret cellars of St Oswald's were no longer mine. Now they belonged to Leon as well.

We went out via a window on the Upper Corridor. I had already turned off the burglar alarm in our part of the School before locking the door carefully behind us. It was late; eleven o'clock at least, and my father's rounds were long finished. No one would come at this time. No one would suspect our presence.

The window gave on to the library roof. I climbed out with practised ease; grinning, Leon followed. Here was a gentle slope of thick, mossy stone tiles, pitching down to a deep, lead-lined gutter. There was a walkway all around this gutter, designed so that a Porter might follow it with a broom, removing the accumulated leaves and detritus, although my father's fear of heights meant that he had never attempted this. As far as I could tell he had never even checked the leadwork, and as a result the gutters were filled with silt and debris.

I looked up. The moon was nearly full, magical against a purple-brown sky. From time to time little clouds smudged across it, but it was still bright enough to underline every chimney, every gutter and slate in indigo ink. Behind me, I heard Leon draw a long, wavering breath. '*Wow!*'

I looked down; far beneath me I could see the Gatehouse, all lit up like a Christmas lantern. My father would be there, watching TV, perhaps, or doing press-ups in front of the mirror. He didn't seem to mind my being out at night; it had been months since he had questioned where I went and with whom.

'Wow,' repeated Leon.

I grinned, feeling absurdly proud, as if I had built it all myself. I grabbed hold of a climbing-rope that I had strung into place a few months before, and hoisted myself up on to the ridge. The chimneys towered over me like kings, their heavy crowns black against the sky. Above them, the stars.

'Come on!'

I teetered, arms spread, gathering in the night. For a second I felt as if I could step right out into the spangled air and fly.

'Come *on!*'

Slowly, Leon followed me. Moonlight made ghosts of both of us. His face was pale and blank – a child's face of wonder. 'Wow.'

'That's not all.'

Emboldened by success, I led him on to the walkway; broad path inked by shadows. I held his hand; he did not question it but followed me, docile, one arm held out across the tightrope space. Twice I warned him; a loose stone here, a broken ladder there.

'Just how long have you been coming here, anyway?'

'A while.'

'Jesus.'

'D'you like it?'

'Oh, *yeah*.'

After half an hour of climbing and scrambling, we stopped to rest on the flat, broad parapet above the Chapel roof. The heavy stone slates kept the day's heat, and even now they were still warm. We lay on the parapet, gargoyles at our feet. Leon produced a pack of cigarettes and we shared one, watching as the town spread out like a blanket of lights.

'This is amazing. I can't believe you never said.'

'Told you now, haven't I?'

'Hm.'

He was lying beside me; hands tucked behind his head. One elbow touched mine; I could feel its pressure, like a point of heat.

'Imagine having sex up here,' he said. 'You could stay all night if you wanted to, and no one would ever know.' I thought his tone was slightly reproachful; imagining nights with lovely Francesca in the shadow of the rooftop kings.

'I guess.'

I didn't want to think of that – of them. The knowledge

– like an express train – passed silently between us. His closeness was unbearable; it itched like a nettle rash. I could smell his sweat and the cigarette smoke and the slightly oily, musky scent of his too-long hair. He was staring up at the sky, his eyes brimful of stars.

Slyly I put out my hand; felt his shoulder in five little pinpoints of heat at my fingertips. Leon did not react. Slowly I opened my hand; my hand trespassed across his sleeve, his arm, his chest. I was not thinking; my hand seemed divorced from my body.

'Do you miss her? Francesca, I mean?' My voice trembled, catching at the end of the phrase in an involuntary squeak.

Leon grinned. His own voice had broken months before, and he loved to tease me about my immaturity. 'Aw, Pinch-beck. You're such a kid.'

'I was only asking.'

'A little kid.'

'Shut up, Leon.'

'Did you think it was the real deal? Moonlight and morons and love and romance? Jesus, Pinchbeck, how banal can you get?'

'Shut *up*, Leon.' My face burned; I thought of starlight; winter; ice.

He laughed. 'Sorry to disillusion you, Queenie.'

'What do you mean?'

'I mean, *love*, for Christ's sake. She was just a shag.'

That shocked me. 'She wasn't.' I thought of Francesca; her long hair; her languid limbs. I thought of Leon and of everything I had sacrificed for him; for romance; for the anguish and exhilaration of sharing his passion. 'You know she wasn't. And *don't* call me Queenie.'

'Or what?' Now he sat up, eyes shining.

'Come on, Leon. Don't muck about.'

'You thought she was the first, didn't you?' He grinned. 'Oh, Pinchbeck. Grow up. You're starting to sound just like her, you know. I mean, look at you, getting all worked up about it, trying to cure me of my broken heart, as if I could ever care that much about a *girl*—'

'But *you* said—'

'I was winding you up, moron. Couldn't you tell?'

Blankly, I shook my head.

Leon punched my arm, not without affection. 'Queenie. You're *such* a romantic. And she *was* sort of sweet, even if she was only a girl. But she wasn't the first. Not even the best I've had, to be honest. And definitely – definitely – not the last.'

'I don't believe you,' I said.

'You don't? Listen, kid.' Laughing, full of energy now, the fine hairs on his arms bleached-blackened silver in the moonlight. 'Did I ever tell you why I got chucked out of my last school?'

'No. Why?'

'I shagged a master, Queenie. Mr Weeks, metalwork. In the shop, after hours. No end of a fuss—'

'No!' Now I began to laugh with him in sheer outrage.

'Said he loved me. Stupid bugger. Wrote me letters.'

'No.' Eyes wide. '*No!*'

'No one blamed *me*. Corruption, they said. Susceptible

lad, dangerous pervert. Identity undisclosed to protect the innocent. It was all over the papers at the time.'

'Wow.' There was no doubt in my mind he was telling the truth. It explained so much; his indifference; his sexual precocity; his daring. God, his daring. 'What happened?'

Leon shrugged. '*Pactum factum*. Bugger went down. Seven years. Felt a bit sorry for him, really.' He smiled indulgently. 'He was all right, Mr Weeks. Used to take me to clubs and everything. Ugly, though. Big fat gut on him. And *old* – I mean, *thirty*—'

'God, Leon!'

'Yeah, well. You don't have to look. And he gave me stuff – money, CDs, this watch that cost like five hundred quid—'

'No!'

'Anyway, my mum went spare. I had to have counselling, and everything. Might have scarred me, Mother says. I might never recover.'

'And what was it—' My head was reeling with the night and with his revelations. I swallowed, dry-throated. 'What was it—'

'*Like?*' He turned to me, grinning, and pulled me towards him. 'You mean, you want to know what it was *like?*'

Time lurched. An adventure-story enthusiast, I had read a great deal about time *stopping still*; as in: '*for an instant time stopped still as the cannibals crept closer to the helpless boys.*' In this case, however, I distinctly felt it *lurch*, like a goods train in a hurry pulling out of a station. Once more I was disconnected; my hands like birds swooping and fluttering; Leon's mouth on mine, his hands on mine, pulling at my clothes with delicious intent.

He was still laughing; a boy of light and darkness; a ghost; and beneath me I could feel the rough boy-warmth of the roof slates, the delightful friction of skin against fabric. I felt close to oblivion; thrilled and terrified; revolted and delirious with irrational joy. My sense of danger had evaporated; I was nothing but skin; every inch a million points of helpless sensation. Random thoughts flitted across my mind like fireflies.

He had never loved her.

Love was *banal*.

He could never care that much for a girl.

Oh, Leon. Leon.

He shed his shirt; struggled with my fly; all the time I was laughing and crying and he was talking and laughing; words I could barely hear above the seismic pounding of my heart.

Then it stopped.

Just like that. Freeze-frame on our naked, half-naked selves; I in the pillar of shadow that ran alongside the tall chimney-stack; he in the moonlight, a statue of ice. Yin and yang; my face illuminated; his darkening in surprise; shock; anger.

'Leon—'

'Jesus.'

'Leon, I'm sorry, I should have—'

'*Jesus!*' He recoiled; his hands held out now as if to ward me off. 'Jesus, Pinchbeck—'

Time. Time lurched. His face, scarred with hate and disgust. His hands, pushing me away into the dark.

Words struggled in me like tadpoles in a too-small jar. Nothing came out. Losing balance, I fell back against the chimney-stack, not speaking, not crying, not even angry. That came later.

'You little pervert!' Leon's voice, wavering, incredulous. 'You fucking – little *pervert*!'

The contempt, the hatred in that voice told me everything I needed to know. I wailed aloud; a long, desperate wail of bitterness and loss, and then I ran, my sneakers fast and quiet on the mossy slates, over the parapet and along the walkway.

Leon followed me, swearing, heavy with rage. But he didn't know the rooftops. I heard him, far behind, stumbling, crashing heedlessly across the tiles in pursuit. Slates fell in his wake, exploding like mortars into the courtyard below. Crossing over from the Chapel side he skidded and fell; a chimney broke his fall; the impact seemed to shudder through every gutter, every brick and pipe. I grabbed hold of an elder tree, spindly branches poking out of a long-blocked drainage grate, and hoisted myself further up. Behind me, Leon scrabbled higher, grunting obscenities.

I ran on instinct; there was no point in trying to reason with him now. My father's rages were just the same; and in my mind I was nine again, ducking the deadly arc of his fist. Later, perhaps, I could explain to Leon. Later, when he had had time to think. For the moment all I wanted was to get away.

I did not waste time trying to get back to the library window. The Bell Tower was closer, with its little balconies half-rotten with lichen and pigeon droppings. The Bell Tower was another St Oswald's conceit; a little arched boxlike structure, which, to my knowledge, had never housed a bell. Down one side ran a steep-slanting lead gutter, leading to an overflow pipe that shot rainwater out into a deep and pigeon-stinking well between the buildings. On the other side the drop was sheer; a narrow ledge was all that stood between the trespasser and the North Quad, some two hundred feet below.

Carefully, I looked down.

I knew from my travels across the roofscape that Straitley's room was just below me, and that the window that gave on to its crumbling balcony was loose. I teetered on the walkway, trying to gauge the distance from where I was standing, then jumped lightly on to the parapet, then down into the shelter of the small balcony.

The window, as I'd hoped, was easy to force open. I scrambled through, heedless of the broken catch that gouged my back, and at once the burglar alarm sounded, a high, unbearable squealing that deafened and disoriented me.

Panicked, I wriggled back the way I had come. In the Quad below, the security lights popped on, and I ducked down to escape the harsh illumination, cursing helplessly.

Everything was wrong. I had disabled the alarm in the library wing; but in my panic and confusion I had forgotten that the Bell Tower's alarm was still on; and now the siren was screaming, screaming like the golden bird in 'Jack and the Beanstalk', there was no way my father could miss it, and Leon was still up here with me somewhere, Leon was trapped—

I stood on the balcony and jumped across on to the walkway, looking down as I did into the illuminated Quad. Two figures stood there, looking up, their giant shadows fanning around them like a hand of cards. I ducked into the shelter of the Bell Tower, crawled forward to the edge of the roof and glanced down once again.

Pat Bishop was watching me from the courtyard, my father at his side.

9

'THERE. UP THERE.' RADIO VOICES ACROSS A FAR DISTANCE. I'd ducked back, of course, but Bishop had seen the move-ment, the round dark head against the luminous sky. 'Boys on the roof.'

Boys. Of course, he'd assumed that.

'How many boys?' That was Bishop; younger then, tense and fit and only slightly red-faced.

'Don't know, sir. I'd say at least two.'

Once more I dared a glance below. My father was still watching, his white face upturned and blind. Bishop was already moving fast. He was heavy, all muscle. My father followed him at a slower pace, his huge shadow doubled and trebled by the lights. I did not bother to watch them any more. I knew already where they were heading.

My father had turned off the burglar alarm. The megaphone was Bishop's idea; he used it on Sports Days and fire drills, and it made his voice impossibly nasal and penetrating.

'*You boys!*' he began. '*Stay where you are! Do not attempt to climb down! Help is on the way!*'

That's how Bishop spoke in a crisis; like a character from some American action movie. I could tell he was enjoying his role; the newly appointed Second Master; man of action; troubleshooter; counsellor to the world.

In fifteen years he has hardly changed – that particular brand of righteous arrogance seldom does. Even then he thought he could put things right with nothing but a megaphone and a few glib words.

It was one thirty; the moon had set; the sky, never quite dark at that time of year, had taken on a sheer translucent glow. Above me, somewhere on the Chapel roof, Leon was waiting; cool, collected; sitting it out. Someone had called the fire brigade; already I could hear sirens in the distance, Dopplering towards us. Soon, we would be overrun.

'*Indicate your position!*' Bishop again, wielding his megaphone with a flourish. '*Repeat, indicate your position!*'

Still nothing from Leon. I wondered whether he had managed to find the library window on his own; whether he was trapped or running silently down the corridors, looking for a way out.

Somewhere above me a slate rattled. There came a slithering sound – his trainers against the lead gutter. And now I could see him too – just a glimpse of his head above the Chapel parapet. As I watched he began to move – so slowly that it was almost imperceptible – on to the narrow walkway that led towards the Bell Tower.

It made sense, I thought. He must have known that the library-window option was impossible now; that low, slanting roof ran right alongside the Chapel building, and he would be in plain sight if he tried. The Bell Tower was higher, but more secure; up there he would be able to hide. I was on the other side, however; if I joined him from where I was standing, I would be instantly visible from below. I resolved to go around, to take the long way across the Observatory roof and join him in the shadows where we could hide.

'*Boys! Listen!*' It was Bishop's voice, so highly amplified that I clapped my hands over my ears. '*You're not in any trouble!*' I turned away to hide a nervous grin; he was so convincing that he almost convinced himself. '*Just stay where you are! Repeat! Stay where you are!*'

Leon, of course, was not fooled. The system, we knew, was run on such platitudes.

'*You're not in any trouble!*' I imagined Leon's grin at that perennial lie, and felt a sudden pain in my heart that I was not there with him to share his amusement. It would have been so fine, I thought; Butch and Sundance trapped on the roof, two rebels defying the combined forces of St Oswald's and the law.

But now . . . It struck me then that I had more than one reason for not wanting Leon caught. My own position was far from secure; a word, a single glimpse of me and my cover was blown for ever. There was no getting round it – after this, Pinchbeck would have to disappear. Of course, he could, quite easily. Only Leon had any inkling that he was anything more than a ghost; a fake; a thing of rags and stuffing.

At the time, however, I felt little fear on my own account. I knew the roof better than anyone, and as long as I kept hidden, I might still escape discovery. But if Leon spoke to my father – if either of them made the connection –

It wasn't the imposture that would provoke the outrage. It was the challenge. To St Oswald's; to the system; to everything. I could see it now; the inquiry; the evening papers; the squib in the national press.

I could have lived with punishment – I was *thirteen*, for God's sake, what could they do to me? – but it was the ridicule I feared. That, and the contempt; and the knowledge that in spite of everything, St Oswald's had won.

I could just see my father standing, shoulders hunched, looking up at the roof. I sensed his dismay; not just at the attack on St Oswald's, but at the duty that now awaited him. John Snyde was never quick; but he was thorough, in his way, and there was no doubt in his mind as to what he should do.

'I'll have to go after them.' His voice, faint but clearly audible, reached me from the Quad below.

'What's that?' Bishop, in his eagerness to play the man of action, had completely overlooked the simplest solution. The fire brigade had not yet arrived; the police, always overworked, had not even looked in.

'I'll have to go up there. It's my job.' His voice was stronger – a St Oswald's Porter has to be strong. I remembered that from Bishop's lectures: *We count on you, John. St Oswald's counts on you to Do Your Duty.*

At a glance, Bishop measured the distance. I could see him working it out; clocking the angles. Boys on the roof; man on the ground; Head Porter in between. He wanted to go up himself – of course he did – but if he left his post, who would wield the megaphone? Who would deal with the emergency team? Who would take control?

'Don't spook them. Don't get too close. Take care – all right? Cover the fire escape. Get on the roof. I'll talk them down.'

Talk them down. There's another Bishop phrase, with its action-man overtones. He, who would have liked nothing better than to climb up on to the Chapel roof – possibly abseiling down again with an unconscious boy in his arms – could have had no inkling of the effort – the astonishing effort – it took for my father to agree.

I'd never actually used the fire escape. I preferred my less conventional routes; the library window; the Bell Tower; the skylight in the glass-fronted art studio, which gave access on to a slim metal joist that ran from the art block to the Observatory.

John Snyde knew nothing of these, nor would he have used them if he had. Small for my age, I was already getting too heavy to balance on glass, or to scramble through ivy on to the narrowest of ledges. I knew that in all his years as a St Oswald's Porter, he had never ventured as far as the fire escape on the Middle Corridor, let alone the precarious complex of gutters and pavements beyond. I was willing to gamble he would not do so now; or that if he did, he wouldn't go far.

I looked across the roofscape in the direction of the Middle Corridor. There it was, the fire escape; a dinosaur skeleton strung out across the drop. It was in poor shape – bubbles of rust bursting through the thick paint – but it looked strong enough to take a man's weight. Would he dare? I asked myself. And if he did, what would I do?

I considered climbing back towards the library window, but it was too risky, too visible from the ground. Instead I used another run, teetering on a long joist between two large art-room skylights before climbing across the Observatory roof and up through the main gully back towards the Chapel. I knew a dozen possible means of escape. I had my keys, and I knew every cupboard, every passage and back stair. Leon and I need never be caught. In spite of myself I was excited; I could almost see our friendship renewed, the silly quarrel forgotten in the face of this greater adventure—

By now the fire escape was safely out of range; however for a minute or two I knew I would be in full sight of the Quad. The risk was small, however. Silhouetted against the moonless sky, there was little chance of my being recognized by anyone from the courtyard below.

I ran for it then, my sneakers holding firm to the mossy slope. Below me, I could hear Bishop with his megaphone – *Stay where you are! Help is on its way!* – but I knew he hadn't seen me. Now I reached the dinosaur's spine, the ridge that dominated the main building, and stopped, straddling it. There was no sign of Leon. I guessed him to be hiding on the far side of the Bell Tower, where there was the most cover, and where, if he kept his head down, he would not be visible from the ground.

Quickly, on all fours, I monkeyed along the ridge. As I passed into the shade of the Bell Tower I looked back, but there was no sign of my father, either on the fire escape or on the walkway. Nor was there yet any sign of Leon. Now I reached the Bell Tower, jumped the familiar well between it and the Chapel roof, then from the comforting flag of shadow surveyed my rooftop empire. I risked a low call. 'Leon!'

No reply. My pale voice ribboned out in the misty night. 'Leon!'

Then I saw him, flattened against the parapet twenty feet ahead of me, head craning like a gargoyle's to the scene below. 'Leon.'

He'd heard me, I knew it; but he did not move. I began to climb towards him, keeping low. It could still work; I could show him the window; lead him to where he could hide and then bring him out, unseen and unsuspected, when the coast was clear. I wanted to tell him that, but I wondered, too, whether he would listen.

I crept closer; below, the deafening yawn of the megaphone. Then, sudden lights harrowed the rooftop in red and blue; for a second I saw Leon's shadow shoot over the roof, then he was down flat again, swearing. The fire engines had arrived.

'Leon.'

Still nothing. Leon seemed mortared to the parapet. The voice from the megaphone was a giant blur of vowels that rolled over us like boulders.

'*You there! Don't move! Stay where you are!*'

I ducked my head over the parapet, visible, I knew, only as a dark protrusion among so many others. From my eyrie I could see the squat form of Pat Bishop, the long neon gleam of the fire engine, the dark butterfly-shadowed figures of the men surrounding it.

Leon's face was expressionless, a mushroom in shadow. 'You little shit.'

'Come on, man,' I said. 'There's still time.'

'Time for *what*? A quick shag?'

'Leon, please. It's not what you think.'

'No, really?' He began to laugh.

'Please, Leon. I know a way out. But we've got to hurry. My dad's on his way—'

A silence, long as the grave.

Below us, the voices, all blurred together like bonfire smoke. Above us now, the Bell Tower with its overlooking balcony. In front of us, the well separating Bell Tower and Chapel roof; a stinking siphon-shaped depression, lined with gutters and pigeons' nests, which sloped down to the narrow gullet between the buildings.

'Your *dad?*' echoed Leon.

Then came a sound from the rooftop behind us. I turned and saw a man on the walkway, blocking our escape. Fifty feet of roof lay between us; though the walkway was broad, the man shook and faltered as if on a tightrope, hands clenched, face stiff with concentration as he inched forward to intercept us.

'Stay there,' he said. 'I'm coming to get you.'

It was John Snyde.

He couldn't have seen our faces, then. We were both in shadow. Two ghosts on the rooftop – we could make it, I knew. The well that separated Chapel from Bell Tower was deep, but its throat was narrow – five feet at its widest point. I'd jumped it myself more times than I could remember, and even in the dark I knew the risk was small. My father would never dare follow us there. We could scramble up the roof's incline, balance along the Bell Tower ledge and jump on to the balcony, as I'd done before. From there, I knew a hundred places for us to hide.

I did not think beyond that. Once more in my mind we were Butch and Sundance; freeze-framed in the moment; for ever heroes. All we needed was to make the jump.

I like to think I hesitated. That my actions were in some way determined by thought, and not the blind instinct of an animal on the run. But everything after that exists in a kind of vacuum. Perhaps that was the very moment when I ceased to dream; perhaps in that instant I experienced all the dream-time I was ever likely to need; an end to dreams for the rest of my life.

At the time, though, it felt like waking up. Waking up *all* the way, after years of dreaming. Thoughts shot across my mind like meteors against a summer sky.

Leon, laughing, his mouth against my hair.

Leon and me, on the ride-on mower.

Leon and Francesca, whom he had never loved.

St Oswald's, and how close – how very close – I had come to winning the game.

Time stopped. In space, I hung like a cross of stars. On the one side, Leon. On the other, my father. As I said, I like to think I hesitated.

Then I looked at Leon.

Leon looked back.

We jumped.

QUEEN

1

St Oswald's Grammar School for Boys

Remember, remember, the Fifth of November,
Gunpowder, treason and plot.

AND HERE IT IS AT LAST, IN ALL ITS KILLING GLORY. ANARCHY
has descended on St Oswald's like a plague; boys missing;
lessons disrupted; many of my colleagues out of School.
Devine has been suspended pending further inquiry (this
means I'm back in my old office, though rarely has a victory
given me less joy); and Grachvogel; and Light. Still
more are being questioned, including Robbie Roach, who is
naming colleagues left, right and centre in the hope of
diverting suspicion away from himself.

Bob Strange has made it clear that my own presence here
is merely an emergency measure. According to Allen-Jones,
whose mother is on the Board of Governors, my future was

discussed at some length at the last Governors' meeting, with Dr Pooley, whose son I 'assaulted', calling for my immediate suspension. In the light of recent events (and most of all in the absence of Bishop), there was no one else to speak for me, and Bob has implied that only our exceptional circumstances have deferred this perfectly legitimate course of action.

I swore Allen-Jones to secrecy about the matter, of course – which means it will be all over the Middle School by now.

And to think we were so anxious about a School Inspection only a few weeks ago. Now, we are a School in crisis. The police are still here, and show no sign of ever being ready to leave. We teach in isolation. No one answers the phones. Waste-bins remain unemptied, floors unswept. Shuttleworth, the new Porter, refuses to work unless the School provides him with alternative accommodation. Bishop, who would have dealt with it, is no longer in any position to do so.

As for the boys, they too sense an imminent collapse. Sutcliff came into registration with a pocketful of fire-crackers, causing the chaos you'd expect. In the world outside, there is little confidence in our ability to survive this crisis. A school is only ever as good as its last set of results, and unless we can pull back this disastrous term, I have little hope for this year's A-levels and GCSEs.

My fifth-form Latin set could probably manage, given that they finished the syllabus last year. But the Germans have suffered terribly this term, and the French, who are now missing two staff members – Tapi, who refuses to come back until her case has been resolved, and Pearman, still absent on compassionate leave – have little likelihood of catching up their lost ground. Other departments have similar problems; in some subjects whole modules of course-work have not been delivered, and there is no one to take charge. The Head spends most of his time shut up in his office. Bob Strange has taken over Bishop's duties, but with limited success.

Fortunately, Marlene is still here, running things. She looks less glamorous now, more businesslike, her hair pulled back from her angular face in a no-nonsense bun. She has no time for gossip nowadays; she spends most of the day fielding complaints from parents and questions from the Press, wanting to know the status of the police investigation.

Marlene, as always, handles it well – of course, she's tougher than most. Nothing throws her. When her son died, causing a rift within her family that never healed, we gave Marlene a job and a vocation, and ever since, she has given St Oswald's her total loyalty.

Part of that was Bishop's doing. It explains her devotion to him and the fact that she chose to work here, of all places. It can't have been easy. But she never let it show. In fifteen years, she's never had so much as a day's absence. For Pat's sake. Pat, who pulled her through.

Now he is in hospital, she tells me; he had some kind of an attack last night, probably brought on by stress. Managed to drive himself to Casualty, then collapsed in the waiting room and was transferred to a cardiac ward for observation.

'Still,' she said, 'he's in good hands. If only you'd seen him last night—' She paused, looking sternly into the middle distance, and I realized with some concern that Marlene was close to tears. 'I should have stayed,' she said. 'But he wouldn't let me.'

'Yes. Hum.' I turned away, embarrassed. Of course it's been a fairly open secret for years that Pat has more than a simply professional relationship with his secretary. Most of us couldn't care less about this. Marlene, however, has always maintained the façade, probably because she still thinks that a scandal might damage Pat. The fact that she had alluded to it now – even obliquely – showed more than anything else how far things have come.

In a school like St Oswald's, nothing is insignificant; and I felt a sudden acute lurch of grief for the ones of us who are still left; the old guard; valiantly keeping to our posts while the future marches inexorably over us.

'If Pat leaves, I won't stay,' she said at last, turning her emerald ring round and around her middle finger. 'I'll take a job in a solicitor's office or something. If not, I'll retire – in any case I'll be sixty next year—' That, too, was news. Marlene has been forty-one for as long as I can remember.

'I've also considered the retirement option,' I said. 'By the end of the year I'll have scored my Century – that is, unless old Strange gets his way—'

'What? Quasimodo, leave the Bell Tower?'

'It had crossed my mind.' Over these past few weeks, in fact, it has done more than cross it. 'It's my birthday today,' I told her. 'Can you believe it? Sixty-five years old.' She smiled, a little sadly. Dear Marlene. 'Where did those birthdays go?'

With Pat gone, Bob Strange took this morning's Middle School Assembly. I wouldn't have recommended it; but with so many of the management team either absent or unavailable, Bob has decided to take it upon himself to bring our ship back into calmer waters. Rather a mistake, I thought at the time. Still, there's no arguing with some people.

Of course, we all know that it isn't Bob's fault that Pat has been suspended. No one blames him for *that*; but the boys dislike the effortless ease with which he has slid into Bishop's position. Bishop's office, always open to anyone who needed him, is now shut. A buzzer device like the one on Devine's door has been installed. Detentions and other punishments are dealt with bloodlessly and efficiently from this administrative hub, but the humanity and warmth that made Pat Bishop so acceptable is noticeably lacking in Strange.

The boys sense this and resent it, finding ever more ingenious ways to show up his failings in public. Unlike Pat, our Bob is not a man of action. A handful of firecrackers thrown under the Hall platform during Assembly served to demonstrate this; with the result that the Middle School spent half the morning sitting in silence in the Hall while Bob waited for someone to confess.

With Pat Bishop, the culprit would have owned up within five minutes, but then, most boys aim to please Pat

Bishop. Bob Strange, with his cold manner and cartoon-Nazi tactics, is fair game.

'Sir? When's Mr Bishop coming back?'

'I said "In silence", Sutcliff, or you will go and stand outside the Headmaster's office.'

'Why, sir? Does *he* know?'

Bob Strange, who has not taught Middle School for over a decade, has no idea of how to deal with such a frontal attack. He does not realize how his crisp manner betrays his insecurity; how shouting simply makes things worse. He may be a fine administrator, but in the field of pastoral care, he's shocking.

'Sutcliff, you're in detention.'

'Yes, sir.'

I would have mistrusted Sutcliff's grin; but Strange didn't know him, and simply went on digging himself deeper. 'What's more,' he said, 'if the boy who threw those crackers doesn't stand up *right now*, then the whole of the Middle School will be in detention for a month.'

A month? It was an impossible threat. Mirage-like, it descended on the Assembly Hall, and a low, slow sound rippled through the Middle School.

'I shall count to ten,' announced Strange. 'One. Two.'

Another ripple as Strange demonstrated his mathematical skills.

Sutcliff and Allen-Jones looked at each other.

'Three. Four.'

The boys stood up.

A moment's silence.

My entire form followed them.

For a second, Strange goggled. It was superb; all of 3S standing to attention in a tight little phalanx; Sutcliff, Tayler, Allen-Jones, Adamczyk, McNair, Brasenose, Pink, Jackson, Almond, Niu, Anderton-Pullitt. All of my boys (except Knight, of course).

Then 3M (Monument's form) did the same.

Thirty more boys standing in unison, like soldiers, looking straight ahead without a word. Then 3P (Pearman's form) stood up. Then, 3KT (Teague). Then, finally, 3R (Roach).

Now every boy in the Middle School was standing. Not a word was spoken. No one moved. All eyes were on the little man on the platform.

For a moment he stood.

Then he turned and left without a word.

After that there wasn't much point in teaching anything. The boys needed to talk, so I let them, popping out occasionally to calm down Grachvogel's class next door, where a supply teacher called Mrs Cant was having a hard time keeping order. Of course, Bishop dominated the conversation. There was no polarization here; no doubt at all of Pat's innocence. All agreed that the charge was absurd; that it wouldn't even make it past the magistrate; that everything had been a terrible mistake. That cheered me; I wished some of my colleagues could have been as certain of it as these boys.

Through lunch-time I stayed in my room with a

sandwich and some marking, avoiding the crowded Common Room and the usual comforts of tea and *The Times*. It's a fact that all the papers have been full of the St Oswald's scandal this week, and anyone entering the main gates must now pass between a shooting gallery of Press and photographers.

Most of us do not stoop to comment, though I think perhaps Eric Scoones spoke to the *Mirror* on Wednesday. Certainly, their short piece had a ring of Scoones about it, with its depictions of an uncaring management and its veiled accusations of nepotism in the higher echelons. However, I find it impossible to believe that my old friend might be the egregious Mole, whose mixture of comedy, gossip and slander has captivated the readers of the *Examiner* for the past few weeks. And yet his words gave me a distinct sense of *déjà vu*; as if the author were someone whose style I knew, whose subversive humour I understood – and shared.

Once again, my thoughts returned to young Keane. A keen observer, in any case; and, I believe, a writer of some talent. Could *he* be Mole? I would hate to think so. Damn it, I *liked* the man; and I thought his remarks in the Common Room the other day showed both intelligence and courage. No, not Keane, I told myself. But if not Keane, then who?

It was a thought that nagged me all through the afternoon. I taught poorly; lost my temper with a group of fourth-formers who seemed incapable of concentration; gave detention to a sixth-former whose only crime, I admitted later to myself, had been to point out an error in my use of the subjunctive in prose translation. By Period 8 I had made up my mind. I would simply ask the man, openly and honestly. I like to think I'm a fair judge of character; if he were Mole, then, surely I would know.

When I found him, however, he was in the Common Room, talking with Miss Dare. She smiled as I came in, and Keane grinned. 'I hear it's your birthday, Mr Straitley,' he said. 'We got you a cake.'

It was a chocolate muffin on a saucer, both raided from the School canteen. Someone had put a yellow candle on top and a cheery frill of tinsel around the outside. A Post-It note attached to the saucer read 'Happy Birthday, Mr Straitley – 65 today!'

I knew then that Mole would have to wait.

Miss Dare lit the candle. The few members of the Common Room who still lingered at this late hour – Monument, McDonaugh and a couple of freshers – clapped. It was a measure of my distraction that I almost burst into tears.

'Dammit,' I growled. 'I was keeping it quiet.'

'Whatever for?' said Miss Dare. 'Listen, Chris and I are going out for a drink this evening. Would you like to come? We're going to see the bonfire in the park – eat toffee apples – light sparklers—' She laughed, and I thought for a moment how very pretty she really was, with her black hair and pink Dutch-doll face. Notwithstanding my early suspicions regarding Mole – which possibility seemed quite out of the question to me at that moment – I was glad she and Keane were getting on. I know only too well the pull of St Oswald's; how you think there's all the time in the world to meet a girl, get hitched, have children, maybe, if she wants them; and then suddenly you find that all of it has passed you by, not by a year but by a decade or two, and you realize that you are no longer a Young Gun but a Tweed Jacket, irrevocably wedded to St Oswald's, the dusty old battleship that has somehow swallowed your heart.

'Thanks for the offer,' I said. 'But I think I'll stay at home.'

'Then make a wish,' said Miss Dare, lighting the candle.

'That I *can* do,' I said.

2

DEAR OLD STRAITLEY. I'VE COME SO CLOSE TO LOVING HIM these past few weeks, with his incurable optimism and his idiotic ways. It's funny how catching that optimism can be; the feeling that perhaps the past can be forgotten (as Bishop has forgotten it); that bitterness can be put aside, and that Duty (to the School, of course) can be as much of a motivating force as (for instance) love; hate; revenge.

I sent my last few e-mails this evening, after School. Roach to Grachvogel, incriminating them both. Bishop to Devine. Light to Devine, in tones of escalating panic. Knight to all, threatening, weeping. And finally the *coup de grâce*; to Bishop's mobile and to his PC (I'm sure the police will be monitoring *that* by now); a last, tearful, imploring text message from Colin Knight, sent from his own mobile phone, which should in due time confirm the worst.

All in all, a job well done, with no need for further action on my part. Five staff members destroyed in one elegant strike. Bishop, of course, could crack at any time. A stroke, perhaps; or a massive heart attack, brought on by stress and the certainty that whatever the outcome of the police investigation, his time at St Oswald's is finished.

The question is, have I done enough? Mud sticks, they say; and all the more so in this profession. In a sense, the police are superfluous. The merest hint of sexual impropriety is enough to sink a career. The rest I can confidently leave to a public weaned on suspicion, envy and the *Examiner*. Already I've started the ball rolling; I wouldn't be at all surprised if someone else took over during the next few weeks. Sunnybankers, perhaps; stout-minded folk from the Abbey Road estate. There will be fires; attacks, perhaps, on lone colleagues; rumours heated to scandalous certainty in the pubs and clubs of the town centre. The beauty of it is that from a certain point I no longer have to take any direct action. One little push, and the dominoes begin to fall all by themselves.

I'll stay, of course, as long as I can. Half the fun is being here to see it happen – though I am prepared for every eventuality. In any case, the damage must surely be irre-versible by now. A whole department in ruins; many more staff implicated; a Second Master hopelessly tarred. Pupils leaving – twelve this week – a trickle that will soon become a flood. Teaching neglected; health and safety poor; plus an imminent Inspection which cannot fail to close the School down.

The Governors, I hear, have been holding emergency meetings every night for the past week. The Head, no negotiator, fears for his job; Dr Tidy is concerned about the potential impact on School finances; and Bob Strange covertly manages to turn everything the Head says to his own advantage whilst maintaining the appearance of complete loyalty and correctitude.

So far (barring a couple of disciplinary *faux pas*) he has managed to take over Bishop's job quite nicely. A Headship may follow. Why not? He is clever (clever enough, in any case, not to appear *too* clever in front of the Governors); competent; articulate; and just bland enough to pass the stringent personality tests applied to all St Oswald's staff.

All things considered, a nice little piece of antisocial engineering. I say it myself (because no one else can), but actually I'm very pleased with the way things have worked out. Remains one small, unfinished piece of business, and I plan to deal with that tonight, at the Community bonfire. After that I can afford to celebrate, and I will; there's a bottle of champagne with Straitley's name on it, and I mean to open it tonight.

For now, though, I am idle. That's the worst part of a campaign such as this; those long, charged moments of waiting. The bonfire starts at seven thirty; by eight the pyre will be a beacon; thousands of people will be in the park; there will be music booming from loudspeakers; screaming from the fairground; and at eight thirty the fireworks will start; all smoke and falling stars.

Just the place for a quiet murder, don't you think? The dark; the crowds; the confusion. So easy here to apply Poe's law – stating that the object that is hidden in plain sight remains unseen longest – and simply to walk away, leaving the body for some poor baffled soul to discover, or even to discover it myself, with a cry of alarm, relying upon the inevitable crowd to shield me from sight.

One more murder. I owe it to myself. Or maybe two.

I still have Leon's photograph, a clipping taken from the *Examiner*, now leaf-brown and speckled with age. It's a school photograph, taken that summer, and the quality is poor, blown up for the front page into a grainy mess of clustered dots. But it's still his face; his cock-eyed grin; his too-long hair; and scissored tie. The headline stands alongside the picture.

LOCAL SCHOOLBOY IN DEATH PLUMMET.
PORTER QUESTIONED.

Well, anyway, that's the official story. We jumped; he fell. Even as my feet touched the other side of the chimney I heard him go – a gutter-rattle of broken slates and a squeal of rubber soles.

It took me a moment to understand. His foot had slipped; perhaps a moment's hesitation; perhaps a cry from below had spoilt his leap. I looked, and saw that instead of landing squarely beside me, his knee had caught the edge of the gully; he'd slip-slid down the slimy funnel; bounced back; and now he was trapped across the mouth of the drop, holding on to the edge of the gutter with his fingertips, one foot stretched acrobatically to touch the far side of the chimney, the other hanging limply into space.

'*Leon!*'

I threw myself down, but I couldn't reach him; I was on the wrong side of the chimney. I didn't dare jump back in case I dislodged a slate. I knew how brittle the gutter was; how nibbled and scalloped its edges.

'Hang on!' I called, and Leon looked up at me, face blurred with fear.

'Stay there, son. I'll get you.'

I raised my head. John Snyde was now standing on the parapet barely thirty feet away. His face was a slab; his eyes holes; his entire body shook. Now he edged forward with clockwork movements; his fear rolled off him like a stench. But he was moving. Inch by inch he crept closer – his eyes screwed almost shut in fear – and soon he would see me, and I wanted to run, I *needed* to run, but Leon was still down there, Leon was still trapped—

Below me I could hear a low cracking sound. It was the gutter giving way; a piece broke off and fell into the space between the buildings. There was a squeal of rubber as Leon's sneaker slid a few more inches down the greasy wall.

As my father approached I began to back away, further into the shadow of the Bell Tower. Lights strobed from the fire engines below; soon there would be people all over the roof.

'Hang on, Leon,' I whispered.

Then suddenly I felt it in the nape of my neck, a distinct sensation of being watched. I turned my head and saw—

Roy Straitley in his old tweed jacket, standing at his window not twelve feet above me. His face was gaudy in the lights; his eyes were startled; his mouth drawn down into a tragicomic mask.

'*Pinchbeck?*' he said.

And in that second came a sound below us; a hollow, ratcheting sound like a giant penny stuck in a vacuum-cleaner pipe—

Then – *crunch*.

Silence.

The gutter had given way.

3

I RAN THEN, AND KEPT RUNNING, WITH THE SOUND OF Leon's fall at my heels like a black dog. Here my knowledge of the roof came into its own; I loped, monkeylike, across my rooftop circuit, cat-leaped from the parapet on to the fire escape, and from there regained the Middle Corridor by the open fire door, and thence, the open air.

I was running on instinct by then, of course; everything suspended but the need to survive. Outside, emergency lights still strobed mystically red and blue from the fire engines parked in the Chapel court.

No one had seen me leave the building. I was clear. All around me, firemen and police, cordoning off the area against the little group of gawkers that had collected on the drive. I was clear, I told myself. No one had seen me. Except, of course, for Straitley.

Cautiously now, I made for the Gatehouse, avoiding the parked fire engine with its bank of red-blue lights and the hopeful ambulance sirening its way up the long drive. Instinct drove me. I made for home. There I would be safe. There I would lie under my bed, wrapped in a blanket, as I always had on Saturday nights, door locked, thumb in mouth, waiting for my father to come home. It would be dark under the bed; it would be safe.

The Gatehouse door was wide open. Light came from the kitchen window; the lounge curtains were open, but light shone from there too, and there were figures standing against the light. Mr Bishop was there, with his megaphone. Two policemen were standing by the patrol car that blocked the drive.

And now I could see someone else there, a woman in a coat with a fur collar; a woman whose face in the lights seemed suddenly, fleetingly familiar—

The woman turned, full-face to me, and her mouth dropped in a great lipsticked 'Oh'.

'Oh, sweetheart! Oh, love!'

The woman, running towards me on kitten heels.

Bishop, turning, megaphone in hand, as a cry went up from the firemen at the far side of the building. *'Mr Bishop, sir! Over here!'*

The woman, hair flying; eyes wet; arms like batwing doors to scoop me in. A sensation of *shrinking*; a tickle of fur against my mouth; and suddenly there were tears; tears boiling out of me as everything came back in a tidal wave of memory and grief. Leon, Straitley, my father – all forgotten; left far behind as she gathered me into the house, to safety.

'It wasn't supposed to be like this, love.' Her voice was shaking. 'It was going to be a surprise.'

In that second I saw it all. The unopened plane ticket. The whispered conversations on the phone. *How much?* Pause. *All right. It's for the best.*

How much for *what*? To give up his claim? And how many scratchcards, how many six-packs and takeaway pizzas did they promise him before he gave them what they wanted?

I began to cry again, this time in rage at their joint betrayal. My mother held me in a scent of something expensive and unfamiliar. 'Oh, sweetheart. What happened?'

'Oh, Mum,' I sobbed, sinking my face into her furry coat, feeling her mouth against my hair, smelling cigarette smoke and the dry, musky scent of her as inside something small and clever slipped its hand into my heart and squeezed.

4

IN SPITE OF MRS MITCHELL'S INSISTENCE THAT LEON WOULD never have gone on the roof alone, her son's best friend – the boy she called Julian Pinchbeck – was never found. School records were searched; door-to-door inquiries made, but to no avail. Even this effort might not have been undertaken if it had not been for Mr Straitley's insistence that he *had* seen Pinchbeck on the Chapel roof – though sadly, the boy had got away.

The police were very sympathetic – after all, the woman was distraught – but secretly they must have believed poor Mrs Mitchell to be slightly off her rocker, for ever talking about nonexistent boys and refusing to accept her son's death as a tragic accident.

That might have changed if she had seen me again, but she didn't. Three weeks later I went to live with my mother and Xavier at their home in Paris, where I was to remain for the next seven years.

By that time, though, my transformation was well under way. The ugly duckling had begun to change; and with my mother's help it happened fast. I did not resist it. With Leon dead, Pinchbeck could not hope or wish to survive. I disposed rapidly of my St Oswald's clothes and relied upon my mother to do the rest.

A *second chance*, she had called it; and now I opened all of the notes, the letters, the parcels waiting in their pretty wrappers under my bed, and made full use of what I found inside.

I never saw my father again. The investigation into his conduct was only a formality, but his manner was odd, and it aroused the suspicion of the police. There was no real cause to suspect foul play. But he was aggressive under questioning; a breathalyser test revealed he'd been drinking heavily; and his account of that night was vague and unconvincing, as if he hardly recalled what had happened any more. Roy Straitley, who confirmed his presence at the scene of the tragedy, had reported hearing him shout, – 'I'll get you' – at one of the boys. The police later made much of this, and though Straitley always maintained that John Snyde was running to *help* the fallen boy, he had to admit that the Porter had had his back turned to him at the time of the incident, and that he could not therefore have known for sure whether the man was trying to help or not. After all, said the police, Snyde's record was hardly untarnished. Only that summer he had received an official reprimand for attacking a pupil on St Oswald's premises; and his uncouth behaviour and violent temper were well known around the School. Dr Tidy confirmed it; and Jimmy added some embellishments of his own.

Pat Bishop, who might have helped, proved strangely reluctant to speak on my father's behalf. This was partly the fault of the New Head, who had made it clear to Pat that his principal duty was to St Oswald's, and that the sooner the Snyde fiasco was cleared up, the sooner they could distance themselves from the whole sorry affair. Besides, Bishop was beginning to feel uneasy. This business threatened both his new appointment and his growing friendship with Marlene Mitchell. After all, *he* was the one who'd befriended John Snyde. As Second Master, he'd encouraged him, believed in him, defended him, knowing that John had a history of violence against my mother, against myself and on at least one documented occasion against a pupil of St Oswald's – which made it all the more plausible that the man, goaded to breaking-point, had lost his head and chased Leon Mitchell across the rooftops to his death.

There was never any real evidence to support the claim. Certainly Roy Straitley refused to do so. Besides, wasn't the man afraid of heights? But the papers got hold of it. There were anonymous letters, phone calls, the usual public outrage that accumulates around any such case. Not that there ever *was* a case. John Snyde was never formally charged. All the same, he hanged himself, in a bed-and-breakfast room in town, three days before we moved to Paris.

Even then I knew who was responsible. Not Bishop, though he was partly to blame. Not Straitley, not the papers, not

even the Head. St Oswald's killed my father, just as surely as
St Oswald's killed Leon. St Oswald's, with its bureaucracy,
its pride, its blindness, its assumptions. Killed them and
digested them without a thought, like a whale sucking up
plankton. Fifteen years later, no one remembers either of
them. They're just names on a list of Crises St Oswald's Has
Survived.

Not this one, though. Last time pays for all.

5

Friday, 5th November
6.30 p.m.

I PASSED BY THE HOSPITAL AFTER SCHOOL, WITH SOME flowers and a book for Pat Bishop. Not that he reads much, though perhaps he should; besides, as I told him, he ought to be taking it easy.

He wasn't, of course. I arrived to find him engaged in a violent discussion with the same pink-haired nurse who had dealt with my own problem not long before.

'Christ, not another one,' she said, on seeing me. 'Tell me, are *all* St Oswald's staff as awkward as you two, or did I just get lucky?'

'I tell you, I'm fine.' He didn't look it. He had a bluish tinge, and he looked smaller, as if all that running had impacted him somehow. His eye fell on the flowers in my hand. 'For God's sake, I'm not dead *yet*.'

'Give them to Marlene,' I suggested. 'She could probably do with cheering up.'

'You could be right.' He smiled at me, and I caught sight of the old Bishop again, just for a moment. 'Take her home, will you, Roy? She won't go, and she's tired out. Thinks something's going to happen to me if she gets a good night's sleep.'

Marlene, I discovered, had gone to the hospital cafeteria for a cup of tea. I caught up with her there, having extracted a promise from Bishop that he wouldn't try and check himself out in my absence.

She looked surprised to see me. She was holding a crumpled handkerchief in one hand, and her face – unusually clear of make-up – was pink and blotchy. 'Mr Straitley! I wasn't expecting—'

'Marlene Mitchell,' I said sternly. 'After fifteen years, I think it's time you started calling me Roy.'

Over polystyrene cups of a peculiarly fishy-tasting tea, we talked. It's funny how our colleagues, those not-quite-friends who populate our lives more closely than our closest relatives, remain so hidden to us in the essential. When we think of them, we see them not as people, with families and private lives, but as we see them every day: dressed for work; businesslike (or not); efficient (or not); all of us satellites of the same lumbering moon.

A colleague in jeans looks strangely *wrong*; a colleague in tears is almost indecent. Those private glimpses of something outside St Oswald's seem almost unreal, like dreams.

The reality is the stone; the tradition; the *permanence* of St Oswald's. Staff come, staff go. Sometimes they die. Sometimes even *boys* die; but St Oswald's endures, and as I have grown older I have taken increasing comfort from this.

Marlene, I sense, is different. Perhaps because she's a woman – those things don't mean so much to women, I've found. Perhaps because she sees what St Oswald's has done to Pat. Or perhaps because of her son, who haunts me still.

'You shouldn't be here,' she said, wiping her eyes. 'The Head told everyone . . .'

'Bugger the Head. It's after hours, and I can do what I like,' I told her, sounding like Robbie Roach for the first time in my life. It made her laugh, though, which was what I wanted. 'That's better,' I said, inspecting the dregs of my now-cold beverage. 'Tell me, Marlene, why does hospital tea *always* taste of fish?'

She smiled. She looks younger when she smiles – or perhaps it was the absence of make-up – younger and not so Wagnerian. 'It's good of you to come, Roy. No one else has, you know; not the Head, not Bob Strange. Not a single one of his friends. Oh, it's all very tactful. All very St Oswald's. I'm sure the Senate were equally tactful with Caesar when they handed him the hemlock bowl.'

I think she meant Socrates, but I let it go. 'He'll survive,' I lied. 'Pat's tough, and everyone knows those charges are ridiculous. You'll see, by the end of the year the Governors will be begging him to come back.'

'I hope so.' She took a sip of her cold tea. 'I'm not going to let them bury him, as they buried Leon.'

It was the first time in fifteen years that she had mentioned her son in my presence. Another barrier down; and yet I'd been expecting it; that old business has been more than usually on my mind in recent weeks, and I suppose she felt the same.

There are parallels, of course: hospitals; a scandal; a vanished boy. Her son was not killed outright by the fall, although he never regained consciousness. Instead, there was the long wait by the boy's bedside; the dreadful, lingering torment of hope; the procession of hopefuls and well-wishers – boys, family, girlfriend, tutors, priest – until the inevitable end.

We never did find that second boy, and Marlene's insistence that he must have seen something was always taken as a hysterical mother's desperate attempt to make sense of the tragedy. Only Bishop tried to help; checking School records and going over photographs until someone (maybe the Head) pointed out that his persistence in clouding the issue would almost certainly damage St Oswald's. Not that it mattered in the end, of course; but Pat was never happy about the outcome.

'Pinchbeck. That was his name.' As if I could have forgotten – a fake name if I ever heard one. But I'm good at names; and I'd remembered his from that day in the corridor, when I'd found him sneaking about near my office on some unlikely excuse. Leon had been there then, too, I thought. And the boy had given his name as Pinchbeck.

'Yes, Julian Pinchbeck.' She smiled, not pleasantly. 'No

one else really believed in him. Except Pat. And you, of course, when you saw him there—'

I wondered if I *had* seen him. I never forget a boy, you know; in thirty-three years I never have. All those young faces, frozen in time; every one of them believing that Time will make the exception for them alone; that they alone will remain for ever fourteen . . .

'I saw him,' I told her. 'Or at least, I *thought* I did.' Smoke and mirrors; a ghost boy who dissolved like the night mists when morning came. 'I was so *sure*—'

'We all were,' said Marlene. 'But there was no Pinchbeck on any of the School records, or in the photo files, or even on the lists of applicants. Anyway, by then, it was all over. No one was interested. My son was dead. We had a school to run.'

'I'm sorry,' I said.

'It wasn't your fault. Besides—' she stood up with a sudden briskness that was all School Secretary. 'Being sorry won't bring Leon back, will it? Now it's Pat who needs my help.'

'He's a lucky man,' I said, and I meant it. 'Do you think he'd object if I asked you out? Just for a drink, of course—' I said, 'but it *is* my birthday, and you look as if you could do with something a little more substantial than tea.'

I like to think I haven't lost my touch. We agreed to an hour, no more, and left Pat with instructions to lie down and read his book. We walked the mile or so to my house; it was dark by then, and already the night smelt of gunpowder.

A few early fireworks popped over the Abbey Road estate; the air was misty and surprisingly mild. At home there was gingerbread and sweet mulled wine; I lit the fire in the parlour and brought out the two cups that matched. It was warm and comfortable; by the light of the fire my old armchairs looked less shabby than usual, and the carpet less threadbare; and around us, on every wall, my lost boys watched with the grinning optimism of the forever young.

'So many boys,' said Marlene softly.

'My gallery of ghosts,' I said, then, seeing her face; 'I'm sorry, Marlene. That was tactless.'

'Don't worry,' she said, smiling. 'I'm not as sensitive as I used to be. That's why I took this job, you know. Of course in those days I was sure there was a conspiracy to hide the truth; and that some day I'd actually see him, walking down some corridor with his gym bag, those little glasses slipping down his nose . . . But I never did. I let him go. And if Mr Keane hadn't brought it up again, after all these years—'

'Mr Keane?' I said.

'Oh, yes. We talked it over. He's very interested in School history, you know. I think he's planning to write a book.'

I nodded. 'I knew he'd been taking an interest. He had notes, pictures—'

'You mean this?' Out of her wallet Marlene drew a small picture, clearly scissored from a School photograph. I recognized it at once – in Keane's book it had been a poor reproduction, barely visible, where he'd circled a face in red crayon.

But this time I recognized the boy, too; that wan little face, owlishly bespectacled, raccoon-like, the school cap crammed down over the floppy fringe.

'That's Pinchbeck?'

She nodded. 'It's not the best likeness, but I'd know him anywhere. Besides, I've been over that picture a thousand times, matching names to faces. Everyone's accounted for. Everyone but him. Whoever he was, Roy, he wasn't one of ours. But he was there. *Why?*'

Once more, that feeling of *déjà vu*; the sensation of something slipping, not quite easily, into place. But it was dim. Dim. And there was something about the small un-formed face that troubled me. Something familiar.

'Why didn't you show the police the photo at the time?' I asked.

'It was too late.' Marlene shrugged. 'John Snyde was dead.'

'But the boy was a witness.'

'Roy. I had a job to do. There was Pat to think of. It was over.'

Over? Perhaps it was. But something about that wretched affair had always felt unfinished. I don't know where the connection had come from – why it had returned to mind after so many years – but now it had, and it wouldn't leave me alone.

'Pinchbeck.' The dictionary gives its meaning as (*of jewellery) flashy, tawdry, counterfeit. A fake.* 'A made-up name, if ever there was one.'

She nodded. 'I know. It still makes me feel funny,

thinking of him in his St Oswald's school uniform, walking along the corridors with the other boys, talking to them, even being photographed with them, for God's sake. I can't believe no one noticed—'

I could. After all, why should they? A thousand boys, all in uniform; who would suspect he was an outsider? Besides, it was ridiculous. Why should a boy attempt such an imposture?

'The challenge,' I said. 'Just for the thrill of it. To see if it could be done.'

He would be fifteen years older now, of course. Twenty-eight or thereabouts. He would have grown, of course. He'd be tall now, well-built. He might be wearing contact lenses. But it was possible, wasn't it? Wasn't it *possible*?

Helplessly I shook my head. I hadn't realized until that moment how much hope I had placed on Knight – and only Knight – being responsible for the recent mischief that has plagued us. Knight was the culprit; the sender of e-mails; the malicious surfer (if that's the word) of internet filth. Knight had accused Bishop and the others; Knight had burnt the Gatehouse; I'd even half-convinced myself that Knight had been behind those articles signed Mole.

Now I saw the dangerous illusions for what they were. These crimes against St Oswald's went much further than simple mischief. No boy could have committed them. This insider – whoever he was – was prepared to take his game as far as it went.

I thought of Grachvogel, hiding in his closet.

I thought of Tapi, locked in the Bell Tower.

Of Jimmy (like Snyde), who took the blame.

Of Fallow, whose secret was revealed.

Of Pearman and Kitty, ditto.

Of Knight; Anderton-Pullitt; the graffiti; the Gatehouse; the thefts; the Mont Blanc pen; the small acts of localized disruption and the final bouquet – Bishop, Devine, Light, Grachvogel and Roach – firing off one after another like rockets into the flaming sky . . .

And once again I thought of Chris Keane, with his clever face and dark fringe; and of Julian Pinchbeck, the pale boy who at twelve or thirteen had already dared an imposture so brazen that for fifteen years no one had believed it possible.

Could Keane be Pinchbeck? *Keane*, for gods' sakes?

It was an astonishing leap of illogic or intuition; and yet, I saw how he could have done it. St Oswald's has a rather idiosyncratic policy on application, based on personal impressions rather than on paper references. It was just conceivable that someone – someone clever – might be able to slip through the network of checks that exist to filter out the undesirables (in the private sector, of course, police checks are not required). Besides, the mere thought of such an imposture is beyond us. We are like the guards at a friendly outpost, all comic-opera uniforms and silly walks, falling by the dozen beneath unexpected sniper fire. We never expected an attack. That was our mistake. And now someone was picking us off like flies.

'*Keane?*' said Marlene, just as I would have done if our positions had been reversed. 'That nice young man?'

In a few words, I filled her in on the nice young man.

The notebook. The computer passwords. And through it all, his subtle air of mockery, of arrogance; as if teaching were simply an amusing game.

'But what about Knight?' said Marlene.

I'd been thinking about that. The case against Bishop was built on Knight; the text messages from Knight's phone to his; maintaining the illusion that Knight had run away, perhaps from fear of further abuse . . .

But if Knight was not the culprit, then where *was* he?

I considered it. Without the calls from Knight's phone, without the incident at the Gatehouse and the messages from his e-mail address, what then would we have assumed and feared?

'I think Knight's dead,' I told her, frowning. 'It's the only conclusion that makes any sense.'

'But why kill Knight?'

'To raise the stakes,' I said slowly. 'To make sure Pat and the others were well and truly implicated.'

Marlene stared at me, pale as pastry. 'Not Keane,' she said. 'He seems so charming. He even got you that cake—'

Gods!

That cake. Till then I'd forgotten all about it. Likewise I had forgotten Dianne's invitation; to see the fireworks, to have a drink, to celebrate—

Had something alerted Keane to her? Had she read his notebook? Had she let something slip? I thought of her eyes, bright with enjoyment in her vivid young face. I thought of her saying, in that teasing voice: *Tell me, are you a professional spy or is it just a hobby?*

I stood up too fast, and felt the invisible finger poke at my chest, insistently, as if advising me to sit down again. I ignored it. 'Marlene,' I said. 'We have to go. Quick. To the park.'

'Why there?' she said.

'Because that's where he is,' I said, grabbing my coat and flinging it over my shoulders. 'And he's with Dianne Dare.'

6

Friday, 5th November
7.30 p.m.

I HAVE A DATE. EXCITING, ISN'T IT? THE FIRST I'VE HAD, IN fact, in years; in spite of my mother's high hopes and my analyst's optimism, I've never really been that interested in the opposite sex. Even now, when I think of them, the first thing that comes into my mind is Leon, shouting – *You little pervert!* – and the sound he made as he fell down the chimney.

Of course I don't tell *them* that. Instead I please them with tales of my father; of the beatings he gave me and of his cruelty. It satisfies my analyst, and now I've even come to half-believe it myself, and to forget about Leon as he jumped the gully, his face freeze-faded to the comforting sepia of the distant past.

It wasn't your fault. How many times during the days that

followed did I hear those words? I was cold inside; racked by night terrors; rigid with grief and the fear of discovery. I believe that for a time I genuinely lost my mind; and I threw myself into my transformation with a desperate zeal, working steadily (with my mother's help) to eradicate every trace of the Pinchbeck that was.

Of course, that's all over now. Guilt, as my analyst says, is the natural response of the true victim. I have worked hard to eradicate that guilt, and I think that so far I have succeeded rather well. The therapy is working. Naturally, I don't plan to tell her the precise *nature* of this therapy of mine; but I do think she'll agree with me that my guilt complex is mostly cured.

One more job to do then, before the final catharsis.

One more glance in the mirror before I meet my bonfire date.

Looking good, Snyde. Looking good.

7

Friday, 5th November
7.30 p.m.

IT USUALLY TAKES FIFTEEN MINUTES TO WALK FROM MY house to the municipal park. We did it in five, the invisible finger urging me on. The mist had dropped; a thick corona surrounded the moon, and the fireworks that popped from time to time above us lit up the sky like sheet lightning.

'What time is it?'

'Seven thirty. They'll be lighting the bonfire any moment now.' I hurried on, skirting a group of small children dragging a guy on a trolley.

'Quid for the guy, Mester?'

In my day, it was pennies. We hurried on, Marlene and I, through a night that was rich with smoke and shot with sparklers. A magical night, bright as those of my childhood and scented with the dusk of autumn leaves.

'I'm not sure we should be doing this.' That was Marlene, sensible as ever. 'Shouldn't the police be dealing with this kind of thing?'

'D'you think they'd listen?'

'Maybe not. But I still think—'

'Listen, Marlene. I just want to see him. Talk to him. If I'm right, and Pinchbeck *is* Keane—'

'I can't believe it.'

'But if it is, then Miss Dare may be in danger.'

'If it is, you old fool, then *you* may be in danger.'

'Oh.' It actually hadn't crossed my mind.

'There'll be police at the gate,' she said reasonably. 'I'll have a quiet word with whoever's in charge while you see if you can find Dianne.' She smiled. 'And if you're wrong – which I'm sure you are – we can all celebrate Bonfire Night together. All right?'

We hurried on.

We saw the glow from the road some time before we reached the park gates. A crowd had already gathered there; attendants posted at each entrance to hand out tickets, and beyond the gates there were more people – thousands of them – a bristling mass of heads and faces.

Behind, the fire was already lit; soon it would be a tower of flame leaping at the sky. A guy, perched on a ruined armchair halfway up the pile appeared to dominate the scene like the Lord of Misrule.

'You'll never find them here,' said Marlene, seeing the crowd. 'It's too dark, and look at all these *people*—'

Sure enough, there were more people at tonight's bonfire than even I had expected. Families, mostly; men carrying children on their shoulders; teenagers in fancy dress; youngsters in alien antennae, waving neon wands and eating candyfloss. Beyond the bonfire was the funfair; arcade games, waltzers and shooting ranges; Hook-a-Duck and the Tower of Fear; roundabouts and the Wheel of Death.

'I'll find them,' I said. 'You just do your bit.'

On the other side of the clearing, almost out of sight in the low-lying mist, the firework display was about to start. A cordon of children lined the area; beneath my feet, the grass was churned mud. All around me, a cocktail of crowd noise, several kinds of fairground music and at our backs, the red pandemonium of the fire as the flames leaped and the stacked pallets exploded with the heat, one by one.

And now it began. There was a sudden scattered sound of applause followed by a – *Whoooo!* from the crowd as a double handful of rockets bloomed and burst, illuminating the mist in a sudden flashgun-flare of red and blue. I moved on, scanning the faces now illuminated in neon colours; my feet shifting uncomfortably in the mud; my throat harsh with gunpowder and anticipation. It was surreal; the sky was in flames; the faces in the firelight looked like Renaissance demons, forked and pronged.

Keane was among them somewhere, I thought. But even that certainty had begun to fade, to be replaced by an unfamiliar self-doubt. I thought of myself pursuing the Sunnybankers, old legs giving way as the jeering boys escaped over the fence. I thought of Pooley and his friends, and of my collapse in the Lower Corridor, outside the Head's office. I thought of Pat Bishop saying; *you're slowing down*, and young Bevans – not so young now, I suppose – and the small but constant pressure of the invisible finger within. At *sixty-five*, I told myself, *how long can I expect to keep up the pretence?* My Century had never seemed further away – and beyond it, I could see nothing but dark.

Ten minutes in, and I knew it was hopeless. As well try to empty a bathtub with a spoon as try to find anyone in this chaos. From the corner of my eye I could just see Marlene, some hundred yards or so away, talking earnestly with a harassed-looking young police officer.

The Community Bonfire is a bad night for our local constabulary. Fights, accidents and casual thefts are rife; under cover of darkness and the holiday crowd almost anything is possible. Still, Marlene looked to be doing her best. As I watched, the harassed young officer spoke into his walkie-talkie; then a swatch of crowd pulled across the pair of them, hiding them both from sight.

By this time I was beginning to feel quite peculiar. Perhaps the fire; perhaps the belated effect of the mulled wine. In any case I was glad to move away from the heat for a while. Nearer the trees it was cooler and darker, there was less noise, and the invisible finger seemed inclined to move on, leaving me a little breathless, but otherwise fine.

The mist had settled lower, made eerily luminous by the fireworks, like the inside of a Chinese lantern. Through it now almost every young man appeared to be Keane. On each occasion, however, it turned out to be some other young man, sharp-faced and with a dark fringe, who glanced at me oddly before turning back to his wife (girlfriend, child). Still, I was sure he was there. The instinct, perhaps, of a man who has spent the last thirty-three years of his life checking doors for flour-bombs and desktops for graffiti. He was here somewhere. I could feel it.

Thirty minutes in, and the fireworks were almost over. As always they'd kept the best till last, a bouquet of rockets and fountains and spinning wheels that made starry night from the thickest fog. A curtain of brilliant light descended, and for a time I was almost blinded, fumbling my way through the mass of people. My right leg ached; and there was a stitch running all the way down my right-hand side, as if something there had begun to unravel, gently releasing stuffing, like the seam on a very old teddy bear.

And then, suddenly in that apocalyptic light I saw Miss Dare; standing alone, some distance from the crowd. At first I thought I'd made a mistake; but then she turned, her face, half hidden beneath a red beret, still lit in garish shades of blue and green.

For a moment the image of her stirred some powerful memory in me, some urgent sense of terrible danger, and I began to run towards her, feet slipping in the soapy mud.

'Miss Dare! Where's Keane?'

She was wearing a trim red coat that matched her beret, her black hair tucked neatly behind her ears. She smiled quizzically as I arrived, panting, at her side.

'Keane?' she said. 'He had to go.'

8

Friday, 5th November
8.30 p.m.

I HAVE TO ADMIT I WAS QUITE NONPLUSSED. I'D BEEN SO SURE Keane would be with her that I stared at her stupidly without a word, watching the coloured shadows flicker across her pale face and listening to the giant beat of my old heart in the darkness.

'Is anything wrong?'

'No,' I said. 'Just an old fool playing detective, that's all.'

She smiled.

Above and around me, the last rockets flared again. Rainforest green this time; a pleasing colour that made Martians of the faces that turned to watch. The blue I found slightly unnerving, like the blue lights of an ambulance, and the red—

Once more, something that was not quite a memory rose

partway to the surface and dived again. Something about those lights; the colours; the way they had shone against someone's face—

'Mr Straitley,' she said gently. 'You don't look well.'

As a matter of fact I'd felt better; but that was the smoke and the heat of the fire. More important to me was the young woman standing at my side; a young woman who all my instincts told me might still be in danger.

'Listen, Dianne,' I said, taking her arm. 'I think there's something you need to know.'

And so I began. With the notebook at first; then with Mole; with Pinchbeck; with the deaths of Leon Mitchell and John Snyde. It was all circumstantial when viewed piece by piece; but the more I thought and spoke about it, the more I could see a picture emerging.

He'd told me himself he'd been a Sunnybank boy. Imagine what *that* must have been for someone like Keane. A smart kid; a reader; a bit of a rebel. The staff would have disliked him almost as much as the pupils did. I could see him now, a sullen, solitary boy, hating his school, hating his contemporaries, making his life in the fantasy world.

Perhaps it had started off as a cry for help. Or a joke, or a gesture of revolt against the private school and what it stood for. It must have been easy, once he'd found the nerve to take the first step. As long as he wore the uniform, he would have been treated like any other of our boys. I imagined the thrill of walking unseen down the solemn old corridors, of looking into classrooms, of mingling with the other boys. A solitary thrill, but a powerful one; and one that had soon darkened into something like obsession.

Dianne listened in silence as I expanded my tale. It was all guesswork; but it *felt* true, and as I went on, I began to *see* the boy Keane in my mind's eye; to feel something of what he had felt and to understand the horror of what he had become.

I wondered whether Leon Mitchell had known the truth. Certainly, Marlene had been completely taken in by Julian Pinchbeck, as indeed had I.

A cool customer, Pinchbeck, especially for such a young lad. Even on the roof he had kept his nerve; escaping like a cat before I could intercept him; vanishing in the shadows; even allowing John Snyde to be accused rather than admit his own involvement.

'Perhaps they were horsing about. You know what boys are like. A silly game that went too far. Leon fell. Pinchbeck ran. He let the Porter take the blame, and he's been living with the guilt for fifteen years.'

Imagine what that might do to a child. I considered Keane and tried to see the bitterness behind the façade. I couldn't do it. There was perhaps some irreverence – a whiff of the upstart – a hint of mockery in the way he spoke. But malice – actual *malice*? It was hard to believe. And yet, if not Keane, then who could it be?

'He's been playing with us,' I told Miss Dare. 'That's his style. His humour. It's the same basic game as before, I think, but this time he's taking it through to the end. It isn't enough for him to hide in the shadows any more. He wants to hit St Oswald's where it really hurts.'

'But *why?*' she said.

I sighed, feeling suddenly very tired. 'I liked him,' I said irrelevantly. 'I still like him.'

There was a long silence.

'Have you called the police?'

I nodded. 'Marlene has.'

'Then they'll find him,' she said. 'Don't worry, Mr Straitley. We might get to have that birthday drink after all.'

9

NEEDLESS TO SAY MY OWN BIRTHDAY WAS A SAD AFFAIR. I understood, however, that it was a necessary stage, and I opened my presents, still waiting under the bed in their gaudy wrappers, with gritted-teeth determination. There were letters, too – all the letters I had previously scorned – and now I gave every word my obsessive attention, combing through the reams of nonsense for the few precious scraps that would complete my metamorphosis.

Dear Munchkin,

I hope you got the clothes I sent you. I hope they all fit! Children seem to grow up so much faster here in Paris, and I do want you to look nice for your visit. You'll be quite grown-up by now, I suppose. I can hardly believe I'm nearly thirty. The doctor says I can't have any more children. Thank goodness I've still got you, my love. It's as if God has given me a second chance.

The packages contained more clothes than I'd ever owned in my entire life. Little outfits from Printemps or Galeries Lafayette, little jumpers in sugared-almond colours, two coats (a red one for winter and a green one for spring) and any number of little tops, T-shirts and shorts.

The police had been very gentle with me. As well they might; I'd had a terrible shock. They sent a nice lady officer to ask me some questions, and I answered them with becoming forthrightness and the occasional tear. I was told several times that I had been very brave. My mother was proud of me; the nice lady officer was proud of me; it would be over soon and all I had to do was tell the truth and not be afraid of anything.

It's funny, isn't it, how easy it is to believe the worst. My story was simple (I've found lies are always best served as plainly as possible), and the police lady listened to it keenly, without interruption or apparent disbelief.

Officially, the School declared it a tragic accident. My father's death closed the matter rather conveniently, even gaining him some posthumous sympathy from the local Press. His suicide was put down to extreme remorse following the death of a young trespasser on his watch, and the other details – including the presence of a mystery boy – were rapidly set aside.

Mrs Mitchell, who might have been a problem, was given substantial compensation and a new job as Bishop's secretary – they had become rather close friends in the weeks that followed Leon's death. Bishop himself – recently promoted – was warned by the Head that any further investigation of the unfortunate incident would be both detrimental to the reputation of St Oswald's and a dereliction of his duties as Second Master.

That left Straitley. Not so different then as now; a man grey-haired before his time, delighting in absurdity, rather slimmer than he is now but still ungainly, a shambling albatross of a man in his dusty gown and leather slippers. Leon never respected him quite as I did; saw him as a harmless buffoon, likeable enough, clever in his way, but essentially not a threat. Still, it was Straitley who came closest to seeing the truth, and it was only his arrogance – the arrogance of St Oswald's – that blinded him to the obvious.

I suppose I should have been grateful. But a talent like mine begs to be acknowledged, and of all the casual insults St Oswald's has thrown at me over the years, I think it is his I remember most vividly. His look of surprise – and yes, condescension – as he looked at me – *dismissed* me – for the second time.

Of course I wasn't thinking clearly. Still blinded by guilt, confusion, fear, I had yet to learn one of life's most shocking and closely guarded truths; that remorse fades, like anything else. Perhaps I *wanted* to be caught that day; to prove to myself that Order still ruled; to keep the myth of St Oswald's intact in my heart; and most of all, after five years in the shadows, to finally take my place under the lights.

And Straitley? In my long game against St Oswald's, it has always been Straitley, and not the Head, who has played the King's role. A slow mover, the King; but a powerful enemy. Even so, a well-placed pawn may bring him down. Not that I wished for that, no. Absurd as it was, I wished, not for his destruction, but for his respect, his approval. I had been the Invisible Man for much too long, the ghost in St Oswald's creaking machine. Now at last I wanted him to look at me – to *see* me – and concede, if not a win, then perhaps a draw.

I was in the kitchen when he finally called at the house. It was my birthday, just before dinner, and I'd spent half the day shopping with my mother, and the other half discussing my future and making plans.

A knock on the door – I guessed who it was. I knew him so well, you see – albeit from a distance – and I had been expecting his visit. I knew he, of all men, would never take the easy solution over the just. Firm, but fair, was Roy Straitley; with a natural propensity to believe the best of anyone. John's reputation cut no ice with him; nor did the New Head's veiled threats; nor the speculations in that day's *Examiner*. Even the possible damage to St Oswald's was secondary to this. Straitley was Leon's form-teacher, and to Straitley, his boys mattered more than anything else.

At first my mother wouldn't let him in. He'd called twice before, she told me, once when I was in bed and once more as I was changing my clothes, discarding my Pinchbeck gear for one of the Paris outfits she'd sent in her innumerable care packages.

'Mrs Snyde, if you could just let me in for a *moment*—'

My mother's voice, her newly rounded vowels still

unfamiliar behind the kitchen door. 'I told you, Mr Straitley, we've had a difficult twenty-four hours and I really don't think—'

Even then I sensed that he was uncomfortable with women. Peering through the crack in the kitchen door I saw him, framed by the night, head down, hands digging deeply into the pockets of his old tweed jacket.

In front of him, my mother; tensed for confrontation; all Paris pearls and pastel twin-set. It disturbed him, that feminine temperament. He would have been happier talking to my father, straight to the point, in words of one syllable.

'Well, perhaps if I could just have a word with the child.'

I checked my reflection in the kettle. Under Mother's guidance, I was looking good. Hair neat and freshly styled; face scrubbed; resplendent in one of those new little outfits. I had removed my glasses. I knew I would pass; and besides, I wanted to see him – to see, and, perhaps, be *seen*.

'Mr Straitley, believe me, there's nothing we can—'

I pushed open the kitchen door. He looked up quickly. For the first time I met his eyes as my very own self. My mother stood close, ready to snatch me away at the first sign of distress. Roy Straitley took a step towards me; I caught the comforting smell of chalk dust and Gauloises and distant mothballs. I wondered what he would say if I greeted him in Latin; the temptation was almost too great to resist, then I remembered that I was playing a part. Would he recognize me in my new role?

For a second I thought he might. His eyes were penetrating. Denim-blue and slightly bloodshot, they narrowed a little as they met mine. I put out my hand – took his thick fingers in my own cool ones. I thought of all the times I had watched him in the Bell Tower; of all the things he had unwittingly taught me. Would he see me now? Would he?

I saw his eyes flick over me; taking in the clean face, pastel sweater, ankle-socks and polished shoes. Not quite what he'd expected, then; I had to make an effort to hide a smile. My mother saw it, and smiled herself, proud of her achievement. As well she might be; the transformation was all hers.

'Good evening,' he said. 'I don't mean to intrude. I'm Mr Straitley. Leon Mitchell's form-tutor.'

'Pleased to meet you, sir,' I said. 'I'm Julia Snyde.'

10

I HAD TO LAUGH. SUCH A LONG TIME SINCE I HAD THOUGHT of myself as Julia, rather than just Snyde. And besides, I'd never *liked* Julia, just as my father had never liked her, and to be reminded of her – to *be* her – now was strange and puzzling. I thought I had outgrown Julia, as I had outgrown Sharon. But my mother had reinvented herself. Why couldn't I?

Straitley, of course, never saw it. To him, women remain a race apart, to be admired (or perhaps feared) from a safe distance. His manner is different when talking to his boys; with Julia his easy manner stiffened a little; became a wary parody of its jovial self.

'Now I don't want to upset you,' he said.

I nodded.

'But do you know a boy called Julian Pinchbeck?'

I have to admit that my relief was marred by a certain disappointment. I'd expected more of Straitley, somehow;

more of St Oswald's. After all, I'd already practically offered him the truth. And still he hadn't seen it. In his arrogance – the peculiarly *male* arrogance that lies at the very foundations of St Oswald's – he had failed to see what was staring him in the face.

Julian Pinchbeck.

Julia Snyde.

'Pinchbeck?' I said. 'I don't think so, sir.'

'He'd be your age, or thereabouts. Dark hair, skinny. Wears glasses with wire frames. He may be a pupil at Sunnybank Park. You may have seen him around St Oswald's.'

I shook my head. 'I'm sorry, sir.'

'You know why I'm asking, don't you, Julia?'

'Yes, sir. You think he was there last night.'

'He was there,' snapped Straitley. He cleared his throat and said, in a softer voice, 'I thought maybe you'd seen him too.'

'No, sir.' Once more I shook my head. It was too funny, I thought to myself; and yet I wondered how he could have failed to see me. Was it because I was a girl, perhaps? A slapper, a pram-face, a toerag, a prole? Was it so impossible to believe such a thing of Julia Snyde?

'Are you sure?' He looked at me sharply. 'Because that boy's a witness. He was there. He saw what happened.'

I looked down at the shiny toes of my shoes. I wanted to tell him everything then, just to see his jaw drop. But then he would have had to know about Leon, too; and that, I knew, was impossible. For that I had already sacrificed so much. And for that I prepared to swallow my pride.

I looked up at him then, allowing my eyes to fill with tears. It wasn't difficult in the circumstances. I thought of Leon, and of my father, and of myself, and the tears just came all on their own. 'I'm sorry,' I said. 'I didn't see him.' And now old Straitley was looking uncomfortable, huffling and shuffling just as he did when Kitty Teague had her little crisis in the Common Room.

'Now then.' He pulled out a large and slightly grubby handkerchief.

My mother glared. 'I hope you're happy,' she said, putting a possessive arm around my shoulders. 'After everything the poor kid's already been through—'

'Mrs Snyde, I didn't—'

'I think you should go.'

'Julia, please, if you know anything—'

'Mr Straitley,' she said. 'I'd like you to leave.'

And so he did, reluctantly, caught between bluster and unease, apologies on one side, suspicion on the other.

Because he *was* suspicious; I could see it in his eyes. He was nowhere near the truth, of course; but his years of teaching have given him a second sight where pupils are concerned, a kind of radar that in some way I must have triggered.

He turned to go, hands in his pockets. 'Julian Pinchbeck. You're *sure* you've never heard of him?'

Mutely, I nodded, grinning inside.

His shoulders slumped. Then, as my mother opened the door for him to leave, he turned abruptly and met my eyes for what was to be the last time in fifteen years. 'I didn't mean to upset you,' he said. 'We're all concerned about your father. But I was Leon's form-tutor. I have a responsibility to my boys—'

Again I nodded. '*Vale, magister.*' It was no more than a whisper, but I swear he heard.

'*What* was that?'

'Goodnight, sir.'

11

AFTER THAT, WE MOVED TO PARIS. A NEW LIFE, MY MOTHER had said; a new start for her little girl. But it wasn't that easy. I didn't like Paris. I missed my home and the woods and the comforting smell of cut grass rolling over the fields. My mother deplored my tomboyish manners, for which, of course, she blamed my father. He'd never wanted a girl, she said, lamenting over my cropped hair, my skinny chest, my scabbed knees. Thanks to John, she said, I looked more like a dirty little boy than the dainty daughter of her imaginings. But that was going to change, she said. All I needed was time to blossom.

God knows, I tried. There were endless shopping trips; dress fittings; appointments at the beautician's. Any girl would dream of being taken in hand; to be Gigi, to be Eliza, to change from the ugly duckling into the gracious swan. It was my mother's dream, anyway. And she indulged it now; crowing happily over her living doll.

Nowadays, of course, little trace remains of my mother's handiwork. My own is more sophisticated and definitely less showy. My French is fluent, thanks to four years in Paris, and although I never quite made the grade as far as my mother was concerned, I like to think I have acquired a certain style. I also have an abnormally high sense of self-esteem, or so my analyst says, which at times verges on the pathological. Maybe so; but in the absence of parents, where else is a child to seek approval?

By the time I was fourteen, my mother had realized that I would never be a beauty. I wasn't the type. *Un style très anglais*, as the beautician (the bitch!) repeatedly pointed out. The little skirts and twin-sets that looked so pretty on the French girls simply made me look ridiculous, and I soon forsook them for the safety of the jeans, sweatshirts and trainers of my earlier youth. I refused make-up and cut my hair short. I no longer looked like a little boy, but it had become clear that I would never be Audrey Hepburn, either.

My mother was not as disappointed as she might have been. Despite her high hopes, we had failed to bond. We had little in common, and I could tell that she was tired of making the effort. More importantly, she and Xavier had finally achieved what they had hitherto thought impossible – a miracle baby, born in the August of the following year.

Well, that clinched it. Overnight, I became an embarrassment. The miracle baby – they called it Adeline – had basically priced me out of the market, and neither my mother nor Xavier (who had few opinions of his own) seemed interested in an awkward teenager. Once more, in spite of everything, I was invisible.

Oh, I can't say I cared. Not about that, anyway. I had nothing against Adeline – who looked like nothing more to me than a squawking lump of pink putty. What I resented was the *promise*; the promise of something that had been barely offered before it was snatched away. The fact that I hadn't wanted it was irrelevant. My mother's ingratitude was. I had made *sacrifices* for her, after all. For her I had left St Oswald's. Now, more than ever, St Oswald's beckoned to me like a lost Eden. I forgot how I'd hated it; how for years I waged war against it; how it had swallowed my friend, my father, my childhood at a single gulp. I thought about it all the time, and it seemed to me then that it was only in St Oswald's that I had ever felt truly alive. There, I had dreamed; there I had felt joy; hate; desire. There I had been a hero; a rebel. Now I was just another sullen teen, with a stepfather and a mother who lied about her age.

I know it now; it was an addiction, and St Oswald's was my drug. Night and day I craved it, finding poor substitutes where I could. Rapidly they bored me; my *lycée* was a dull place, and the most daring of its rebels only dabbled in the most adolescent of misdemeanours: a little sex, a little truancy and a number of basically uninteresting drugs. Leon and I had covered far more exciting ground together years before. I wanted more; I wanted misrule; I wanted *everything*.

I was unaware at the time that my behaviour had already begun to attract attention. I was young; angry; intoxicated. You might say St Oswald's had spoiled me; I was like a university student sent back to kindergarten for a year, smashing toys and turning over tables. I delighted in being a bad influence. I played truant; I mocked my teachers; I drank; I smoked; I had hurried (and, for me, joyless) sex with a number of boys from a rival school.

The crunch came in a most distressingly *ordinary* way. My mother and Xavier – who I'd assumed were too goggle-eyed over their miracle child to care much about the down-to-earth kind – had been watching me more closely than I had thought. A sweep of my room had provided the excuse they were seeking: a five-gram block of workaday resin, a packet of condoms and four Es in a twist of paper.

It was kids' stuff, that was all. Any normal parent would have forgotten all about it, but Sharon simply mumbled something about my previous history, removed me from school and – the final indignity – booked me in with a child psychologist, who, she promised, would soon bring me to rights.

I don't think I am a naturally resentful person. Whenever I have lashed out, it has always been after almost unbearable provocation. But this was more than anyone could stand. I wasted no time in protesting my innocence. Instead, and to my mother's surprise, I cooperated as best I could. The child psychologist – whose name was Martine and who wore dangly earrings with little silver kitties – declared me to be progressing nicely, and I fed her every day until she got quite tame.

Say what you like about my unconventional schooling, but I do have quite an extensive general knowledge. You can thank St Oswald's library, or Leon, or the films I've always watched – in any case I knew enough about mental cases to fool a kitty-loving child psychologist. I almost regretted the ease of the task; found myself wishing they had given me more of a challenge.

Psychologists. They're all the same. Talk to them about anything you like, it always gets down to sex in the end. After an impressive show of reluctance and a number of nicely Freudian dreams, I confessed; I'd been having sex with my father. Not John, I said; but my *new* father, which made it all right – or so *he* said, although I myself had been having second thoughts.

Don't get me wrong. I had nothing (as such) against Xavier. It was my *mother* who had betrayed me; my mother I wanted to hurt. But Xavier was such a convenient tool, and besides, I made it sound mostly consensual, so that he would get off with a lighter – maybe even a suspended – sentence.

It worked fine. Too fine, perhaps; by then I'd been working on my routine and incorporated a number of embellishments to the basic formula. More dreams – I don't dream, as I said, but I do have quite a vivid imagination – a number of physical mannerisms, a habit of cutting picked up from one of the more sensitive girls in my class at school.

Physical examination provided the proof. Xavier was duly ousted from the family home, a generous allowance was promised to the soon-to-be divorcée and I (thanks in part to my brilliant performance) was stuck in an institution for the next three years by my loving mother and the kitty-wearing Martine, neither of whom could be convinced that I was no longer a danger to myself.

You know, there is such a thing as doing a job too well.

MATE

1

Friday, 5th November
Bonfire Night, 9.15 p.m.

'WELL, THEN,' HE SAID. 'I SUPPOSE THAT'S THAT.'

The fireworks were over and the crowd had begun to disperse, shuffling slowly towards the exits. The cordoned area was almost empty; only the smell of gunsmoke remained. 'Perhaps we ought to find Marlene. I don't like to think of her waiting alone.'

Dear old Straitley. Always the gent. And so *close*, too; certainly he'd come closer to the truth than my mother, or my analyst, or any of the professionals who had tried to understand my teenage mind. Not quite close enough – not yet – but he was almost there, we were in the endgame now, and my heart beat a little faster at the thought. Long ago I'd faced him as a pawn and lost. Now, at last, I challenged him as a Queen.

I turned to him, smiled, and said, '*Vale, magister.*'

'*What* did you say?'

She had turned to go; in the glow of the embers she looked very youthful under her red beret, her eyes pinned with dancing firelight. 'You heard,' she said. 'You heard me then, didn't you, sir?'

Then? The invisible finger prodded me gently, almost sympathetically. I felt a sudden urge to sit down and resisted it.

'You'll remember in time,' said Miss Dare, smiling. 'After all, you're the one who never forgets a face.'

I watched him as he worked it out. The mist had thickened; now it was hard to see beyond the closest trees. At our backs, the bonfire was nothing but embers; unless it rained it would continue to smoulder for two or three days. Straitley frowned, burnished like a wrinkled totem in the dim light. A minute passed. Two minutes. I began to feel anxious. Was he too old? Had he forgotten? And what would I do if he failed me now?

Finally, he spoke. 'It's – it's Julie, isn't it?'

Close enough, old man. I dared draw breath. 'Julia, sir. Julia Snyde.'

Julia Snyde.

Such a long time since I'd heard that name. Such a long time since I'd even thought of her. And yet here she was again, looking just like Dianne Dare, looking at me with affection – and a touch of humour – in her bright brown eyes.

'You changed your name?' I said at last.

She smiled. 'Under the circumstances, yes.'

That I could understand. She'd gone to France – 'Paris, was it? I suppose that's where you learned your French.'

'I was an apt pupil.'

Now I recalled that day in the Gatehouse. Her dark hair, cut shorter than it is now, the neat, girlish outfit, pleated skirt and pastel sweater. The way she'd smiled at me, shyly then, but with knowledge in her eyes. How I'd been sure she'd known something—

I looked at her now in the uncanny light and wondered how I could have failed to miss her. I wondered what she was doing here now, and how she had changed from Porter's girl to the assured young woman she was today. Most of all I wondered just how much she had known, and why she had hidden it from me, now and all those years ago.

'You did know Pinchbeck, didn't you?' I said.

Silently she nodded.

'But then – what about Keane?'

She smiled. 'As I said. He had to go.'

Well, serve him right, the little sneak. Him and his note-books. My first glance should have warned me; those lines, those drawings, those whimsical little observations on the nature and history of St Oswald's. I remember asking myself then whether it wouldn't have been better to deal with him straight away; but I had a lot on my mind at the time, and anyway, there wasn't much – besides that photograph – to incriminate me.

You'd think a budding author would have been far too busy with his Muse to go messing with such ancient history. But he had – plus he'd spent time at Sunnybank Park, though he was three or four years ahead of me, and wouldn't have made the connection immediately.

I hadn't myself for a while, you know; but some-where along the line, I must have recognized his face. I'd known it *before* I joined Sunnybank Park; remembered watching as a gang of boys cornered him after school; remembered his neat clothes – suspicious for a Sunnybanker – and, most of all, the library books under his arm that proclaimed him a target. I'd known right then it could have been me.

It had taught me a lesson, watching that boy. *Be invisible,* I'd warned myself. *Don't look too smart. Don't carry books.*

And if in doubt, run like hell. Keane hadn't run. That had always been his problem.

In a way I'm sorry. Still, after the notebook, I knew I couldn't let him live. He'd already found the St Oswald's picture; he'd talked to Marlene, and most of all there was that photograph, taken from God knows what Sports Day at Sunnybank, with Yours Truly at the back (the Thunderpants mercifully out of sight). Once he'd made that connection (and he would have done, sooner or later), it would have been a simple matter of going through Sunnybank's photo archive until he found what he was looking for.

I'd bought the knife some months before – £24.99 from Army Stores – and I have to say it was a good one; sharp, slim, double-edged and lethal. Rather like myself, in fact. A pity I had to leave it, really – I'd meant it for Straitley – but retrieving it would have been a messy business, and besides, I didn't want to be wandering around a public park with a murder weapon in my pocket. No chance of finding any prints on the knife, either. I was wearing gloves.

I'd followed him to the cordoned area, just as the fireworks were starting. Here there were trees, and in their shelter the shadows were doubly dark. There were people all around, of course; but most of them were watching the sky, and in the false light of all those rockets, nobody saw the quick little drama that played out under the trees.

It takes a surprising amount of skill to stab someone between the ribs. It's the intercostal muscles that are the trickiest part; they contract, you know, so that even if you don't strike a rib by accident, you have to get through a layer of tensed muscle before you do any real damage. Going for the heart is equally risky; it's the breastbone, you see, that gets in the way. The ideal method is through the spinal cord, between the third and fourth vertebrae, but you tell me how I was expected to locate the spot, in the dark, and with most of him hidden under a great big Army Surplus parka?

I might have cut his throat, of course, but those of us who have actually tried it, rather than just watching the movies, will tell you that it's not as easy as it looks. I settled for an upward thrust from the diaphragm, just below the wishbone. I dumped him under the trees, where anyone seeing him would assume he was drunk, and leave him well alone. I'm not a biology teacher, so I can only guess – blood loss or a collapsed lung – as to the technical cause of death, but *he* was pretty damn surprised about it, I can tell you.

'You killed him?'

'Yes, sir. Nothing personal.'

It occurred to me that perhaps I was genuinely ill; that all this was a kind of hallucination that said more about my subconscious than I wanted to know. Certainly I'd felt better. A sudden stitch dug painfully into my left armpit. The invisible finger had become an entire hand; a firm, constant pressure against my breastbone that made me gasp.

'Mr Straitley?' There was concern in Miss Dare's voice.

'Just a stitch,' I said, and sat down abruptly. The muddy ground, though soft, seemed astonishingly cold; a cold that pulsed up through the grass like a dying heartbeat. 'You killed him?' I repeated.

'He was a loose end, sir. As I said, he had to go.'

'And Knight?'

There was a pause. 'And Knight,' said Miss Dare.

For a moment, an awful moment, my breath caught. I hadn't liked the boy, but he was one of mine, and in spite of everything I suppose I'd hoped—

'Mr Straitley, please. I can't have this now. Come on, stand up—' She put a shoulder under my arm – she was stronger than she looked – and hauled me upright.

'Knight's dead?' I said numbly.

'Don't worry, sir. It was quick.' She wedged a hip against my ribs, half-hoisting me to my feet. 'But I needed a victim, and not just a body, either. I needed a *story*. A murdered schoolboy makes front-page news – on a slow day – but a *missing* boy just keeps on giving. Searches; speculation; tearful appeals from the distracted mother; interviews with friends; then as hope dwindles, the dragging of local ponds and reservoirs, the discovery of an item of clothing and the inevitable DNA testing of listed paedophiles in the area. You know how it is, sir. They know, but they *don't* know. And until they know for certain—'

The cramp in my side came again, and I gave a smothered gasp. Miss Dare broke off at once. 'I'm sorry, sir,' she said in a gentler voice. 'None of that's important now.

Knight can wait. It's not as if he's going anywhere, is it? Just breathe slowly. Keep walking. And for God's sake, *look* at me. We don't have much time.'

And so I breathed, and I looked, and I kept walking, and slowly we limped, I hanging like an albatross around Miss Dare's neck, towards the sheltering trees.

2

Friday, 5th November
9.30 p.m.

THERE WAS A BENCH UNDER THE TREES. WE STAGGERED there together across the muddy grass, and I collapsed on to the seat with a jolt that set my old heart twanging like a broken spring.

Miss Dare was trying to tell me something. I tried to explain that I had other things on my mind. Oh, it comes to us all in the end, I know; but I'd expected something more than this madness in a muddy field. But Keane was dead; Knight was dead; Miss Dare was someone else, and now I could no longer pretend to myself that the agony that flared and clawed at my side was anything remotely resembling a stitch. Old age is so undignified, I thought. Not for us the glories of the Senate, but a rushed exit in the back of an ambulance – or worse, a doddering decline. And still I fought it. I could hear my heart straining to keep moving, to keep the old body going for just a little longer, and I thought to myself; are we ever ready? And do we ever, really believe?

'Please, Mr Straitley. I need you to concentrate.'

Concentrate, forsooth! 'I happen to be rather preoccupied at the moment,' I said. 'The small matter of my imminent demise. Maybe later—'

But now that memory came again, closer now, almost close enough to touch. A face, half-blue, half-red, turning towards me, a young face raw with distress and harsh with resolve, a face, glimpsed once, fifteen years ago—

'Shh,' said Miss Dare. 'Can you see me now?'

And then, suddenly, I did.

A rare moment of overwhelming clarity. Dominoes in line, rattling furiously towards the mystic centre. Black-and-white pictures leaping into sudden relief; a vase becomes lovers; a familiar face disintegrates and becomes something else altogether.

I looked; and in that moment I saw Pinchbeck; his face upturned, his glasses strobing in the emergency lights. And at the same time I saw Julia Snyde with her neat black fringe; and Miss Dare's grey eyes under her schoolboy's cap, the flashes of the fireworks illuminating her face and suddenly, like that, I just knew.

Do you see me now?

Yes, I do.

I caught the moment. His jaw dropped. His face seemed to slacken; it was like watching rapid decay through time-lapse photography. Suddenly he looked far older than his sixty-five years; in fact in that moment he looked every bit the Centurion.

Catharsis. It's what my analyst keeps talking about; but I'd never experienced anything like it until then. That look on Straitley's face. The understanding – the horror – and behind it, I thought perhaps, the pity.

'Julian Pinchbeck. Julia Snyde.'

I smiled then, feeling the years slip from me like dead weight. 'It was staring you in the face, sir,' I said. 'And all the time you never saw it. Never even guessed.'

He sighed. He looked increasingly ill now; his face was hung with sweat. His breath rattled and churned. I hoped he wasn't about to die. I'd waited too long for this moment. Oh, he'd have to go in the end, of course – with or without my killing knife I knew I could finish him easily – but before that, I wanted him to understand. To see and to know without any doubt.

'I see,' he said. (I knew he didn't.) 'It was a dreadful business.' (That it was.) 'But why take it out on St Oswald's? Why blame Pat Bishop, or Grachvogel, or Keane, or Light – and why kill Knight, who was just a boy—'

'Knight was bait,' I said. 'Sad, but necessary. And as for

the others, don't make me laugh. Bishop? That hypocrite. Running scared at the first breath of scandal. Grachvogel? It would have happened sooner or later whether I had a hand in it or not. Light? You're better off without him. And as for Devine – I was practically doing you a favour. More interesting is the way in which history repeats itself. Look how fast the Head dropped Bishop when he thought this scandal might damage the School. Now he knows how my father felt. It didn't matter whether he was to blame or not. It didn't even matter that a pupil had died. What mattered most – what *still* matters most – was protecting the School. Boys come and go. *Porters* come and go. But God forbid that anything should happen to besmirch St Oswald's. Ignore it, bury it, and make it go away. That's the School motto. Isn't that right?' I took a deep breath. 'Not now, though. Now, at last, I've got your attention.'

He gave a rasp that could have been laughter. 'Perhaps,' he said. 'But couldn't you just have sent us a postcard?'

Dear old Straitley. Always the comedian. 'He liked you, sir. He always liked you.'

'Who did? Your father?'

'No, sir. Leon.'

There was a long, dark silence. I could feel his heart pumping. The holiday crowd had long since dispersed, and only a few scattered figures remained, silhouetted against the distant bonfire and in the near-deserted arcades. We were alone – as alone as we could be – and all around us I could hear the sounds of the leafless trees; the slow, brittle creaking of the branches; the occasional sharp tussle of a small animal – rat or mouse – in the fallen leaves.

The silence went on so long that I feared the old man had gone to sleep – that, or had slipped into some distant place to which I could not follow him. Then he sighed, and put out his hand towards me in the darkness. Against my palm, his fingers were cold.

'Leon Mitchell,' he said slowly. 'Is *that* what this is all about?'

3

Bonfire Night
9.35 p.m.

LEON MITCHELL. I SHOULD HAVE KNOWN. I SHOULD HAVE known from the start that Leon Mitchell was at the bottom of this. If ever a boy was trouble incarnate, he was the one. Of all my ghosts he has never rested easy. And of all my boys he haunts me most.

I spoke to Pat Bishop about him once, trying to understand exactly what had happened and whether there was something more I might have done. Pat assured me there wasn't. I was at my balcony at the time. The boys were below me on the Chapel roof. The Porter was already on the scene. Short of *flying* down there like Superman, what could I have done to prevent the tragedy? It happened so fast. No one could have stopped it. And yet hindsight is a deceitful tool, turning angels into villains, tigers into clowns. Over the years, past certainties melt like ripe cheese; no memory is safe.

Could I have stopped him? You can't imagine how often I have asked myself that very question. In the small hours it often seems all too possible; events unspooling with dream-like clarity as time and again the boy falls – fourteen years old, and this time I was *there* – there at my balcony like an overweight Juliet, and in those small hours I can see Leon Mitchell all too clearly, clinging to the rusty ledge, his broken fingernails wedged into the rotting stone, his eyes alive with terror.

'*Pinchbeck?*'

My voice startles him. A voice of authority, coming so unexpectedly out of the night. He looks up instinctively – his grip breaks. Maybe he calls out; begins to reach up; his heel stropping against a foothold that is already half rust.

And then it begins, so slow at first and yet so impossibly fast, and there are seconds, whole *seconds* for him to think of that gullet of space, that terrible darkness.

Guilt, like an avalanche, gathering speed.

Memory, snapshots against a dark screen.

Dominoes in a line – and the growing conviction that perhaps it was me, that if I hadn't called out just at that precise moment, then maybe – just maybe—

I looked up at Miss Dare and saw her watching me. 'Tell me,' I said. 'Just whom do you blame?'

Dianne Dare said nothing.

'Tell me.' The stitch-that-wasn't clawed fiercely into my side; but after all these years the need to know was more painful still. I looked up at her, so smooth and serene; her face in the mist like that of a Renaissance Madonna. 'You were there,' I said with an effort. 'Was *I* the reason Leon fell?'

Oh, how clever you are, I thought. *My analyst could learn a trick or two.* To throw that sentiment back at me – hoping perhaps, to gain a little more time . . .

'Please,' he said. 'I need to know.'

'Why's that?' I said.

'He was one of my boys.'

So simple; so devastating. *One of my boys.* Suddenly I wished he'd never come; or that I could have disposed of him, as I'd disposed of Keane, easily, without distress. Oh, he was in a bad way; but now it was I who struggled to breathe; I who felt the avalanche poised to roll over me. I wanted to laugh; there were tears in my eyes. After all these years, could it be that *Roy Straitley blamed himself?* It was exquisite. It was terrible.

'You'll be telling me next he was like a son to you.' The tremor in my voice belied the sneer. In fact, I was shaken.

'My lost boys,' he said, ignoring the sneer. 'Thirty-three years and I still remember every one. Their pictures on my living-room wall. Their names in my registers. Hewitt, '72. Constable, '86. Jamestone, Deakin, Stanley, Poulson –

Knight—' He paused. 'And Mitchell, of course. How could I have forgotten him? The little shit.'

It happens, you know, from time to time. You can't like them all – though you try as best you can to treat them the same. But sometimes there's a boy – like Mitchell, like Knight – who, try as you may, you can never like.

Expelled from his last school for seducing a teacher; spoilt rotten by his parents; a liar, a user, a manipulator of others. Oh, he was clever – he could even be charming. But I knew what he was, and I told her as much. Poison to the core.

'You're wrong, sir,' she said. 'Leon was my friend. The best friend I ever had. He cared for me – he *loved* me – and if you hadn't been there – if you hadn't yelled out when you did—'

Her voice was fragmenting now, becoming – for the first time I had known her – shrill and uncontrolled. It occurred to me only then that she planned to kill me – absurd, really, as I must have known it from the moment of her confession. I supposed I ought to be afraid – but in spite of that, in spite of the pain in my side, all I could feel was an overriding sense of *irritation* with the woman, as if a bright student had made an elementary grammatical mistake.

'Grow up,' I told her. 'Leon didn't care about anyone but himself. He liked to exploit people. That's what he did; setting them off against each other, winding them up like toys. I wouldn't be surprised if it had been his idea to go up on the roof in the first place, just to see what would happen.'

She drew a sharp breath like a cat's hiss, and I knew I'd overstepped the mark. Then she laughed, regaining her control as if it had never been lost. 'You're fairly Machiavellian yourself, sir.'

I took that as a compliment, and said so.

'It is, sir. I've always respected you. Even now I think of you as an *adversary* rather than an enemy.'

'Be careful, Miss Dare, you'll turn my head.'

She laughed again, a brittle sound. 'Even then,' she said, her eyes gleaming. 'I wanted you to see me. I wanted you to *know*—' She told me how she'd listened in at my classes, gone through my files, built her store from the discarded grains of St Oswald's generous harvests. For a time I drifted as she spoke – the pain in my side receding now – recounting those truant days; books borrowed; uniforms pilfered; rules broken. Like the mice, she'd made her nest in the Bell Tower and on the roof; collecting knowledge; feeding when she could. She had been hungry for knowledge; she had been ravenous. And all unknowing, I had been her *magister*; singled out from the moment I first spoke to her that day in the Middle Corridor, now singled out again to blame for the death of her friend, the suicide of her father and the many failures in her life.

It happens, sometimes. It's happened to most of my colleagues at one time or another. It's an inevitable conse-quence of being a schoolmaster, of being in charge of susceptible adolescents. Of course, for female members of staff it happens daily; for the rest of us, thank God, it is only occasional. But boys are boys; and they sometimes fixate upon a member of staff (male or female) – sometimes they even call it love. It's happened to me; to Kitty; even to old Sourgrape, who once spent six months trying to shake off the attentions of a young student called Michael Smalls, who found every excuse to seek him out, to monopolize his time, and finally (when his wooden-faced hero failed to live up to his impossible expectations) to disparage him on every possible occasion to Mr and Mrs Smalls, who eventually removed their son from St Oswald's (after a set of disastrous O-level results) to an alternative school, where he settled down and promptly fell in love with the young Spanish mistress.

Now, it seemed, I was in the same boat. I don't pretend to be Freud or anyone, but it was clear even to me that this unfortunate young woman had somehow *chosen* me in much the same way that young Smalls had chosen Sourgrape, investing in me qualities – and now, responsibilities – that were quite out of proportion with my true role. Worse, she had done the same with Leon Mitchell, who, being dead, had attained a status and a romance to which no living person, however saintly, might hope to aspire. Between us, there could be no contest. After all, what victory can there ever be in a battle with the dead?

Still, remained that irritation. It was the *waste*, you see, that troubled me; the confounded waste. Miss Dare was young, bright, talented; there should have been a bright, promising life stretching out ahead of her. Instead she had chosen to shackle herself, like some old Centurion, to the wreck of St Oswald's; to the gilded figurehead of Leon Mitchell, of all people, a boy remarkable only by his essential mediocrity and the stupid squandering of his young life.

I tried to say so, but she wasn't listening. 'He would have been somebody,' she said in a stubborn voice. 'Leon was special. Different. Clever. He was a free spirit. He didn't play to the normal rules. People would have remembered him.'

'*Remembered* him? Perhaps they would. Certainly I've never known anyone leave so many casualties behind him. Poor Marlene. She knew the truth, but he was her son and she loved him, whatever he did. And that teacher at his old school. Metalwork teacher; a married man, a fool. Leon destroyed him, you know. Selfishly; on a whim, when he got bored of his attentions. And what about the man's wife? She was a teacher, too, and in that profession it makes you guilty by association. Two careers down the drain. One man in prison. A marriage ruined. And that girl – what was her name? She can't have been more than fourteen years old. All of them victims of Leon Mitchell's little games. And now me, Bishop, Grachvogel, Devine – and you, Miss Dare. What makes you think *you're* any different?'

I had stopped for breath, and there was silence. Silence so complete, in fact, that I wondered if she had gone away. Then she spoke in a small, glassy voice.

'What girl?' she said.

4

Bonfire Night
9.45 p.m.

HE'D SEEN HER IN THE HOSPITAL, WHERE I HAD NOT DARED go. Oh, I'd wanted to; but Leon's mother had been there at his bedside the whole time, and the risk was unacceptable. But Francesca had come; and the Tynans; and Bishop. And Straitley, of course.

He'd remembered her well. After all, who wouldn't? Fifteen years old and beautiful in that way that old men find so inexplicably heart-breaking. He'd noticed her, first for her hair and the way it fell across her face in a single swatch of raw silk. Bewildered, perhaps, but more than a little excited by the drama of it all; the real-life tragedy in which she was a player. She'd chosen black, as if for a funeral, but mostly because it suited her, for after all, Leon wasn't actually going to *die*. He was fourteen, for pity's sake. At fourteen, death is something that only happens on TV.

Straitley hadn't spoken to the girl. Instead he'd gone to the hospital cafeteria to bring Marlene a cup of tea, whilst waiting for Leon's visitors to leave. He'd seen Francesca on her way out – still fascinated perhaps by that hair as it moved like an animal across her lower back – and it had crossed his mind that the roundness at her stomach looked more pronounced than the usual adolescent tubbiness; in fact with those long, slim legs and narrow shoulders, that weight around her abdomen made her look more than a little—

I breathed deeply, using the method my analyst had taught me. In for five beats; out for ten. The scent of smoke and dank vegetation was very strong; in the mist my breath plumed like dragonfire.

He was lying, of course. Leon would have told me.

I said it aloud. On the bench the old man lay very still, denying nothing.

'It's a lie, old man.'

The child would be fourteen years old by now, as old as Leon when he died. Boy or girl? Boy, of course. Leon's age; with Leon's grey eyes and Francesca's dappled skin. He wasn't real, I told myself – and yet that image refused to be dismissed. That boy – that imaginary boy – with a hint of Leon in the cheekbones, a hint of Francesca in the plump upper lip . . . I wondered, had he known? Could he possibly *not* have known?

Well, what if he had? Francesca didn't matter to him.

She was just a girl, he'd told me so. Just another shag, not the first, not the best. And yet he'd kept this secret from me, from Pinchbeck, his best friend. Why? Was it shame? Fear? I'd thought Leon above those things. Leon, the free spirit. And yet—

'Say it's a lie and I'll let you live.'

No word from Straitley; just a sound like that of an old dog turning over in his sleep. Damn him, I thought. Our game was practically over, and here he was trying to introduce some element of doubt. It annoyed me; as if my business with St Oswald's were not simply a matter of pure revenge for my broken life, but some altogether messier, less noble affair. 'I mean it,' I said. 'Or our game ends now.'

The pains in my chest had subsided now, to be replaced by a deep and languorous cold. In the darkness above me I could hear Miss Dare's rapid breathing. I wondered if she was planning to kill me now, or whether she meant simply to let Nature take its course. As it happened I found I wasn't especially interested either way.

All the same, I wondered dimly why she cared. My assessment of Leon seemed hardly to have slowed her down; but my description of the pregnant girl had stopped her in her tracks. Clearly, I thought, Miss Dare hadn't known. I considered what this might mean to me.

'It's a lie,' she repeated. The cool humour in her voice

was gone. Now every word crackled with a lethal static. 'Leon would have told me.'

I shook my head. 'No, he wouldn't. He was scared. Terrified it would affect his university prospects. Denied everything at first, but his mother got the truth out of him in the end. As for myself – I'd never seen the girl. Never heard of the other family. But I was Leon's form-tutor. I had to be told. Of course both he and the girl were under-age. But the Mitchells and the Tynans had always been friendly, and with support from the parents and the Church, I suppose they could have managed.'

'You're making this up.' Her voice was flat. 'Leon wouldn't have cared about any of that. He'd have said it was banal.'

'Yes, he liked that word, didn't he?' I said. 'Pretentious little oik. Liked to think the normal rules didn't apply to him. Yes, it was banal, and yes, it frightened him. After all, he was only fourteen.'

There was a silence. Above me, Miss Dare stood like a monolith. Then, at length, she spoke.

'Boy or girl?' she said.

So, she believed me. I drew a long breath, and the hand pressing against my heart seemed to give way, just a little. 'I don't know. I lost touch.' Well, of course I did – we all did. 'There was some talk of adoption at the time, but Marlene never told me, and I never asked. You, of all people, should understand why.'

Another silence, longer, if anything, than the previous one. Then, softly and despairingly, she began to laugh.

I could see her point. It was tragic. It was ridiculous. 'It takes courage sometimes, to face up to the truth. To see our heroes – and our villains – as they really are. To see ourselves as others see us. I wonder, Miss Dare, in all that time you say you were invisible, did *you* ever really see yourself?'

'What do you mean?'

'You know what I mean.'

She'd wanted the truth. And I gave it now, still wondering for what stubborn purpose I was putting myself through all this, and for whom. For Marlene? For Bishop? For Knight? Or simply for Roy Straitley, BA, who had once tutored a boy called Leon Mitchell with no more or less favour or prejudice than any other of my boys – or so at least I fervently hoped, even with the drag of hindsight and that small, persistent fear that perhaps some part of me had *known* the boy might fall – had known, but had factored it into some dark equation, some half-considered attempt to slow down the *other* boy, the boy who pushed him.

'That's it, isn't it?' I told her softly. 'That's the truth. You pushed him, then thought better of it and tried to help. But I was there, and you had to run—'

For *that* was what I thought I'd seen, as I peered short-sightedly from my eyrie in the Bell Tower. Two boys, one facing me, the other with his back turned, and between us the figure of the School Porter, his wavery shadow flicking out across the long rooftop.

He'd called out, and the boys had fled; the one with his back to me plunging ahead of the other so that he came to a stop almost opposite me in the shadow of the Bell Tower. The other was Leon. I recognized him at once, a brief glimpse of his face in the harsh lights before he joined his friend at the edge of the gully.

It should have been an easy jump. A few feet, and they would have reached the main parapet, allowing them a clear run right across the main School roof. An easy jump for the boys, perhaps, though I could see from John Snyde's lumbering progress that he was far from capable of following them there.

I could – I *should* – have called out then; but I needed to know who the other boy was. I already knew he was not one of mine. I know my boys, and even in the darkness I was sure I would have recognized him. They were balanced together on the edge of the drop; a long finger of light from the Quad illuminated Leon's hair in scarlet and blue. The other boy was still in shadow; one hand outstretched as if to shield his face from the approaching Porter. A low, but nevertheless violent discussion seemed to be under way.

It lasted ten seconds, maybe even less. I could not hear what they said, though I caught the words *Jump* and *Porter* and a smattering of shrill, unpleasant laughter. I was angry now; angry as I was at the trespassers in my garden, the vandals at my fence. It was not so much the trespass itself, or even that I had been called there in the middle of the night (in fact I'd come of my own accord, on hearing the disturbance). No, my anger ran deeper than that. Boys misbehave; it's a fact of life. In thirty-three years I've had ample demonstration. But this was one of *my* boys. And I felt much as I imagine Mr Meek to have felt, that day in the Bell Tower. Not that I would have shown it, of course – to be a teacher is principally to hide rage when it is truly felt, and to feign it when it is not – all the same, it would have done me good to have seen the look on the faces of those two boys as I called out their names from out of the dark. But for that, I needed *both* their names.

I already knew Leon, of course. In the morning, I knew he would identify his friend. But the morning was still hours away; just then it would be as clear to the boys as it was to me that I was helpless to stop them. I could imagine their response to my angry call – the laughter, the jeers as they sprinted away. Later, of course, I would make them pay. But the legend would endure; and the School would remember, not their four weeks' litter duty or five-day suspension, but the fact that a boy had defied old Quaz on his own turf and – even for a few hours – had got away with it.

And so I waited, squinting to make out the second boy's features. For a moment I glimpsed them as he stepped back to make the leap; a sudden slice of red-blue light showed me a young face twisted by some harsh emotion; mouth drawn, teeth bared, eyes like slots. It made him unrecognizable; and yet I knew him, I was sure of it. A St Oswald's boy. And now he took the jump at a run. The Porter was approaching fast – his broad back partly eclipsing my field of vision as the roof dipped towards the gully – and then in the sudden blur of movement and the shutterclick of lights I'm sure I saw Pinchbeck's hand connect with Leon's shoulder – just for a second – before they went over together into the dark.

Well, of course, it wasn't *quite* like that. Not from where I was standing, anyway, but close enough all the same. Yes, old man, *I* pushed Leon, and when you called my name I was sure you'd seen me do it.

Perhaps I even *wanted* someone to see it; someone to acknowledge my presence at last. But I was confused; appalled at my act; uplifted at my daring; incandescent with guilt and rage and terror and love. I would have given anything for it to have happened the way I told you; Butch and Sundance on the Chapel roof; the last stand; the last look of complicity between friends as we made our brave leap to freedom. But it wasn't like that. It was nothing like that at all.

'Your *dad*?' said Leon.

'Jump!' I said. 'Go on, man, jump!'

Leon was staring at me, face streaked with fire-engine blue. 'So that's it,' he said. 'You're the *Porter's* kid.'

'Hurry up,' I hissed. 'There isn't time.'

But Leon had seen the truth at last; the look I so hated was back on his face, and his lips were curling with cruel mirth. 'It's almost worth getting caught for this,' he whispered, 'just to see their faces—'

'Stop it, Leon.'

'Or what, Queenie?' He began to laugh. 'What are you going to do, eh?'

There was a horrible taste in my mouth; a taste of sour metal, and I realized I had bitten my lip. Blood ran down my chin like drool.

'Please, Leon—'

But Leon was still laughing in that gaspy, affected way; and for a terrible instant I saw through his eyes; saw fat Peggy Johnsen, and Jeffrey Stuarts, and Harold Mann and Lucy Robbins and all the freaks and losers from Mr Bray's class, and the Sunnybankers with no future beyond the Abbey Road estate, and the pram-faces and slappers and toerags and proles, and worst of all I saw myself, clearly, and for the first time.

It was then that I pushed him.

I don't remember this part as clearly. Sometimes I tell myself it was an accident. Sometimes I almost believe it was. Perhaps I expected him to jump; Spiderman does it across twice that distance; I'd done it enough times myself to be absolutely sure he wouldn't fall. But Leon did.

My hand on his shoulder.

That sound.

God. *That sound.*

5

Bonfire Night
9.55 p.m.

SO, AT LAST, YOU'VE HEARD IT ALL. I'M SORRY IT HAD TO BE
here and now. I was quite looking forward to Christmas at
St Oswald's – not to mention the Inspection, of course. But
our game is done. The King is alone. All our other pieces
have left the board and we can face each other honestly, for
the first and last time.

I believe you liked me. I think you respected me. Now
you know me. That's all I really wanted of you, old man.
Respect. Regard. That curious *visibility* that is the automatic
birthright of those living on the other side of the line.

'Sir? Sir?'

He opened his eyes. Good. I was afraid I'd lost him. It
might have been more humane to finish him off, but I
found I couldn't do it. He'd seen me. He knew the truth.

And if I killed him now, it would not feel like victory.

A draw, then, *magister*. I can live with that.

Besides, there was one last thing that troubled me; one question left unanswered before I could declare an end to the game. It occurred to me then that I might not like the answer. All the same, I needed to know.

'Tell me, sir. If you saw me push Leon, why didn't you say so at the time? Why protect me when you knew what I'd done?'

I knew, of course, what I wanted him to say. And silently, I faced him now, squatting low enough at his side to catch even the smallest of whispers.

'Talk to me, sir. Why didn't you tell?'

For a time, there was silence, but for his breathing that rattled slow and shallow in his throat. I wondered then if I'd left it too late; if he planned to expire out of sheer spite. Then he spoke, and his voice was faint, but I heard him well. And he said: '*St Oswald's.*'

She'd said *no lies*. Well, I gave her the truth. As much of it as I could, anyway, though I was never sure afterwards how much of it I had spoken aloud.

That's why I kept the secret for all these years; never told the police what I'd seen on the roof; allowed the business to die with John Snyde. You have to understand; Leon's death on School premises was terrible enough. The

Porter's suicide made it worse. But to involve a child – to *accuse* a child – that would have catapulted the sorry affair into tabloid territory for ever. St Oswald's didn't deserve that. My colleagues, my boys – the damage to them would have been incalculable.

And besides, what precisely *had* I witnessed? A face, glimpsed for a split second in treacherous light. A hand on Leon's shoulder. The figure of a Porter blocking the scene. It wasn't enough.

And so I'd let the matter lie. It was barely dishonest, I told myself – after all I hardly trusted my own testimony as it was. But now here was the truth at last, returning like a juggernaut to crush me, my friends – everything I'd hoped to protect – beneath its giant wheels.

'St Oswald's.' Her voice was reflective, barely audible across a cavernous distance.

I nodded, pleased she'd understood. After all, how could she not? She knew St Oswald's as well as I did; knew its ways and its dark secrets; its comforts and its little conceits. It's hard to explain a place like St Oswald's. Like teaching, you're either born to it or you're not. Drawn in, too many find themselves unable to leave – at least until the day the old place decides to spit them out (with or without a small honorarium taken from Common Room Committee funds). I have been so many years in St Oswald's that nothing else exists; I have no friends outside the Common Room; no hopes beyond my boys, no life beyond—

'St Oswald's,' she repeated. 'Of course it was. It's funny, sir. I thought maybe you'd done it for me.'

'For *you*?' I said. 'Why?'

Something splashed against my hand; a droplet from the nearby trees, or something else, I wasn't sure. I suddenly felt a surge of pity – surely inappropriate, but I felt it nevertheless.

Could she really have thought that I had kept silent all these years for the sake of some unimagined relationship between us? That might explain a number of things: her pursuit of me; her all-consuming need for approval; her ever more baroque ways of gaining my attention. Oh, she was a monster; but in that moment I felt for her, and I reached out my clumsy old hand towards her in the darkness.

She took it. 'Bloody St Oswald's. Bloody vampire.'

I knew what she meant. You can give, and give and give – but St Oswald's is always hungry, devouring everything – love, lives, loyalty – without ever sating its interminable appetite.

'How can you bear it, sir? What's in it for *you*?'

Good point, Miss Dare. The fact is I have no choice; I am like a mother bird faced with a chick of monstrous proportions and insatiable greed. 'The truth is that many of us – the old guard, at least – would lie or even *die* for St Oswald's if duty demanded it.' I didn't add that I felt as if I might actually be dying there and then, but that was because my mouth was dry.

She gave an unexpected chuckle. 'You old drama queen. You know, I feel half inclined to give you your wish – to let you die for dear St Oswald's and see how much gratitude you get for it.'

'No gratitude,' I said, 'but the tax benefits are enormous.' It was a lame quip, as last words go, but in the circumstances it was the best I could do.

'Don't be an ass, sir. You're not going to die.'

'I'm turned sixty-five, and can do as I please.'

'What, and miss your Century?'

'*It is the game,*' I misquoted from somewhere or other. '*Not he who plays it.*'

'*That* depends what side you're on.'

I laughed. She was a clever girl, I thought, but I defy anyone to find a woman who *really* understands cricket. 'I need to sleep now,' I told her drowsily. 'Up stumps and back to the Pavilion. *Scis quid dicant—*'

'Not yet, sir,' she said. 'You can't sleep now—'

'Watch me,' I said, and closed my eyes.

There was a long silence. Then I heard her voice, receding now like her footsteps as the cold drew in.

'Happy birthday, *magister.*'

Those last words sounded very distant, very final in the dark. The Last Veil, I told myself glumly – at any point now I could expect to see the Tunnel of Light Penny Nation's always talking about, with its celestial cheerleaders urging me on.

To be honest I've always thought it sounded a bit ghastly, but now I thought I could actually *see* the light – a rather eerie greenish glow – and hear the voices of departed friends whispering my name.

'*Mr Straitley?*'

Funny, I thought: I'd expected celestial beings to be

rather less formal in their address. But I could hear it clearly now, and in the green glow I could see that Miss Dare had gone, and that what I had taken for a fallen branch in the darkness was in fact a huddled figure, lying on the ground not ten feet away.

'Mr Straitley,' it whispered again, in a voice as rusty – and as human – as my own.

Now I could see an outstretched hand; a crescent of face behind the furred hood of a parka; then a small greenish light, which I recognized at last as the display screen of a mobile phone, illuminating his face. And it was a *familiar* face; the expression strained but calm as he began, patiently, still holding the phone with what looked like an agonizing effort, to crawl across the grass towards me.

'*Keane?*' I said.

6

Paris. 5ième arrondissement
Friday, 12th November

I CALLED THE AMBULANCE. THERE'S ALWAYS ONE NEAR THE park on Bonfire Night in case of accidents, fights and general misadventure, and all I had to do was phone in (using Knight's phone for the last time), reporting that an old man had collapsed and leaving instructions that would be at the same time precise enough to allow them to find him and vague enough to give me a chance to get away in comfort.

It didn't take long. Over the years I have become rather an expert at quick getaways. I got back to my flat by ten; at ten fifteen I was packed and ready. I left the hire car (keys in the ignition) on the Abbey Road estate; by ten thirty I was fairly certain it would have been stolen and torched. I'd already wiped my computer and removed the hard drive, and now I disposed of what was left along the railway tracks on my way to the station. By then I had only a small case of Miss Dare's clothes to carry; I left them in a charity bin where they would be laundered and sent to the Third World. Finally I dumped the few documents still pertaining to my old identity into a skip and bought myself a night at a cheap motel and a single rail ticket home.

I have to say, I've missed Paris. Fifteen years ago, I never would have believed it possible; but now I like it very much. I am free of my mother (such a sad business, two burnt to death in an apartment fire); and as a result I am the sole beneficiary of rather a neat little inheritance. I've changed my name as my mother did hers, and I've been teaching English for the last two years at a comfortably suburban *lycée*, from which I have recently taken a short sabbatical to complete the research that will, I am assured, lead to my rapid promotion. I do hope so; in fact I happen to know that a little scandal is about to erupt (regarding my immediate superior's on-line-gambling problem) which may offer me a suitable vacancy. It isn't St Oswald's, of course; but it will do. For now, at least.

As for Straitley, I hope he survives. No other teacher has earned my respect – certainly not the staff at Sunnybank Park, or at the dull Paris *lycée* that succeeded it. No one else – teacher, parent, analyst – has ever taught me any-thing worth knowing. Perhaps this is why I let him live. Or perhaps it was to prove to myself that I have finally surpassed my old *magister* – though in his case survival carries its own double-edged responsibilities, and what his testimony will mean to St Oswald's is hard to tell. Certainly, if he wishes to save his colleagues from the present scandal, I see no alternative but to raise the spectre of the Snyde affair. There will be unpleasantness. My name will be mentioned.

I have little anxiety on that front, however; my tracks are well hidden, and unlike St Oswald's, I will emerge from this once again unseen and undamaged. But the School has weathered scandals before; and although this new development is likely to raise its profile in a most disagreeable way, I imagine it may endure. In a way, perversely, I hope it does. After all, a sizeable part of me belongs there.

Now, sitting in my favourite café (no, I *won't* tell you where it is), with my demitasse and croissants on the vinyl tabletop in front of me and the November wind snickering and sobbing along the broad boulevard, I could almost be on holiday. There's the same sense of promise in the air; of plans to be made. I should be enjoying myself. Another two months of sabbatical to go, a new, exciting little project to begin, and, best of all, *strangest* of all, I am free.

But I have dragged this revenge of mine behind me for so long that I almost miss the weight of it; the certainty of having something to chase. For the present, it seems, my momentum is spent. It's a curious feeling, and spoils the moment. For the first time in many years, I find myself thinking of Leon. I know that sounds strange – hasn't he been with me all this time? – but I mean the *real* Leon, rather than the figure that time and distance have made of him. He'd be nearly thirty now. I remember him saying: *Thirty, that's old. For Christ's sake, kill me before I get there.*

I never could before, but now I can see Leon at thirty; Leon married; getting a paunch; Leon with a job; Leon with a child. And now, after all, I can see how *ordinary* he looks, eclipsed by time; reduced to a series of old snapshots, colours faded, now-comic images of fashions long dead – *my God, they used to wear that gear?* – and suddenly and ridiculously I begin to weep. Not for the Leon of my imagination, but for my own self, little Queenie as was, now twenty-eight years old and heading full-tilt and for ever into who knows what new darkness. Can I bear it? I ask. And will I ever stop?

'Hé, *la Reinette. Ça va pas?*' That's André Joubert, the café owner; a man in his sixties, whip-thin and dark. He knows me – or thinks he does – and there is concern in his angular face as he sees my expression. I make a shooing gesture – '*Tout va bien*' – leave a couple of coins on the table and step out on to the boulevard, where my tears will dry in the gritty wind. Perhaps I will mention this to my analyst at our next appointment. On the other hand, perhaps I will miss the appointment altogether.

My analyst is called Zara, and wears chunky knitwear and *l'Air du Temps*. She knows nothing of me but my fictions, and gives me homeopathic tinctures of sepia and iodine to calm my nerves. She is full of sympathy for my troubled childhood and for the tragedies that robbed me, first of my father, then of my mother, stepfather and baby sister at such an early age. She feels concern for my shyness, my boyishness, and for the fact that I have never been intimate with a man. She blames my father – whom I have presented to her in the garb of Roy Straitley – and urges me to seek closure, catharsis, self-determination.

It occurs to me that perhaps I have.

Across the boulevard, Paris is bright and sharp around the edges, stripped raw by the November wind. It makes me restless; makes me want to see precisely where that wind is blowing; makes me curious as to the colour of the light just over the far horizon.

My suburban *lycée* seems banal next to St Oswald's. My little project has been done before; and the prospect of settling down, of accepting the promotion, of fitting into the niche, now seems altogether too easy. After St Oswald's I want more. I still want to dare, to strive, to conquer – now even Paris seems too small to contain my ambition.

Where, then? America might be nice; that land of reinvention, where just to be British confers automatic Gentleman status. A country of black-and-white values, America; of interesting contradictions. I feel that there might be considerable rewards to be gained for a talented player such as myself. Yes, I might enjoy America.

Or Italy, where every cathedral reminds me of St Oswald's and the light is golden on the dust and the squalor of those fabulous ancient cities. Or Portugal, or Spain – or further still, to India and Japan – until one day I find myself back in front of St Oswald's main gates, like the serpent with its tail in its mouth, whose creeping ambition girdles the earth.

Now that I come to think about it, it seems inevitable. Not this year – maybe not even this decade – but some day I will find myself standing there, looking in at the cricket grounds and the rugby fields and the quads and arches and chimneys and portcullises of St Oswald's Grammar School for Boys. I find this a curiously comforting thought – like the image of a candle on a window-ledge burning just for me – as if the passing of Time, which has been ever more present in my thoughts these past few years, were simply the passing of clouds across those long golden rooftops. No one will know me. Years of reinvention have given me protective colours. Only one person would recognize me, and I do plan to wait until long after Roy Straitley has retired before I show my face – *any* of my faces – around St Oswald's again. A pity, in a way. I might have enjoyed a final game. Still, when I come back to St Oswald's I'll make sure to look for his name on the Honours Board among the Old Centurions. I have a definite feeling it will be there.

3

14th November

I THINK IT'S SUNDAY, BUT I'M NOT QUITE SURE. THE PINK-haired nurse is here again, tidying up the ward, and I seem to remember Marlene here too, sitting quietly on the chair beside my bed, reading. But today is really the first day that time has run its natural course, and that the tides of unconsciousness which have ruled my days and nights for the past week have begun to recede.

Miss Dare, it seems, has vanished without trace. Her flat has been cleared; her car was found torched; her last pay packet remains untouched. Marlene, who divides her time between the ward and the School office, tells me that the certificates and letters submitted at the time of her application have been revealed to be fake, and that the 'real' Dianne Dare, to whom her Cambridge languages degree was offered five years ago, has been working at a small publisher's in London for the past three years, and has never even heard of St Oswald's.

Naturally, her description has been circulated. But appearances can be changed; new identities forged; and my guess is that Miss Dare – or Miss Snyde, if that's still her name – may be a long time in eluding us.

I fear that on this subject I have not been able to help the police as much as they would have liked. All I know is that she called the ambulance, and that the medics on board administered the on-the-spot care that saved my life. The next day, a young woman claiming to be my daughter delivered a gift-wrapped packet to the ward; inside they found an old-fashioned silver fob watch, nicely engraved.

No one seems to be able to remember the young woman's face; although it is true that I have no daughter, or any relative fitting that description. In any case, the woman never returned, and the watch is just an ordinary watch, rather old and slightly tarnished, but keeping excellent time in spite of its age and with a face that, if not precisely handsome, is certainly full of character.

It is not the only gift I have received this week. I've never seen so many flowers; you'd think I was a corpse already. Still, they mean well. There's a spiny cactus here from my Brodie Boys with the impudent message: *Thinking of you.* An African violet from Kitty Teague; yellow chrysanthemums from Pearman; a busy Lizzie from Jimmy; a mixed bouquet from the Common Room; a Jacob's Ladder from the sanctimonious Nations, a spider-plant from Monument (perhaps to replace the ones Devine removed from the Classics office) and from Devine himself, a large castor-oil plant that stands at my bedside with a kind of shiny disapproval, as if asking itself why I'm not dead yet.

It was close, so I've been told.

As for Keane, his operation lasted several hours and took six pints of donated blood. He came to see me the other day, and though his nurse insisted he remain in his wheel-chair, he looked remarkably well for a man who has cheated death. He has been keeping a notebook of his time in hospital, with sketches of the nurses and caustic little observations on life on the ward. There may be a book in it some day, he says. Well, I'm glad it hasn't stifled his creativity, at least; though I've told him that nothing good ever comes of a teacher turned scribbler, and that if he wants a decent career he should stick to what he's really good at.

Pat Bishop has left the cardiac ward. The pink-haired nurse (whose name is Rosie) professes to be heartily relieved. 'Three Ozzies at the same time? It'll turn my hair grey,' she moans, although I have noticed that her manner has softened considerably towards me (a side-effect, I suppose, of Pat's charm) and that she spends more time with me now than with any of the other patients.

In the light of new evidence, the charges against Pat have been dropped, although he is still under a suspension order signed by the New Head. My other colleagues have a better chance; none of them were officially charged, and so may well return in due course. Jimmy has been reinstated – officially for as long as it takes the School to find a replace-ment, but I suspect that he will continue to be a permanent fixture. Jimmy himself believes that he has me to thank for this second chance, although I have told him several times that I have nothing to do with it. A few words to Dr Tidy, that's all; as for the rest, just blame the approaching School Inspection, and the fact that without our dim-witted but mostly capable handyman, a great many of St Oswald's small but necessary cogs and wheels would have long since seized up completely.

As for my other colleagues, I hear that Isabelle has gone for good. Light, too, has left (apparently to begin a business management course, having found teaching too demanding). Pearman is back, to the secret disappointment of Eric Scoones, who saw himself running the department in Pearman's absence, and Kitty Teague has applied for a Head of Year job at St Henry's, which I have no doubt she will get. Further afield, Bob Strange is running things on a semi-permanent basis – though the grapevine tells me he has had to bear with a significant amount of indiscipline from the boys – and there are rumours of a redundancy package being put together (a generous sum) to ensure that Pat stays away.

Marlene thinks Pat should fight – the Union would certainly back his case – but a scandal is a scandal, regardless of its outcome, and there will always be people who voice the usual clichés. Poor Pat. I suppose he could still get a Headship somewhere – or better still, a post of Chief Examiner – but his heart belongs to St Oswald's, and his heart has been broken. Not by the police investigation – they were just doing their job, after all – but by a thousand cuts; the phone calls left unreturned, the embarrassed chance meetings; the friends who changed sides when they saw the way the wind was blowing.

'I could go back,' he told me, as he prepared to leave. 'But it wouldn't be the same.' I know what he means. The magic circle, once broken, can never quite be restored. 'Besides,' he went on. 'I wouldn't do that to St Oswald's.'

'I don't see why not,' said Marlene, who was waiting. 'After all, where was St Oswald's when *you* needed help?'

Pat just shrugged. There's no explaining it, not to a woman; not even one in a million, like Marlene. I hope she'll take care of Pat, I thought; I hope she'll understand that some things can never be fully understood.

Knight?

Colin Knight remains missing, now presumed dead by everyone but the boy's parents. Mr Knight is planning to sue the School and has already thrown himself into a number of muscular, well-publicized campaigns – calling for a 'Colin's Law' to be passed, including compulsory DNA-testing, psychological evaluation and stringent police checks on anyone planning to work with children – to ensure, he says, that whatever happened to his boy can never happen again. Mrs Knight has lost weight and gained jewellery; her pictures in the newspaper and on the daily TV bulletins show a brittle, lacquered woman whose neck and hands seem barely capable of supporting the many chains, rings and bracelets that hang from her like Christmas baubles. For myself, I doubt her son's body will ever be found. Ponds and reservoirs have yielded no trace;

appeals to the public have raised a great deal of well-meaning response, many hopeful sightings, much goodwill – but no result. *There is still hope*, says Mrs Knight on the TV news, but the reason the television is still running the story is not for the boy (whom everyone has written off) but for the riveting spectacle of Mrs Knight, rigid in Chanel and armoured in diamonds, still clinging to that delusion of hope as she stiffens and dies. Better than *Big Brother*. I never liked her in the old days – I have no reason to like her now – but I do pity her. Marlene had her job to sustain her as well as her affection for Pat; more importantly, Marlene had her daughter, Charlotte – no substitute for Leon, but all the same a child, a hope, a promise. Mrs Knight has nothing – nothing but a memory that grows ever less reliable as the days pass. Already the tale of Colin Knight has grown in the telling. Like all such victims, he has become a popular boy in retrospect, loved by his teachers, missed by his friends. An outstanding student who could have gone far. The photo in the paper shows him at a birthday party, aged eleven or maybe twelve; smiling brashly (I don't think I *ever* saw Knight smile); hair washed; eyes clear, skin as yet unblemished. I barely recognize him, and yet the reality of the boy no longer matters; *this* is the Knight we will all remember; that tragic image of little-boy-lost.

I wonder what Marlene thinks of it all. After all, she too has lost a son. I asked her today, in passing, as Pat was collecting his things (plants, books, cards, a barrage of *Get Well* balloons). And I asked her, too, a question that has remained unasked for so long that it took another murder to give it voice at last.

'Marlene,' I said. 'What happened to the baby?'

She was standing by the bed with her reading glasses on, scrutinizing the label on a potted palm. I meant Leon's child, of course – Leon's and Francesca's – and she must have known it, because her face became abruptly still, taking on a careful lack of expression that reminded me briefly of Mrs Knight.

'This plant's very dry,' she said. 'It needs watering. God knows, Roy, you'll never manage to look after them all.'

I looked at her. 'Marlene,' I said.

It would have been her grandchild, after all. Leon's child; the hopeful shoot; the living proof that *he* had lived, that life goes on, that spring comes round – all clichés, I know, but such are the small wheels upon which the big wheels turn, and where would we be without them?

'Marlene,' I repeated.

Her eyes went to Bishop, who was talking to Rosie some distance away. Then, slowly, she nodded. 'I wanted to take him,' she said at last. 'He was Leon's son, and of course I wanted him. But I was divorced; too old to adopt; I had a daughter who needed me and a job that took time. Grandmother or not, they'd never let me take him. And I knew, too, that if I saw him – even once – I'd never be able to let him go.'

They had put the baby up for adoption. Marlene had never tried to find out where he'd gone. It could have been anywhere. No names, no addresses are exchanged. He could be anyone. We might even have seen him without knowing it, at an interschool cricket match, on a train, or just passing in the street. He could be dead – it happens, you know – or he could be right here, right now, a fourteen-year-old boy among a thousand others, a young half-familiar face, a flop of hair, a *look*—

'It can't have been easy.'

'I managed,' she said.

'And now?'

A pause. Pat was ready to go. Now he approached my bedside, unfamiliar in jeans and T-shirt (St Oswald's masters wear a suit) and smiled.

'We'll manage,' said Marlene, and took Pat's hand. It was the first time I'd seen her do that; and it was then that I understood I'd never see either of them at St Oswald's again.

'Good luck,' I said, meaning goodbye.

For a moment they stood at the foot of my bed, hand in hand, looking down at me. 'Take care, old man,' said Pat. 'I'll see you around. God, I can hardly even see you now behind all those bloody flowers.'

5

Monday, 6th December

APPARENTLY I'M NOT WANTED. OR SO BOB STRANGE TOLD ME when I turned up at work this morning. 'For God's sake, Roy. It won't kill the boys to miss a few Latin lessons!'

Well, maybe not; but I happen to care about my boys' results, I happen to care about the future of Classics in School, and besides, I feel a lot better.

Oh, the doctor said what doctors usually say; but I remember Bevans when he was just a little round boy in my Latin class, with a habit of perpetually removing one shoe during lessons, and I'll be damned if I'll let him order *me* about.

I found they'd put Meek in charge of my form. I could tell *that* from the noise that drifted down through the floor of the Quiet Room; an oddly nostalgic accumulation of sounds, among which Anderton-Pullitt's persistent treble and Brasenose's resonant boom were immediately recognizable. There was laughter, too, drifting down the stairwell, and for a moment it could have been any time – any time at all – with the sound of boys laughing, and Meek protesting and the smell of chalk and burnt toast coming up from the Middle Corridor and the distant *blam* of bells and doors and footsteps, and the peculiar slithering, sliding sound of satchels being dragged along the polished floor, and the heels of my colleagues tap-tapping their way to some office, some meeting, and the dusty golden air of the Bell Tower shining thick with motes.

I took a deep breath.

Ahhh.

It feels as if I have been away for years, but already I can feel the events of the past weeks dropping away, like some dream that happened to someone else a long, long time ago. Here at St Oswald's there are still battles to be fought; lessons to be taught; boys to be instructed on the subtleties of Horace and the perils of the ablative absolute. A Sisyphean task: but one with which, as long as I am still standing, I mean to continue. Mug of tea in one hand, copy of *The Times* (open at the crossword page) tucked neatly under one arm, gown flapping dustily against the polished floor, I make my way resolutely towards the Bell Tower.

'Ah. Straitley.' That'll be Devine. There's no mistaking that dry, disapproving voice, or the fact that he never calls me by my first name.

There he was, standing by the stairs; grey suit, pressed gown and blue silk tie. Starchy doesn't *begin* to describe his stiffness; his face wooden as a tobacconist's Indian in the morning sun. Of course, after the Dare business he is in my debt, and that, I suppose, makes it worse.

Behind him, two men, suited and shod for administrative action, stood like sentinels. Of course. The Inspectors. I'd forgotten, in all the excitement, that they were due today, although I had noticed an unusual degree of reserve and decorum amongst the boys as they arrived, and there were three disabled parking-spaces in the visitors' car-park that I was sure hadn't been there the previous night.

'Ah. The Inquisition.' I sketched a vague salute.

Old Sourgrape gave me one of his looks. 'This is Mr Bramley,' he said, gesturing deferentially towards one of the visitors, 'and this is his colleague, Mr Flawn. They'll be following your lessons this morning.'

'I see,' I said. Trust Devine to arrange *that* on my first day back. Still, a man who will stoop to the Health and Safety manoeuvre will stop at nothing, and besides, I've been at St Oswald's for too long to be intimidated by a couple of Suits with clipboards. I gave them my heartiest smile, and riposted at once. 'Well, I'm just on my way to the Classics office,' I said. 'It's so important to have a space of one's own, don't you think? Oh, don't mind him,' I told the Inspectors, as Devine set off down the Middle Corridor like a clock-work gazelle. 'He's a bit excitable.'

Five minutes later we reached the office. A nice little space, I have to say; I've always liked it, and now that Devine's lot have had it repainted, it looks even more welcoming. My spider-plants are back from whatever cupboard Devine had consigned them, and my books pleasingly arranged on a series of shelves behind my desk. Best of all, the printed sign saying 'German Office' has been replaced by a neat little plaque which reads simply, 'Classics'.

Well, you know, some days you win, some days you lose. And it was with a certain sense of victory that I sailed into room 59 this morning, causing Meek's jaw to drop and a sudden silence to fall over the Bell Tower.

It lasted a few seconds; and then a sound began to rise from the floorboards, a rumbling sound like a rocket about to take off; and then they were on their feet, all of them; clapping and cheering and yelling and laughing. Pink and Niu; Allen-Jones and McNair; Sutcliff and Brasenose and Jackson and Anderton-Pullitt and Adamczyk and Tayler and Sykes. All my boys – well, not quite *all* – and as they stood there, laughing and clapping and yelling my name, I saw Meek stand too, his bearded face lighting up in a genuine smile.

'It's Quaz!'

'It's *alive!*'

'You're back, sir!'

'Does that mean we *still* don't get a proper teacher this term?'

I looked at my fob watch. Snapped it shut. On the lid, the School motto:

> *Audere, agere, auferre.*
> To dare, to strive, to conquer.

Of course I have no way of knowing for sure if it was Miss Dare who sent it to me, but I am sure it was. I wonder where she is – who she is – now. In any case, something tells me that we may not have heard the last of her. The thought does not trouble me as once it might. We have met challenges before, and overcome them. Wars; deaths; scandals. Boys and staff may come and go; but St Oswald's stands for ever. Our little slice of eternity.

Is that why she did it? I can almost believe it was. She has cut a place for herself in the heart of St Oswald's; in three months she has become a legend. What now? Will she return to invisibility – a small life, a simple job, perhaps even a family? Is that what monsters do when the heroes grow old?

For a second I let the noise increase. The din was tremendous; as if not thirty but three hundred boys were running riot in the little room. The Bell Tower shook; Meek looked concerned; even the pigeons on the balcony flew off in a clap of feathers. It was a moment that will stay with me for a long time. The winter sunlight slanting through the windows; the tumbled chairs, the scarred desks, the schoolbags strewn across the faded floorboards; the smell of chalk and dust, wood and leather, mice and men. And the boys, of course. Floppy-haired boys, wild-eyed and grinning, shiny foreheads gleaming in the sun; exuberant leapers; inky-fingered reprobates; foot-stampers and cap-flingers and belly-roarers with shirts untucked and subversive socks at the ready.

There are times when a percussive whisper does the trick.

At other times, however, on the rare occasion that a statement really needs to be made, one may sometimes resort to a shout.

I opened my mouth, and nothing came out.

Nothing. Not a peep.

Out in the corridor the lesson bell rang, a distant buzz that I sensed rather than heard beneath the classroom roar. For a moment I was sure that this was the end; that I had lost my touch as well as my voice; that the boys, instead of jumping to attention, would simply rise up and stampede at the sound of the bell, leaving me like poor Meek, feeble and protesting in their anarchic wake. For a moment I almost believed it as I stood at the door with my coffee mug in my hand and the boys like Jack-in-the-boxes jumping with glee.

Then I took two steps on to my quarterdeck, laid both hands on the desk-top, and tested my lungs.

'Gentlemen. *Silence!*'

Just as I thought.

Sound as ever.

ACKNOWLEDGEMENTS

Once again I owe a profound debt of gratitude t
people – agents, editors, proof-readers, marketi
typesetters, booksellers and reps – who have worl
to bring this book on to the shelves. A special pl
Honours Board goes to Hockey Captain Serafi
honourable mention also to Netball Captain Brie
to Jennifer Luithlen for away matches; to
Liversidge for her editorial contribution to tl
Magazine, and to Louise Page for promoting the
the world outside. House points are granted
Secretary Anne Reeve and to Head of IT Mark
The Art medal goes once more to Stuart Hayg
French prize (albeit in a disappointing year) t
Janson-Smith. Prefects' badges are awarded to K
Anouchka Harris, and the 'mrs joyful prize for ra
goes (for the third consecutive year) to Christophe
Last of all, sincere and affectionate thanks to

511

Brodie Boys (I said you'd go far), to my erstwhile form 3H, to the members of the Roleplay Club and to all my colleagues at LGS, too numerous to mention. And for any of you who may fear to meet yourselves in the pages of this book, rest assured: *you're not there.*

A full programme of events for this term may be found on the School website at joanne-harris.co.uk